Forgotten Life

Forgotten Life

by

BRIAN ALDISS

I think, therefore I am.
I dream, therefore I become.

LONDON
VICTOR GOLLANCZ LTD
1988

First published in Great Britain 1988
by Victor Gollancz Ltd,
14 Henrietta Street, London WC2E 8QJ

British Library Cataloguing in Publication Data
Aldiss, Brian
  Forgotten life.
  I. Title
  823'.914[F]

ISBN 0–575–04369–5

Typeset at The Spartan Press Ltd,
Lymington, Hants
and printed in Great Britain by
St Edmundsbury Press Ltd, Bury St Edmunds, Suffolk

for

MARGARET

još svaki dan

He walked; all round the slumb'ring Glade
 Shone the *SUBLIME*. Through elm and birch
Old cottages led to the Church
 While winding Stour a sail display'd
By many a sunlit mound and bend.
 But on goes he with inward muse,
And still the *DARKNESS* him pursues;
 He murmurs, "Stay, I have no Friend,
No Love, no *ABSOLUTION* claimed,
 And all that IS is ever maimed".

"The Calm" from
A Summer Stroll Through Parts of Suffolk
William Westlake 1801

Of all persons, those in distress stand most in need of our good offices. And, for that reason, the Author of nature hath planted in the breast of every human creature a powerful advocate to plead their cause.

In man, and in some other animals, there are signs of distress, which nature hath both taught them to use, and taught all men to understand without any interpreter. These natural signs are more eloquent than language; they move our hearts, and produce a sympathy, and a desire to give relief.

There are few hearts so hard, but great distress will conquer their anger, their indignation, and every malevolent affection.

Essays on the Power of the Mind
Thomas Reid, Edinburgh, 1820

Lo, how it guards the son from War's alarms,
The loving Shelter of a Mother's arms;
Snatch him too young away and count the Cost,
A tortured Spirit, rostered with the Lost.

from "Miss Montagu's Portrait"
William Westlake, 1790

Book One

ANGEL

I

It was almost roses, roses, all the way. The fans kept on laughing and joking, even into the asperities of JFK Airport.

SPEAK TO US GREEN MOUTH, cried their noble banners, in priceless fan embroidery, too overwhelmed to give punctuation a single hem-stitched thought.

RAZZMATAZZ FOR TAZZ.

"Don't leave us! We'll make ya President!"

What measure was the unit of laughter? The *ha*? A million units of *ha* were expended as the admiring throng gladly, proudly, lugged Green Mouth's luggage to the First Class Check-In. Every one of the faithful needed to lay a plump hand on the sacred suitcases.

More units, as baggage moved on the metal loop away into concealed realms, piece by precious piece. More units, as the throng shuffled slowly towards Duty Free Zone and final farewells. More units, pained now, before they could possibly say goodbye to her. A little chorus of units trickled among the streams of *ha*-less humanity filling the lounges.

Green Mouth was always at the centre of the chorus, triumphal, regal. Almost silent herself, the catalyst against whom the *ha*-units she generated beat in vain. It was a fine performance, Dr Clement Winter told himself. He should not worry. There was no real cause for worry.

The noise, the banners, the nervous mirth, provoked Green Mouth continually to smile her grim smile, and to chuckle her grim chuckle, which even the most admiring could not effectively imitate. Laughter was not for her but for the acolytes. Chuckles were power-based, laughter was weakness. She floated slowly towards SHOW PASSPORTS, stately as a cinema butler, be-ringed hand up to shoulder to adjust green cloak.

Some of those jostling near asked her questions, harmless things intended as no more than tribute. To these questions, Green Mouth tossed remarks of some brevity: "We'll have to see about that." "That's one for my agent." "What do you think?" "We'd all like to know that."

Each little coded reply provoked more units of *ha*. The throng loved, thrilled to, such effortless arrogance. They ate them like dog biscuits. And of course there was grief in every *ha*, for Green Mouth was about to desert them.

Green Mouth was deserting them. She was now leaving the United States of America behind, leaving it forsaken to make out on its own as best it could. The mere idea was *ha*-inducing. So Clement told himself, squeezing out his amusement as the throng elbowed him.

The fans had a fantasy ready to account for the desertion. Green Mouth had been Called. Tazz of Kerinth had called her on telepathic beam. A New Cause awaited Green Mouth. So she was about to leave Planet Earth for another galaxy, wrapped in her ample green cloak, wearing that neat little tiara — handmade by admirers in Churubusco, Indiana — in among her blonde curls. This was what they told each other, among *ha*s, to console themselves for the cruel facts of life.

No wonder the mundane passengers, outside the charmed *ha*-ing circle, turned momentarily to stare. Envy must account for those surly looks.

At the inescapable moment of parting, a group of the laughingest fans, calling themselves the Inner Circle of Kerinth, who had travelled with Green Mouth and Clement all the way from Boston, unfurled their largest banner. It bore the slogan featuring in the publisher's current publicity campaign: GREEN MOUTH SEZ IT ALL. A bugle *ha-ha*ed, sky high.

Clapping, cheering. *Ha*-ing, weeping. Other passengers pushed out of the way. Special people only in this throng — men and women, or rather, boys and girls, weighty around stomach and hips, protuberant of buttock and breast, most having achieved, if not maturity, avoirdupois, all be-badged if not actually in fancy costume, all addicts of Green Mouth's pre-pubertal planet. Cameras and videocams at the alert, all clustered about their heroine for the last shot, a last kiss, an embrace or, failing those, a mere touch.

How fortunate that she was, in her forty-sixth year, so statuesque that she could withstand their ardour, like a rock in a surging tide, or perhaps Brünnhilde standing in for Andromeda on her rock. She could recall all the names of the faithful — all their first names. She had a word for each personally, even if it was only " 'Bye." Her little Hispanic editor from Swain Books Inc. was thanked last and with greatest warmth. Against his lips, as he stood on tiptoe, were crushed most enthusiastically those pursed green lips. Clement turned away. When he looked again, she and the camp-followers were parted. The desertion was made flesh.

The *ha* count dies. The fans are swept aside by brisk business passengers equipped with the latest brief-cases. They look deflated, tawdry, as they furl up their banners. Alcohol and drugs and hangovers increase their sorrow. Some weep, some begin to skip or dance.

None of this matters. The hall is already peopled with eccentrics, drawn to this parting of the ways like cats on a quayside. Some speak out for various religions, thrusting pamphlets on the unwary. Some tout lost or mislaid causes. Some cry aloud injustices in various distant homelands. Some merely try to sell earrings. Big blacks skate grandly by on wooden wheels, Flying Dutchpersons able to ignore the world, their ears plugged with microsound. Although accustomed to the U.S.A., Clement remains amazed at how busy airports are on Sundays.

The Kerinth fans are lost now. Mother has gone away, her sons and daughters are scattered. They drift off to drink calorific shakes in nearby bars, pink, green, brown, or Your Choice.

A last imperial wave of braceletted wrist and Green Mouth is through the final barrier. Clement follows humbly, given status by being i/c documents. Green Mouth seats herself on a plastic seat. Two nearby English passengers shrink away.

"Buy a bottle of Smirnoff, Clem — to take home to Michelin," says Green Mouth. She is not above such mundane details, but she stares ahead as if she had not spoken. He moves towards the Duty Free. He understands she wishes to be alone with her carbonated emotions. She has to come back to Earth before she can leave terra firma.

Clement Winter was a thin man, which suited his self-effacing qualities. There was about him an air of one for whom life has been slightly insufficient, or who has been slightly insufficient for life. He wore a striped light jacket with matching tie, a white shirt, and a pair of blue trousers. His hair was not chestnut enough to notice and now, in his fiftieth year, somewhat frayed about the edges. His hands hung from his sleeves. Only in his face, running a little to fat, was there a lively darting thing; it was as though his head had generally had more luck than the rest of him.

He purchased the vodka his wife wanted and returned to her via the bookstall, where *War Lord of Kerinth* was in the No. 2 Bestsellers slot. *War Lord of Kerinth* had 1.5 million copies in print hardcover, each wrapped in its sizzling jacket by S. S. Bronbell and stamped with the legend cooked up at Swain by the little Hispanic editor, "Green Mouth Sez It All". As he passed the stall, Clement saw a middle-aged woman in a smart ice-blue suit take a copy over to the checkout point. She did not even glance at the price. The volume, bulked up as it was, resembled a glutinous box of chocolates.

No one could mistake Green Mouth. She sat upright in her plastic seat, a dowager duchess at least, her ample mouth that brilliantly repellent green, the same shade echoed about her eyes, her eyelashes tinted gold. He sat beside her, tucking the vodka into a carrier. Her distinctive hand-luggage, bearing its open green mouths, came between them.

"Sheila," he said.

The name, he considered, was like a projectile, a component of some vast SDI programme of the mind, bursting into her personal umwelt, carrying with it unwelcome news of her ordinary humanity. She responded only with a grunt, possibly a grunt of pain, completely *ha*-free.

"You were wonderful," he said. Using the past tense on her like a can-opener. She had to start getting back sometime. There was jet-lag. There was reality-lag. Best to keep them separate.

"Wonderful," he repeated, choosing more of a dying fall this time. And then their flight was called in an electronic voice as soft as the cooing of doves.

On the Boeing, muzak was playing: "Don't Cry for Me, Argentina". As Clement hung the green cloak on a rail, he glanced through into Economy, where the hordes were fighting to stash away liquor in overhead lockers, mussing each other's hair and tempers in the process. Every year, as civilisation ticked by, thousands of gallons of alcohol were ferried back and forth across the Atlantic, each precious bottle of the stuff requiring a human attendant. It was one of the paradoxes of modern living which kept living modern.

Clement hoped that when the hostesses had seen to his wife's minor problems, which always cropped up, and preferably had recognised her, and more preferably had read all her books, she would remove the viridian lipstick and deflate back into being Sheila Winter again. She always said she liked to travel anonymously; and that was fine, as long as everyone knew who you were.

Sure enough, as he returned to his seat, or armchair as Pan-Am liked to call it, the hostesses were flocking round with the champagne, professing to be fans of Kerinth, every one. 1.5 million copies hardcover certainly wasn't hay. And to think the first Kerinth novel, *Brute of Kerinth*, had been published originally in a paperback edition of no more than sixty thousand copies. Not so much wonderful as a miracle — their personal miracle.

Green Mouth was gracious as always. Sure, she'd love to visit the flight deck after dinner. Sure, she always flew Pan-Am. Champagne was poured again. They drank. Clement drank. Good for Kerinth; it stood between him and Economy.

She still retained her Green Mouth face even when her eyes closed. She must be tired after four days in Boston of constant limelight and the tour before that. Never more than six hours' sleep a night. Much drink, taken without flinching. Saying nice things about Swain. Hearing nice things from Swain. All energy-sapping. But never a word of complaint.

Her face, under its paint, was large, brown, homely, and lightly creased. The teeth had been fixed so that she did not look as once she had like something that had just run in the Grand National. Sheila Winter was rather a handsome woman, though there was a heavy jaw, speaking of determination, perhaps of rather a glum kind. In her ears were little *mazooms* of emerald, designed for her by a French fan in California. Not so little, either. They threatened to execute a pincer movement along the planes of Green Mouth's cheeks, just as — how often — *mazooms* had menaced the World of Kerinth before brave Tazz had tamed one of them.

Without opening her eyes, she ran her green nails along his jacket sleeve. "Wonderful," she said.

Once the plane was airborne, the captain spoke over the intercom, telling the passengers at what height they would be travelling and at what time they were due to hit the coast of Ireland — at which announcement all the English passengers looked alarmed. But the champagne came round again, and the feline hostesses, and Green Mouth began to talk without looking at Clement. She was delivering a monologue. Clement felt no need to reply; he understood. The weary brain was off-loading like a computer. Sheila had been travelling round the States for twenty-three days, promoting the latest Kerinth novel from coast to coast in eighteen cities. And for the last four days she had been incarcerated in the Luxor Hotel in Boston (where Clement had joined her), as Guest of Honour at the XIX Fantacon, known in her honour as the Kerincon, the constant target of attention for five thousand fans, many of them attired only in leopard skin and sword.

She had gone without sleep. She had lived on pills. She had rarely ceased drinking or talking. She had given interviews. She had answered endless questions — often the same questions — with good grace. She had received gifts. She had signed many of the 1.5 million copies of her book. She had made a two-hour long speech, full of attractive pathos about her happy childhood and not lacking in *ha*-quota either. She had thrown a wildly expensive party in her hotel suite for publishers, friends, and special fans. She had been laid more than once by her diminutive Hispanic editor, all in the spirit of fun. She had posed for photographs for *Locus* and anyone else who asked. She had smiled her grim smile most of the time. She had smoked almost incessantly, showered often, and accepted with an amusing speech the High Homeric Fantasy Award for being Top Priestess of Epic Fantasy.

No wonder her brain wanted to talk. The sump had to be drained, the gurge regurgitated.

High above the grey and tedious Atlantic, she paused once to emit a simultaneous yawn and belch.

"But how are you feeling?" Clement asked.

Her hand sought his, and then she looked at him through cloudy eyes. "Fucking awful, darling," said Green Mouth.

She was returning to reality. He summoned the hostess for some more champagne.

Monday morning. Home again. Shoes off time. Safe. Secure in the Victorian brick wilderness of North Oxford. Their square-windowed house in Rawlinson Road was shielded from the gaze of passers-by by an enormous horse chestnut tree which some absent-minded builder had forgotten to destroy while he had the chance, possibly during the celebrations attendant on Queen Victoria's Jubilee.

The hired chauffeur stacked their luggage in the hall and left.

Sheila went into the front room and reclined with care on the sofa under the lace-curtained window. Her green lipstick and eye shadow had been removed in the toilet of the 747. She now looked merely pale, merely enervated, merely English.

"Are you going to make us a cup of tea?" she called.

Clement was taking the cases upstairs.

"Good idea. Hang on a moment." Michelin, who lived with them, was out.

The time was 10.50. Or alternatively, 5.50 New York time.

His head rang.

In their bedroom, he set down the cases and opened one of them. In it, approved by Customs, lay Green Mouth's latest prize, the High Homeric Fantasy Award, sculpted in fibre glass.

To please her, possibly to revive her, he took it downstairs and placed it on a table before her. She smiled wanly.

"Oh, that!" said the Top Priestess of Epic Fantasy. It is magnificent. It consists of a bust of Homer with two little cupid wings sprouting from his grey locks, just above his ears. This is no mere *ha* flim-flam. This is a literary award, bestowed by earnest young judges of the various sexes. On the back of the revered Greek story-teller's head are etched the titles of the ten Kerinth novels and the one collection of short stories, with their dates of publication.

What's more, this award is electronic. Inside the skull is concealed a lithium battery smaller than a dime. Clement switches on. Homer's blind eyes light up. The wings flap at a dignified pace. Homer nods.

Sheila smiled. "Wonderful, but . . . tea?"

He brought her tea in her Libra mug, accompanied by two Hedex, and sat on the edge of the sofa clutching his own mug.

"You could go up and lie on the bed."

She nodded, clasping the mug between stubby fingers, looking down into the tea. "I wonder if Michelin made any biscuits."

After they had sipped for a while in silence, she yawned and looked rather sullenly round the room, as if to orient herself.

It was not a remarkable room, except that successive owners had spared the elaborate Victorian fireplace, before which an electric fire now stood. Sheila had chosen a blue, green and gold decor, and had not pushed the green too heavily. The wallpaper was a dark blue, the chairs and sofa were green and gold. Gold birds fluttered in the folds of blue and green curtains. A large rococo-framed gilt mirror hung above the mantelpiece. To the left of the fireplace stood a glass cabinet housing some of Sheila's awards for fiction, including the International Otherworld Fiction Award sculpture of Tazz riding a mazoom. In the bookcase to the other side of the fireplace, above the sets of Dickens, Galsworthy, and Dornford Yates, her own books were on display, with *Brute of Kerinth,* the first in the series, facing outwards into the room.

Postcards from all over the world were ranged along the mantelshelf, like illustrations from other people's lives lived under bright blue skies. Photographs of Green Mouth mixing with important people hung framed on the wall behind the door. Beneath them was a small eighteenth-century side-table bearing a large Chinese vase converted into a table-lamp. Similar conversions involved the mock gas brackets which projected from the wall over the fireplace. The white leather rhino which served as a footrest — present from a grateful and enriched publisher in Germany — had never seen the forests of Sumatra.

The stillness in the room was also in a sense man-made. The Winters had had all the windows double-glazed, to shut out noise from the street.

To the rear of the room, by a curtained archway leading through to the conservatory, a music stack with discs, records and cassettes waited in an alcove. There hung an enormous gouache, painted for a bygone dust jacket, of Gyronee, Queen of Kerinth, standing bolt upright with a spear and a sort of dog, gazing into the purple future.

Beyond the queen stood a bureau at which Sheila often sat to answer her fanmail. Her study suite was upstairs on the first floor. Clement's little study was up another flight, on the second floor, under the eaves that pointed in the direction of the University.

"Back to reality," she said, setting down her mug. "I suppose Michelin is in Summertown shopping."

"She'll be back soon. Shall we have a snort of something?"

"Shall we? Just wine for me."

"Wine it is." He went through to the kitchen and uncorked a bottle of Mouton Cadet, whistling as he did so.

Michelin had collected up the mail and piled it on the dresser. As he put the corkscrew back into the drawer, Clement looked it over. Most of the letters were for Sheila, addressed to her under her famous pseudonym; most of them came from the United States. Sorting casually through the collection, he found some bills and a small package addressed to him. He recognised his sister Ellen's writing.

The package was registered. Evidently Michelin had signed for it. He frowned, but made no attempt to open it just yet. Like Sheila, he felt a reluctance to allow the real world back in: the world of bills. On Kerinth, bills were never presented or paid; no-one worked, except peasants. Sisters, if they sent packets, sent them by hand — probably by a messenger on a telepathic erlkring. The messenger would arrive in a lather, perhaps seriously wounded, and the packet would contain something portentous. A lover's heart, perhaps, as in *The Heart of Kerinth*.

Was Ellen sending him something equally vital?

He suppressed such questions, left the package on the dresser, and went back into the front room to Sheila, carrying the bottle and two glasses.

After the first glass, she fell asleep. He spread a tartan rug gently over her. He stood regarding her. With her eyes closed she looked character-less, despite the noble nose and noticeable chin.

Taking the opportunity, Clement went quietly upstairs to his study. There his dead brother's papers awaited him, stacked on the desk, tumbling out of boxes on the floor; the mortal remains of Joseph Winter in folders and old brown paper bundles. For all practical purposes, Joseph in death had taken over Clement's study.

When Sheila had made her remark, commonplace enough, about coming back to reality, she had spoken, Clement thought, with contempt as well as resignation. Reality for him meant something different, something with the texture of puzzlement, for to enter his study was to feel himself entangled in the affairs of his late brother.

Some time soon, he would have to drive over again to his dead brother's flat. It was two months since Joseph had suffered his final heart attack. His flat remained, ensconced in that limbo of small London streets where

Chiswick subsides ignobly into Acton amid a welter of little furniture dealers, junk shops, discount stores, and auto repair shops. There Joseph Winter had lived in his semi-academic obscurity with a succession of women, while books and documents had piled up round him.

Clement felt only mild curiosity about the women. The books and documents, willed to him, were his responsibility. He had collected some, almost at random, culling them from wardrobes and mantelpieces. He was also engaged with a series of secondhand booksellers, trying to screw from them a tolerably fair price for Joseph's old volumes, some of which, dealing with Joseph's subject, South East Asian history, were of value.

The question of the books could be resolved. They were the subjects of a mere financial transaction. It was the unpublished work, particularly that dealing with Joseph's private life, which presented more than a problem, a challenge, which made Clement feel that his own life was being called into account.

Clement slumped in his chair, forearms resting on his knees, so that his hands dangled in space.

"Joseph," he said aloud — quietly, bearing in mind that Sheila was asleep — "what am I going to do about you?"

Since the brothers had never known what to do about each other in life, it appeared unlikely that the question would be resolved now, when one of them had folded up his mortal tent and stolen away.

II

Clement Winter left his house shortly after nine the next morning, keeping an eye open for his next-door neighbours, the Farrers, whom he detested. It was a Tuesday, quite a sensible, neutral day of the week — the day, in fact, when he usually held his clinic; but this week as last he had cancelled it, using the excuse of his American trip. Which was as well; jet-lag still made him feel slightly dissociated. Both his legs ached, the left in particular. He walked consciously upright, but a little stiffly.

This walk was his daily exercise. The car remained in the garage. He had changed his more daring American rig for a familiar light grey suit from Aquascutum, as better suited to the environs of Carisbrooke College.

Sheila was still in bed, presumably divesting herself of her Green Mouth personality at leisure. Though he guessed she would soon be working again. Michelin had taken her breakfast up on a tray: orange juice, a mixture of Alpen and All-Bran, two slices of brown wholemeal toast, and a mug of best Arabian coffee with cream. Clement had looked in on her after his breakfast and had taken her the *Independent*. They had murmured endearments to each other.

Now he was playing the role of one more Oxford don, greying, distinguished, as he walked down the Banbury Road to Carisbrooke.

Boston had been cold and rainy. Oxford was remarkably hot. A June heatwave lay over the British Isles. The newspapers were already circulating tales of old ladies fainting in the streets. In Oxford, Clement reflected, it would be old dons.

As he entered the college grounds, a slightly falsetto tooting sounded behind him. Turning, he saw a blue car of no significance drawing into the car park. His research assistant, Arthur Stranks, waved at him from the driver's seat.

Out of politeness, Clement turned back, and stood waiting while Arthur parked the car and climbed out, to walk sideways towards his boss so as to keep the car within his sight.

"Isn't she a beauty?" he said. "I bought her last week, er, in Kidlington, zero miles on the clock. Cheri's mad about her."

"I'm not much of an expert on cars," Clement said, searching the new acquisition for some kind of distinguishing mark. He recalled that previously Arthur had driven a dilapidated Mini with printed jokes in the rear window. "What is it?"

"She's the new Zastava Caribbean," Arthur said, standing on tiptoe in his trainers, a habit by which he expressed enthusiasm as well as elasticity. "Jugoslav-made, newly imported. The Kidlington garage is the only garage in all Oxfordshire where you can buy it. Sole agents. Er — Cheri and I will be able to drive everywhere in it."

"Except, presumably, the Caribbean."

Arthur laughed good-naturedly. "We'll see about that," he said.

They walked along together.

"I've promised not to drive too fast," Arthur said. "Not with Cheri in her condition."

Clement recalled that Mrs Stranks, who had changed her name from Cherry to Cheri — to be more interesting, her husband said — was newly pregnant.

In Clement's room, the accustomed piles of papers and books awaited him. He looked about with a show of pleasure. Here at least, he could bring some sense and order into life.

Arthur Stranks blinked a welcome through his glasses and nodded his head a bit.

"I hope the New York conference was a success? Fun? You get the material you needed?" His manner was solicitous.

"Some of it, some of it. I had a long conversation with Prof Stauffer and I've brought back photocopies of a bundle of his material."

Arthur looked interested and did some more nodding. He had tidied the room while Clement was away, and the old box files now stood in military array under the wide window. The photograph of Willy Wilkes-Smith, the late Master of Carisbrooke, Clement's friend, still hung awry behind the door. Clement went over and straightened it.

Two stacks of wire baskets, six baskets tall, stood on the broad central table. They contained documents, together with photographs and cuttings culled from European and transatlantic sources. One day, with the aid of Arthur, a secretary who came twice a week, and a computer, all this paper, with which the room was slowly filling, would be processed into more paper: into, to be precise, Clement's next work, a study entitled, *Adaptability: Private Lives in Public Wars*. The title was a compromise between the academic respectability he had already achieved and the popular acclaim he felt he deserved; of course the publishers would probably change it anyhow.

"Er, the breakdowns of the VD figures have arrived from the National Archives in Washington. Came on Thursday."

"Good." He began to open letters. "How's Cheri? Any morning sickness?"

"Cheri's fine. Great."

They looked at each other across the room, expressionlessly. Clement, in a fit of good will, put down the letter he was holding and commenced to tell Arthur something about the Modern History conference he had attended before flying to Boston to meet Green Mouth.

Clement, who was rather a distant man, discovered in Arthur a desire to get a little too close in their relationship. Also, there was the generation gap, much though he might try to discount it — indeed, he disliked the very phrase. At forty-nine, Clement was conscious of his age. His once curly hair now harboured ash to dilute its previous chestnut and, even more regrettably, was thinning in a silly fashion, behind and in front. His ruddy cheeks had become patchily sallow, in a way that made him uncomfortable before his mirror. Although no hypochondriac, he imagined himself due for a heart attack at times, and had cut down accordingly on the College port. Caring little about politics, he still clung to his liberal socialist principles, born in the early days of Harold Wilson, the first Prime Minister he had voted for, and believed those principles helped keep his faculties from ossifying.

Arthur Stranks was twenty-two and sallow to start with, a stubby young bespectacled man with a pleasant air of wishing to please. His dark hair was cut flat on top; the Scrubbing Brush Cut was how Clement and Sheila thought of it. As if to assert a wildness of character acquaintances would not otherwise have suspected him of possessing, Arthur had a small tattoo on his left wrist, a bird of prey with something resembling a rat in its beak, probably holding some arcane sexual significance, thought Clement. He knew his assistant for one of Mrs Thatcher's conformists, tethered to his job and monetarist respectability, but there was another side to Stranks, a side represented in part by Mrs Stranks, Cheri, a rather silent lady of sidelong glances, sighs, and a self-evident bosom, who was always to be seen — at least by Clement — in very tight stone-washed jeans. Regarding Stranks, Clement found himself thinking of the bird with the rat and of Cheri.

Stranks had made it clear from the first that he considered it a privilege to work for Dr Clement Winter. In an early attempt to be friendly, Sheila and Clement had taken the Strankses to Covent Garden to Janáček's opera *Jenůfa*. A few months later the Strankses had invited the Winters to what was at first described simply as "a concert". After accepting, Clement discovered that it was a rock concert.

When the day came, Sheila was too busy finishing a novel to go out. She had excused herself, and Clement had gone on his own with Arthur and Cheri to the Birmingham National Exhibition Centre to see Tina Turner live.

He was the only person in the audience in a suit.

The show, the noise, the audience, the enthusiasm, had overwhelmed him. Until that evening, he had never heard of Tina Turner. She was a light coffee-coloured lady wearing a tight-fitting white two-piece which laced up over her exuberant breast, and, even more effectively, a huge wig like a lion's mane. As she screamed her songs at the audience, the mane shook with fervour. The stage could barely contain Tina Turner. She prowled and stamped about it, shrieking her strange love laments, as if seeking a way of getting at the audience and devouring it.

She was a marvellous and, to Clement, a terrifying spectacle. His ideal of feminine beauty had been formed at about the age of ten, when he distinctly recalled rubbing a pubescent penis against a photograph of Miss Hedy Lamarr. Hedy Lamarr had been presented as static, even icy, with the best bits (as he had put it to himself) always chastely concealed. This secretiveness, this pretended show of privacy, had enhanced Hedy Lamarr's stunning beauty. All such artifices were flung out to allow Tina Turner's beauty full play. He was looking at a new age, heralded triumphantly by the singing, the stamping, the tossing mane.

And, like the other males in the audience, Clement was filled with lust. That was what he found terrifying. Savage though Tina might appear, barbaric though the noise was, he saw or imagined a delicacy to her limbs, her hands with their long red claws. In particular, there was a sunny good humour about the whole performance from which it took him days to recover.

The audience, clapping and shouting, was another matter. Art and Cheri beside him were suddenly half-naked, which was to say in T-shirts; paying him no attention, they became part of the mass-mind. Clement, too, dropping his jacket on the floor, also gave in. The whole great cavern became a pool of amplified noise and heat and emotion. And Tina Turner, her carnivorous teeth gleaming at the fun of it all.

The next morning found Clement out of sorts with himself. He sent his suit to the cleaners in Summertown. There were worlds which were not his.

Since then, Clement had kept a mental distance from his assistant. He feared that Stranks and his wife, who had really looked astonishing in that T-shirt, might invite him again into those lower depths. And was affronted that they never did.

Now he averted his eyes from the sinister tattoo, and called his attention back to the reason that had brought them to this untidy room.

"Better pick up the threads again," said Clement, after they had talked for some while. He rubbed his hands together, staging enthusiasm, but doing no more than frown at his chair.

"How's Sheila?" Arthur needed more conversation before starting work. "Er — her side of things go okay?" He had the habit of beginning most sentences with "Er", often accompanied by a quick and useless adjustment of the spectacles.

"Oh, her tour went like a bomb. She's good on television, and they're respectful to the English accent, you know. Especially in the south. She's a bit exhausted — no wonder."

"Should think so. She likes America?"

"Very much so. Whiskey sours. And of course she is so popular there. The Americans have an enthusiasm we lack."

"They're not so critical, are they?"

Clement found this rather an unfortunate remark, but all he said, as he sat down, was, "You and Cheri must come round again soon. Sheila will tell you all about it."

The last time Arthur and Cheri had come round to Rawlinson Road had been quite a success. He had read a couple of Green Mouth novels; no doubt the essentially conservative nature of epic fantasy had its appeal. Clement had spent much of the evening talking to Cheri. It had not been unpleasant. He remembered now that at sight of the tiny swimming pool she had said brightly, "I must bring my costume next time."

Arthur was still postponing a move towards the table.

"Er, I was reading about Zola in one of the weeklies."

"Oh yes?"

"Emile Zola. . . . Seems as if when he was writing his novels he was transported into a sort of totally different thingey — state of being. Rather like being possessed — a state of possession. Terrible visions, intense nightmares, dreams of er, sexual ecstasy, intimations of murder. Quite different from his normal life. A different plane of being. . . . I wondered if — excluding the murder business, of course — if other writers also experienced that kind of transformation. . . . A different frame of mind entirely."

Clement laughed briefly. "You'd have to ask my wife that question."

Something in Clement's tone caused Arthur to fall silent. He retreated to his own desk. His trainers made squeegee noises on the parquet flooring.

This was a signal for Clement to resign himself to work. He pulled various items from his briefcase, arranging them on the table before him.

The main bulk of work on *Adaptability* was already finished, although some chapters required last minute revision. There were appendices to be drawn up — mainly Arthur's task — the vexatious notes to be gone over, and various references to be checked. He would be only a few months over his publisher's deadline. Yet, he realised, the trip to the States, the appearance at the symposium — where American full professors seemed to lead such affluent lives — and the outing to see his wife in action at Fantacon XIX, had unsettled him. He regarded the cordilleras of paper before him without appetite. They certainly would not be printed up in an edition of 1.5 million.

He found himself thinking again of his dead brother. He owed Joseph something. Consanguinity could not be denied.

Sighing, he began to sort through some newspaper cuttings which Arthur had amassed while he was away. One of them caught his attention. It was a brief account, cut from the *Independent*, of a massacre which had occurred in the Lisenitsky Forest, on the outskirts of Lvov, in the Ukraine, in September 1943.

The details were brief but clear. Following the fall of Mussolini, Italy surrendered unconditionally early that September. Italian forces were still fighting alongside the Nazis. Many of them were left politically and physically stranded by the armistice. 229,000 Italians were serving on the Eastern front. 89,000 of them were killed or disappeared without trace. The Germans were hard-pressed by the Russians after the failure of their Sixth Army to take Stalingrad. When 2,000 Italians refused to fight at the front and demanded repatriation, the Germans, ruthless as ever, simply rounded them up in a sand pit and shot them all. Trees were then planted over the site to conceal it. Over forty years later, the site had been discovered by some children from Lvov.

It was only a small incident in a long war; but it touched closely on the theme of Clement's book, the break-up of families and relationships throughout Europe as the result of two world wars. In his years in Berlin, Clement had counselled women whose husbands or sons had disappeared into the vast battlefields of the Soviet Union, never to be heard of again.

Making a precis of the facts on a file card, Clement handed it over to Arthur to store the entry in the computer. After some thought, he scribbled a line to the *Independent* correspondent in Moscow, asking for verification and, if possible, amplification of the facts. The sole witness to the massacre, according to Tass, quoted in the paper, was a woman who had been a schoolgirl of sixteen at the time.

This was only one of a number of similar massacres. In Babi Yar, outside Kiev, the Nazis had massacred 200,000 of their so-called enemies. In Katyn, near Smolensk, Russians had murdered over 4,000 Polish officers.

What had that schoolgirl been doing, wandering innocently in the woods near Lvov? And what effect had sight of that massacre had on her later life? According to her testimony, some of the Italian soldiers had been playing guitars. He saw her through the double-glazed windows of his room, wandering among the willows on the banks of the Isis. She had crept nearer to see who could be playing guitars so happily in the middle of a war. Then came the rifle shots and the cries. She stood behind a tree, fearful. Then she had run for home and not dared to speak of what she had heard and seen.

Clement received these destructions with binocular vision. They happened a long time ago in a distant place. They were also contemporaneous, happening close at hand. Violence remained in the air. Most people in Europe were governed by force. It was inevitable that savagery would break out again. Even understanding was no defence against that.

Since that schoolgirl witness had been born, Hitler's evil empire had been destroyed. Other evils had sprung up. Her own town, Lvov, had passed from Poland to become part of the Soviet Empire. The century had produced new states of doubtful legality. The new states raised armies which marched or clashed along the shifted frontiers. The victors exacted duties, levies, and taxes — above all a moral tax — on those within their borders.

He sighed and turned back to his desk. Under all his horror at the massacres lay a fascination he sought to conceal even from himself. The fascination kept him at his work. Such massacres as the schoolgirl witnessed represented a rare time when life became greater than the imagination. Generally, the reverse was true.

Over coffee in the common room, Clement bumped into Harry Raine, Master of Carisbrooke. Raine, tall, decrepit by design, spare, thin of jowl, began to talk immediately about problems of invigilation. "The day of examining and being examined is upon us. You timed your return from the feverish charms of the New World well," he told Clement, with his ghostly smile.

He dislikes me, Clement thought, because my wife makes a lot of money from her writing and I never say a word against it.

He was not sure if this were really so, since Harry sometimes gave the impression — it was something in that ghostly smile which displayed the

26

strangely grouped grey teeth — of disliking everyone. But he never asked after Sheila.

She's too much a challenge to his antiquated set of values, Clement thought. And he doesn't like women either. Hence his hugely pompous manner — enough to put off any sensible girl.

Going home that evening, Clement Winter walked to the shops in Summertown, met a few acquaintances, chatted, and collected from the delicatessen smoked herring, bean salad, and a brand of walnut ice-cream which Sheila particularly enjoyed. He was aware that he was probably duplicating Michelin's efforts earlier; but he wished to reassure his wife that the good things of life had not necessarily stopped just because they were back in England again.

As he entered Rawlinson Road, he passed his neighbour, John Farrer. Farrer was short and bald and given to tweed suits with heavy lace-up shoes when not wearing city clothes. He was "in insurance", and his whole demeanour from the plodding walk onward summed up the banality of the Here and Now, in Clement's opinion. This would have been insufficient to stop the Winters from speaking to him; it was John Farrer who had decided not to speak to, and even to ignore the existence of, his neighbours. They passed by on the pavement, within a foot of each other, staring straight ahead.

Clement could not resist it. He winked as they were passing.

The wink was to say, "Bourgeois Man, you wear your silly thick jacket, even in a heatwave. Right down to your soul you're overdressed." It was also to say, "Aren't we comic, carrying on this silly feud when we are neighbours?"

It was also to say, "I believe I'm superior to you because I can see the funny side of all this. . . ."

The wink was not returned. Stony-faced, the banality of the Here and Now marched on by. Clement turned in at his own gate.

His house, like many of the others in this most superior road, was an example of bland but condescending English architectural manners, with no one feature overwhelming another. Nor did it vie with the neighbouring houses — with the Farrers' house, for instance. All the same, its essential features had been assembled in such a way that it appeared different from any of the others in the street, and the façade was crowded with too much detail, the windows too large, the porch too heavy, the gables too pointed, for complete discretion. I'm prosperous, the house said, as Clement went in, and I think you should know it.

When he entered the house, he found his wife sitting in the kitchen by the Aga, in a familiar attitude when talking, with one arm bent and tucked behind her head, chatting over the phone to a friend, recounting the ardours and triumphs of the American tour. A cold cup of coffee stood on the table by her. It took Clement only a moment to deduce that the friend at the other end of the line was Maureen Bowler; internal evidence suggested as much. Sheila used a special voice when talking with her feminist friend.

Sheila was wrapped in her blue towelling robe, resting her bare feet on the table. She smiled and waved at Clement without interrupting the flow of her conversation. She was saying, "I told them that my idea of the fantastic was not just yesterday's fantastic, which has become familiar through constant use — unicorns and all that — but something really fantastic, like a whole world on which every living organism has achieved consciousness. . . . Yes, that's it, like the planet Amarnia in *Kerinth Invaded*. And then Larry Ivens got up and tried to argue that nothing was fantastic any more —"

He went over to the refrigerator and put the herring and ice-cream in it. Going to the walk-in larder, he took a bottle of white wine from the stone floor. Uncorking it, he poured two glasses, one of which he passed to Sheila. They made toasting gestures to each other and drank; Sheila in addition waggled her toes.

He took his glass upstairs, where Joseph's papers awaited him. It was noticeably warmer on the second floor. He stood about, opened a window, and then switched on the radio. From Radio Three came the sound of a fellow with an abnormally high voice singing about somewhere called Wenlock Edge. Clement switched him off again, and stood surveying the collection of papers and boxes accumulated here.

His American trip had merely postponed a decision he must now make. He must decide to what use to put his brother's life now that his brother had finished with it. There was also Joseph's flat in Acton, with all his books and possessions, to be disposed of.

Indecision was not a habit with him. Yet he pottered about now, the very picture of indecision. He had to admit it: Joseph worried him.

Joseph had been the adventurous one. Clement had had no adventures in life. His social work, his analysis in West Berlin, his visiting professorships in the States — all had a sheltered quality, compared with Joseph's way of knocking about the world on next to nothing.

Clement had gone to university, unlike his brother and sister, or anyone else in the Winter family. His parents would never have aspired so high. Yet the three years in Birmingham — so he felt, looking back — had been largely wasted, as far as living was concerned. He had made few friends, joined few societies, played no games. He had filled up his days with work, poisoning himself with coffee and the cigarettes he now loathed.

Introspectiveness had led him to become absorbed in the deficiencies of the human character. Within those labyrinths, Clement found himself able to exercise endless patience, like a naturalist in dense jungle, content to wait for hours, and to endure a thousand insect bites and stings, in order to glimpse some rare species. Such a species was now delivered to him in the shape of his elder brother's papers, and he didn't know what to do with them, or what pattern to extract from them.

After graduating, he had done social work in London and Coventry, later specialising in psychiatric work at the Maudsley Hospital, where he came to deal with post-war trauma victims. The war, like a heavy monsoon, had made some people and ruined others, and the losers formed a long queue at Clement's door, demanding attention.

That queue had captured his intense compassion. He had gone to study in Berlin, and there underwent a course of analysis with T. F. Schulz, emerging as a qualified analytical psychologist in 1969. It was in Berlin he had met the young Sheila Tomlinson, long before she set foot on Kerinth.

Back in England, the queue of the maladjusted still awaited him. Marriage to Sheila did not greatly disrupt work on the queue. Only when their one child, Juliet, died, did Clement exert himself and change the course of his career, becoming a professor of sociology in 1973, and publishing his best-received work, *Personality and Aggression*, in 1974. Later, he worked at the Tavistock Institute of Human Relations. By then Sheila was enjoying her first literary success, and Clement had to take a certain amount of teasing, much of it only superficially good-natured, from his colleagues. Academics hated fantasy, feeling themselves surrounded by it; nor were they more cordial to success.

The situation had been better in the States, where success was still regarded as a fun thing, and where he had taken several visiting fellowships in the late seventies. Carisbrooke College, less conventional than older Oxford colleges, had made him a fellow in 1981.

Joseph had followed a less academic course.

Clement's temperate qualities enabled him to enter keenly into the problems of others. But those problems had merely been traffic through the plain of his own life. His one adventure, apart from the determination needed to get to university, had lain in marrying Sheila; she, too, had been part of that traffic, born the month Paris fell to the German invader, seeking a stability she had lost, and willing to find a substitute for it in Clement's cautious embrace.

Twelve years Clement's senior, Joseph had been just old enough to see action in the war, swept overseas in the struggle which had convulsed the world. In Clement's considered opinion, years of soldiering had awoken something primitive in his brother's nature, a rebellious and, from some points of view, admirable quality, which had enabled him ever after to live an independent life of struggle, punctuated by periods of insolvency and hazardous travel in the Far East. And of course many affairs with women. Joseph had never settled for anything; nor had he settled down. He had never been able to settle down. That some of his existential problems remained unresolved seemed evident from the muddle of papers in Clement's room; he had left scattered evidence of his existence, almost as a challenge to his brother, whose duty in life it was to understand.

Clement's training, as well as his analytical disposition, enabled him to see how reluctant he was to face his own lack of involvement in Joseph's affairs. He had been far — often physically far — from the crucial events in Joseph's career.

He took from the drawer of his desk an envelope containing a letter and photograph Joseph had sent him in the early eighties. He was sorry to think that they had arrived in response to his duplicated form. When he was embarking on the research required for *Adaptability*, Clement had sent out the forms to large numbers of people, inviting memories of the beginning of the war in 1939. He had been impersonal; his brother's response had been personal and immediate.

Joseph had taken the printed question literally. His reply, in his hasty handwriting, concerned only the declaration of war, when he had just turned thirteen. On that day, 3rd September 1939, when Britain and France declared war on Nazi Germany, his sister Ellen was almost nine; Clement was little more than a toddler. Their parents, Ernest and Madge Winter, were in their late thirties or early forties.

Madge Winter had taken the photograph on the family box Brownie. It was in black-and-white, with a white margin. Time had made it crisp and slightly concave. In Joseph's writing on the back of the snap was the legend, "Taken an hour after war was declared."

The family was standing by the old square Morris. Ellen, in a check print dress, was holding baby Clement and grinning. Joseph, in holiday shorts, was wearing a large cap and grinning. Father looked sternly out of the car window, elbow and forearm disclosing a rolled-up shirt sleeve. His expression suggested he was mulling over his favourite phrase, 'That's what you get. . . .' Behind the car, part of a ruin could be seen. They had been holidaying on the north coast of Cornwall, by Tintagel, King Arthur's castle.

"I respond to your form at once, because the more obstinately 1939 gets forgotten by the population at large, the more obstinately I remember it," Joseph had written in his reply to the form.

Even there, Clement reflected, Joseph revealed his character. Good-natured, rather self-mocking, yet in some way challenging, going against the grain.

"There was a car park on the cliff top, large and open, and almost deserted except for our Morris and someone's caravan. The caravan was drawn up so that it enjoyed views of the Atlantic. Rather a battered old thing, if I remember rightly (does one ever remember rightly?). Father pulled up next to it. We got out and Ellen and I ran to look at the cliffs, followed by cautionary screams from mother.

"A fat man climbed out of the caravan, strolling across to engage my father in conversation. I went over to them after a while, in order to observe the fat man at close quarters. He smoked a pipe and wore a panama hat. Also old grey flannel trousers held up by braces, unless I invent that bit. He seemed a jolly man, although he and father were talking seriously about the international situation. It was a Sunday, and father showed him something in the newspaper.

"The fat man said that his wife had turned him out of the caravan while she prepared lunch — speaking laughingly, he added that there wasn't room for two large people inside when she was busy. He waved to her, I remember, and the woman looked out and waved back, with an extra wave for me.

"She was cooking sausages and mash, and had their radio tuned to the Home Service. The radio said there was to be a special announcement. 'This'll be it,' said the fat man to father, calling to his wife to turn the volume up.

"Mother and Ellen were walking off towards the ruins with the baby — with you. I stood beside father, staring out to sea. The sun was shining. It was a beautiful day and the sausages smelt good.

"I felt anxious. Perhaps I prayed. I was pretty religious at that age. Kids used to be. It seemed unlikely to me that Hitler would halt the invasion of Poland just because we asked him to, powerful though we believed Britain to be at that time. In a minute, up came the voice of Neville Chamberlain, to inform us that a state of war existed with Nazi Germany. The solemnity of his tone as much as the words impressed me deeply. I looked up at father. He just continued to stare out over the Atlantic. The fat man swore — politely, because I was there. His wife went on frying sausages.

"She called her husband in for lunch after a while. I could hardly believe it. I imagined everything stopped when war began. We shook hands with the fat man. I was proud because he shook hands with me very readily and told me to do well. He dipped into a pocket and gave me sixpence before disappearing. While this comforted me father was annoyed with me for accepting it. He thought the man was common. No one had sausages for Sunday dinner, even on holiday, he said.

"He headed for the ruins to break the news to mother. I followed. The sunlight and the sea remained completely unaltered."

Clement folded the letter along its old crease-lines, and reinserted it in its envelope. That had been one enormous difference between him and Joseph: the war. It had for ever separated them.

His gaze alighted on the small package from his sister. As he took up his paperknife to open it, Sheila entered the room carrying the wine bottle, and sat down on his sofa.

"How was Maureen?"

"Oh, she's still working to abolish marriage, the legalised way in which men suppress women." They both laughed. Since her separation from a drunken husband some years ago, Sheila's friend Maureen Bowler had become a noted feminist.

"You'll take life easy for a few days, Sheila, darling? You need a rest after all the Green Mouth excitements in the States."

"Perhaps we'll fly down and have a few days in Marbella next month, if it's not too hot. I'm not doing anything too serious at present. But I phoned Mrs F."

Mrs F. was Mrs Flowerbury, Sheila's faithful secretary.

"There's a pile of stuff awaiting attention in my study. Mrs F. swore she was prepared to come even on Sunday."

"Silly woman!"

"Well, her children are away and her husband's got this contract in the Gulf. I think she's glad to come here to fill in the time. As you know, some people have peculiar attitudes to time. . . ."

They chatted and drank wine for a while, until Sheila told Clement to open up Ellen's package.

From the wrapping he lifted seven venerable envelopes. They were accompanied by a letter from Ellen, penned in her small grey house in Salisbury on small grey notepaper.

Holding up the paper, Clement read aloud. "'Knowing that you are working on Brother Joseph's papers, I am sending you seven letters which he wrote to me from India. I was only fourteen at the time, he was my idolised elder brother. The letters have become fragile with time, like the rest of us. Treasure them well. I definitely' — underlined — 'want them back before long.' And she ends with love to you and me, and a P.S. saying the dog is in good health."

"Nothing about Jean?" Sheila asked.

"She doesn't mention Jean." Jean was the only child of the marriage between Ellen and Alwyn Pickering. She had become divorced three years earlier and was the source of excited anxiety to her mother, in which capacity she vied with Jessie, the dog.

Of the seven envelopes Ellen had sent, two were plain. Five were official, with the words ACTIVE SERVICE printed boldly on them. All seven bore four anna stamps and Indian postmarks, dating from the time when Joseph was a soldier on his way to fight the Japanese in Burma. His age was eighteen, although he had passed himself off for a year older than he was.

"They're antiques!" Sheila exclaimed.

"We all are."

"Speak for yourself."

Switching on his desk light, Clement began to read the letters in order, passing each to Sheila as he finished it.

Even as he read, he thought, "I can't simply use Joseph as a witness in my book. He'll have to have a book to himself and I'll have to write it. I can start with his war service."

The frayed letters, now over forty-two years old, were written in various inks and pencil on various pieces of paper. All testified to a close link between brother and sister, excluding little Clem.

Dimapur, India
3rd Oct. 1944

Dearest Ellen,

Just a note to tell you that your loving brother is on the fringes of something triffic. Or trifficesque. An adventure. Like the ones we used to have together, imagining we were in the wilds. Now I am really going to be in the wilds. The real wilds. The wildly wild wilds.

In fact if you could see me at present you'd guess something wild was in the wind. I'm sitting writing to you in a broken down old tent, relic of the Great War or the Crimea, in a terrible transit camp in a place called Dimapur, on the threatened eastern fringes of India. Look it up in your school atlas. The flies are dreadful, the whole camp is like an entrance to hell. Except hell is not as hot as Dimapur.

We arrived here late last night, off the train from a place further north called Tinsoukia, four days after leaving Calcutta. I had been sixteen days on the move, shunted here and there by an inefficient administration, sleeping in trains (sometimes on the wooden luggage rack) and even on hard concrete station platforms among the natives. There were six of us arriving at 2 a.m. this morning, exhausted, to a not very friendly reception. Orderly corporals are a bad lot at the best of times. This one said he could do nothing till eight this morning. We had to sleep on the tables in the mess. So we did, for about three hours. (The mess is a concrete floor and a thatched roof, by the way.)

At six, as day was dawning, we were woken by the cooks. Cooks are worse than corporals. We had to get up then while they prepared breakfast. Later on, we checked into this most derelict of tents and here we are. I've had a snooze. Now this note. We haven't the faintest idea what will happen next — except that we are on our way to Burma to fight the Japs. I shall not name that country again. It's against regs. Take it from me that it is less a country, more a state of mind. The Id of the modern world.

The food would make you sick, but we're used to it.

There was a notice on Dimapur station which said NEW YORK 11,000 MILES, TOKYO 5,400 miles, LONDON 8,300 MILES. That's how far we are from civilisation.

Our detail is under command of a cheerful sergeant called Ted Sutton. He's from Yorkshire, a brickie foreman in civvy life, and one of the best men I ever met. Nothing upsets him, nor can you put anything over on him. Privately, I worship Ted and his cheerfulness. I'd follow him anywhere. No doubt I shall have to.

I'm very cheerful. The awfulness is exciting. But I'm also a bit fed up (or *chokka*, as we say here). I wanted to get to China. You know how I've always been mad about things Chinese. It's quite close. Chunking's the place to be — Chiang Kai-shek's capital. Constantly bombed by the Japs, full of filth and mud, so I heard from a chap in a bar in Calcutta who'd been there. That's where I long to be. (Okay, I'm daft, but it can't be worse than — where we're going. . . .) I volunteered twice, knowing the Chinese are bound to be short of radio ops. But no joy. Funny, the Chinese aren't trusted. Yet they're our allies. (I saw some beautiful Chinese girls in Calcutta but never mind that!)

Oh, we're supposed to parade or something. I'll post this here or God knows when there will be another chance. Here we go! Love to all.

Dear Ellen,

Some address, eh? Some place!

Plenty of through traffic, as you might expect. We're literally perched on the edge of a road. And what a road! I wish you could see it. It would satisfy your craving for "mad things"!

I wrote to you last from another world. Something has happened since then; that old world has gone. This is a different world — a sub-world of men only and grave intentions and festering discontent and rationed food and that particular brand of "organised chaos" in which the British Army specialises. Well, before I get too philosophical, I'd better tell you how we got to Milestone 81.

Was there ever such a day — or such a road! We started out from Dimapur (if you got my letter from there, which I doubt, because the camp was so appalling they probably burn all letters), where this road begins. It runs on to Kohima and Imphal — famous, legendary names, local equivalents of Valhalla. We travelled in a three-tonner, eight of us. All I could do was stand looking out of the back and marvel, along with a bloke from Warrington called Fergy. Some of the others — amazing! — weren't interested, and didn't look. I bet you would have done.

Like the Burma Road, this road has been built by coolie labour — is *still* being built, because owing to landslides and rockfalls it is never completed. It's been hacked out of jungle-clad mountainside. I've never seen such mountains. Jagged, steep — someone's going to have to fight over mountains very similar. Many trucks have driven over the edge. It's easy — just a moment's lack of concentration. . . . You can see the skeletons of crashed trucks down in the valleys, far below. Sometimes we passed strings of men, almost naked, with buckets balanced on poles over their shoulders — down far below, or far above the road. And here and there, too, working by the little threads of river in the valleys, peasants — bent in typical peasant posture, working. Even war brings them no relief from work.

It's a one-lane road, with lay-bys every so often to let convoys pass each other. Each milestone marked — each an achievement.

At Milestone 81, I got decanted, and here I am. A real soldier now. In a WAR ZONE.

Royal Signals is strong here, along with other units of the famous British 2 Division. We are now part of the multi-racial Fourteenth Army, more familiarly known as the Forgotten Army. The Forgotten Army. The name clings like mustard gas. Everyone here grumbles like fury. I have to hide the fact that I'm enjoying it all.

Later. Sorry, interruption. I was talking about the people I now must work with. They have every right to grumble. They are more or less resting after the battle of Kohima. "One of the worst British battles of the war." Kohima's only a few miles ahead of us. It's now safe in British hands, what's left of it, and all the Japs there are dead. Very few prisoners taken.

The chaps complain because they think they should be sent home, or at least be given leave in India. Instead they face another campaign. And they have only me to tell it to. I think they hate me — inexperienced, pale-skinned, and having missed the hard bits. . . . Most of them have already served three years out here. No home leave. Offered no prospect at all of getting home as long as the war with Japan lasts . . . which could be a century.

Morale's low. You get the idea. They romanticise themselves as the Forgotten Army. Very bitter. I was still in the Fourth Form when they came out here.

"What bloody good are you going to be, Winter?" That's what one bloke asked me yesterday. I can't say how many times I've been told to "get some service in" — which I am doing. Trouble is, we all go about in the bare bluff, as they say, and everyone here is baked dark brown. I'm conspicuous because as yet I'm still lily white from England. Another week or two of this sun should cure that!

The only person who has been friendly so far is a Birmingham man, Bert Lyons, whose father owns a bicycle shop. He and I had quite a good talk by the light of a small lantern last night. Bert seems to have the same kind of sense of wonder as you and I. He's also a radio op.

The Japs are still marching on India. Though we turned them back at Kohima, they are still regarded as almost unbeatable. Bert says it's because they can live on so little — a handful of rice a day. Whereas we are decadent. He says the British Empire is finished. The Japs took over Malaya, Singapore, the Dutch East Indies, and Burma itself so easily. It's incredible. Are they going to rule half the world? Slim, the commander of the Forgotten Army, calls them "the most formidable fighting insects on Earth". I guess dealing with Japs is a bit like that — fighting giant invading insects from another world. The tales of their cruelty are legendary.

Before reaching Milestone 81, we reinforcements had a chance to talk to some troops who had been in Orde Wingate's Chindits — heroes all — and they were in no doubt about just how tough all encounters with the

Jap were likely to be. (If they got wounded in the jungle, these Chindits were given a shot of morphine and left with a revolver — to shoot themselves rather than fall into Jap hands.)

Anyhow, I'm now a member of "S" Signal Section — their sole new recruit. The other reinforcements are spread throughout the division. I've not been through "S" section's harrowing experiences, about which they constantly tell me. Am I welcome? Certainly not. I'm a representative of "The Blight" (Blighty), the country thousands of miles distant which has ignored them and their exploits for so long. Thank God for Bert Lyons. "Don't worry, we're all *puggle*," he says — *puggle* being our word for *le cafard*. . . .

Such mighty things happening. Conversation so trivial — apart from those terrible experiences — some of which I now know by heart. God, what these poor so-and-sos have been through. And more to come.

I'm off on duty now. Love to all.

Milestone 81. Assam
13th Oct. 1944

Dear Ellen,

Hope to hear from you some day. Letter from Mum, which I'll answer soon. Perhaps you could show her this one to be going on with. The chaps here have mainly given up writing home.

We're still waiting to move forward. I'll then have to be careful what I say. Of course our letters are censored by one of the officers for safety's sake.

I'll tell you what our billet is like. Very picturesque, I assure you.

I'm lodged in a tent consisting of a spread of brown tarpaulin over a patch of steep hillside. Lodged is the word. When I got here from Dimapur, five men already occupied the tent. If you can call it a tent. They made room for me, and so I found lodgement on the outer side, just about.

My bed or *charpoy* is home-made. I can't say I'm proud of my handiwork, but it'll do. A bit Robinson Crusoe! It consists of a ground sheet stretched across four bamboo poles which are lashed together with old signal wire. This masterpiece is balanced on empty jerry cans, stacked so that the bed is roughly level on the uneven ground. My mosquito net is secured to ropes overhead, so low that the net is uncomfortably close to my face. Never mind — I can see the stars at night.

Apparently we are 4,300 feet above sea level. It's as if we were perched on the top of Ben Nevis. From my charpoy, I can see a hill whose peak is a thousand feet higher than we are. It towers above us, jungle-clad all the way. Not long ago, it swarmed with Japs. By propping myself up on one elbow, I can see the great road, winding and winding on for miles, always carrying its slow crawl of convoys. What a window on the world! Behind me, on the slope where we are perched, is an untidy waste land, only partly cleared. It was also Jap-infested until recently. In it still remain all the vantage points, fire bays, and tunnels the Japs dug. They were killed by grenades and flame-throwers, and their bodies walled-in where they lay. No wonder the hillside has a thriving rat population. . . .

I was asleep last night when a rat jumped on to my charpoy and ran across the net over my face. I struck out violently at it — and dislodged my charpoy from its pile of cans. Consequently I was pitched right out of the tent, where I rolled some way down the slope, naked as the day I was born. The other blokes just laughed or swore because I had woken them. I had to laugh myself.

Mum asks if we have any entertainment. Three nights ago, the Army Cinema rolled up and showed us Margaret Lockwood in *The Wicked Lady*, which I now know nearly by heart. The men just sat about on the hillside, watching. You should — or shouldn't — have heard what they said they'd do to Margaret Lockwood. Out here, a white woman is almost a mythological creature.

Can't be bothered to write more. I like this place — it's so weird, though everyone takes it for granted. We haven't even got a NAAFI, where you might linger over a beer or a coffee.

One entertainment is to watch the agile Naga women climb up and down the steep hillsides to harvest tea in the distant valley. They don't look as good as Margaret Lockwood. They scale the slopes with huge wicker baskets secured to their backs by wide leather straps running round the forehead. It's a tough life, and they can't let the war get in their way. Do they consider their surroundings beautiful, I wonder?

Love to all.

Milestone 81. Assam (Nagaland)
18th Nov. 1944

Dear Ellen,

Still in the same spot. This outdoor life must be depraving: what do you think? Yesterday I stole something. . . .

My orders were to report to the MO for various injections — TAB and so on. The MO — how typical of an officer — had appropriated for himself what passes out here for a "cushy billet", a bungalow belonging to a tea planter who is now probably sitting out his life in

New Delhi (unless the Japs got him). It felt quite odd to be "indoors". The waiting room in which I was made to kick my heels for a good half-hour actually boasted a couple of cane armchairs and a *crammed bookcase*. What an anachronism! Books! On one shelf was a paperback with a title that immediately attracted me. I started reading it there and then.

Right after the first page, I knew that that book had to become part of the booty of war. "Loot what you can" is an ancient warrior's slogan. Even a 1/3d. Pelican. By the time the doctor summoned me, it was safe inside my bush shirt. The book is Olaf Stapledon's *Last and First Men*, and tells of the rise and fall of poor suffering humanity over the next few billion years. (Are we rising or falling just now?)

Stapledon is an even better companion than Bert Lyons. He'll come into action with me (we're due to go forward soon). He provides an antidote to the triviality of daily conversation (which is in contrast to the majesty of our surroundings), which centres largely round the subjects of Kohima, sex, and the possibilities of getting home. Only Stapledon and his preoccupations seem a match for these stirring times. A cure for transience.

End of true confession. Sorry to write in pencil.

Love to all.

                                              Milestone 81. Nagaland
                                              30 Nov. 1944

Dear Ellen,

Many thanks for the letter with all the sordid details of your birthday. Or at least some of them. You're really getting a big girl — and who is this fellow Mark who is taking such an interest in you? Full details please. The mouth organ sounds like a great attraction.

Sorry I wasn't with you to have a slice of that cake. Rations or no rations, Mum obviously did well. Our rations here are awful. I won't go into details, but I'm always hungry. Everything we eat has to come down that winding road from Dimapur which I described to you earlier. Sometimes the ration wagon rolls over the cliff-side. Then we go short. The chaps in my tent talk about cooking up rats, and swear that rats and canned Indian peas taste good — but that's just to impress the newcomer in their midst, I hope.

Forgive this awful colour ink — all I could find.

Rumours abound. We are at last about to move forward into action. So they tell us.

"I heard the Captain say
We're going to move today.
I only hope the blinking sergeant-major knows the way. . . ."

This camp, now so familiar, is temporary. Everything is temporary along the Dimapur road. Maybe one day they will let it all revert to jungle. The air's so fresh and good here and I'm secretly so excited.

It's not only the air that's fresh. So's the water. Washing is quite an adventure. I wish I could draw. Facilities are just about nil at Milestone 81. Our only place to wash is at the mouth of a huge cast-iron pipe which snakes down the hillside and terminates here at a concrete base. The pipe vibrates with power and water gushes forth, splashing everywhere. In order to wash, you have to strip off entirely and then fling yourself into the stream. It's like jumping in front of a cannon! It's easiest to take the full force of the water smack in the chest — difficult to do because slippery green algae grow on the ever-wet concrete.

The water's freezing cold. It's come down from five thousand feet in a great hurry. Soaping is mighty difficult. However, my hardened campaigner friends tell me that it could be the last running water we'll see for months. (They're ever optimistic.)

We've just been issued with new chemical stuff called DDT. We've had to dip our shirts in it and run the liquid along the seams of our trousers. This will prevent lice and other nasty things at a time when it looks as if we shall be unable to wash clothes for months at a stretch.

You see what a funny life your brother leads. It's better than school. And to toughen us up, we've been made to climb down into the valley and back, with kit. I tried to get a piggy-back off one of the Naga women, but no luck. We can't climb the mountain above us, because that's where the Nagas live and they must not be disturbed.

Yours till the cows come home.

Manipur, I think
20th Dec. 1944

My dear Ellen,

Guess what? It's Christmas Day! Yes, 20th December.

The world has done one of its marvellous changes. Everything is different. I'm different. I'm rolling forward into ACTION. Imagine! This green and dusty world is slipping towards jungle warfare. . . .

We knew something was up on the fifteenth and sixteenth. Our unit on

40

that day had its collective haircut. Weren't knights of old shriven before battle? Shriven and shorn? Well, at least we've been shorn.

Ahead of us lie danger and a desperate land full of terrors and destitute of barbers. . . .

The very next day — we packed up everything and started rolling forward. A whole division, 2 Div, moving to our forward positions before the actual assault.

At the last minute, the CO addressed us, gave us a briefing. "You will all be proud to fight for king and country. . . ." He doesn't know his men. But he concluded by quoting Shakespeare:

> And gentlemen in England now abed
> Shall think themselves accursed they were not here,
> And hold their manhoods cheap while any speaks
> That fought with us upon St Crispin's Day.

Among the common soldiery was many a moist eye. Amazing to see us all respond to poetry. Or maybe it was funk.

I have to scribble these lines just to tell you about the journey, hoping not to anger the censor. Because it really was legendary — legendary! Not to be measured in miles or the time on a clockface. A move across a great division, like the division between life and death —

— Into a land without civilians. Without civilisation. Not a place for ordinary human life. You couldn't buy a ticket to get here.

A mysterious mountain country — without living inhabitants, without real roads, without towns, without flags or currencies. The writhing, thunderous, plenitudinous route to war. A newly invented route, patched together out of lanes, jungle tracks, *chaungs* (a *chaung* being a sandy stream bed reliably dry in the dry season). On this gallant road we embarked at a dim and secret hour of night, with even our voices muffled, for every sound carries in the thin air. We're travelling from Milestone 81 — home! — to a rendezvous in the country I can't name, called Yzagio. This rather imaginary highway we travel is christened the Tiddim Road. Six months ago, it was all dense jungle and raging rivers. And in Japanese territory.

If you will have nothing of this legend, then I have to admit that this way of the conquerors lasts only about two hundred miles. On it, my girl, we left the old mundane world behind.

After we had passed the blackened remains of Kohima — like all you ever imagined of the Great War — we went from Nagaland into the old state of Manipur. Ragged and brutalised Imphal went by, possessed

41

solely by pigs and vultures. The mountains became more gigantic, the way more unlikely, like something in a dream. All our vehicles proceed at a crawl, in bottom gear most of the time. Headlights are muffled. We ourselves wear a secret, anonymous air. Dispatch riders patrol up and down the convoy, seeing to it that the trucks keep even distance, neither too far from nor too close to the next vehicle. All this in a great fog of dust, the very material of secrecy.

I'm travelling in a three-tonner with some of "S" Section and its stores. The stores include immense rolls of barbed wire. So excited was I last night that I climbed over the barbed wire as we moved, until most of me was out on the cab roof, from where I got a fine view of the shrouded nomansland all round us. In that awkward position I fell asleep.

Shouting and noise. Daylight. I awoke. I was hanging far over the side of the vehicle, between cab and body, my legs trapped in a roll of barbed wire, *upside-down*. In my sleep I had slipped right off the smooth cab. But for the embrace of the wire, I would certainly have fallen to the ground and been run over in the dark.

That was this morning. I live to tell the tale. God knows where we are. In place or time — because today we were served our Christmas dinner. Imagine, 20th December! Very surrealist.

We ate in an empty grain store, all built of bamboo and dry leaves. Being a greedy little thing, you'll like to know what we got for this monster feast. Well, it was probably better than you will do on the 25th. We started with chicken noodle soup, followed by canned chicken, canned mutton, sausage stuffing, beans, potatoes and gravy, all washed down by two cans of beer, and followed by Christmas duff with sauce and canned pears. Then coffee. A marvellous blow-out!

By way of presents, each man got a handful of sweets and biscuits and half a bar of Cadbury's chocolate. The CO then made a brief speech and offered us this toast: "To our wives and sweethearts!" (The old meanie didn't say anything about *sisters.* . . .)

This meal has marked not only the putting away of the old order but the imposition of half-rations. Fancy — the food was bad enough at Milestone 81. But from now on all food has to be supplied by air, so half-rations it is.

Soon it will be dark. That's the end of Christmas Day and then we'll be on the wonderful road again. I tell you these things. Try to understand. Something really extraordinary is happening to your old brother.

God knows when this'll be posted but — Happy Christmas!

Dear Ellen,

How are things at home? How is the mouth organ player? You all seem very far away. There are great psychological barriers in communicating rather than in just firing off letters for their own sweet sakes. To be honest, I'm not sure if the outer world exists any more.

And I've got other problems. . . . For instance, I was hauled up before an officer I had better not name (he will probably read this letter before you do) in the Censorship office. Apparently I have been giving too much away in my letters and endangering security. (You might be a Jap agent in England, sending all my letters on to High Command in Tokyo, or something similarly daft.) There I stood, rigid at attention in my soiled jungle greens; there he sat immaculate in khaki, putting me right. On such situations the British Empire is founded.

In future any references to place names or troop movements will be deleted from my letters. There is to be no further attempt to convey a picture of what is happening in these possibly most exciting days of my life. I made a protest, but it's like butting your blinking head against an advancing tank. Any attempts to evade regulations will be punished.

It was hard enough in the first place, trying to describe life here to you. Now I'm *forbidden* to try to convey a picture! So here's what may prove to be my last try.

I mean the picture is like one of those marvellous Brueghels (in this culturally deprived area I have even forgotten how you spell that weird Flemish name. . . .). Is there one called *The Conversion of St Paul*? Where there are thousands of people on horseback and on foot in the tall mountains and, although St Paul is having his moment right in the middle of the picture, no one is taking a blind bit of notice. We're doing this incredible thing and no one's taking a blind bit of notice — just grumbling about where their next packet of fags is coming from. . . .

Later. Oh, *burps*. Now the first day of 1945. No celebrations last night, bringing more complaints. Fancy wanting to celebrate. I was collared to shift heavy stores. Too exhausted then to do anything more than sleep.

We're at a place called — but I named it once and daren't do so again or they'll keelhaul me under the nearest 3-tonner. Great amassment of vehicles. People all strolling round, brown as berries, smoking among the branchless trees. (Hope that doesn't give our positions away.) Half-rations. God in his heaven, CO in his mobile home. Only the Japs missing from the picture. (You could perhaps get Dad to send me some ciggies if he's feeling generous.)

Oh, I can't concentrate. Something comes between us, and you know who he is.

Well, I'll just tell you how we got here. I think it was the night after I last wrote that we got on the road again, the whole division, all very orderly. (I don't tell you which division, so it's safe. . . .) I was more careful about how I travelled, not wanting to meet my end yet — dying for your country should not entail being run over by your own 3-tonner! Yet the sight of endless trucks trundling like elephants in convoy is irresistible. Are they off to the Elephants' Graveyard or a solemn heavyweight orgy? Some stops, some starts, yet on the whole a steady funeral pace. Huge chunks of landscape phantasmal in the dusty dark.

Sleep, huddled in a silly position on a crate. Waking next morning very early to behold a wondrous sight.

> Is dawn a secret shy and cold,
> Anadyomene, silver-gold?
> Are we still on terra firma
> Or merely moving into — another land?

Answers in the affirmative c/o The Censor, please. The convoy was winding about the endless mountains, intruding into a Chinese landscape. Mountains filled our view, heaps of them. Beyond each mountain, more mountains, thickly afforested. Clouds floated *below* us, lit by the early sun. Clouds and smaller clouds of dust. For wherever the mountains went, there too went the road, coiling tirelessly — and, for all its inexhaustible miles, covered with X Div vehicles. What an astonishing sight! My first experience of travelling mountainous country. We could see the road winding above and behind us; it was the way we had come. And there it all was to be seen and enjoyed. We were outdoors, and not sitting inside at desks, over boring lesson books.

Green, blue, gold, were the colours of the distance. Closer at hand, only the sandy grey of dust and vehicles. The trucks in their passage threw up dust over all the trees lining the way. Everything without wheels stood absolutely motionless, as if breeze had never been invented, as if the dust had killed off the jungle.

So we made our advance over that marvellous ——— Road, across the mountains of Manipur and those of the ——— Range, until we reached the more level ground on which our present site (no names, no pack-drill) stands. We are parked in a scraggy and ant-infested forest, while the division sorts itself out in order of battle and puts in maintenance on all vehicles.

Later. Sorry to go on in pencil, but I'm now in the signal office. On duty but little traffic coming over the wires, so I'll continue for a while.

It's hot. I'm sweating.

The signal office is a 3-ton lorry, its flap at the rear raised horizontally to extend the floor-space. You climb into the lorry by a rusty ladder with three widely spaced wooden rungs. Inside, at the end nearest the cab, sits the Signal Master in all his glory. He's an officer (of course). He has a table with a field phone. Before him are piles of paper, code names, references, maps, diagrams, documents.

To one side of the lorry are two long narrow tables on which stand four Fullerphones. These chesty, unhappy little instruments play an important role in keeping the division in touch with itself and with other nearby units. On the floor are four piles of Fullerphone boxes, and on these the Fullerphone operators have to sit. They are translating the buzzings in their earphones into words on paper — as I'm doing between scribbling to you.

A tarpaulin is attached to the outside of the lorry and extended so as to provide shade for the Counter Clerk. He's an important man. At the moment it's our Corporal Pine. The Corp shuffles and sorts and distributes the endless stream of messages which pass through our hands, dealing them out to us operators or to various other lowly degrees of messenger.

With him sits the Superintendent, crooning times and cyphers into the ear of his phone. Here too sits our orderly, patiently waiting — at present it's Steve. This morning it was old Gaskin. Steve smokes stylishly, cradling one elbow in the palm of his hand, relaxed until the counter clerk calls on him to take a message on foot to one of the local gods hiding nearby behind acronyms, ADMS, ARQS, CLAD, DELS, and the like.

A camouflage net covers this lazy yet busy scene. Flies buzz everywhere.

Oh, yes. Nearby is another tent, upon which snakelike lines of cables converge. It's our telephone exchange, a place of urgency, stuffed with winking lights and brass plugs. This is the tent whose ropes you trip over, swearing, in the dark.

Dispatch riders and cable-layers lurk nearby, somnolent as lizards. Only lizards don't smoke.

Bert's my relief. He's working another Fullerphone. By now, I am pretty well accepted by the rest of "S" Section. They respect the fact that I nearly fell off the truck one night, and that I was hauled up before the Censor (they mostly gave up writing home long ago — part of the myth

45

of the Forgotten Army). They are no longer astonished that I can send and transmit Morse almost as rapidly, as stylishly, as they. What they can't get over is the fact that I appear to be enjoying myself. Nor can I.

Love to all.

III

Clement folded Ellen's letters carefully back into their envelopes and took them over to the window sill, to tuck them in Box File No. 2, in which he kept anything of his brother's relating to the war period.

"Good letters," Sheila said. She had sat immobile, as was her way, to read them through. "Joe's excitement comes through. He seems to have had no qualms about going to war."

"That's true." Glancing out of the window, he saw Alice Farrer in her front garden next door. Holding her green watering-can, she was sprinkling the roots of her pseudo-acacia. It was her excuse to have a good look at what was happening in the street. The fact that very little ever happened did not deter her. She used her nose as a tracking device to follow two girl students who walked slowly along the pavement, talking, completely unaware of her.

"He had made up his mind by then there were worse things than going to war." He spoke as he turned back into the room. He was fascinated by Alice Farrer only to the extent that he could say honestly that nothing she did would ever interest him.

"Such as what, exactly? His unhappy childhood?"

"That, too, I suppose. But I was thinking of an incident he once told me about. Maybe he told me twice. It was about something which had made a great impression on him. It took place outside Calcutta, and so it would have happened just before the first of these letters to Ellen. In any case, the incident was too horrific for him to wish to report it to a little sister.

"The group he was in was led by the Sergeant Sutton he mentions in one of Ellen's letters. After travelling across India from Bombay, they reached a transit camp somewhere on the outskirts of Calcutta. Joe gave me a vivid account of the squalor, and of seeing a water buffalo dying in the railway marshalling yards — shunting yards, we used to call them — surrounded by vultures, who set about tearing it to shreds while it still had life.

"Owing to some confusion in the rail timetables, not uncommon in those days of crisis, with the Japanese army at the gates of India, Joe's detachment had to leave their train and go to this camp somewhere nearby. It was just a collection of ragged tents beside a railway

47

embankment, no signs of discipline or cleanliness anywhere. Full of flies and filth.

"Joe and Sutton went to the office to apply for money to continue their journey to Burma. I suppose at that time the movement of troops would be towards the east only, across India to the war zone. He said it was like a peristaltic movement. Everyone was drawn into it. But he and Sutton found that this camp was full of deserters, who had got that far and then jumped off trains at Calcutta, rather than face the Japanese. Deserters ran the camp. There was nowhere they could go — they certainly couldn't make it back to England. So they stayed put, waiting for the war to finish. If the camp was inspected, the deserters simply melted into Calcutta, where no one could find them. They lived by making false returns to various legitimate units nearby. The money was spent on food, booze, and whores. The whores came into the camp — quite against army regulations, of course."

He glanced out of the window again. "The old bitch next door is watering her tree once more. Anyhow, Joe and Co had to stay in the deserters' camp that night. The camp was run by a renegade RSM, a Glasgow man, an alcoholic. He approached Sergeant Sutton, inviting him to stay there, since he wanted a sergeant under his command. Joe thought there was some talk of a drug racket, I don't know what.

"They had a crisis in the camp. I've never told you this, have I? The RSM had an NCO with him who was severely ill from amoebic dysentery and complications. He died the night Joe was in the camp. The RSM sent a detail of four men out at midnight with storm lanterns to bury the body under a railway bridge, where it wouldn't be discovered. They hadn't got a padre for any kind of service, because all padres were officers, and an officer would have had them rounded up and shot.

"Sergeant Sutton said to Joe and the others, while the burial was going on, 'Do you want to stay here or go on to Burma?' All the detachment, fresh out from England, were profoundly shocked by what was happening. Of course, the idea of Burma was also not to be taken lightly. So Joe said to Sergeant Sutton, 'What do you think, sarge?'

"And the sergeant said, 'I'd sooner be killed in battle than stay in this fucking sink of iniquity another night.' Next morning, they marched back to the Calcutta station — Howrah, I think it was called. They swore to the RSM that they would say nothing about the illegal camp, and of course they kept their word.

"Joe derived a profound moral from that episode. I've always thought of him as very courageous — not heroic, I don't mean, but courageous — and he probably saw the war itself as somehow cleaner or more honest than the fear which was the reason for the camp's existence. He saw how easily men could deteriorate."

Sheila had moved over to the window and was gazing out at the sunlit street.

"It makes a good story. Terrifying. It would make a play. Did the RSM threaten them before letting them leave? With a gun, I mean?"

"I don't know about that."

"I think he'd have to. Burying the body at dead of night is a nice touch, but they could have left the body out for the vultures. Would that be a quicker way of disposing of the body?"

"Sheila, this really happened."

"Yes, I know."

When she had gone downstairs to get on with her own work, and he heard her typewriter tapping in the room below his, he thought of how her mind was at work on the story. It would probably surface, with added drama, in a future Kerinth novel. He merely wanted to strengthen the story, not add to it. He wanted it clear and as it had been, over forty years ago. Yet even he, telling it to Sheila, had added something. The bit about the whores coming into the camp seemed all too likely; but that had not been anything Joseph had told him. He remembered now that Joseph had said, in passing, that the deserters got fearfully drunk on palm wine every night, in order to escape from their miserable circumstances. Had he said palm wine? It was difficult to remember.

Precision was not the only function of memory.

All the untidy clutter of papers in his room came from Joseph's flat in Acton. He had to get clear in his own mind his brother's early years. Then he could make decisions on how to deploy the material.

He picked up from his desk a photograph he had taken a year before Joseph's death, showing Joseph and Sheila walking together on Port Meadow. In the background was Joseph's girl friend — his final girl friend — Lucy Traill.

Joseph was laughing, his mouth open, his face creased with humour. His tall, spare figure was leaning slightly forward. He liked to walk briskly. His hair, as always too long, was a streaky white and grey.

It was his wife's features that Clement mainly studied. Because of the aspect of stillness in Sheila's nature, she photographed well. Her broad face and well-defined nose and mouth were in evidence as she smiled at whatever the joke was. He thought, "No photograph can ever do her justice. Nor for that matter does my memory. I fail to set up a moving picture of her in my mind. That's why I'm always eager to see her again, even if she has been out of the room for less than an hour. How I love

49

that face! I couldn't explain to anyone what it means to me, to see it every day.

"I must be over-dependent on her. Why aren't I more detached, as I am with others — with Arthur Stranks, for instance? Sheila would probably be shocked if she knew with what intensity I love her face and the woman. What a weakling I am! And she went to bed with that wretched little Hernandez. . . ."

He was wasting time. To celebrate the publication of *War Lord of Kerinth*, he was arranging a party for Sheila in nine days' time, on the Thursday of the following week. He made a few phone calls to local friends, inviting them to come. Then he returned to the question of his brother.

In Box File No. 2 lay a battered exercise book, in which Joseph had sought to retain some of his memories of the war years, in particular his time in Burma. The letters to his sister explained why Joseph had scarcely written home at all during the Burmese campaign. The censorship would not permit him to give a truthful account. And the censor already had an eye on Joseph. Joseph perhaps recalled Frederick the Great's epigram that the common soldier had to fear his officer more than the enemy.

The battered exercise book was of Indian origin, bound in a coarsely woven cover. The narrative it contained was undated. The handwriting, in miscellaneous inks, some now badly faded, varied sufficiently for Clement to infer that the greater part of the account had been composed shortly after Joseph's division had returned from Burma to India for rest and recuperation.

This was his brother's first attempt at anything like an historical narrative, his first step towards the historian he was later to become. To lend the original narrative a clearer perspective, Joseph had inserted a few passages later, generally of a reflective nature. For an instance, the battle of Dien Bien Phu in 1954 was mentioned.

First came the title. Joseph had made it deliberately grandiose.

A BRIEF HISTORY OF THE CAMPAIGN OF
2ND BRITISH DIVISION
UNDER GEN. NICHOLSON
AGAINST THE JAP ARMY AND
THE RECONQUEST OF MANDALAY
1944–1945
By Signalman Joseph Winter

*

Nights were filled with gunfire when the various units of 2 Div crossed the River Chindwin, against stiff opposition from the Japs situated on the eastern bank. Those nights were climatologically beautiful. The Burmese moon is like no other moon. It woke unvoiceable yearnings in the men involved in the great struggle.

Of all those beautiful dangerous nights, one in particular stands out.

I had had to be away from my unit, and a driver was sent in a Jeep to collect me and catch up with the advance. He was in no mood to hurry; I could not make him hurry; and darkness overtook us before we had done much more than start on our way forward. The sun plunged down into the earth and the stars immediately shone forth overhead, streaming along in the grip of the galactic current.

We were two insignificant creatures in a machine on a plain that ran clear to the Irrawaddy. The driver had no intention of driving by night. We ate K-rations and slept one on either side of the jeep rolled in blankets, with the marvellous sky unfettered overhead. Far from being dwarfed by it, I felt that it filled me and made me vast; I was indivisible from it. A war was passing over the starlit land with its "bright and battering sandal", and I was part of its great process.

Burma was beautiful, a country worth fighting for. Nothing else was asked — at the time, I was eighteen years of age.

We woke at dawn with a bird calling. We were chilly in our thin uniforms before the sun came up. We brewed up mugs of tea, ate a hunk of bread, and moved on. "Bloody cold," we said.

Nothing was to be seen all round us but plain and, distantly, tops of trees. I found no way in which we could share the magnificent experience of the night; perhaps such exciting experiences are always enjoyed alone — unless one has a girl there. In any case the driver was a man of few words.

The track across the plain led us to the River Chindwin, where a Bailey bridge had been built. It was strongly guarded. Men lounged about, brown-naked to the waist, smoking, rifles on their shoulders, sweat-rags tied round their necks. We called out cheery greetings as we crossed that splendid river, its name honoured in the East. Fine dust hung in the air, sun shone on the water as it ran dark and flat between its sandy banks. It was as peaceful a scene as you could wish. Only two nights earlier, men had died at that spot.

Myingyang, the town on the far side of the river, had been almost completely destroyed in the fighting. Smoke still drifted among the ruined trees. Everything — remains of houses and bungalows — took on tones of black; smoke issued from their gaping black mouths. Tree stumps still burned quietly.

Black also were the piles of corpses gathered up neatly here and there and now left to ripen like grapes in the sun. They were swollen as if about to burst, and stank with the powerful smell of death. So much for the remains of the Japanese Army.

The Jeep driver stopped at one of the biggest piles. He went over to it and helped himself to a pair of boots from one of the dead. I cannot say how this offended me. A fat porker was feeding among the corpses, scarcely able to waddle. The driver, kicking the animal out of the way, beckoned me over. I would not leave the Jeep. He selected the pair of boots he wanted, dragging them off the corpse, kneeling in the sunlight to do so. He fitted the boots on to his own feet before coming back to the vehicle. I could not look the man in the eye.

To everything that happened at that period in time, an extra weight of significance was added. It was as though I travelled back through time to witness the traits of man and nature at their most basic, as though our movement through trees was also a movement through centuries. My understanding of the world, which had hitherto been rather childish, or child-based, advanced greatly, so that everything that happened, down to the movement of my own muscles, was surrounded by a nimbus of truth, in which the ugly was perceived as being as sacred as the beautiful. The blessed sunlight contributed to this revelatory mood.

I was a little mad in the nights, as in the days. The world turned — I heard its axis rotate. One night early in the campaign we were bivouacked by the improvised road which, in the wet season, served as a river bed. A Burmese moon shone through the trees — the moon seeming always to be at the full, when Chinese Buddhist thought has it that the Yin (female) influence is at its most strong. I could not sleep, pent in my little bivouac, for an overwhelming feeling of excitement, so was forced to get up and walk among the dust-saturated trees and shadows. Muffled trucks and guns rumbled out of the silver darkness and into the opaque distance. I stood by the road, unable to leave it, letting the dust settle on me. The behemoths, with dim orange headlights for eyes, were the sole occupants of this world.

Of course what I longed for then — there and then — in my hot little heart, was love or, less abstractly, a woman to love.

Greater than the Chindwin is the river into which it flows, the unmeasurable, immemorial Irrawaddy. The waters of the Irrawaddy are fed both by tributaries rising nearby and distant tributaries which rise in regions of rock and ice up in the Himalayas, so that, like life itself, the river consists of alternating currents of warm and cold streams; and no swimmer can tell which he will encounter next, the warm or the cold. Just to stand looking at the Irrawaddy after the weeks and miles of drought we had put behind us was to drink deep, and to feel its flow as something profound — a main artery in the life of the planet.

For a brief period after rejoining my unit I was able to swim alone in the great river, flinging myself in from the sandy bank, for once unmindful of Japs, snakes, and signal offices. The river immediately took hold of one with its dark effortless power. A river-steamer had been sunk in mid-stream, and lay at an angle on the river-bed with all its superstructure in the sunlight. Long tresses of weed, anchored to its bows, pointed tremulously downstream. It was possible to reach the boat after prolonged battles with the currents, and the water, green as lizard skin, suddenly gave way to scaly hull. With a heave, I was there, over the railings and lying fish-naked on the slant of deck. Ferns and small trees grew on the deck house, giant bees toasted themselves on the scrc planking. There it was possible to squat, dangling one hand in the race, a part of that stationary voyage upstream, Captain of the Wreck.

Solitude was precious, because rare. Most of the time, we men of the Forgotten Army crowded together. Life was gregarious for safety reasons. Those of us on "S" Relief grew to know each other very well. Despite our uncertain movements, our routine was fixed. It went in three-day cycles: first day, afternoon shift from 1 p.m. till 6; second day, morning shift from 8 a.m. till 1 p.m., and night shift from 6 p.m. till 8 the next morning; third day, off duty after 8 a.m. to sleep, probably with guard or similar duties in the afternoon or evening. This routine, or something like it, was to be mine for almost three years, in action or out of it. In Burma, night duty generally meant no sleep at all, with signals being passed all the time. Sometimes, it was possible to doze for half-an-hour, head on your arm at the table; more rarely, you could curl up under a blanket in a corner of the office for an hour.

During the Mandalay campaign, my job was to work that prehistoric line instrument, the Fullerphone. About the size of a shoe-box, and black, the Fullerphone scarcely resembled a weapon with which to defeat the ferocious Jap Army. It held none of the glamour of a wireless set. Being solely a line instrument, it had to be connected with forward units or rear units — brigade or Division HQ — which entailed, in a mobile war, the perpetual laying of cable.

The Fullerphone gave off a misanthropic buzz. But it did send and receive morse. We worked at up to eighty letters a minute. We held the various units of the advance together. We kept everyone in touch. We were good.

When coming off the all-night shift, after perhaps twelve hours of intensive work by dim lights, we did not expect comfort. Sometimes, we had an hour in which to pack up everything, take down the signal office, and start another move. At the best of times, we could get breakfast and then sleep.

The cooks were compelled to wait for us until we came off duty. This did not please them, since sometimes, inevitably, we were late. The food — probably a fried egg and a soya link and a mug of tea — would be cooling or cold. Washing our mess tins was a particularly dismaying business. Two dixies filled with what had been hot water stood at the entrance to the mess area (we sat on the ground or on logs to eat); one dixie was for washing mess tins and "eating irons", the other for a post-wash rinse. By the time we got to them, the liquid in the dixies resembled a particularly rich vomit. Water was scarce. We had to use what was there. Since we had nothing on which to dry tins and cutlery, we used our mosquito nets; by the end of the campaign, the nets had developed a ripe aroma.

Sleep after a busy night was not always easy. Our bivouacs were pitched over slit trenches, and so stood out away from shade, since no one attempts to dig slit trenches, an unrewarding occupation at the best of times, near the roots of trees. Temperatures under the canvas rose as rapidly as the sun. Inside our fragrant mosquito nets, necessary to keep off flies, the heat was suffocating. We fricasséed as we slept.

And there was a local defiler of sleep. Central Burma is the habitat of the Morse Code bird. The Morse Code bird sits in the leaves of the palm tree outside signalmen's tents and utters random bursts of Morse Code. Dit dit-dit-dit dit-dah-dit-dit dit-dah dah dit. . . . Endlessly, meaninglessly, while the weary brain of the operator who has been passing Morse all night perforce tries to transcribe the bird's nonsense. Full grown men have been known to run naked, screaming, from their trenches, trying to drive the offender away. No raven of Edgar Allan Poe's was ever more ill-omened than the Morse Code bird.

Few animals were to be seen; the birds were mainly those of the kind that earned their living by eating the dead. We passed through a copse outside Myingyang where Japanese troops lay scattered in death. Turkey-like vultures with creamy feathers ran among them, guts so swollen with food that they could scarcely hop into the lowest branches of the trees to escape us. The Japanese, British and Indians had between them made of Burma a terrible waste; ordinary life was suspended while the evil dream of war went by, first in a tide one way, then in a tide the other.

Our portion of tide moved forward about once a week. At one period, we pitched camp near Yeu. The four or five bivouacs of "S" Relief were clustered near two large palms tethered to the ground by thickets of vines and creepers. Before us was open land, looking towards a canal; behind was a thicket, very noisy at night with the sound of things scuttling through the dead undergrowth. We were nervous in that camp, not knowing exactly where the enemy was. As the sun was setting on our first evening there, we heard noises in the topknots of the palms. Looking up, we saw black snakes dangling far above us. We came to realise that the snakes were the tails of some kind of big cat. The Cockneys among us became particularly nervous; war was one thing, tangling with wild life quite another.

The night was moonlit, the heartbreaking moonlight of a still Burma night, when the Moon hangs like a sacred gong in the next field but one, ancient with wisdom, gold with desire. I lay awake under my mosquito net, my rifle by my side. After a while, crashing noises sounded from the nearest tree. A shadow fell outside the bivouac. One of the cats was standing there.

· Because we had camped so near to the tree for purposes of conceal-ment, and because we had arrived in the dark the previous night, we had not dug slit trenches as usual. Our slender cover was propped up on poles in order to make it easier to enter and leave the tent. The big cat strolled in. I lay there, resting on one elbow, afraid to move. The cat came closer. It looked in at me. Only the net separated our faces. Neither of us spoke. Then it walked out the rear of the tent and was gone.

What communication could I have had with it?

That camp remains in memory my favourite. It was one of the few sites where there were Burmese nearby. They had not fled at our approach. They had harvested the crop on the field by whose perimeter we stayed and were busy threshing grain while we were there. We watched the operation with interest, talked to them, called to the women, and offered them cigarettes. Beyond the field of stubble was a grain field, the crop very much broken down, and beyond that was a canal, with low-growing blossom trees on its banks and nine inches of water flowing in it. The whole neighbourhood was attractive, with small white pagodas here and there like silver pepper-pots set randomly on a lawn.

But it was water that was the attraction. Water we had not seen for six weeks at that time. Sweat and dust alone had kept our bodies clean. It was possible to lie in the canal and be almost totally submerged in water. All the relief went for a bathe that first day. Thereafter, they considered that nine inches of water was too tame, and so I went alone, accompanied only by Sid Feather's rhesus monkey, Minnie. Minnie ran beside me on her long lead like a dog. In the water, she would enjoy a swim and then come and perch on my shoulder to dry herself. I lay there prone, watching a busy kingfisher which fished in the water from one of the low trees. The sun burned overhead, war was miles away. I communed with nature.

The trouble with communing with nature is that she does not commune back. One day, when returning through the flattened cereal crop from the canal, I almost stepped on a great snake, straw coloured, basking in the sun. It reared up to strike. Minnie immediately scaled the nearest tree, which happened to be me, and stood on the top of my head, screaming furiously and throwing handfuls of my hair at the snake.

Perhaps Minnie saved the day. The snake did not strike. It suddenly made off, shaking out its long coils. I watched it thrash its way through the burnished stalks. It was six or more feet long. It made its way rapidly across the field. Shaken, I walked back to camp. Minnie remained clinging to my ears until we were in safer surroundings.

The fear of snakes always haunted us. Army training in India taught us that the first thing we did on waking was lean out of bed and tip our boots upside down, in order to eject any nasties which might have lodged there during the night. It was a habit which took years to break, even in relatively scorpion-free England.

Although I never became fond of the army, I found a developing passion for the natural world, that great green system which encompassed us. It could bring my heart up from my boots. Burma is a varied country, by no means all jungle as some imagine. Its variety was beautiful and the Burmese appeared to have lived in harmony with its variety, embellishing it with their pagodas, and not overwhelming it — as India was overwhelmed — with humankind. But the Burmese had by and large vanished, taking cover like rabbits under the wing of war. We entered their buildings, moodily looking for souvenirs and poking about, rifles in hand, in the manner of invading soldiery. Some of the wooden houses were enchanting. I remember one in particular, with a verandah contained behind an ornamental rail. Of the four stilts on which it stood, only three remained. Inside, all was as it had been. Although chairs remained in place, everything listed to starboard, like a sinking ship.

In this surreal landscape, the British were surreal objects. The ethos of the Forgotten Army was to look as wild as possible. We wore trousers with puttees and boots, to keep out insects, and bush hats. Our torsoes were mahogany brown, our backsides alabaster white. It was the custom to tie bits of the coloured signal scarves dropped with our airborne rations round our hats to serve as puggarees, and to grow our hair long. "In the depths of the Burmese jungle lived a strange white race. . . ." For me, this costume remained a kind of dressing up; for the older members of the Army, it had become second nature. Many of them described themselves as *puggle*. It was the sun, the heat, the awful food, they'd tell you.

The maddest in "S" Relief was Steve Dutt. It was rumoured that his father was a general; Steve was just a private and an orderly. A sweet-natured man, he was never heard to raise his voice in conversation. He would sit about, listening to our talk, smiling, stroking his moustache. His recreation was to drill himself as if he were a platoon. On these occasions, he put on a sergeant-major's voice.

"Steve Dutt, Steve Dutt, harten-shun. As you were. Wait for it. Steve Dutt, harten-SHUN. Salooope arms. By the right, quick — wait for the order, Dutt. Quick — MARCH. Ep, ep ep, right, ep. Let's see you swing that arm. Plenty of bullshit. Keep in line.

"Steve Dutt, Ri-ight TURN. Chin up. Look to your front, man. Harbout TURN. Ep, ep, ep, right, ep."

And so on. True, we all on occasions drilled ourselves, but it was Steve Dutt who drilled himself continually, for a half-hour at a time, up and down in whatever clear ground there was. We would hear him at night, outside the bivouacs. No one thought anything of it.

"By the right, number. One, two, three, four, five — six. As you were. Wake up, Dutt, you know what comes after five, don't you? Dutt, by the right, number. One, two, three, four, five, SIX, seven, eight, nine, ten. Pick up your dressing. Squad, diss— I want to see you smartly away. Diss-MISS."

Then he would come in. "Sergeant put me through it today," he'd say cheerfully, lighting up a cigarette.

A few of us in "S" Relief had small lanterns. We would sit and chat in the entrance of someone's bivvy after dark. We spoke our own lingo of English and fractured Urdu. The conversation would often turn to London. There were frequent arguments about which number bus ran through Cockfosters, or where it went after it left the High Street.

My mates were homesick, and would talk about "our mum" doing this or that, or "my old woman" doing this or that, or how they went down to see the Spurs play every Saturday. Their small home worlds were continually resurrected. Homesickness was something I never felt. The present was too vivid.

Another favourite topic was how forgotten we were in this unearthly part of the world, and how we never featured in the news. It was the rule to find nothing good about overseas. To declare that one felt passionately about Burma would have been to invite ostracism, or else the scornful, "Wait till you've got a bit of service in."

The man I was most fond of in "S" Relief, after Bert Lyons, was Ron Grade. Ron was a slow-spoken farmer from Pinner way. One of his eyes was beyond his control and would wander about in the course of conversation. Ron was the only man with a camera; perhaps it was a sign of the interest he took in the world for which the others cared little.

Ron never ran out of film. He seemed to photograph everything, dead Japs, distant landscapes, "S" Relief in transit. It must have been his roving eye. The few snaps I have of those times come from Ron's camera. He photographed us when at last we reached the Mu river. So delighted was "S" Relief by the charm of running water that Sid Feather drove us to bathe every time we were off duty.

Since the spirit of Romanticism is connected with ruin and destruction, the Mu site must be one of the most romantic places to choose for a swim. Two railway bridges had once crossed the river at this point, a low wooden bridge and a grander one, metal on sturdy brick piers. Both bridges had been blown up by the British in their retreat from Mandalay. Both had been blown up with engines and rolling stock on them, so that the invading Jap should have no use of them.

The wooden bridge had disappeared — swept downstream or eaten by ants. What remained to mark the spot was a small tank engine, only half-submerged by the river in its shrunken dry season state.

The greater bridge had left greater remains. Two stout double piers had not fallen in the doubtless hasty explosions, so that between it and the eastern, Mandalay-bound shore, a totally unworkable span of line had stayed in place, slightly buckled and laden with two locomotives and a selection of carriages and trucks which straggled back to the land. Vegetation was already devouring the rearmost trucks.

The next span, the one which, in the wet season, would cover the mid-point of the Mu, had fallen down. Left balanced on its pier were a locomotive and tender. The tender stood with its tail in the air on top of the pier; the engine, to which it remained attached, hung down, buffers clear of the water by some feet. There it dangled, in that precarious position, for three years of war. The metals were too hot to touch — that we knew from the sunken tank engine, on which we could climb only after splashing it with cooling water.

We went every day to the surviving narrow, green, fast-running channel of the Mu, rushing deeply entrenched in its bed of sand; and every day the engineering ruin presided over our pleasures.

In her book, *The Pleasure of Ruins*, Rose Macaulay remarks, "The ascendancy over men's minds of the ruins of the stupendous past, the past of history, legend and myth, at once factual and fantastic, stretching back and back into ages that can but be surmised, is half-mystical in basis. The intoxication, at once so heady and so devout, is not the romantic melancholy engendered by broken towers and mouldered stones; it is the soaring of the imagination into the high empyrean where huge episodes are tangled with myths and dreams; it is the stunning impact of world history on its amazed heirs."

Our three-year-old ruin was also part of world history; it had already become a symbol of the end of a myth, the myth of white supremacy. We did not know it then, but never again would the British ride from Mandalay to Dimapur in their first class carriages, relegating the Wog to the third, as if the land belonged to them. The Forgotten Army might — indeed, would — drive the Jap from Burma; but it was beyond even our powers to restore the country to the British crown. The tide of history had turned and, whatever his later victories, the white man had been defeated — in many cases with remarkable ease, in Hong Kong, the N.E.I., Singapore, and Burma. The British, not the most pragmatic of races, recognised their defeat in victory, and left their former colonies and dependencies with comparative good grace, so that some measure of good will attached to their memory. Not so the Dutch and French. The latter, in particular, clinging to Indo-China — a struggle in which the Americans soon rashly involved themselves — would bring further chaos to the regions of S.E. Asia, with the battle of Dien Bien Phu breaking out not ten years after the time we bathed below the broken bridge over the Mu.

I still have a faded photograph of the bridge, with "S" Relief naked below it. Ron took the photograph.

Ron was not just a keen photographer. He was a pleasant man to be with — one of those people who, by some inner quality, make us feel slightly better than we are.

Ron never showed irritation or swore like the rest of us. "S" Relief benefited from his presence when the battle for the Chindwin was on.

The Japs held the east bank of the Chindwin, the British the west. The fighting continued for several nights and days. Our signal office kept moving, sometimes only half a mile at a time. The firing could clearly be heard. In that period, the section had to be split up, and the detachment I was on worked six nights out of nine, passing messages all the while. In the day we had guard duty. It was a time of maximum exhaustion, and the Morse Code birds were at their most punitive. The constant hammer of shellfire, like a maniac pounding his sleepless pillow, was rendered more unreal by the brilliant sunlight; recalling my uncle's experiences of World War I, I had believed warfare was conducted to the accompaniment of rain, or at least the famous North European drizzle.

During this crisis period, Ron and I were sent on detachment to run a radio link on our own. This was the only time we encountered live Japs; on other occasions, we had seen them, reassuringly, trotting along with the naked point of a bayonet at their backs, prisoners.

There was no "front" in the accepted sense. For forward momentum to be sustained, the tanks had to drive forward as fast as possible, giving the enemy no chance to rest or recoup. Any odd contingents of Japs left behind, separated by freak of war from the main body, could be mopped up later. So there was no way of telling when Japs might not pop up and surrender or, more likely, attack. Ron and I were dumped under three large trees with empty expanses on one side and a *chaung* on the other. We had some rations and water and the wireless set, and were told that a truck would collect us "within twenty-four hours". Till then, the set was to be continually manned and, for our own safety, we were not to show a light, except for the one on the 22 set.

The night was moonlit and still. We had dug ourselves a trench in the sandy soil and were crouching over the set together. Ron had the headphones on and was receiving when I became certain I heard a low voice from the direction of the *chaung*. I took up a firing position with my rifle, and nudged Ron. Coolly, he went on scribbling down the message with his right hand, while taking up his rifle in his left.

When the message finished, he signed off and took up position beside me, still wearing headphones. We were in moonlight, dappled by the filtering branches of the trees. I felt that this made us highly visible; in fact, it was probably a help in dimming out the tiny downward-directed light on the set. We crouched together, aiming into the dark.

Bushes grew round the banks of the *chaung*. Night birds scuttled in the dry undergrowth. We began to think our nerves were playing us up, and that the slight breeze accounted for the supposed voices. Certainly the bushes were swaying slightly. I stared fixedly at them — to become suddenly aware that three figures stood behind their uncertain shapes, heads and shoulders showing.

I squeezed the trigger and fired at once. Ron fired at the same moment.

The rifle kicked against my shoulder. The world seemed full of noise. Above that noise I heard a shrill cry. I ceased fire.

A long silence fell. Gradually the noises of the furtive birds in the undergrowth returned. Neither Ron nor I dared to get up.

Another message was offered over the wireless. Ron gave the wait signal, and then we rose and went forward together, rifles raised.

The Japs had run off, all but one. He lay face downwards in the sand of the *chaung*. Next morning, we examined him in a squeamish way. A bullet had gone through his chest. He was a poor thin diseased specimen.

Then I was glad it was Ron with me. We argued a bit about which one of us had shot him, but did not pursue the matter too far. Ron said laughingly, "You must have shot him. With my wandering eye, I'm not much of a marksman." Neither of us wanted full responsibility.

Not until several years later, when I was back in England, did the nightmares come. Then I woke screaming. The Japs were after me again. And again it would be moonlight. But those nightmares, like so many other things, gradually worked their way through the system and were dissipated into thin air.

Ron and I ate our frugal breakfast a few paces away from the dead Jap. About midday, the linesmen showed up in their truck and took us back to Signal HQ. We reported the Jap, and were briefly regarded as heroes by the rest of "S" Section. But there was a war to be going on with, and the incident was soon forgotten — except in the fertile beds of Ron's and my memory.

Japanese resistance broke. The Chindwin was crossed, and bridged by long Bailey bridges. We were now on the famous Road to Mandalay, still a good cobbled road, its miles marked by two waves of war, burning villages from which Japs had just retreated, and the rusty carcasses of old cars, abandoned during the retreat towards India, three years earlier. In contrast to this thrilling chaos, the trees with which the sides of the road were planted looked suburban, painted as their trunks were with whitewash up to a height of four feet.

This was the habitat of death. The victorious Japs were victorious no longer. Their units were in retreat, their soldiers often starving and diseased. Very little mercy was shown them; their reputations were too ghastly for that; for too long, the British had looked on them as both superhuman and subhuman. "Though kings they were, as men they died."

We drove among the paraphernalia of defeat: burnt-out Japanese trucks by the roadside, overturned 8-wheelers, scattered ammunition, dead bodies, vehicles and buildings burning quietly to themselves in the middle of nowhere. We drove. The infantrymen slogged it all on foot, every mile. We were now about 400 miles from the old base, Dimapur.

Even when in grimly victorious mood, the Fourteenth Army remained bitter. Newsreels were shown with the odd film show, so that we were accustomed to seeing coverage of triumphal Allied advances in Italy, France and Belgium. Entry into towns was always marked by pretty girls rushing out to present the soldiers with wine or flowers or, even better, kisses. These were the traditional rewards of liberators. The miserable "towns" we liberated, sometimes little more than names on Ordnance Survey maps, were utterly deserted. No pretty girls came running to us. The fruits of victory had a bitter taste.

Since time immemorial, the prizes for soldiers after a battle have been loot, drink, and women. In that respect, ours was a remarkably chaste war.

Three Indian soldiers were caught raping a Burmese woman. She was very irate about the whole business and said, "Just when I was getting interested, they gave up." We took this story for truth at the time.

At this stage in the great upheaval of nations, the division I was to join in the future, 26 Indian Division, was in action in one of the worst areas of Burma, the dreaded Arakan, mopping up the Japs on Ramree Island. Such names as Arakan and Ramree acquired a special and dread significance.

The object of 2 Div's immediate attention was Mandalay. The Japs were now withdrawing from round the city, where they could muster eight divisions against our five. Commander Bill Slim's plan was to switch IV Corps, to which we belonged, from the north to the south to attack Meiktila while XXXIII Corps attacked from the north. Meiktila was a focus for road, rail, and air communications south of Mandalay; Mandalay was of relatively little strategic but of immense symbolic importance, its name known all over the world — a poor man's inland Singapore.

Mandalay fell towards the end of March after an intense struggle. In Meiktila, even Japanese hospital patients were ordered to fight to the death. The Japs fought in strong-points, alleys, and cellars. They were all exterminated by bullet, bayonet, or flame-thrower.

When I rolled into Mandalay in our signal truck, I was all but prostrate from dysentery, though still working. The city had once been a seat of Buddhist learning, and its hill was covered with white icing pagodas, many of them damaged in the fighting. The thick walls of Fort Dufferin were also much damaged. But Slim had given orders that Mandalay should not be bombed.

It was an empty city, doomed and desolate. The smell of corruption hung over it, while birds sat on trees overhead, waiting. Stray dogs wandered about the streets, many of them suspiciously fat, but disconsolate. Perhaps they, like us, felt a sense of anti-climax.

Before we left Burma, there was one more adventure. 2 Div had completed its task with the defeat of the Japanese in the plains and the retaking of Mandalay. It was the task of other units to drive the Japs south towards Rangoon and, if possible, eliminate them entirely. We were to be flown out — an unusual operation in those days on that front.

I was one of the rear detail. Four of us manned a skeleton signal office in a small tent. After we had passed the last traffic, we closed down for good. There was now no one to answer our signals.

The radio and line apparatus we loaded into a Dodge truck, which set off into the wilderness. We returned to pick up our kit. We had camped under a large tree with generously spreading branches. For the flight back to a base in Bengal, we were allowed only 40 lbs. of personal kit; the rest had to be dumped — *pegdoed*, in our corruption of Urdu. A lot of pegdoing went on in India and Burma. So we got our packs on our backs and our kitbags on our shoulders with our bivouacs and mosquito nets, and started to walk to the airfield. Behind us, a wind whipped up dust, fluttering the pages of the books, so lovingly accumulated, which I had been forced to pegdo. Stapledon's *Last and First Men* was left behind. The wind grew stronger, whipping about our legs, reminding us that the monsoons were on the way to revivify the torn land. Out of their hiding places among tossing bushes came dark figures, rushing forward and seizing the abandoned loot. Partridge raised his rifle, half in fun. Before the tree was out of sight, the Burmese had borne all our pegdoed possessions away.

The airstrip was marked only by a small windsock, rippling in the new winds. The strip consisted of a runway of knee-high grass perhaps two hundred yards wide and a mile or more long. Perhaps it had once been designed as a fire-break. Nothing was to be seen but grass and trees, stretching across the plain. No one else was about, not a shack, not a truck, no personnel in sight. We had water and rations but no means of communication with the world.

The four of us settled in the shade of the trees and waited, smoking, chatting. Idle chat. I had found no way of communicating my inward feelings to my friends, sensing that anything I said on an emotional level would be laughed at. Nor did I impart my feelings to my parents; my few letters home were miracles of superficiality. Now, under the trees, I found myself alone in having some regrets at leaving Burma. With a great victory behind us and the unknown ahead, here was surely an hour of communing. We continued to talk in trivialities, all perhaps afraid to reveal our true selves.

One thing we vowed, sprawling in the shade, was that when we got back to the Blight we would tell everyone what we had been through. We would — as the expression had it — "grip them ragged". The Ancient Mariner would have nothing on us. It can be seen that this process of telling all would have had great therapeutic value. I was with three men who were about to be sent home after long service abroad; for myself, I had still a lot of time to serve out. So I never knew if the requisite grips were applied. But for me, returning to Blighty when the war had been over some while, and put out of mind, I found that no one wished to hear. The jungle experience was too alien.

Why did no novelists or poets spring up to celebrate the experience of Burma from the common soldier's point of view? It was an undemocratic war. Only officers spoke about it later — heroes like Bernard Fergusson and "Mad" Mike Calvert, and of course Slim's own fine book on the campaigns, *Defeat into Victory*. They all stuck to autobiography or fact. Hardly a poet spoke up. There was Alun Lewis, but he shot himself before going into action.

One of Lewis's poems tells how:

> But leisurely my fellow soldiers stroll among the trees.
> The cheapest dance-song utters all they feel.

It's a lie, an officer's snotty lie; Lewis did not know what he was talking about. Delightful irony reposed in singing those "dance-songs". Their superficiality, like our chatter, served to cover momentous upheavals of feeling. "Paper Doll" and "Moonlight Cocktail" had marvellous surreal effect in our jungle hideouts.

We woke the next morning under the great trees, eating a hunk of bread and marmalade for breakfast without washing. The place was as waterless as a desert — and as deserted. No sign of our plane, and the monsoon-bearing wind blew stronger. The smell of smoke came to us.

Hour succeeded hour. We strolled about in the sun, hats off — it was our pride that we never got sunstroke or wore topis, as an earlier generation of regular soldiers had done. The smoke could be seen. It thickened until gradually it shrouded the blue sky. A forest fire was approaching. We could hear its roar and crackle. It was as if a stampede of animals was coming our way.

What were we to do? There was no escaping from our position. The fire was approaching at brisk walking pace, burning up the trees in huge brands on either side of the airstrip, triumphant and furious. Rapidly it came, and still no rescuing plane.

We moved into the centre of the grass strip. Jungle blouses went on, to protect our skins from flying sparks. The sky was black, the whole forest on either side blazing red. We crouched to the ground. The heat seemed to swell about us.

The fires on either side moved parallel with each other like friendly rival expresses. Linking them across the open space ran a wave of flame, consuming the grass, turning what was green black, leaving behind it cindered ground. It dashed towards us like a rip tide.

Standing, we heaved our kit on to our backs. As the wave reached us, we jumped. That is how you evade a forest fire. You jump over it.

"So much for fucking Burma," said Bert Lyons.

There we stood, in a land of black ash. The great fire swept majestically on, about its own purposes, leaving smouldering destruction on either flank. We looked at each other and laughed. Then we lit up cigarettes.

"Where's that bloody plane?" we asked.

We spent another night out in the open, on the burnt earth. Next morning, an aged Dakota with the American star on its wings landed on the black airstrip; we climbed readily enough into its hold, and soon were flying westward, over the Chin Hills towards India and a quieter life.

History is what happens to contemporary events when they have receded enough for us to draw a moral from them. What is the moral of the Burma campaign?

That change is all. Three years after the victory of the Forgotten Army, Burma was granted independence. Although the Japanese had packed their bags and left, Britain was unable to regain the confidence of the Burmese people, who had twice seen their fair country reduced to a battlefield — Burma, that most religious of countries. Nor could the brave Indian Army be relied on to hold down Burma by force. India was being returned to the Indians. That was the British will: while behind that will was American pressure; righteous to a fault about British and Dutch Far East possessions, the United States nevertheless let itself be led into another war that has been seen since to have caused more damage and destruction in Vietnam, Cambodia, and surrounding regions than even the Japanese dreamed of.

Nineteen thousand men of British and Commonwealth origin — the greatest number being Indian other ranks — died in the Irrawaddy crossings by Mandalay and Meiktila. In the earlier battle of Kohima, over two thousand men of British 2 Div, for which I was a pale-skinned reinforcement, died. All told, in Burma, there were seventy-one thousand British and Commonwealth casualties. Japanese casualties have been numbered at 185,000.

A memorial was erected to the British dead at Kohima. On the memorial is carved a free translation of a Greek epitaph, which reads:

When you go home
Tell them of us and say
For your tomorrow
We gave our today.

Sadly, it was no one's tomorrow, despite the brave words. The British got out. The Burmese then sank under a repressive regime. Various kinds of struggle still divide it. Visitors from outside are scarcely welcome.

The bamboo grows beside the rivers where once we so bravely, so fruitlessly, drove from Milestone 81, through Kohima and Imphal, down the Tiddim Road, across Chindwin and Irrawaddy, to a ruined Mandalay. A lot of tomorrows lie buried along the route.

IV

Clement sat over his brother's old exercise book for a while, engaged in unconstructive musings. Then, sighing, he made a few phone calls. As he was setting the phone down, the intercom buzzed. It was Michelin.

"Your supper's all ready, Clem. And I'm just off out."

"Got another party?"

"Yes, another party. . . ."

"Oh, well, enjoy yourself."

He went downstairs slowly, dragging his steps so that anyone observing him might imagine there was something weighty on his mind. Downstairs, where the temperature was cooler, Sheila was in the conservatory pouring herself another glass of white wine.

"Where's your glass?"

"Oh, I left it on my desk upstairs."

"Doesn't matter. I'll get another. It's so hot, Michelin has laid a table outside by the pool for us. She's just gone."

"Another party. . . ."

"Good drinking evening."

She was pouring wine slowly into the glass she had taken from the cabinet, letting the neck of the bottle chink once against the rim of the glass to emphasise the benefaction of what she was doing. It seemed to him, watching her, that her strong nose was slightly less sharp this evening, as if a certain watchfulness, apparent in her manner during their time in the States, had now relaxed.

Passing him the brimming glass, she said, "If you go outside, I'll bring the food. It's all ready."

The garden was still mainly in sunlight, slanting over the old brick walls. The little pool was in the shadow cast by the Farrers' house next door. But it was warm there, and in the patio area Michelin had laid a pink linen cloth on their white conservatory table.

"Did you have a dip?" he asked, when she emerged with avocados.

"I spent a whole hour on the phone catching up with news since we've been away." She passed on various items of gossip.

"The film contract's come alive again," she said.

"I don't believe it."

They chatted about the Kerinth film contract with Obispo Artists. A letter had been awaiting her from Tarleton Broker, film agent in London for the Green Mouth novels. A deal with Obispo had been on and off for over a year; now they were involved with a director-producer called Calvin Boas Lee, whom both Sheila and Clement had met, and liked tolerably. Now the deal was alive. Tarleton had a contract ready. After they had demolished most of Michelin's strawberry shortcake, Sheila produced Tarleton's letter, and they read it over between them.

"So I'll go up to London on Thursday and work over the contract page by page with Tarleton."

"Looks as if you're going to be rich and famous. Even more of both."

She pulled a face at him. "Don't say it. It frightens me. Poor me. Everyone will hate me even more."

"Love you even more."

She squeezed his hand. "I'll keep my head. Promise."

"Don't count your chickens, love."

"That's right. . . ."

Thursday, the day that Sheila took the train up to London to see her film agent, was also the day of the week when Clement drove to Headington for his regular appointment with a fellow analyst. This analyst, a Jungian like Clement, was a Czech exile called Mrs Vikki Emerova. They had known each other for some years, and occasionally met in the Department of Psychiatry in the Warneford, or at official functions. He always addressed her as Mrs Emerova, and she him as Dr Winter.

Clement's clinic, which these days he held only once a week, was in central Oxford. Mrs Emerova had a downstairs room in a small Edwardian house with a neglected garden off Headington High Street. Headington was full of similar houses with similar rooms, each occupied by people much like Mrs Emerova. The Emerovas of this world sat in chairs listening to the woes of people sitting opposite them. Anything could be said to them. One could talk in intimate detail about sexual perversions, or one could enter on a lengthy diversion concerning politics. One could be fearfully academic or downright coarse. The Mrs Emerovas would never flinch.

Unnatural though this arrangement might appear, many of the academics of Oxford, burdened with personal problems, made their pilgrimage weekly to the shabby rooms in the discreet houses of Headington.

In the back garden at Mrs Emerova's were three ancient apple trees, and nothing else. The grass did not seem to grow. It was never short and never particularly long. Perhaps, Clement surmised, there were special nurseries — garden centres, they were called nowadays — in the wilds beyond Headington, in Wheatley and Holton and Horspath and Garsington which supplied special grass seed for analysts' gardens, guaranteed to lull their clients with its monotony. His own clinic had no garden.

Once a year, in the Headington spring, the three ancient apple trees burst into blossom. Hope sprang into the breasts of the analysands. Christ may have died for them, God might have created the world for them. . . . All was possible. . . . But come the autumn and the fruits were as green and acid as the lives of those who looked out upon them from Mrs Vikki Emerova's window.

"But she had it off with him in the next room. This was in Boston. In our hotel — the well-named Luxor Hotel. A little Spanish type, five feet one and pretty weedy, I'd say. Always had a smarmy sort of grin for Sheila. I watched him. I saw him last year and was friendly. Arthur Hernandez. More properly Arturo, I'm sure. Her editor at Swain Books — not that he seems to do much editing. Those guys have generally tried their hand at writing, had no joy at it, but ever after think they have special insights into writers' lives. He's probably straight out of university, probably only twenty-three or twenty-four — half her age. No real experience of life. They probably did it last year too, and I never found out. There I was, being nice to him. Oh, of course he was all over me when I arrived at the Luxor from New York. By that time, they'd probably been doing it all round the States. It's the sense of betrayal. . . . I can't see how Sheila could possibly — And all the time he was 'Green Mouth' this and 'Green Mouth' that. I said to him, 'Look, when we're not performing in public, couldn't you relax and call her Sheila? Green Mouth is only her trade name.' And he said, 'Oh, I do zees only to show respect.' Respect, and the whole time he was bloody well shafting her. I mean, there are rules about these things, and the Americans know that as well as anyone else. I've never been anti-American. Rather the reverse. Of course, Arthur Bloody Hernandez is probably from Puerto Rico. I wondered if I wrote to Swain and complained if they'd sack him. Sheila is their most valuable property. They wouldn't want to lose her. Of course, I suppose they might argue that it was Arthur Hernandez, damn him, by offering his services, who kept her there instead of with a bigger organisation. I know Random House made overtures. They have business arrangements with her publisher on this side of the Atlantic.

Maybe I should try to persuade her to — no, I couldn't do that. It wouldn't work."

"You feel more anger against him than against Sheila?"

"Really, I don't blame her. Well, not much. I have always been generous. Quite generous — in fact, more generous in that respect than she's ever been with me, by a long chalk. It was just a passing fancy — well, no real harm done. One must have a perspective, yet all the while the other person just goes on acting however they feel like, without restraint. I really don't think Sheila has much power of self-analysis. You can see that in her novels. No kind of self-analysis. Her characters, even the sensitive ones, just barge ahead and *act*. She is very warm natured. All credit for that. I do try to be generous. Even when I walked in and caught them at it — there was her big soft white bum, Mrs Emerova, she on top and you could hardly see him at all, except for two nasty little thin hairy legs, like a beetle crushed by a cream puff — I'll never forget it. You may — you should — try to be detached but it still hurts deeply to catch your wife *in flagrante delicto*, and on top, too. Jealousy is hard to eradicate. She gave me such a look. I simply backed away into the sitting room. Knocked over a vase of flowers. Couldn't think what to say. At such a time, you find yourself completely at a loss. Now why should I have felt such a fool? I suppose it's because — there's a whole tradition behind it, a whole rich tradition. The cuckolded male is a figure of fun, even to himself. It's not so bad for a woman who catches her husband at it. She tends to engage more sympathy, don't you consider? It's something to do with the shape of the sexual organs, basically, I suppose. The male equipment looks a lot funnier than those rather pretty little purses you women have. I just stood there shaking but, in a minute, out *he* came, all dishevelled and looking a bigger fool than I felt, tucking in his shirt. When he saw me, he made a dash for the door to the corridor, so I ran after him and managed a good kick up the arse to help him on his way. That was the most satisfying bit of the whole affair. I rather hurt my left leg doing it."

"Kicking him satisfied you?"

"What do you think? Then out *she* came, dressed, but hair dishevelled. Wanted a drink and a cigarette. Did I tell you she smokes when she's on these tours? Cigars if nothing else is available. She's like a demon. Well, it is all a bit testing. I sympathise with her and I do see why she's got to do it. And I said to her, quite quietly and decently, 'I know you're under pressure but this has got to stop', and she said, in a sort of level voice, 'I'm enjoying it too much to stop.' That's what she said. 'I'm enjoying it too much to stop.' As cool as you like, Mrs Emerova. I'll tell you the effect that sentence had on me, shall I? She never wrote a sentence half as powerful. It just destroyed me. I suppose I didn't look any different. She gave me a drink from the drinks cabinet and I drank it. But something went inside me. I still feel . . . of course I do. It was bad enough to be told she was enjoying it. One does enjoy these affairs. The surreptitiousness, the sense of. . . . But to rub it in. . . . And then to say point blank that she meant to continue, whatever I felt about it. What I felt about it didn't matter to her in the slightest. How can you recover from that? It's so unlike her. Generally she's so considerate. But perhaps she's been like that all the time. I mean, how long have we been married — and all the time she was secretly quite indifferent to what my feelings were if they got in the way of her pleasure? 'I'm enjoying it too much to stop. . . .' Christ, what an insult. It's as if I'm bleeding inside and yet, now we're back home, I have to continue as normal. We both continue as normal, as if nothing had happened. It's grounds for divorce, isn't it?"

"Do you want a divorce?"

"I don't know. I don't know what I want. It's a crowning insult, isn't it?"

"Did she mean it as an insult? Was she not also upset at that moment?"

"I should hope she was! Isn't it at such moments that the truth slips out? How often had they had it off together? Not just in Boston, New York, Philadelphia, Chicago, Salt Lake City, Los Angeles. Can you imagine, they might have done it in Salt Lake City? Ugh. . . . At least I seem to have put paid to Hernandez. I made sure they weren't alone together for the rest of the time we were there. And I don't think he had the appetite for it after being found out. Men don't, do they? There are rules to the game, you know, and if you're caught out, fine, then however much it costs you say you're sorry and you stop. You stop, don't you, for the sake of the other person's feelings? Isn't that the rule? You and the other woman know you run that risk. If found out — all over. Finish. Isn't that the rule?"

"Do you think of it as a game with rules?"

"There are rules, aren't there? Remember your ethology. In everything there are rules, in every species. Otherwise civilisation falls apart. Even when two nations threaten each other, rules remain. If that wasn't so, then the planet would have been destroyed long ago. Even nations which hate each other obey rules, almost unwittingly. How much more so between individuals. How am I going to live now? Am I supposed to go on as if nothing had happened?"

"What has really happened? Sheila returned to England with you, didn't she?"

"I can't talk to you, Mrs Emerova. You're supposed to offer me something, you know. A therapist is supposed to use his or her own feelings in the service of the patient. That's me. How should I best behave in this mess?"

"Do you feel it is a mess? Your marriage is continuing, isn't it?"

"It's continuing, yes. But for how long? What's she thinking? Is she longing for Hernandez every moment of the day? 'I'm enjoying it too much to stop.' It puts me off my stroke, I don't mind admitting. Yes, I do mind admitting it. I feel that when we have intercourse she'll just be thinking of him all the while, and making comparisons."

"Does that make you feel inferior?"

"Oh, Christ, it makes me feel bereaved. Our calling has little defence against bereavement. How am I to know what she's thinking?"

"May you not suppose that she wants everything to continue as normal?"

"What right has she to hope that? I'm the one who should be deciding about that! Instead, I'm arranging for a party for her next Thursday, to celebrate her latest effusion. . . ."

"Doesn't that suggest that you both want everything to continue as normal?"

"Well, it can't continue as normal, can it? That's not possible. Not while I still have so much anger inside me. Okay, under the stress of the tour, when she's the cat's whiskers and the whole world's bending an ear to her, I quite understand that then she's feeling so good that she wants the odd extra bit of adulation — I mean, this guy Hernandez, he has no interest in her as such, he's only interested because she's the grand and glorious Green Mouth who brings so much money into his company, whose new novel has got 1.5 million copies in print. It's impersonal on both sides, in a way, all part of the big Green Mouth act — I *understand* that, it's my business to understand. Good for her! But 'I'm enjoying it too much to stop. . . .' Am I supposed not to feel angry and hurt because I'm an analyst? What do you expect?"

"If you accept that she is having to undergo a big act, then perhaps this hurtful thing she said was also a part of the big act and has no further meaning? Couldn't it just have been Green Mouth speaking?"

"Big Mouth, you mean."

"Well, I'm afraid that it's ten past twelve. Just gone. . . ."

"I meant to ask you about my brother."

"Can we talk about him next week?"

＊

Clement got to Carisbrooke in time for lunch. As he collected a plate of plaice and pommes frites, he saw that he would be sitting next to George Forbes, the Medieval History Fellow, with whom conversation was no bore.

"What did you make of *Playing for Time?*" George asked.

"Yes, very funny. I took it with me for light reading on my trip. I'll let you have it back. He used to live just near here, you know."

"You're looking a bit battered."

"Worse than usual? What about you?" Such remarks as George's were perfectly acceptable, coming from George. He spoke in a kind of conspiratorial way. He was a sturdily built man with a beaky face and high cheek bones, on which there rested a high colour. He had a shock of white hair. A handsome-looking man, Clement thought. Also, he voted Labour, which Clement considered was to be prized in a Professor of Medieval History.

"I'm fresh as a daisy," George said, smiling to show it was not true. "I've been invigilating. Ten more days and I'm off to Stanford. What's the matter?"

"Oh. . . ." He picked at his fish. "Usual boring problem. . . . Domestic, blah, blah, blah. Let me ask you something, George. Don't you regard life as a game to be played according to the rules? Wouldn't you say that? I mainly mean unwritten rules."

Without ceasing industriously to demolish his fish, George said, "We live in a post-Christian society where the written rules were brought down from Mount Sinai by Moses. We subscribe to the idea that it is wrong to murder or steal. 'Do not adultery commit, Advantage rarely comes of it', etcetera. These days, there's less of a consensus than there was, say, before the world wars. It's harder to know by what rules the other chap's playing."

"You don't quarrel with the idea of life as a game, though?"

"A bloody unsporting one." George removed a bone from his mouth. "A philosopher would say your question was without meaning."

"It's true we impose the idea of a game. For most of the people I see, 'game' has comforting connotations. It implies that there will be a half-time, and someone will be looking on to see fair play. It's an antidote to injustice. People hate injustice."

"No. They like it. They are happy to put up with it. Otherwise, they'd all vote more sensibly."

"I've got a spot of injustice at the moment. I'm supposed to sort out Joseph's life, as if I was capable of sorting out my own."

"I thought you chaps were used to that kind of situation. Doubtless it's rather different if it's your brother. Comes a bit too close to home. Are you going to have some pudding?"

73

"All his papers have been dumped on me. I can't just throw them away, can I?"

"How about letting the dead bury the dead?"

"That comes well from an historian. He wants — wanted — me to do something with them. I don't know whether I'm supposed to write his biography or what. Or just put out a collection of his letters or miscellaneous pieces. . . . He wasn't all that well known, that's the trouble."

"I suppose that Joseph Winter is quite a respected name in some circles. Trouble is, his chosen field was the Far East, wasn't it? Pity he didn't play safe and go for the Tudors and Stuarts, where the big money is."

"His involvement was with the East."

"I didn't mean to belittle him. I just meant that it's a rough old world and there are hierarchies in historical circles as in everything. Really, the study of things far eastern is in its infancy. The documents aren't easily available — or extant, in many cases. No prestige attaches. He wrote the standard history of Sumatra, didn't he?"

"Yes, C.U.P. Sells all of ten copies a year."

George pushed his plate to one side and sipped his wine. "Your brother did something in the East during the war, didn't he? Remind me."

Clement said, "He served in the Forgotten Army."

George spread wide his hands in a despairing gesture. The two men looked at each other. Then they began to laugh.

"Come round and have a drink this evening and advise me," Clement said. "I'd like you to view the documents. Make it six o'clock and we'll have a bit of a tipple. My wife should be back by then."

George Forbes arrived in Rawlinson Road shortly after six, wearing an old cream jacket Clement recalled from previous summers. The two men sat by the swimming pool for a drink and a gossip; then Clement led the way up to his study, and the bundles of Joseph's papers.

"It's a bit of a clutter as yet."

"My brother inherited the family business. I don't suppose he'll leave any papers, thank God."

Boxes full of notes and notebooks presented a problem. George nosed here and there, muttering to himself.

"Literacy, the curse of the thinking classes. . . ."

Clement sat at his desk and watched. "One owes one's brother something. We were never all that close. Joseph was twelve years my senior. The war came between us, that Grand Canyon between generations. I admired him from afar."

George presented himself as a solid block between Clement and the window, as he leafed through one of the notebooks. He read out, "'War. Why is war so popular? Because it allows us to cease being rational. (Not only war itself but armed forces, the acolytes of war, also irrational, organised as secret societies, end product death and disability.) Instead, more like animals, being aware of sacrifice, blood flowing, substitute of primitive courage for passage of time. Intellect tells us to hate war; an older thing sees in it a dangerous release. Like a drug.' Good enough in its day, possibly. Bit dated now. Not the stuff for the eighties."

"There are a lot of essays in that box which appear never to have been published." Clement felt embarrassed and got up to pour them more wine.

After reading spasmodically, George said, "Trouble is, Joseph was really a popular author without being all that popular. All these Thai dynasties— they're too remote for the average reader. Why don't you turn all this material over to the Far East Library, and let them sort it out?"

"Have a look at his wartime stuff. That's in a different vein."

Ignoring the invitation, George said, shuffling in a box, "And I believed it was only in plays that men wrote on the backs of envelopes. . . ."

"I thought of trying to write Joseph's biography. It might get some events in my own life clear."

George gave him a sage look. "Would it add to your reputation? Even in College? Bit obscure. . . ."

A touch of colour entered Clement's sallow cheeks.

"I feel I want to give him a chance. . . ."

George's expression showed what he thought of that remark. The evening sun was slanting in at the window, illuminating the dust on bundles of old newspapers.

"For instance," said Clement, going over to another box by the window, and selecting from it a black binder containing a number of typed sheets, "there's this. It's a record of a British post-war operation which, as far as I've checked, has never been written about. Joseph links the personal — sometimes very personal— with the historic. It gives a clear picture of what conditions were like in Sumatra in 1945–46, after the Japanese were beaten. Would you like to take a look?"

George was already glancing at his watch and sighing.

"All those damned exam papers waiting to be marked. I'd better get back. Thanks all the same. Maybe another time."

After George had gone, Clement wandered through to the rear of the house, touching items of furniture as he went, sometimes only with an extended finger. Michelin had laid a supper table for two in the dining room. He preferred not to glance at it, turning instead into the wide kitchen which opened from the rear hall. There he poured himself a Smirnoff, trickling the vodka on to the rocks at the bottom of his glass and tempering it with a little white Cinzano.

Clutching this glass, sipping at it, he made his way slowly into the garden, across which long westerly shadows had fallen. The shadow of the great Norway maple, growing two doors away in the Phillips' garden, and a living memorial to the time when North Oxford had been pleasant farmland, was cast on the kitchen and guest bedroom wall as if to emphasise the redness of the brick. This wall was pitted with holes and rusted nails, scars and gouges, like a landscape of the past, where previous generations of householders had encouraged green things to scale the heights up to the bedroom window. Various bees and flies took refuge there in the autumn, living out October in increasingly rickety state, on this sunniest of walls. Now it was the ragged pattern of the maple which dominated the brick face.

Generating half-articulated thoughts, Clement stood gazing at the brick. He had another life which had never been lived, a life strangled somewhere in those tangled years of his childhood and adolescence, when he had been possessed by a wish to "get on", and had sacrificed the chance of journeys to foreign lands by sitting for his various degrees. By so doing, he had become successful in a modest way, if being part of the academic environment was success; certainly in Sheila's Kerinth there were other criteria for success — a strong sword arm, cunning, hatred of scholars, power, magic, virility. . . . The ragged pattern on the kitchen wall seemed to stand momentarily for all the ragged coastlines he had never sailed to as sun was setting across torn sea, mysterious land. He had presided over the rebuilding of other lives; now here was his brother's, lying in fragments. How could it be meaningfully put together, put together in such a way as to express a certain muted exhilaration, romantic but submerged, which belonged to the Winters?

Why had Sheila not come back on the five o'clock train as she usually did? What was she up to now? Other houses could be seen from where Clement stood — the backs of houses in Staverton Road; the families there seemed to be working as they should. Old Badger, the Bursar of St Arnold's, was a funny little ineffectual man, yet his existence, at least from the outside, appeared to run in a perfectly smooth and pleasant way. Of course Badger, looking from one of his upper windows and seeing a fellow of Carisbrooke drinking vodka in his back garden by his swimming pool, might be thinking identical thoughts.

76

Sheila did not arrive until eleven-thirty, disgorging from a taxi with some style. She had caught the ten-five from Paddington.

Dragging a large carrier bag labelled Dickins & Jones, she entered talking and put her free arm round Clement's neck as she kissed him.

"I caught the train by the skin of my teeth. Jessica Bishop was on it. The taxi was so slow — traffic in the West End was worse than ever this evening. The taxi driver did his best. He told me he was going to retire to Clacton next week. Clacton's probably full of retired taxi drivers."

He recognised her chattery London persona, a mock-up perhaps of a woman Sheila would have liked to be, still not integrated into her personality.

"Have you bought yourself another outfit?"

She twirled the carrier bag and then dumped it on the sofa. "I'll tell you about that later. Calvin Boas Lee is a bastard. After Tarleton wrote to me, he got a phone call from Calvin in Hollywood to say he would be over in London today. So Tarleton booked us a table for three at Sidebottom's. You know how these people are — one o'clock came and went and Calvin did not show."

He noted the Americanism, as she went into a long description of what they had done and not done, and how stingy Tarleton had been about phoning the Hollywood office for information. As she talked, she went to stand by the fireplace, hands on hips.

Clement had been playing Wagner; she turned down the volume.

"So eventually Tarleton said that we couldn't let the Sidebottoms down — he's friendly with them and takes all his best clients there. So we went down for a bite and it was after two before we arrived. Of course we had to have champagne to soothe ourselves. And you, Clem, why have you not eaten supper? You were being moody, weren't you? I ought to have phoned you from Sidebottom's, and this is your way of reminding me."

"I just didn't feel hungry."

"Well, then I'm sorry. Have some toast and pâté now. I'm going to have a cup of tea and then I'm going to stagger to bed. It's been a hard day and I'm absolutely exhausted, and Calvin's a bastard of the first water. And the second and third, and however many waters there are."

"So does this mean the film deal's fallen through?"

"Who knows what it means?" she said wearily, turning to march into the kitchen, her figure momentarily framed in the dark doorway and then encompassed by it.

"What else did you do in town?" he called through.

"Nothing. What do you think I did?" Her voice came accompanied by the sound of the kettle filling from the cold tap. "I'll show you the new outfit in the morning. I expect you'll hate it."

Clement decided to have a cup of tea with her and forgo his pâté for the pleasure of going to bed at the same time she did. Perhaps she might not want that, although she sounded amenable enough.

After the usual ritual of turning out the lights and chaining the front door, they took their tea upstairs. All was peaceful in the street. She talked intermittently about her agent, Tarleton, and his marital problems, as they washed and undressed. After they had scrambled into bed, under the king-size duvet, Clement clasped her to him, feeling her considerable bulk roll readily towards him. He kissed her and murmured in her ear.

"Oh, that's how it is," she exclaimed, putting on a light girlish intonation. "I thought you were just a little bit huffy with me downstairs. A general huffiness ever since I came in. Favourite pupil had mis-behaved."

"Is that really how you see yourself?"

"I couldn't help being late. I didn't do it to annoy. Or did you think I was hanging about on Paddington station on purpose?"

He preferred not to pursue that line of thought, and said so, slipping his hand down under the duvet instead. Yet he heard the edginess in his own voice.

"I can't think what it is you see in me," Sheila said, in a mock-naive chirping voice.

He growled. "This neat little box of tricks so cunningly hidden where none but I may find it."

"Oh, that's what it's all about, is it? Is that all I mean to you? Is that what you were waiting for?"

"You ask as many questions as Mrs E. Had you forgotten I still fancy you?"

Despite the dark, she moved her head back as if to get a better look at him.

"What's that mean?"

"You seem to have forgotten what happened in Boston with that Spanish gigolo!" He had not meant to say it.

She lay back with her head on the pillow. He could feel the emotion warm in her, without being able to read its content. Anger welled up in him. Unsatisfied, they fell apart. Her refusal to speak seemed to smother them. But, as he was about to withdraw his hand from her thighs, pity for her and all her difficulties overcame his anger.

With compassion in him, he felt able to make love to her. She did not resist.

Afterwards, when he heard Sheila sail on relaxed breathing into the caverns of sleep, he thought to himself, soothingly, "It'll be all right. She never admits when she's in the wrong. I'll just have to forget about it. Bury it. That's best. She will never refer to it again if I don't; I know that. It means much less to her than it does to me. We're different people.

"What a mess. Half the time, she's Green Mouth, leading that other life in that dream world of hers. I must take it easy. There's no need for it to infect me. It's such a misery. . . . Why can't people just screw and be done, for the simple pleasure of it? . . . But I suppose that's what she did with the little Hispanic sod. Don't go over it all again. Think of something else. Remember how she was in Berlin."

There was always another circle to descend, down to the smallest circle that could never be reached — his self. Before that was the newly activated circle of his lost brother. He found himself lying there addressing Mrs Emerova; and he and she were back in their familiar chairs, in the darkness.

"I wonder why it is I find myself upset about Joseph? After all, his wasn't an easy or a very successful life. Perhaps I envy him because he's out of it all. Or perhaps I'm jealous of the way he's got out of it and left all this stuff — his problems — for me to resolve. What do you think?"

"If you find yourself offering so many alternatives, could it be something more important to you than any of them?"

"It's as if I've had no life — no, as if I've only lived through other people, and now he's offering me another substitute life, his secret life, well. . . ."

"And do you want the life he's offering you?"

"I partly admire, partly despise the all-consuming love he had for a Chinese woman. It seems to have haunted him."

"Is that what you want in the way of love? Do you feel Sheila gives you a lesser kind of love than the Chinese woman gave Joseph?"

"Yes — I mean no. I don't really believe in all-consuming love. It's a Romantic myth. Perhaps I envy him the myth. He was very much a man who lived with myths. My life seems devoid of myths. It's stuffed with contemporary history instead. For two brothers we were very separate. . . ."

"But now he's trying to come closer and you don't want it?"

"Well." He laughed. "It's a bit late to try and come closer now, eh? He should have tried that when he was alive."

"That sounds rather like your father, doesn't it?"

Clement was silent a long time. Bloody Mrs Emerova, with her irrelevancies, disrupting his line of thought. There was so much hatred and disappointment in various relationships that it was difficult sometimes to see your way.

"Anyhow, this great love of his. It failed, didn't it? He couldn't see it through. He wasn't quite determined enough."

"Is that how you see it?"

"How do you see it?"

"I want to see it through your eyes. I think that for some reason it is important for you to believe that neither he nor your father loved you enough, or was capable of loving enough. . . ."

"You confuse me. There are so many points on which we disagree. Sometimes I can't help wishing I was anywhere but here."

"Far away from me, eh? Like Joseph in Sumatra. . . ."

V

The past immediately becomes history. Even yesterday has undergone a magical transformation; it may still exist in memory, in stone, in documents, in old newspapers waiting to be disposed of. But it lacks breath. It has become part of death's kingdom.

The Sumatra I remember does not exist any more. As far as I am aware, no novelist or poet celebrated the Sumatra I knew. It remains alive only in my memory. And alas, my memory is faulty.

Long after I had returned to England from Sumatra, many years after, the chance arose to return there. I had in mind what Marcel Proust said in the circumstances, that it was impossible ever to return to a well-loved place, for what we sought was a time as well as a place. I knew it, yet, when the opportunity arose, I gladly took it, marvelling that it was possible for me to return at all.

From Singapore I flew to Medan, the capital city of Sumatra. Polonia airport was little different. Except that it had previously — thirty years earlier — lain outside town. Now it was in the suburbs. Medan had grown.

Much had changed. I had known Medan as a sleepy town, a town of shadows and silences. The population had expanded enormously since then, and had taken on some of the trappings of modernity. No longer did bullock carts lumber along the Kesawan. The population now relied on two- or three-wheeled vehicles for its daily errands. Exhaust fumes poisoned the air. Hooting and tooting, motor-cycles wove their way along the crowded streets.

As I walked through the town, a fever gripped me to revisit the parts of the town I had once known and in particular to set foot again in those places sacred to the love that had existed between Mandy and me. I remembered a short story of Thomas Hardy's in that melancholy vein in which I once delighted, with a title such as "Interlopers at the Knap" or "A Tryst at an Ancient Earthwork", in which a man goes back to his hometown in Wessex and finds it much changed, although he himself feels youthful as ever.

In Wessex, the stones had become worn, the shops had lost their paint, the old coaching inn was ruinous and unwelcoming. In Medan, a similar erosion seemed to have taken place under the burden of population; though I felt myself to be as lusty as ever, thirty years had weighed heavily on the city. Unlike any town in Hardy's Wessex, it bore an additional burden: it had changed hands.

When, on the 5th October, 1945, 26 Ind Div Signals landed at the port of Emmahaaven, we imagined we were visiting a Dutch possession, an island one thousand miles long which was part of the N.E.I., the Netherlands East Indies. In fact, the island never returned to Dutch hands. The world had changed, independence movements had started up everywhere. Thirty years later, a great many evidences of Dutch rule had disappeared under Indonesian nationalism, as tropical temples disappear under encroaching jungle.

The map I bought had not one familiar name on it. Indonesian names had taken over from Dutch. The outlines of the town were blurred. The centre had been disfigured by extra roads and one-way streets. Even the atmosphere had been rerouted, renamed, and reconstituted.

The compulsions of pilgrimage overcame me. Three places I badly needed to visit were the grocery store where Mandy and I had first met, my apartment where we had first kissed, and the bungalow where our love had been consummated. Clutching my map, I set out on foot through a bewildering maze of streets, the lives of whose inhabitants spilled untidily on to the thoroughfare. Pigs, derelict automobiles, laundry, were the ordinary furniture of any ordinary road, round which the inhabitants made their way. I was dazed by it all. Nothing was the same. This was the measure of thirty years of freedom and progress, that a stranger should choke and weep from the foulness of the atmosphere. Most of the men I passed smoked cigarettes in self-defence.

Nothing was the same. I soon became lost. The map, turn it about as I might, was no help. And then I found myself by a landmark I knew. Presenting a clean wall to the broken street and pavements was the Deli Cinema.

The cinema, built in the streamlined style of the thirties, with curves for corners, had just had a new coat of paint. It glowed with prosperity. The reason was clear. It was showing such masterpieces of the cinema as *Shark Invaders Destruction* and *Ghost Devils of the Pacific*. Just as when I knew the cinema in the forties — when I had taken Mandy there — its speciality was fantasy, generally horror fantasy. Whatever else had changed with independence, with freedom, with the population explosion, an appetite for ephemeral sensation had remained constant.

With this landmark, I was able to find my way to the first of my three objectives, the grocery store. It was, in fact, just round the corner. This was the first hint I had that my memory too was feeling the effect of thirty years, for I had imagined the store to be at some distance from the cinema. Did I not recall shadowy silent streets, walked with her arm on my sleeve at night? Yet here I was, standing in front of the store. It was now shuttered and closed. Next door, a butcher's thrived. An old cart was parked outside its door. Useless to ask passers-by where the people had gone who once lived here; they knew nothing.

Just to have seen the store gave me some satisfaction, although I was burdened with the passage of thirty years, the length of a generation. The years had been longer than I imagined. The Sumatrans thronging past me were young. One and all, they looked too busy, too hard pressed, to wish to speak to a foreigner with very few words of Besar Malay at his command.

Now I could get to one of the two remaining objectives, for the bungalow where we made love in those indolent afternoons was only a few streets away. It was baffling enough, though. One street had been blocked off. New streets had been pushed through, and buildings reorientated to face another way. A low wooden building in which I had worked with Intelligence had disappeared, to be replaced by a shoddy office block.

I walked for a long while, hot and bewildered. I had forgotten the name of the street with the bungalow; it had certainly not been called Jl Irian Barat, as the map seemed to indicate. All was confusion. I nearly got run over by a three-wheeled van. I found myself walking round the outside of a large bustling enclosed market, negotiating refuse, broken boxes, parked lorries, and knots of people. Nowhere was that certain bungalow with a palm (possibly two?) and a flowering — tree? — shrub of some sort? — at its gate.

Time had to pass and weariness set in before I accepted the idea that the line of little bungalows had gone, probably to make way for the market. There remained only my apartment to visit, where Mandy and I had first kissed. That, being further from the centre of town, was less likely to have suffered change.

Clutching the address carefully written on a card, I tried to get a taxi. Six taxis stood outside the Pardede Hotel, their drivers playing cards and smoking in the shade of a palm.

They were used to foreigners and their whims. One of them, who spoke a good smattering of English, agreed to take me on my quest.

Directing him to the right area was complicated. We drove about fast one-way systems while I looked out for landmarks. The house in which I had my apartment had stood on the edge of a wide open space with jungle at the far side of it and a distant view of the railway line. It had been built in a distinctive Dutch style.

There were no open spaces. I could not understand the way the railways ran, or the meandering River Deli, now used for a refuse dump. Replica Dutch houses stretched for street after street.

Finally, I asked the driver to pull into a side street. Something here seemed familiar in the general layout. Close behind the house had been a sleepy kampong. Of course it would be gone now; one might expect that. Modern housing would take its place. If we had come from that direction, then this would be the road behind my house and — why, this would be the very house, this one on the corner. Some of the grounds must have gone, shaved off to widen the road. I hesitated at the gate. Had it really looked like that? Search my memory as I would, I did not recall exactly the features of the house.

The taxi-driver had become very partisan on my behalf. He violently wished that I should find "my old home".

"This is yours, sir? Your old home?"

Thirty years had gone by. "This is it," I said.

He immediately took charge, marching past the gate and up to the front door. He rang the bell. The garden was pretty, with plenty of flowering shrubs. Back to me in a rush came the memory of how happy I had been in Sumatra. And what a situation I was in now.

A young woman answered the bell. While she listened to the driver's explanation, which was helped out by plentiful gestures towards me, the rest of the family joined her at the door, their faces bursting out on either side of her hips, her knees, her shoulders, dependent upon age and size.

The woman and a man I assumed to be her husband now came forth and beckoned me inside with welcoming smiles. There was nothing for it but to smile in return and enter the house.

Of course, this was the front. I had always entered by a door at the back, where a staircase led straight up to my room. I had almost never come in by this door. . . . But, wait, surely there had been a modest washplace just inside this door, with a stoup where you squatted and poured cold water over yourself. It wasn't there; this could not have been the house.

The family was friendly and inquisitive. There were the young couple, an older woman, a granny, and several children of radiant looks.

Through the driver, I explained that I had once lived here, that the British had once occupied Sumatra and got rid of the Japanese.

The young couple, who did most of the talking, looked confused. They knew that the Dutch had once occupied the island. They had never heard of the British or Japanese being here.

In the modern tropics, most of the population is young. The sense of history is something that belongs to chilly northern lands. They had only the present tense.

I had lived in a part of the house, I explained as Sumatran coffee was brought. Upstairs. I had the two rooms at the top of the stairs.

Would I care to see the rooms again?

Well, I would. That should prove definitely whether or not I was in the right house.

Grandpa was in the rooms upstairs, sleeping.

Then I could not possibly disturb. . . .

No, no, they would send the children up first.

So I found myself in the hall and — escorted by the whole family, climbing the stairs. Conviction came over me. The stairs, the turn in the stairs, were familiar. This was the very place where I had been so tortured, so madly happy.

Children came out on the landing to greet me, dragging Grandpa with them. We gravely gave each other greeting. I entered the room.

It was after all only a faded eroticism which had got me to that room; nothing particularly noble. I felt I had arrived under false pretences. Yet, no matter what, I had arrived. This was the room. It smelt right. And I had travelled through the years and miles to return here. There was a certain triumph to the moment.

And as they all stood back to have a good look at me, I remembered a story about Flaubert, and the erotic enjoyment he had had with a woman in a little hotel in Marseilles. Years later, when on his way to Tunis to collect material for *Salammbô*, he went in search of that little hotel — from motives exactly the same as mine, I suppose — and could not find it. He hunted all over, and finally discovered that it had been turned into a toyshop, with a barber's shop above it. Flaubert went upstairs and asked for a shave. He recognised the wallpaper. It was the wallpaper of his old bedroom, where he had made love.

Now here I was, in a room where I had been with Mandy. And in that flash of remembrance, as I walked towards the window — even as I said, ecstatically, "Yes, yes, this is my old room" — I knew it was nothing of the sort. It was merely a similar room. For my old bedroom had a balcony, and this room had no balcony.

Yet the view out of the window — something there, the disposition of the house next door, remained familiar. No, no, I was mistaken. I remained smiling out of gratitude, and made for the door. There I drew up short. A cupboard stood on the landing. I had forgotten the cupboard but surely in my time there had been a cupboard just there . . . hadn't there?

As I went down the stairs with the children hopping about me, I thought, well, of course they would have pulled down that old-fashioned bathroom beside the door. They must have a newer bathroom elsewhere. This must be the house. How could I forget?

And as for the balcony. . . . Well, in the tropics things fall down, balconies fall off. . . .

I gave them all a grateful farewell. The driver drove me back to the hotel.

Had I been where Mandy and I had once been? I could not tell. Since the doubt still remains it is as well that I enjoy the mists of uncertainty.

Everything was different when we arrived in Sumatra in 1945. Everything there seemed fresh and pleasant after the wastes of India. From the start, we had a more romantic view of the tropics, with small islands green in blue water and the surf white where it beat against the sand. The jungle grew down to the edge of the water, where palm trees canted out over the breaking waves.

We had been warned that the island was occupied by head-hunters and cannibals. We saw neither; it was the nationalists we had to worry about — a more urban breed. Another breed was present on the quayside, to disconcert us as we disembarked: the Japanese.

After the encounters with the Japanese in Burma, we still felt vengeful towards them. Here were these men of the 25th Japanese Army in smart uniforms and polished boots, marching about and guarding our stores. Their arrogance, however, had disappeared, and they were under the surveillance of a single Indian soldier, his rifle slung casually over his shoulder.

At this period, very few Dutch had come ashore, while British and Indian troops were also thin on the ground. Japanese troops were used for policing duties, and sometimes permitted to keep their weapons. This ordinance from On High seemed bizarre if not downright mistaken to those of us who had seen active service with the now-disbanded Forgotten Army. On one occasion, two friends and I sat down to coffee in a little Chinese teashop in Padang. We were armed with sten guns, which we carried over our shoulders. Some Indian troops belonging to the Rajputana Rifles sat at another table. At a third table was a party of Dutch, also armed. At a fourth table sat a group of Indonesians, while two

Japanese in uniform sat huddled at the rear at a table for two. We were all being served by patient Chinese, who sensibly devoted their talents to making money. But for them, one felt, shooting might break out at any time.

Partly because of such paradoxes, the port of Emmahaaven and the town of Padang pleased us. The Indonesians pleased us immediately, with their light brown skins and sophisticated air — as it seemed to those weary of that Stone Age poverty which makes India the capital of Beggardom. After India, the variety of clothes was impressive, with men sometimes in silks and sarongs instead of the ubiquitous shorts, and women in long skirts with blouses and waistcoats. The many Chinese women wore either a *cheongsam* or provocative pyjamas. Everyone looked clean, and their general air of mild prosperity was echoed in the pleasant houses, many of them timber-made and raised off the ground. The hovels which cluster round Indian towns like soiled skirts were missing. One could observe solid tables in rooms, spread with a cloth, and rugs on the floor. Outside some houses were dovecotes; more frequent were cages with pretty birds singing away their captivity.

On our arrival, everyone appeared friendly, waving and smiling — but tact is a virtue with which to greet any visiting army. Why should they not appear easy? At least the Japanese were going, and the population lived in a climate where fruit and vegetation could not but continue to grow.

Although we had our duties to do, like any other army we took what pleasure we could in our spare time. There was an old semi-derelict swimming pool by the coast, just outside Emmahaaven. The trees had grown in the years of Japanese neglect, so that the water was generally shaded and cool. I often borrowed a Jeep and swam there with two friends who were willing to make the effort and travel this far from Padang — I should explain that baking days and stifling nights meant that many of us had little energy, and spent the days resting when not working. I was fortunate in that the heat gave me energy.

Pleasant though it seemed, the swimming pool was ill-fated. One day, we met two orderlies from the Medical Corps, pale of body and just out of England. After a swim, we set out to explore the little stream which, feeding the pool, meandered among trees and moss-covered rocks. We came on a nasty-looking snake, preparing to strike at eye-level from the branch of a tree. One of the medics exclaimed with delight. It was a green horned viper, he said.

Pulling off his neck-rag, he gripped it between his fists and thrust it at the viper. The creature struck. Quickly, the medic dragged it from the tree and knotted the fabric about its head, so that the snake was a helpless prisoner. We were naked. He hurried back to his clothes and thrust the imprisoned reptile into a trouser pocket. The rest had had enough of snakes, and returned to the safety of the pool, while the medic and his friend, with shrieks of delight, looked for more snakes.

Next day, we learned that the orderly was dead. While he was taking the viper back to his quarters, it had somehow escaped and bit him through the fabric of his trouser pocket.

Only a few days later, another escapade ended in grief. A sergeant in Intelligence took a Dutch girl friend to the swimming pool. They drove in a Jeep after sunset — at a time when the curfew was about to come into effect. They parked the Jeep so that its lights shone on to the surface of the pool, an area of light among the surrounding shadows. They dived in and swam. A few moments later, they were fired on by a light machine gun. Both were killed. A patrol of South Wales Borderers dragged their bloody bodies out of the water.

From then on, the swimming pool was placed out of bounds.

I remained in Padang only three months. My travels in the East left me strangely restless. I wanted more travel. I wanted I knew not what. I had applied for a posting to China, for China to me represented the grand epitome of things eastern and exotic; the application was turned down. I then applied for a posting to Intelligence, to replace the dead sergeant. I was accepted. Such a posting was possible only in an out-of-the-way spot like Sumatra, where reinforcements were almost impossible to come by. Intelligence was down in strength; they took me on and promoted me to sergeant. A week after transfer, I was posted to Medan.

It is Medan and how I met Mandy there on which I want to concentrate, so I will pass over that marvellous overland journey of five hundred miles which took me across the highlands of Sumatra to the capital city. I have never forgotten it, though I have forgotten the names of the driver and cook who accompanied me. We travelled in a Dodge truck up into the wild mountains which form the backbone of the island, sleeping overnight near Lake Toba — taking sentry duty turn and turn about during the night.

Toba was like a miracle, a lake fifty miles long, lying peacefully in the crater formed by a volcano which had erupted a million years B.C. In the lake was the island of Samosir; what its history could have been, if it had any, I could not guess. Although the dawn was chilly, the driver and I had a brief swim in the lake's clear waters, while the cook stood guard.

"You buggers must be mad," he said, as we emerged.

But on me was the madness of exhilaration.

We were fired at in Parapat, where we rashly tried to buy a chicken, but escaped unhurt, to arrive in Medan, hot and filthy, some thirty-two hours after we had left Padang. A month later, another truck taking the overland route was ambushed. From then on, nobody drove between Padang and Medan. British forces kept to the towns.

Medan impressed as being nearer civilisation. Despite the emergency and an early curfew, shops were open and had glass in their windows — a sophistication not achieved in Padang. Many were run by Indians (especially Sikhs) and Chinese.

Again there was the familiar task imposed by an unfamiliar city: to learn the way around, to learn the names of the streets, to learn how to get to the more desirable nooks. And again the romance of geography overcame me. Here was a distant place — and I was living in it, on a day to day basis, in danger of taking it for granted.

I was given two rooms in the upper floor of a pleasant house, once in Dutch hands, then Japanese. My main room had a balcony with an agreeable open view, jungle visible in the distance. I entered by the rear door, along a path fringed by pleasant flowering bushes. The rear staircase — once presumably a servants' stair — led directly up to my rooms. The rest of the house was occupied by assorted sergeants.

My travel documents instructed me to report immediately to a Captain Zajac, a tall demented-looking Pole with ferocious moustaches. It was said of him that when the Germans invaded Poland, where the Zajacs held vast estates, he and his elder brother had set fire to their mansion rather than let it fall into enemy hands and had walked south to join the British in India. On the way, they had been joined by other Poles. Over one hundred of them had finally gathered at the frontier.

By then, Zajac's elder brother was dead.

Zajac had collected a medal in the Arakan while losing most of his left ear in a fanatical attack on a Jap bunker. Hatred seemed to be his chief motivation. In consequence, I discovered, he was beloved by his group of men. But he hated me because I was a replacement for the sergeant, his old comrade, who had been killed in Emmahaaven swimming pool. He gave me a complicated order involving Allied war graves. I was forced to admit that I had had no Intelligence training and, in consequence, could not carry out the order.

He gave me a furious bollocking. I ought to be on a charge. I had no business volunteering for a job I could not carry out, etc.

The telephone interrupted his raving. At the end of the call, as he replaced the receiver, he said to me, in a mild tone of voice as if losing his temper was beyond his capacity, "Dismiss, now, sergeant, and I will send for you when I need you."

I saluted and dismissed.

While I waited to be sent for, I made it my business to understand the local situation. The troops were showing their civilian dispositions, and had settled as well as might be into situations best suited to them. Since there were almost no facilities provided by the over-stretched S.E. Asia Command, of which we were an outpost, small private enjoyments had been carved out, many of them centering round the RAPWI camp and the Dutch women there. RAPWI stood for Repatriation and Aid, (Prisoners-of-War Indonesia), and therefore embraced all Dutch and foreign nationals who had fallen into Jap hands during their swift advance through the N.E.I. in 1942.

These unfortunates were largely displaced persons, unable to take up their old tasks on plantations and so on while the Emergency prevailed; many wanted nothing better than to get on the little steamer, the *Van Heutz*, which called at Belawan Harbour twice a week, ferrying people to Singapore for the commencement of the long voyage back to Holland and Europe. Meanwhile, most were prepared to celebrate their comparative liberty in the commonplace ways.

Eedie was a large cheerful girl. It was her height that first won my interest. I was six foot one and she was six foot two. I had never had a girl-friend bigger than I before. She was going about with a handsome Irish corporal in the RAOC, but a couple of dances was enough for her to change her mind. She found I had a Jeep at my command, and that was enough. We drove all round Medan that night, drinking in the few bars that were open, talking and laughing furiously, pouring out personal histories of the war to each other — therapy of a necessary kind. Driving her back to the RAPWI camp, I was cut off by the curfew and spent the night on her bedroom floor. But only for about ten minutes. After that, Eedie relented and allowed me into a much more comfortable place.

Medan was an unruly town. Discipline tightened up only when the "extremists", as we called the nationalists of Soekarno's Liberation Army, went on the attack. Otherwise, morale was low enough to permit a certain amount of individuality. The Irish RAOC corporal went gunning for me, weeping and cursing in semi-public places over my absconding with his Dutch lady friend. In some respects, Medan resembled the Wild West.

It was a difference of opinion between Eedie and me, rather than any of Corporal Paddy's threats, which spoilt our harmony. The Dutch had reason to be grateful to the British, and were in fact more friendly towards us than vice versa. They also had cause to dislike us, since they depended on us and the British were reluctant to allow Dutch reinforcements into the country. Any such move was greeted with reprisals from Soekarno. *Merdeka!* (Freedom) was scrawled everywhere, and bullets flew. In Java, pitched battles were fought at Surabaja and elsewhere. The British were more prepared than the Dutch to play a waiting game.

Intelligence was under pressure to discover how news of pending arrivals of Dutch troops reached Soekarno, and the Port Authority at Belawan was tightened — to no effect. The *Van Heutz* reached Belawan from Singapore. Forces there sympathetic to Soekarno radioed the news ahead.

This matter of politics came between Eedie and me.

"You're pigs, all of you, worse than the fucking Germans," she told me one evening as we sat smoking outside the RAPWI hall. "We know that you want to have Sumatra under the Union Jacket, just like in India and Burma." She always called it the Union Jacket.

"Why do you think we want this stinking dump? We've got enough on our bloody hands. We wouldn't have it if the Dutch gave it to us."

"Oh, yes, you would. How much of the globe is already inside your greedy hands? You'd have it okay, you bet." She laughed scornfully. We were partly drunk.

"Oh? Well then, it isn't yours to give, is it? You rely on us, don't you? Otherwise, if we weren't here, you lot would be kicked out, lock, stock and barrel."

"That's only because —"

"And another thing. You don't call us Germans. You Dutch are nearer the fucking Germans than we are, aren't you? You live next fucking door. Who do you think freed the fucking Netherlands?"

"Well, it wasn't you, so just shut it up. You want Sumatra back, just because it was yours once before in history."

"Oh, piss off, you Dutch bint. Come to bed."

"Not with you, you're bloody drunk. It comes from your fucking ears."

So a little frostiness intervened. As so often with drunken arguments, I did not mean a word I said, and yet the underlying resentment had to be given voice. The British had no good reason to be in Sumatra to begin with.

VI

About a mile from my billet, in a modest side street, stood the cinema called the Deli, after Medan's main river. It was commandeered for the military, although men could take girl friends, one per man. Performances were always crowded.

The idle Japanese Army had spent its three-year occupation looting and collecting what booty it could. 26 Division was busy forcing it to disgorge. Food, valuables, furniture, and, above all, drink, arrived spasmodically at the sergeants' mess. They had acquired a vast store of movies, the more appropriate of which were shown in the Deli. Thus did I see many vintage films, many ancient themes.

One evening, while Eedie was avoiding me, I went with another sergeant, Charlie Frost, to a showing of *The Great Gabo*, a melodrama about a ventriloquist's dummy which takes over the ventriloquist.

We emerged from the Deli with the crowd, everyone in sombre green uniform, with a defiant variety of headgear and lengths of hair, everyone armed. Our footsteps echoed in the narrow streets as we dispersed. On one corner, respectfully back against the wall, stood a white man in white ducks in company with three Chinese, a man and two women, all dressed European style. As Charlie and I passed them, one of the women asked in a lively voice, and with bright glances at us, "Was it a good film?"

Thus I made the acquaintance of Ginny and her sister Mandy, and Jean Mercier and Wang.

The garrison trooped by as we stood talking. When the street was empty, the man asked, "Would you care for a drink?"

Soldiers meet only a certain cross-section of any civilian population. Of that cross-section, those most willing to talk to soldiers are crooks, priests, and prostitutes. Charlie and I were highly suspicious of this man with a French accent, but we went along with him and the others. They all lived just round a corner or two, in what had been a grocery shop before the Japanese arrived. The ground floor was arranged with old bamboo chairs and tables. Very little had been done for the decor, beyond the hanging of a few bright Chinese calendars. Our new friends had moved in only four months ago, after the British released them from internment.

There are times in childhood when a boy sees a girl and is overcome by a mysterious yearning, of whose nature he is kept unaware since the time is not yet ripe. A similar yearning overcame me when I sat down on those wicker chairs and found myself conversing with two Chinese ladies. Despite my life-long admiration of all things Chinese, my only intercourse with a Chinese girl had been — how secretly, how boldly! — in Calcutta, with a pretty creature who charged me ten rupees for the pleasure.

Jean was a cheerful and fatherly man, a rubber planter whose plantations lay to the east, outside Palembang. He was French Swiss, and married to Ginny. Mandy was Ginny's younger sister and married to Wang. Jean and Ginny had a baby boy, Sammi; Mandy and Wang had two little children, Fat and Tek, generally looked after by an inferior aunt.

Jean's nationality had puzzled the Japanese authorities. If he was French, then he was an enemy alien; if he was Swiss, then he was neutral. How could he be both? By insisting on speaking English rather than his native French, Jean persuaded the Japanese that he really was Swiss, and therefore entitled to a simple internment, rather than imprisonment with the Dutch. The other three of the party were Japan's hated enemy, Chinese. But no, they also were Swiss, according to Jean's continued claims. The Japanese were, on occasions, sticklers for what was correct. Besides, Wang, although he spoke little English, was from Hong Kong, and had a British passport. So the four had lived for three years, chafing at their confinement, in a small house in the street where I was now billeted — in which time both couples had had children born to them. The British had released them recently, and established them in this part of Chinatown.

All this emerged, with many other details, over innumerable cups of coffee and innumerable cigars. Ginny's bold move of talking to us in the street led Charlie and me to think of ourselves as specially chosen to look after these four unfortunates with no home and no immediate prospect of getting back to the rubber plantations where they all worked.

We soon drew closer to the four Merciers, as we called them. I saw more of them, for I was idle. Soon, I was calling on them every day, as well as in the evening, with Charlie. Charlie Frost was a good old Cockney, with a little wife he had rashly married on his embarkation leave, who now pined for him, or not, in a terraced house in Lewisham. We became friends simply by accepting each other, without questions. I cannot say whether that was a working class ethic or part of the alchemy of wartime. I know that I greatly admired Charlie and his immense solid respectability. His father was in the coal business, I remember.

The Merciers told us stories of Medan under the Japanese, and how public executions had been carried out in the main square. Sometimes the Japanese were correct and polite. At other times, they behaved with inhuman brutality.

Gradually, by unspoken means, Charlie and I were accepted into the little Mercier group. Ginny was twenty-four and Mandy twenty-two. Wang was about the same age, and Jean thirty.

Jean was generally calm, always genial. He and Ginny conversed in English, since she had no French and he no Cantonese. He had no wish to leave Sumatra. He just wished for normal conditions to return, and to work on the plantation with his pretty wife looking after the home. Jean was a tall thin man — we were all thin — always immaculately dressed in white ducks and white shirt.

Wang was lazy and good-natured. He alone did not look half-starved. He liked the current condition of uncertainty, since it meant he did not have to work — although after a while he did get a menial job in a restaurant.

Of the two sisters, Ginny was the more vivacious. Being the older, she was inclined to boss her sister about; yet after all their internment the two were close friends. Both had attended Hong Kong University, and were well educated. Mandy — whose Chinese name was Wang Lim Hwa — was the prettier, with a sweet kitten shaped face and deep dark eyes. Ginny was always laughing, and soon hung on my arm and treated me as if she were a youthful aunt of mine. I adored her, though my feelings for her sister were warmer, darker.

They were proud of their English friend. Soon, while Jean went out to haunt offices for news or shifts in policy, Ginny and Mandy were riding round in their friend's Jeep to do the shopping, or simply for the pleasure of it, their cotton dresses blowing carelessly in the wind. I was certainly proud of them, although there was no kudos to be had from associating with Chinese women, unlike Dutch women; rather the reverse, to be frank. Most of my Army colleagues regarded them as "natives".

Jean and Wang trusted me to take care of their wives. Aware of that trust — trust is strong in times of war — I stood and watched as they shopped for tiny slices of cheese or tried on hats, laughing delightfully at each other as they did so. I was adult now, and the sten hanging on my shoulder was there to protect them as well as myself.

After the long months in India and Burma, female company was an oasis in the desert. I soon became aware of the considerable differences between the two sisters. While Ginny, as I have mentioned, touched me openly, swung on my arm in company, laughing, physical contact with Mandy was more secret. At first it was an affair of bare arm accidentally touching bare arm, nothing more. Yet it developed into a strange code, the meaning of which I told myself I could not understand.

They were animated and cheerful young women, happy to be free at last from their semi-captivity, glad to have a stranger's attention. The shabby grocery store was always a place of laughter and the babble of tongues — and, almost from the start, shy deer glances from Mandy.

Ginny always wore light Western-style cotton dresses. Mandy wore the same by day. In the evenings, perhaps when Charlie and I took the girls to the cinema, she would put on a yellow or blue silk *cheongsam*, ankle length, with a slit up to the knee. Then she looked most seductive. A dance hall opened in town, sign of reviving peaceful intent, and we escorted the ladies there. Jean and Wang came along but did not dance; they appeared proud to see us dancing with their wives. And as I held that slender and lively body in my arms, I saw the lecherous glances of other men, as they lumbered round the floor with their large Dutch ladies.

Unlike the Dutch, the Chinese were happy to have the British and Indian troops in Sumatra. Not only did they feel that the British were on their side (a feeling the British in no way reciprocated), but the current impasse suited them. They foresaw a time when the British would leave, when things would be worse for them, under the Dutch, or considerably worse, under the Indonesians — who, as Muslims, were known to be anti-Chinese. This was the time for them to be carefree, and enjoy young male company: someone new, after the secondhand years that had passed. Someone to take them to the Deli Cinema and indulge their girlish fantasies.

So my feelings towards Medan developed. It became the most delightful town I ever knew. In its centre were huge shady trees, overgrown and blowsy. Over everything hung a great quiet, broken only by bullock carts creaking by, the odd military vehicle, occasional outbursts of gunfire. People walked at a leisurely pace. The shops were almost empty. The heat was benevolent.

That is how I prefer to remember Medan, tumbledown after three years of utter neglect — yet was not that tumbledown quality how I now saw the whole world. Tumbledownness was a positive quality, defying the rage to be modern. Tumbledownness pointed towards the past, that mysterious past whose history awaited an historian. So Medan remains in memory, and perhaps that particular Medan remains in my memory alone:

> Within the surface of Time's fleeting river
> Its wrinkled image lies, as then it lay
> Immovably unquiet, and for ever
> It trembles, but it cannot pass away.

as Shelley said of a more renowned city.

The illusion that I had managed to detach myself from the army grew daily. Then the South Wales Borderers went into action, and I was once more the focus of Captain Zajac's attention.

In an attempt to persuade the Indians of our division to desert, the Indonesians — the extremists — promised any man who went over to their side with his rifle and ammunition a place in a kampong, a woman, and protection.

One of the first to take advantage of the offer was a certain Corporal Bill Jones of the SWB. Not only did he desert with his revolvers: he loaded some Bren guns and a few boxes of ammunition into a Dodge truck and drove it into the Indonesian lines.

It was a coup for the Indonesians, and a disgrace for the South Wales Borderers. Jones lived a high life in the kampong. He was a flamboyant character, and not above shooting some of his old mates if needs must. Mandy, Ginny and I saw him once when we were shopping. He drove into the centre of town in a large black car, with a heavily armed escort before and behind him in two Japanese trucks. He too was shopping.

His name became legendary and his old regiment swore to wipe him out.

News reached headquarters that Jones was currently in a certain section of town held by the extremists. This section had as its headquarters a cinema called the Rex.

For once the British went on the attack. The few armoured vehicles in the area were mustered and the Borderers moved in after dark. They had a personal interest in this operation.

The operation was almost a complete success. The Indonesians were not prepared for a pitched battle. Twelve of them were killed, as against two Borderers. Several houses were set on fire and many more damaged. The Union Jack was raised over the Rex. Jones escaped to fight another day.

Captain Zajac summoned me and we stood before a large scale map of Medan. "Here's the river. The Rex is only three streets away. There's a Sikh temple here. This is the extent of the sector we have cleared. The fires have been put out. Today at twelve hundred hours we blow up this bridge over the Deli. You and I are going along to watch proceedings. It'll cause some inconwenience to the locals, but they can put up with that. It means the area can't be infiltrated again if we just keep a good contingent of Rajputs in the temple area. The Borderers have guard posts here and here."

Sappers did a neat job of blowing up the road bridge precisely at twelve hundred hours. Another sector of town could now be safely held. Zajac and I patrolled the streets, which were pleasant and tree-lined by the river, until we came to the Rex. Here the officer paused on the steps.

The exterior was burnt and the glass doors shattered. An Indian corporal stood on guard, rifle at the slope.

"We'll soon get this place patched up. Rewenge is sweet and so is Claudette Colbert, eh?" It was a joke.

"We could use a second cinema, sir."

"Precisely. But Army Ciné is down on strength. You appear to be a spare bod, sergeant. So you are now going to be in charge of the Rex, starting very conweniently from now. For the time being, you will be answerable direct to me. That may change ewentually. Meantime, you will be receiwing a list of your duties. Two Indian orderlies will be attached to you for cleaning duty. Understood?"

"You mean I'm in charge of this place?"

"Correct."

"Sir."

Everyday affairs in Medan had been lent a spice of excitement, even a note of sophistication, one might say, by the fringes of violence which edged them. Once Charlie and I had been fired on when returning home from the Merciers just before curfew. But to thrust into a vulnerable area was another matter. However, the novelty of the situation was a compensation. A cinema was mine, a whole kingdom of magic.

When the list of my duties arrived, I found that I was to live in the Rex, making my own accommodation. My previous accommodation was to be quitted by eighteen hundred hours.

This news I conveyed to the Merciers when I went to have lunch with them.

Ginny screamed with laughter. "You will be able to play films to yourself all day! Can we come?"

Mercier said, "Will you be safe? Blowing up the bridge has not made British troops more popular."

"The Rajputs are providing a guard at present. My duties don't include stopping the building from being blown up."

I had the afternoon in which to shift my belongings across town. As I went out to the Jeep, sweltering in the sun outside the ex-grocery, Mandy came along too.

"Could I come with you and see your billet before you leave it? I haven't seen that part of Medan since we lived there."

I hesitated. "Will Wang mind? Does your sister want to come along too? How about Jean?"

Perhaps only hindsight suggested that I knew something transforming was about to happen, and wished to postpone its arrival.

To all my questions she demurely answered no and climbed into the passenger seat of the Jeep, showing as she did so an enticing display of leg. She sat there, looking ahead, exquisite and neat. Hot and sweating, I climbed into the driver's seat and started up.

The streets as ever were almost empty, dreaming in sun and shade. The native traffic policeman at the entrance to the Kesawan had nothing to do. When we reached our lines, the MP did not rise from his seat in his guard hut. Recognising me, he waved me on, accompanying the wave with a wolf whistle.

I stopped by the rear door of my billet as usual, walked beside her among the fragrant shrubs, said nothing.

"We live for three years only two doors away, you know," Mandy said, indicating their old house among the trees. "Isn't that funny coincidence?"

It was all I could do to reply. A strange excitement, a mixture of delight and apprehension, filled me.

Opening the back door, I indicated the stairs. She preceded me up them, walking in a leisurely way as if there were nothing at all on her mind.

"Is like our old house," was all she said. "Only not so crowded. Twenty-four people have to live in our old house. Terribly noisy, with the babies crying."

"Of course." I managed to add, "Here's my room," and she went in.

Five weeks had passed since I met the Merciers, five weeks on the hazy time scale of the tropics. In that time, I had never been alone with Mandy. Although I had thought voluptuously about her, they were merely thoughts; I swamped them with the knowledge that she was the mother of two infants and that I was in a delicate international position of trust. But when she turned towards me, I could not extinguish the expression on my face, lit with desire.

She smiled, showing those pearly little teeth. When she smiled broadly, one of them was revealed as pointed.

"Is a nice room for one person. Maybe a little lonely for you, so far away from home."

She walked across the room and went on to the balcony. I stood where I was. After a minute, she turned and came back to me, still with perfect self-possession.

"I wanted to tell you that I love you, that's all."

We put our arms round each other.

Of course, on my part there was simple need. After two years away from England, the unsatisfactory affair with Eedie, at this point not entirely dead, had only whetted my longing for love. Love was the magic word, the trigger to deliver one to the freedoms of happiness, the magic potion made all the tastier by the knowledge that, in the circumstances, it was almost impossible to find. Had I found it? Well, the omens were good.

As we lay on my bed, Mandy spoke of her dissatisfactions with Wang. He was so indolent. He would not work. He had even enjoyed being interned, since that mainly entailed lying on his bed all day doing nothing. He had wept when they were released, since he thought that meant he would have to work again. He was good for nothing but giving her babies, and she did not want any more babies.

Poor Mandy! It was not clear to me, thank God, to see at that time that she was much like Eedie, only wanting a good time and a little excitement after the boredom of the previous three years. I was the nearest available male. But love is so often a matter of proximity, and a question of need as much as personality.

In those days — even in that distant place — adultery was still regarded as a serious affair. The effects of the war in breaking down old moralities had still to be felt; it was hard to live under one creed when one had been brought up in another. This certainly applied to me, who had been educated in an almost Victorian regime.

We tore ourselves away from each other at last. I loaded a few pieces of furniture into the Jeep, and we drove back into town. I dropped Mandy at the corner of her street and went on to the Rex. That night, Charlie and I went to the Merciers as if nothing had happened.

Charlie was not immune to the charms of Mandy and Ginny. As we came away before curfew, he frequently said, "Cor, those two girls. . . . That Mandy . . ." as if words had deliberately failed him. My urge to tell him the truth was very strong. But I dissembled. I dissembled with him, I dissembled with the Merciers. I played the simple, the innocent — the sort of person I had been before that first day.

Mandy proved ingenious. She and Ginny had an elder sister, a rather formidable lady always referred to as Miss Chew. She was a schoolteacher, and lived several streets away from the others in part of a little Dutch-type bungalow. Mandy arranged for us to meet there in the afternoon, from two-thirty to four-forty-five.

The bungalow's front door was sealed up. It was a matter of entering from the rear door. Miss Chew's single room was stacked with furniture, piled to the ceiling and allowing only a narrow way to walk round the single bed, on which a board could be placed to convert it into a table. A bird in a cage sang on the single window-sill.

It sang to us as we made love. For two afternoons we held off, doing no more than kiss, cuddle, and pour our hearts out to one another. Oh, what we said — the history of our different races, the history of the war, could be extrapolated from our confessions. She had been born in the port of Amoy, and at once Amoy became a place I needed to visit and a name synonymous with pleasure.

Then we could hold off from each other no longer. It was not to be expected that, in the sumptuous heat, and in that gauzy claustrophobic room with the light filtered through lacy curtains, we could abstain from the feast we so badly needed. The external world was nothing to us. Even the faint sounds of Chinese opera, played on a distant gramophone, served only to emphasise our distance from others, and our delicious proximity. It was a delightful paradox that to this retiring and quiet girl — "rather a mouse," the unobservant might have said — there was no coyness. Indeed, she led me, this experienced married woman. Standing up abruptly, with a smile which perhaps implied some kind of apology or permission asked, she pulled her cotton dress over her head, slipped out of brassiere and panties, and stood before me naked.

"Take your clothes off," she said.

Doing so, removing my damp shirt and trousers, flinging them aside, I had a chance to gaze at the generous breasts on the delicate figure, the dark nipples, and the mound of Venus lightly thatched with dark hair. After years had passed, I recognised how we took it for granted that we were both so thin, so under-nourished. Now we were to provide each other with the nourishment of our embraces.

"I'm ashamed I'm so skinny for you."

"The nearer the bone the sweeter the meat, my love."

And so it was.

Four-forty-five arrived so swiftly.

"I will see you this evening."

"I can't face it."

"You must pretend."

"But they'll guess —"

"No, they won't. You must not say a word to Ginny. Pretend! Look so innocent as you always do."

And in the sergeants' mess at teatime, I underwent more pretence. Most of the sergeants were, as they put it, "fixed up" in the RAPWI. My predilection for the two Chinese girls had not gone unnoticed.

"They'll land you in trouble, Joe, boy, you'll see. They've all been sleeping with Jap soldiers. You want to fix yourself up with a Dutch *bibi*."

"Leave him alone, he's an old soldier, aren't you, Joe? The longer you stay out here, the whiter they look. The great thing is to get it regular."

"You're having it off with both of 'em, aren't you, mate?" said Bragg.

"Every night," I said.

"Chinese bints are useless in bed," Bradbury said. "No passion. Just lie there and let you do all the work. You'd be a lot better with a Sumatra pusher."

"Leave him alone. He's getting it free. He doesn't have to pay like you, Brad. You're getting it free, aren't you, Joe?"

"A few cigarettes occasionally," I suggested.

Curiously enough, it was not until afterwards that the full realisation dawned on me that I had loved Mandy deeply. Oh, I knew at the time that I was "crazy" about her; I simply failed to take account of how deep it went. Perhaps many lovers suffer from the same peculiar torment. After the affair is finished, they waken to the realisation that the one they loved was more precious than they knew, and irreplaceable.

I also suffered guilt. I was aware that I had left her in a dangerous situation and that possibly — with a little more effort — we might have come to a happier ending.

The longing I experienced, which I cannot say has ever died entirely over the years, was for Mandy herself and all that she represented, and also for that delicate, lithe body of hers which, because it was the first female body to which I had unlimited access, still retains its delightful intimacy in my memory. I longed for it fiercely at the time, and tried to drown its sovereignty over me with the imprint of other bodies.

With Mandy I crossed the thresholds which have no definite name. There is after all more than one kind of bridge across from boyhood to manhood. And in those age-old satisfying rhythms we practised, while our bodies made their funny noises together, we signified another safe crossing, a trans-racial crossing which took us beyond language into a different kind of world of which we never spoke, I suppose because the words were not there. I sometimes thought that Mandy really envied her more lively sister, who had won herself a European; now that Mandy had her own European, she had in some way gained equality.

And I — I was defying all the colour prejudices of my fellows. I had made a definite choice. My friends I had not chosen; they just happened to be in the army, as I was. Mandy I had chosen, and had defied moral laws as well as prejudices to have the secret enjoyment of her.

The Indonesians, when they held the Rex, had erected a look-out hut on the flat roof of the cinema, since the position commanded a good view of the surrounding area. I got my two orderlies to clear the rubbish out of this room and slept there. In Padang, the nights had been as stuffy as the days, but in Medan after dark came a merciful cool breeze. It was pleasant to lie up there on the roof, to fall asleep in a reverie of Mandy.

Below my room was an administrative office which I converted into a living room with the furniture from my previous billet. Not that I anticipated doing much living there.

While the doors of the cinema were being repaired, I got busy sorting out the films held on the premises, with the aid of a casual and chain-smoking captain from Army Ciné, who came round in the mornings. There were some Indian and Chinese films, which we planned to hand over to our friends in the Rajput Rifles. Also, such Hollywood products as — I recall — *By Candlelight*, *Dawn Patrol* with Errol Flynn, *Victoria the Great* — the only English film, with Anna Neagle — *Rebecca of Sunnybrook Farm*, *Man Hunt*, with lovely Joan Bennett, *The Man in the Iron Mask*, *The Bank Dick*, with W. C. Fields, and other rather fusty stories from the thirties. But we knew we had a grateful audience, and the chain-smoking captain promised more up-to-date films from Singapore in a week or two.

"Ever seen *Citizen Kane*, sergeant?"

"No, sir. Who's in it?"

"It's an Orson Welles film. The men wouldn't like it."

"I don't know, sir. They certainly liked *Sergeant York*."

He laughed and strolled away, still smoking.

Medan, stagnant Medan, immovably unquiet, remained as it was while the weeks went by. The fighting continued in Java, but Sumatra was spared such bloodshed; it appeared to be a rule that matters were always decided in Java, where political power resided. Our local extremists remained quiet, doing little more than bombard us with an irregular news-sheet called *Merdeka Times*. The British, for their part, stayed put, and refrained from importing more Dutch troops. The Japanese army was slowly sent in small parcels to Singapore, and thence by — we hoped — uncomfortable troopship home. And the RAPWI was slowly emptied as its occupants took their longed-for passage on the old but seemingly reliable *Van Heutz*. Prostitutes were never allowed on the streets of Medan, but I noticed with superior satisfaction that more and more local girls, a flower neatly woven into their hair, called on the sergeants, leaving their little wooden sandals at the doorstep when they arrived.

VII

There was at that time a song very popular in the sergeants' mess, and constantly played on our gramophone, called "The Very Thought of You", in which the lines "I see your face in every flower, Your eyes in stars above", captured much of what I felt about Mandy — and at the same time failed to capture so much. At least her eyes were mentioned, for I was under the spell of those beautiful Chinese eyes as much as her other parts; they seemed to hold all mystery and meaning. I gloried in her foreignness, and felt I could not possibly have loved her so much had she come from any other land.

She taught me much about love. For her mother had trained her to use her body to best advantage in passion. The muscles of her pelvic floor could move in a way foreign to most women in the West. It is they who afterwards — afterwards — disappoint.

Often we laughed in the middle of our love-making. The hours of two-thirty to four-forty-five are sultry ones in Medan, and our bodies, oiled with sweat, often made outrageous noises as they pressed together. Perhaps this is why love affairs are rarely kept secret in the East: the bodies involved involuntarily give themselves away.

One morning after attending to the cleaning of the Rex following the previous night's show, I strolled down to the bazaar to buy cigars. By no means the least enjoyable feature of life in Medan was the fact that large juicy cigars were to be had very cheaply; had they been boxed, labelled, and exported to the Netherlands, as happened before the war, they would have cost rather more than the equivalent of a penny apiece. I was about to go into the tobacconist when I came face to face with Ginny, out for a morning shop.

"So, there you are! Now perhaps you can keep me company and protect me with that gun of yours."

"Am I to protect you from the Indonesians or the British?"

"From all men. You're such a wicked lot."

We went into a street where there was a small market, and Ginny fussed over some cabbage.

"I have to go to hospital tomorrow," she said, glancing quickly up at me. She was very different from her sister, and her movements were more birdlike.

"Ginny — what's the matter with you?"

"Oh, my womb is shifting about or something. The specialist is going to take a look at it." She spoke lightly but inspected me solemnly. "I don't want you to hurt Mandy. Be careful and kind, eh?"

"Whatever do you mean?" I felt a blush beginning.

She took my arm with one hand, swinging a net with the cabbage she had bought in the other, stepping out and saying lightly, "You need not pretend with me, Joe. Mandy always asks the advice of her sisters. Miss Chew of course also knows what goes on in her bungalow. You are shocked?"

"Staggered. Ginny, I'm sorry — I mean, I really am sorry when you've all been so good —"

She laughed. "You British are so prudish. I always heard it, *non?* But happily you were not so prudish for long, Mandy says to me. Now don't be shocked that I know. I will keep your terrible secret, I promise."

I could not look at her. "I feel so bad."

"Don't feel so bad. Come in this shop and you can buy me a duryan ice-cream if you like."

We went into the shop she indicated and sat down at a table. It was dark, and a small Chinese girl served us.

She held my hand. "The times are so dreadful. Don't feel bad. Be happy while you are able, *non?*"

"Oh, Jesus, Ginny, you don't understand, I do feel bad, but at the same time I am happy — wildly happy. I love you but I love your sister even more. I know it's wrong. . . ."

She shook her head. "Yes, it's wicked. But enjoy it. I just have to warn you — Mandy loves you very seriously. She's full of wild fantasies about you."

"What do you mean?"

"Just fantasies."

The ice-cream arrived. I looked at her and smiled. "Once I get used to it I know I'll be delighted that you know. I haven't told anyone. Not even Charlie."

"But he's your friend. . . . And I thought what a good actor he was!"

"You're speaking out now because you're going into hospital. Is it serious?"

"No, no, of course not. . . . Listen, Joe, the British will leave Sumatra soon, you realise."

"Some day, sure."

"They cannot just sit here, *non*? It's impossible. When all the Japs are gone, then you also will go. In a matter of weeks. What about Mandy then?"

"That's all in the future. . . ."

She sighed and took a dainty sip of the ice-cream. She was thin, even by the standards of the day. Her arms looked so fragile.

"Ginny, I have great respect for your husband and should not say this, but I do think you are an absolute darling."

I received one of her sunny, mischievous smiles. "'An absolute darling. . . .' Well, that's nice. And for my part, you know, I quite envy my little sister. There — that's what you wish me to say, *non*?"

"It's what I like to hear, *non*?, but it's too late to try and seduce me." She laughed with me.

The films discovered in the stores of the Rex proved to have Dutch sub-titles. No one minded that. We had to show *Dawn Patrol* and *The Bank Dick* several times. We had good attendances; the cinema was marginally more comfortable than the worn Deli. And the Indonesians made no attempt to recover their lost ground. Perhaps they were prepared to wait for us to go.

Newer films from Singapore never arrived. Singapore was now regarded as the great Land of Plenty. To get leave there was bliss, according to all accounts. We continued to be short of almost all supplies. It was said that the only nutritional quality in our bread was the small beetles found in every loaf. The 26th Indian Division was more forgotten than the Forgotten Army had ever been.

Nor did replacements come through when men left for repatriation. It became apparent that, as Ginny forecast, we were going to withdraw from the island sooner or later, leaving the Dutch to manage as best they could. It was their quarrel, not ours, and someone higher up — probably Slim or Lord Louis Mountbatten — had recognised the fact.

Ginny lingered for several days in hospital. As the wife of a Swiss, she qualified for a bed in the British Field hospital. I went with Mandy to see her, pale and large-eyed against the pillow.

"My god, we are all so fragile," Mandy said, as we left.

A week after her operation, Ginny was discharged. She had had cancer of the womb, and a hysterectomy had been performed. She lay on a couch, smiling and pleasant with everyone, but unable to nurse little Sammi, and scarcely able to move from her cushions.

I noticed that Sammi was beginning to form words. It was a puzzle to imagine what language he would speak, since he was addressed regularly in Cantonese, French, English, and — by several of the people living in the house with the Merciers — Malay. That linguistic uncertainty reflected the general uncertainty under which we lived. Every so often, our CO would have us on parade and give us a pep talk, or the sergeants would be sent for and told to tighten up the discipline of the men. But the rot had set in. Stalemate had been reached and there was no disguising it. Britain was getting out of India and Burma; she could hardly be expected to hold the N.E.I. for another power.

Mandy and I still clung to each other. Behind our barricades of furniture we kept the world at bay. But gradually a new note entered our conversation, embodied in that inscrutable question, What was going to happen to us all?

She pressed, I evaded.

"Why don't you say anything? I suppose you don't care what will happen to us soon enough."

"Don't say that, Mandy. I care, but what can I say? I'm in the bloody army. I have no control over my fate. I do what I'm told."

"So you say! You never have any orders, just a good life."

"I can't explain the army to you. I am not as free as you think. One day I'll get my marching orders and then I'll have to go, same as anyone else."

"And what you think happens to me, please?" Great eyes regarding me.

"Everyone wants us to go. Things will be better for you once we've left. You'll be free to return to Palembang with Wang. Life will get better again."

She stifled a sob and sat up, turning her pale damp back to me.

"Yes? You like to think me back in Wang's bed again? My God, is that all you care?"

"We've had a happy time — we're still having it, but soon things must change. Then I have to go my way and you yours. You know old Wang is very kind, really."

"You Europeans are all alike. You lead an Eastern girl on then you just leave her when it will suit you. How many thousand times I hear that same story?"

We began meeting at Miss Chew's every other day.

"I'm so busy," I explained. "We're going to have a proper beer bar in the foyer. The carpenters are in and I have to watch them."

"Beer, drink. . . . My God! Listen, what is the use? Never mind beer and drink, what will happen to us?"

"You know the answer. It hurts, but you know as well as I. I'll miss you, but life will go on for you as before, except better. I'm the one who has to face the violent changes."

She smacked me lightly on the thigh. "Life as before, you say? What do you know? You go back to peaceful Britain. The violence will be here, you understand? Real violence with blood and many, many people dead. Mainly Chinese. The Indonesians are mad murderous fanatics. They hate Chinese people, just like the bloody Nipponese. Oh, I can't tell you! They wait now, they just wait. . . . Once you are gone, then they start to kill off all foreigners except only Malay people. You think they give back Jean's plantation in Palembang? No, they keep it for themselves. Us they push in the face, into the sea, to swim for China."

I had no answer.

In the evenings, after dark had descended on the city, our little group, the Merciers, Charlie, and I, would sit outside the old grocery and chat, and I would pass Jean a Dutch cigar. The evenings were peaceful under the arcade, apart from the mosquitoes. A short distance away was the barrack where the Ambonese lived. The Ambonese were Indonesian mercenary troops faithful to the Dutch, good fighting men and good singers too. They had their women with them in barracks, and would sit at the open windows strumming guitars and singing songs which had travelled round the world, such as "Aurora" and "La Cucaracha". Sometimes they played a great Malay favourite, "Terang Boelan". At such moments, I chafed that I could not take Mandy into my arms and carry her fast on to the nearest bed.

There we would sit, enjoying the cooler air which followed sunset, until the *satay* man was heard, progressing slowly down the next street, clicking his wooden clickers to announce his wares. When he appeared with his wooden trolley, freighted with steaming soup and the charcoal fire over which the sticks of *satay* sent out an appetising smell, we bought our supper from him. It saved cooking. Eating *satay* in those circumstances seemed to me one of the heights of bliss, the pleasures of Mandy apart.

Terrible anxieties overcame me. I had no idea what to do. I asked Jean for his opinion of the situation.

"Some days I think maybe I'll get back to the plantation, *non*? Then it doesn't look so good. The overland route to Palembang is closed. The British won't let me go by sea, though I could pay — the ships are too crowded. A fine idea, *non*? Doesn't anyone build ships now the war is supposed to be over? The Swiss office remains closed."

"If — when we leave, you'll be part of the Republic of Soekarno's Indonesia. Doesn't that scare you a bit?"

"*Merdeka!*" he said, ironically. "Sure, it scares me, but what can I do?

I'm not Dutch, who they hate. I hope they'll let me and Wang and the ladies go back to work. They'll want rubber production, and it needs real skilled work to bring a plantation to productivity, *non?* So we hope always for the best."

"Why don't you just give up and go to Singapore where you'll all be safe?"

"Singapore? You crazy? You heard how crowded it is? Who could live in such a place? I like open air, me. Besides, all my capital investment is in Palembang. I leave here, I lose it, okay?"

"But you'd be safe in Singapore. What about the others?"

"We've got nothing, Joe. All we've got is here. You might as well suggest going back in Suisse — in Switzerland."

"What's wrong with Switzerland?"

He dropped his voice. "You're not a child, *non?* You know what prejudice exists in Europe. Do you think I'd want to take Ginny back there? We'd both be — what's the word in English? — ostracised. What would she do in Suisse? I belong in the East with her. It's my commitment, *non?*"

If anything, Jean increased my anxieties, by showing me clearly the nature of the trap that was closing round them, round Ginny and Mandy. I still found it difficult to believe in the violence of the Indonesians. Yet only a few years later, Bertrand Russell, one of the few people in the West who seemed at all disturbed by the situation in Indonesia, said that the Soekarno government had killed as many as ten million Chinese. The government had declared them to be Communists, and so not a finger had been lifted in the West. At that time, the Chinese under Chairman Mao were nobody's friends.

The subject was not going to go away. A few days later, Mandy resumed it.

"You like Medan, I think, Joe? Don't I often hear you say how it's nice, warmer than England and so on, *non?*"

She smiled, with a hint of that sharp tooth. "My God, you look so careful. . . . These days, you know you look pretty careful. Listen, I just had this thought. Maybe you don't go with the rest of the army when they leave Medan. You stay here, draw your pay and get some work in this nice place."

"On Jean's plantation, I suppose? I wouldn't know a rubber tree if it came up and bit me."

"Oh, you are so comical. Maybe here in a bank, in the big Dutch bank in the Kesawan. You are Englishman — the Indonesians would not harm you."

"I couldn't work in a bank. I wouldn't be any good. I've had no training." Her suggestion threw me into a panic. I liked Medan: but the thought of being stuck in it on my own in the chaos that would undoubtedly follow as the Indonesians and Dutch fought it out was extremely alarming.

I fell back on my old line of defence.

"You don't understand the army."

"Oh, this damn army! Do they own you lock, stock and barrel, yes? Listen, can't you speak to your officer? The Polish person. Ask him. Ask him if I can come to Singapore with you. I can pay to come on your troopship. Or go in disguise, who knows?"

"Forget it, my darling. These are all fantasies."

But a few days later came the words I had already anticipated, lying awake late into the night.

"Sadly, Joe, you don't love me any more."

Sulkily, "You know I do."

She threw herself naked on top of me and seized my shoulders. "Then why not marry me and get me out of this place? Then I will love you for ever, I swear!"

A kind of depression seized me. I went and lay on my bed on the roof of the Rex and wallowed in gloom. It was not Mandy who depressed me, but rather the tissue of circumstance in which she and the Merciers were caught. To whom did Sumatra belong? To those who lived here? But some of the Dutch in the RAPWI camp, awaiting a ship to take them to Europe, had farmed here for four generations. Much of the prosperity of Sumatra was owed to Dutch enterprise.

And Chinese enterprise had also contributed to the prosperity. I thought again of the first days in Padang, when British, Indian, Dutch, Japanese and Indonesian forces had sat armed together in the Chinese café. The memory clung like a parable. There seemed to be a kind of pleasant neutrality in the Chinese temperament, a moderation in general, which made the Chinese ill targets for retribution. Of course, this was long before Chairman Mao's Cultural Revolution; but even that bout of madness was over comparatively quickly, to be followed by a prevailing Chinese wish for law and decency.

Everyone seemed convinced that a bloodbath would follow the withdrawal of British troops. Yet the same was said of India, and the Indians could scarcely wait to see us gone.

In my naivety, I had imagined that, following the end of the terrible war, everyone would rejoice in peace, and insist that there was no more fighting. Couldn't laws be passed to that effect? Weren't fifty-five million dead enough?

As for dear Mandy, I would have been happy — proud — to marry her. How exciting it would be to set up house somewhere with her and two Chinese children, provided she could get a divorce. I was vague about Chinese divorce. Where would we live? What would my father do if I returned home with a Chinese wife and two kids? The house would fall down. . . .

I longed to be assimilated by her Chinese-ness, to learn Cantonese, to be in a real Chinese city. Perhaps we could go to Amoy, once the fighting there died down. . . . But how would I go about all that?

The world's unsatisfactoriness was bad enough; there was also my own unsatisfactoriness to cope with.

I was twenty years of age. Gloom at that age was a passing thing, just one colour in the dramatic spectrum of emotions. The phone rang.

It was Army Ciné, to announce that a delivery of films was arriving at the port of Belawan, from Singapore. I recognised the drawling voice of the chain-smoking officer, Captain Morrison. He ordered me to go down in the Jeep to collect it. A convoy would be leaving the city for Belawan the following morning at 1030 hours, and I was to join it.

"Sir."

That evening, Charlie and I went round to the Merciers as usual. I told them my news.

"New films, hurrah!" said Jean. "You must give us all free seats, Joe. I want most to see *Hollywood Canteen* with the Andrews Sisters."

"*Bataan*," said Charlie. "I missed it in Calcutta."

"Oh, *Gilda*, please," said Mandy. "It stars Rita Hayworth and I'm just mad about her."

"*Devotion* for me," I said. "It stars Ida Lupino and I'm mad about her. How about you, Ginny?"

Ginny, still lying on her sofa, said, "I think that best would be *Brief Encounter* — a tragic love story. . . ."

I gave her a glance. She returned an innocent smile.

When I said that I was going down to Belawan with a convoy the following morning, there were exclamations of alarm. Several vehicles had been shot up on the coast road.

"The good old SWOBS will see that nothing happens," Charlie said. "The extremists have only got pluck enough to pick off single vehicles. It'll be okay."

"I have the morning off," Wang said. "Can Mandy and I come along with you, Joe, for the ride?"

"It isn't exactly safe. . . ."

"Oh, do let us come," said Mandy, adding her mite. "It would be so lovely to have a sight of the sea."

So it was agreed, with concealed reluctance on my part. I much liked the easy-going Wang, but there seemed a good chance that if he discovered how I was carrying on with his wife he might stick a knife into me. I had heard tales about the Chinese.

It rained the following morning, the downpour sounding thunderous on my flimsy bedroom roof. Shivering, pulling on a shirt, I looked out and saw everywhere leaking roofs and streaming gutters. Poor Medan — for over three years it had had no maintenance, no repair. Under the assaults of a tropical climate, it was falling slowly apart.

In an hour, the rain was over and the sun shone forth with its usual vigour. In ten minutes, everything was bone dry.

The convoy for Belawan assembled from the RAPWI camp. Some more lucky Dutch, mainly women, were off to catch the boat home. I was late arriving with Mandy and Wang. Ginny had taken a turn for the worse, and I drove her back to the field hospital.

She looked so pale. "You need a milder climate," I said.

"Hong Kong would be nice now," she said, "with maybe the first typhoon of the season blowing in from the Pacific. . . . Even Lake Toba would do. The air's fresh by the lake."

I kissed her and left. I feared for her. She would be a wonderful sister-in-law.

The convoy started off only a few minutes late. The South Wales Borderers were there in strength, with Bren carriers leading and tailing the procession of three five-ton lorries, a private car, and several Jeeps, all loaded with civilians. Dispatch riders patrolled the convoy, seeing to it that the vehicles remained close together.

Once there had been fields and cultivation on either side of the Medan-Belawan road. Now it was wilderness, with the jungle drawing nearer. Several *Merdeka* flags flew on wayside huts; only the odd kid or dog ran out to greet us as we went by in our cloud of dust. Mandy and Wang were wildly excited by the ride. I had a conviction that we were going to be shot at, but the journey passed without incident, and we arrived safely at Belawan.

In some respects Belawan was the very opposite to Emmahaaven. The hills sloped jungle-clad down to the water's edge in Emmahaaven, and there was a deep-water anchorage. The Belawan coastline was more ambiguous, being of shallow descent from land to water, and that margin concealed by low-lying mangrove swamps, through which water and mud trickled. No one could say where Sumatra really began or ended. So shallow was the sea for some miles out that a channel to the docks had to be regularly dredged through treacherous sandbanks. This of course had not been undertaken since the outbreak of war; ships of any draught had in consequence to moor two or three miles out to sea, with shallow-bottomed landing craft to transport passengers or cargoes between shore and ship.

There, two miles out on the listless flood, the celebrated *Van Heutz* lay at anchor. It had arrived from Singapore the previous day. Seeing it, the Dutch raised a gallant cheer.

The military ranged themselves protectively round the lorries as the latter were unloaded. A few buildings and go-downs stood forlornly on the dock, their windows broken or missing. Someone had raised a Union Jack over the RTO's office for the occasion; it was an encouraging sight, limply though it lay against its mast in the still heat. Leaving Mandy and her husband by the Jeep, I made my way towards the office through the melée of women shrieking as they tugged at their respective bundles of luggage.

My name was called. I looked round and there was Eedie, a blue scarf tied round her head, carrying an enormous wicker trunk.

"I'm going, Joe, leaving this fucking place at last," she said. She put down the trunk and embraced me mightily. She was still an inch taller than I was. I looked into her broad honest face, beaded with sweat, with the tiniest blond down on her upper lip; all differences between us were forgotten in this moment of reunion and parting. I thanked God that her mad Irishman was not there to see her off.

"Oh, he buggered off last night," she said, when I asked about him. "He's on duty today. Now it's a new life, God be thanked. Three years and seven months in this stinking part of the world — and I only came for a month's holiday with my uncle. Now — no uncle, youth gone, and just this trunk full of all that I possess in the world, just! Oh, but what's that? Soon I'll see snow again, wonderful snow, and pancakes and flowers and Tampax. And no yellow or brown people."

She kissed me again vigorously.

"You'll be going home soon, Joe. Write to me. I give you my address. Maybe you can come and see me in Maastricht. Listen, I know you have a Chinese girl friend now, isn't it? Take my advice, don't get too entangled. Just have fun, old boy, okay?"

"I am having fun," I said, a little unsteadily. She was writing down her address on a damp piece of paper.

"The Orientals are Orientals — okay in their place, that's all.

Remember what your Kipling said, eh? 'East is East and West is West, and never the two shall meet.' He was right, you know."

"Things are different these days, Eedie."

She prepared to hump her trunk again. "Okay, I'm a racist. After all the Nips did, anyone would be. I still have nightmare of being raped. When I get back to Holland, I hope never to see another Oriental again."

We gave each other a farewell kiss and a hug. Someone was shouting for everyone to get a move on. "Whatever you do, take care of your darling self, Eedie."

"Goodbye, fucking Sumatra!" she shouted, joining the crowd.

I stood there rather misty-eyed.

British and Indian MPs and soldiers were directing the excited crowd. I could see that it would take a while, allowing for the usual army bullshit, before they were all embarked in the landing-craft and the craft got away safely towards the distant ship. I went over to the RTO to collect the crate of films. Eedie's parting words were still very much in my mind.

When I had signed for it, two sepoys helped me carry the crate back to the Jeep.

"How I wish we were getting on that boat too," said Mandy. Wang said nothing. He sat where he was in the back of the vehicle, shading his eyes with his hand, gazing out over the leaden water.

VIII

The crate of film was dumped in the foyer of the Rex, where two Indian carpenters were working on building a counter and shelves for the beer bar. They were using old wood ripped from a commandeered building down the street, and complaining of its hardness. The whole foyer was strewn with tools and wood.

I had specifically been given orders by the chain-smoking Captain Morrison not to open the crate on my own account. That was his business. Accordingly, I left it where it was and went to do something else.

The Rex was pleasant during the day, when it was empty. It had its own smell, an aroma of cigars and cigarette smoke, but also a slightly exotic flavour, lent it by a disinfectant we bought locally with Japanese guilders and used in the lavatories; frangipani, perhaps. I liked it in this peaceful state, with the screen blank — the curtains having long since disappeared, probably appropriated for bedding in the days when the Indonesians ran the place.

It was enjoyable to wander about the aisles, thinking of all the fantasy lives which had briefly endured here. One of my orderlies had found an old local Indian lady who came every day and patched the worst worn seats in exchange for a few cigarettes. British Players were her preference; Indian Players were not at all to her taste. She was at work now, and I exchanged *namastes* with her. She was a portly lady, grey-haired and wrapped in a grey sari, who suffered some difficulties with her stomach when she bowed to me. I took those bows as my right, without thought. But no doubt she had done a lot of bowing in her humble life.

Sometimes, I would take a stroll down the road to see the friendly Rajputana Rifles. They lived in an old temple which had in its courtyard a slimy green swimming pool, full of enormous green frogs. In the pool the Rajputs would disport themselves or do their *dhobi*. Despite their coaxing invitations, I would never join them. I took tea with them. They brewed up a particularly thick delicious tea, the leaves boiled up in a black dixie together with a pound of sugar and condensed milk. It was like soup. I was thinking of going down there when Captain Zajac arrived.

He surveyed the muddle in the foyer, irritably smoothing the end of his moustache, and then said, in mild tones, "Why have you not opened this crate of film, sergeant? It's your job, isn't it?"

"Sir, strict orders from Captain Morrison, sir."

"Why's there all this mess here?"

"Men having trouble with the wood, sir. All tidy for this evening's performance. *The Bank Dick*, again, sir. Very popular."

"What's the matter with the wood?"

"Too hard, sir."

"Well, get this crate opened."

"Would you like me to phone Captain Morrison about it, sir?"

I stood rigid as I spoke. He fixed me with a hard cold Polish eye, despite his command of English unsure as to whether I was being impolite. Gradually he relaxed, and his manner became less waspish.

"I don't like slackness, sergeant."

"Sir."

He turned away, perhaps in disgust. The two carpenters resumed their singing, which they had stopped in order to listen to the exchange. The Rajput guard had followed Zajac in, perhaps under the same sort of impulse that moves dogs to follow strangers.

I was looking out through the new glass doors into the street. A big black civilian car stopped. A corporal in a bush hat jumped out and stood cradling a sten gun, staring into the cinema. With a start I recognised him. It was Corporal Jones, the deserter.

"Down, everybody!" I flung myself to the floor, seeing from the corner of my eye that Zajac immediately did the same, turning to face the danger as he did so. The carpenters dived behind their half-built bar.

Jones hesitated. It crossed my mind as I scrabbled for my revolver that he could hardly see in; the foyer being rather dark and the street full of light, the glass doors would present him only with a reflection of the street. But he must have glimpsed a movement. As he fired, the panes of glass splintered and bullets went ricocheting about the place.

I got my revolver up. One shot rang out, then a second. Jones dropped his gun. The look on his face suggested he had heard something that shocked him deeply. He turned and fell to his knees. Someone fired some wild shots from the black car, then it accelerated forward and was lost from my line of sight. A battered truck followed. Men were firing from it at random. Another fusillade of shots rang out, but those I scarcely heeded; the Rajputs were firing at the fugitives. I was running forward after Zajac, who had fired before I could do so.

Jones was on the pavement, head touching the stone, making some kind of a cry.

Zajac stood over him, arms akimbo, still nursing his revolver and smiling grimly.

"Well, I don't suppose the Borderers will thank me for finishing their task for them."

"They'll be glad to see him on his knees, sir. Good shooting."

"Go and get Colonel Glyn Williams of the Borderers on the phone. Tell him — ask him — if he would care to come round here. Then get the Ambulance Unit, fast."

"Sir." I stood staring down at the mighty Jones, at his sweat-stained bush shirt. His blood was trickling out under him, gathering in a rivulet and running into the gutter. He paddled at it with one hand, as if in wonderment. I went inside to the phone, my legs a trifle shaky. A shrill noise was coming from the inside of the cinema. The old patching lady was having hysterics, and the two carpenters were splashing water in her face.

"You'd better get back on bloody duty," I said to the Rajput guard, who was trembling privately to himself. "You were meant to be out there."

He clutched my arm. "Very bad man — kill us all."

"I don't think he'll kill anyone else now. It's okay. *Thik-hai*. Thank god Zajac was here — I've had no target practice since Madras. . . ."

I wound the crank of my field phone vigorously, and eventually a lazy afternoon operator replied. I heard myself yelling at him.

A few minutes later, we found that the Rajputs had managed to wound the driver of the Jones truck, which had run into a tree. It contained cans of petrol and grenades. Jones had intended to pick a quiet time of day and burn down his old HQ.

He died in hospital two days later. The Borderers threw a party in celebration for Captain Zajac. Sportingly, he took me along and we both got agreeably drunk.

August came, bringing thunderstorms. The hot days dragged by. And still I met with my love in the ambushed afternoon, and still the future drew nearer to destroy us.

It was impossible to decide why I hung back from thinking about marrying her, supposing she should get a divorce from Wang — which she said would not be difficult. The years of war had made me feel old; it would be a relief to settle down and be domestic. I had no great desire to return to England.

The obstacles in my way I have already mentioned. I dreaded the opposition and opprobrium the army would bring to any request of mine to get married. I had never heard of such a thing happening, although I guessed I should immediately find myself posted to some inaccessible spot, with never a chance of seeing her again.

There was another more intangible objection which always eluded me. But one day, rooting about a secondhand stall in the native quarter, I came across a worn anthology of English poetry, and bought it. Almost the first poem at which I opened the book was a poem by William Blake:

> He who bends himself to joy
> Doth the winged life destroy:
> But he who kisses the joy as it flies
> Lives in eternity's sunrise.

I could not get the lines out of my mind. Doth the winged life destroy. Yes, we had the winged life and, despite ourselves, we were destroying it. I explained it to Mandy, but she would hear nothing of the matter.

"Blake is dead," she said. "Why listen to him? What does this Blake know of our circumstances? Did he ever kiss me? Was he fucked by me? It's simple — we love each other and should be married together. I know you hate the pretence. We should be free."

"I know, I know. Don't talk about it."

"I must. I lie awake at night thinking about it. There's only one tragedy waiting in the future otherwise, my God. Why does Ginny not recover? Isn't it because she sickens with worry for Sammi and herself and all of us? And at least she has a European husband. Well, that's all I want, this pretty one with the pretty prick here."

"Please, Mandy. I can't talk. I think — I think — Oh, you must blame me, but I am just too immature to deal with it all."

She kissed me and rubbed her nose against my cheek. "I am such an old nag. Now you see how I nag Wang, my God. No wonder no one wants me. You better get back to England before this whole great place goes up in smoke — *Merdeka* smoke!"

Oh, the love we made. Oh, the way we had of torturing each other. And all the time I hadn't even the sense to take Charlie into my confidence. It would not have been possible to have explained my tangled feelings to anyone. Only Blake would have understood.

She was offering me a whole fascinating, foreign way of life and I was too palsied to take it. Why my thousand hesitations?

Back came the answer: Doth the winged life destroy. . . .

The hot days dragged by. Despite the rumours that had been flying, the order to quit Sumatra, when it came from ALFSEA, was something of a surprise. By now, all the Dutch who wished to be repatriated had gone, and the Japanese Army had been sent packing back to Tokyo. In three weeks, we also must be gone.

Various troopships would take off various units. All war material would be sold to the Dutch forces remaining in the islands. Various categories of immovable equipment were to be destroyed. Discipline must be maintained throughout the remainder of the Occupation. It was estimated that all British forces would be cleared from the Medan-Belawan area by 1200 hours on 15th September, 1946.

Indonesian intelligence was, as usual, excellent. Scarcely had the orders been posted on the various unit noticeboards than a procession of extremists was organised. It marched down the Kesawan and round the centre of town, with banners waving saying MERDEKA and BRITISH QUIT, and large portraits of President Soekarno. The British did nothing to quell the procession. They were already starting to pack and to celebrate, each according to his lights.

Rumours flew that we should get a special medal for the Sumatra campaign — "A thumb downturned on a field of shit brown," someone suggested. Other rumours said that we should get no medals since the whole campaign had been a disgrace to the British flag, and we could expect to go on jankers when we got to transit camps in Singapore.

Suddenly there was too much to do and too much to talk about. When Captain Morrison came round again, I asked him if the Rex was to be regarded as in the immovable equipment category, to be destroyed.

"Certainly not, Sergeant Winter. What do you take us for? The Rex and the Deli will be handed over in perfect working order."

"I see, sir. Who to, sir? The Dutch or the Indonesians?"

"To the proper authorities. I'm not sure who."

The orders of course brought to a head my most pressing problem. If I was to act, then I had to act immediately, or the chance would be gone. And it seemed to me that there was someone who could help me if he would — the peevish Captain Zajac, who had been more friendly since our triumphant encounter with Corporal Jones. After I had thought out my approach, I went to talk to him.

"I suppose you will be thinking of returning to England, Sergeant Winter?" he said, when I reported to him in his office. He had a map of Sumatra on one wall and a map of a part of Poland on the other.

"No, sir. I still have time to serve, sir. It's something else I came about."

"Sit down, then. By the look of you it is something serious."

"Yes, sir. This is confidential. I have a romantic involvement with a lady." Even to me the phrase sounded absurd, but it did not pay to speak ordinary English to an officer.

"I see." The moustache stirred. "Locally, you mean?"

"Yes."

"In Medan?"

"Yes."

"You've got three weeks to enjoy yourself, then."

"This is a more permanent sort of affair, sir. She's Chinese. I wondered if you would book a passage for her on the *Van Heutz*. I mean, I'd pay, of course, but it does need a special arrangement, which you as an officer could manage. If you felt able. . . ."

"You want to meet her in Singapore. Is that the case?"

"Well, we may be kicking about in Singapore for some time, sir, don't you think?"

"You're not thinking of marrying this Chinese lady, are you?"

"Sir, the Chinese are going to have a bad time under Indonesian rule. Everyone says so. She would be safer in Singapore, a British colony. Besides, she has just had news that cousins of hers have arrived there, to avoid the fighting in Amoy or thereabouts."

"All Chinese have endless cousins. You shouldn't get involved, Winter."

"However that may be, sir, it happens that I *am* involved, and so I've come to you as my senior officer to ask if you'd do this thing for me. There's nothing illegal in it. It's just a question of priorities."

"'A question of priorities'. . . . We have commitments here only to the Dutch. Not to any other races. Oh, maybe to Europeans. Perhaps the odd Indian, in certain cases. No one else."

"The Chinese fought with us in Burma, sir."

"No other commitments," he said, firmly.

"Well, I have a commitment, sir."

"Is she pregnant, do you mean?"

"No. Not pregnant."

He stared down at his blotting paper. Then he looked up with a sardonic grin. "Is this slant-eyed hussy pretty?"

"I find the lady very pretty, yes. There's a sailing of the *Van Heutz* from Belawan on 13th September, sir, just before we all pull out. The authorities might not let her go after that — the island's going to be a prison, as far as I can make out. If you could see your way to booking her a single passage. . . ."

He stood up.

"Leave it with me."

I rose to my feet, red in the face.

"Does that mean yes or no, sir?"

"I'll think about it."

"Why can't you say yes or no to me, Captain Zajac? It's no skin off your nose to make a decision, is it? You only have to put her name down on a list — one of those endless army lists."

His mouth set angrily at this outbreak, but he said with surprising meekness, "Give me her name, Winter, and I'll get my orderly to ring through to the RTO straightaway. Thirteenth, you said?"

"Thank you, sir. Thanks very much."

I saluted and left. They could not resist wielding their power. Zajac was less awful than most officers; and he as a permanent exile had more excuse than most to be awful.

Feeling considerably worked up, I went for a drink in the sergeants' mess. Again the longing to tell everyone what was going on; but such was my peculiar moral code that I was still bound to silence. I would have been mortified if Charlie Frost found out how I had abused my friendship with the Merciers.

Bradbury was making a speech. The three native mess orderlies, Ali, Thomas, and Chan, were moving about silently, serving drinks to all concerned.

"Come in, stranger," said Bradbury, interrupting himself when he saw me. "We're just into the question of what constitutes immovable equipment and how we should best destroy it, to keep it out of the hands of the Indos. Now then, gents, on this subject of liquor. We have built up quite good stocks from what the Japs disgorged. Enough probably, to last a hard-drinking mess like this for six months, taking it easy."

"I never saw you taking it easy," said Blizzard, and there was general laughter.

"Thank you. Now, I have a few questions to ask you about leaving this valuable liquor behind. Do we want the squarehead Dutch to drink it?"

"No," went up the cry.

"Do we want the bloody wogs to drink it?"

"No."

"Do we want the yellow-skinned Chinks to drink it?"

"No."

"Do we want the extremists to drink it?"

"No-oo."

"Then we have to drink it all ourselves."

"Ye-es." And Bragg was shouting above the noise, "Let's have a party every night till we leave."

The vote was passed *nem con*. Ali, Thomas, and Chan went on filling up glasses amid the uproar, their faces inscrutable.

I downed a couple of whiskies and then went to tell Mandy my good news.

I was five minutes late when I entered the rear door of Miss Chew's little bungalow. Mandy was sitting on the bed, dwarfed by the stacks of tables and chests of drawers which lined the room. She had already drawn the curtains, so that the room existed in twilight. With the window shut, it seemed hotter than ever.

She immediately read something in my looks and manner. We sat together and kissed and caressed each other. Then I told her of my conversation with Zajac.

To my surprise, she burst into tears. I had seen the odd tear, but never a full-scale weep, and was properly dismayed by it. With my arm round those brittle shoulders, she gradually lay against me and began to talk.

She had decided that she had been utterly mistaken in trying to take advantage of me. She should long ago have listened to what I said. She knew at heart that she was not fit to be my wife, quite apart from the fact that she was already married and burdened with two children. She knew all the things that the British said about the Chinese, calling them Chinks, and saying they were slit-eyed and cowardly. More weeping.

I asked where all this nonsense had come from, but she would say nothing.

"Well, whether you marry me or not, there's going to be a ticket for the *Van Heutz* on the thirteenth. You'll have to go. And before that you'll have to say something to Wang."

"I can't go. I can't possibly, my God. What for I go? Better I stay here and be killed and finish with everything."

"Mandy — we can get married in Singapore. Not here, but it's civilised there." I heard my own voice ringing in my ears. I did not know I intended to say any such thing, but there it was, cool as anything, born perhaps of protectiveness, shame, and desperation.

She became rigid. Then she started to mop her little nose.

. "You don't really want to marry me. It's too much for you, I know." She knelt beside me on the bed, looking up, looking down, sniffing intermittently. "I know it's all too much. I understand, Joe."

"Then listen. I know you must fear what Wang will do. Simply tell him that you are going on a holiday to Singapore to see your cousins from Amoy."

"He won't believe that. He will know I am going to join you."

"How will he know if you don't tell him?"

"Oh, Joseph, he has known all about our affair all along. How could I not tell him, when he is my husband?"

This casual remark left me utterly deflated. I had no response to it. If there is anything worse than scheming it is having the scheming found out — and proved to be for nothing.

She then said, speaking rapidly while I floundered, "Then I will accept the ticket. I will take the kids to Singapore, where my cousins will be happy to look after them. It will only be a holiday. If you are there, we can go to Happy World and similar enjoyment places. I will just stay for one month. In that time, I can see how conditions are back here. If too bad, then others follow me. Maybe Ginny comes over for a holiday to recuperate her health. It's a good arrangement. Nobody gets hurt. . . . Now we make love to celebrate and I do a special thing to you you most like."

What could I say?

"It's a deal," I said.

Every day saw scenes of drunkenness as the British celebrated their coming departure. The Indonesians sensibly held their hand and waited. Our vehicles and weapons were sold off to the Dutch who were remaining. Advance parties began to leave on the *San Salvrino* and other troopships. Zajac and I were delegated as part of the rear; we should be among the last to leave.

I closed the Rex down, said goodbye to the Rajputs, and took a temporary room in the sergeants' mess for safety, just in case of a last minute attack. Tension grew. So did the drinking.

Ginny was determined to throw a proper Chinese banquet for Charlie and me. So weak was she that she could do no cooking. In the end, she had to settle for a modest affair. Charlie and I spent a day shopping, buying farewell presents for Jean, Ginny, and Wang, as well as taking them a Jeepload of groceries from the store of loot in the sergeants' mess. Whatever happened, Jean was cool and collected as ever, and showed no agitation. He said that an Indonesian official had promised that he might get his plantation back once the Dutch had left. When that would be, no one could say.

The British had one small trick up their sleeve. The rear party was geared to leave on the fourteenth, a day before the time announced. Thus we hoped to avoid any last minute acts of violence. Zajac told me this late on the thirteenth. For once security had functioned properly. By that time, Mandy should have left on the *Van Heutz* — but the *Van Heutz* had been inexplicably delayed, and had not reached Belawan. It was not unusual for the ship to suffer delays; the poor old lady, feeling her age, was always undergoing mechanical repair.

So the next day it was Mandy who said a tearful goodbye to me, flinging her arms about my neck and kissing me over and over.

"We'll be together in a very few days," I said. "I'll find out the time the ship arrives and I'll be waiting for you on the quayside in Singapore. That's a promise."

"Please, please be there. I'm so frighten of what may happen. I would die if I never saw you again."

I drove Captain Zajac down to Belawan, with the rear of the Jeep filled with luggage that was mainly his. As if news had got about, there were people on the wild road, waving and smiling and shouting "*Merdeka!*", happy to see us go, just as they had once been glad to see us arrive.

With a minimum of delay, we were loaded on to the landing craft in the docks, which then made a slow progress out to sea. I had charge of the luggage. Zajac, as an officer, was taken out in a faster and more elegant craft.

Once aboard the *San Salvrino*, we underwent the usual wait, two miles out from harbour. Sumatra was now reduced to a flat and unpromising line of mangroves; far in the background floated remote and lofty mountains, some of their peaks clothed in cloud.

It was impossible to blot from my mind the question of Mandy — and the whole problem of Ginny and Jean's future in the new Sumatra. Ginny had said goodbye so bravely, with her usual bright smile. But who could say what lay in their future? I had decided that, whatever my doubts, they must be subordinated to rescuing Mandy. Once she had left the country, the others would be tempted to follow, and remove themselves to safety. There were surely plenty of places in Malaysia where an experienced planter like Jean Mercier would be welcome.

As, at last, the *San Salvrino* upped anchor, I knew with a heavy heart that a period in history was over, and that Sumatra, for good or ill, would never be the same again. I also realised that I was probably the only one who would come to tell its story: for already I felt that here were tragic times, and that the ignorant British ought to know something about a place for which they currently cared less than nothing.

I could not wrench my vision from those shores where my emotions had been so exercised. Tears burned in my eyes. No one has felt the true hollow tooth of sorrow who has not sailed from the place they love; the movement of a ship is as remorseless as time. At last impatient with my own melancholy, I broke away and took a turn round the deck.

Everyone else was jubilant at our departure.

As we swung about, to head in the general direction of Singapore, I observed out to sea a ship I recognised immediately as that steamer upon which so many futures had depended, the *Van Heutz* itself. It lay with a decided list to starboard. There was no sound of engines emanating from it, no movement on its deck.

We drew nearer, eventually passing within a few hundred yards of the other vessel. The truth was already apparent. The *Van Heutz* had stuck on a sandbank and was abandoned.

The spectacular and busy harbour of Singapore formed as great a contrast to Belawan as you might find within such a short distance. On disembarkation we were driven by lorry to Nee Soon Transit Camp in the centre of the island. As soon as I could, I was out of camp again, and making enquiries of the port authorities. I was told it was hoped to tow the *Van Heutz* back to Singapore, where the damage to its propellers could be repaired. There were many shifting sandbanks in the Belawan area, which would soon be properly charted and marked by buoys.

On the following day, I was down at the docks again. All round about, Singapore was furiously at work, remedying three years of neglect and oppression. Shipyards and factories were opening again. Immense though the flow of refugees was into the old grey city, there was work for everyone, and the Chinese worked with a great will. I had no interest in anything but the waters of the harbour. The roads were congested with shipping. Among those ships about midday came a cripple, towed by a pair of Chinese-manned tugs, the *Van Heutz*.

How insignificant that steamer looked now, the ship which had played such a large part in the history of so many lives. It was rusted and patched and leaky; strange to think that anyone had placed their future hopes on it. But for the war, it would have been dispatched to the scrapyard before this. Instead, it was moored against a distant wharf for repair. Two days later, the foreman told me that the *Van Heutz* would not be sailing again until the following week.

A week! It was a villainous stretch of time. I had no way of getting in touch with Mandy except by letter — which would have had to be delivered by the *Van Heutz* itself. She had no way of getting in touch with me. She did not know my address. We had parted — for all the heartache, I now saw that we had parted so casually, so certain that we would be in each other's embrace again within no more than a few hours. We had not reckoned on the Tumbledown Factor. . . . Now as never before in this time of dismay I realised that I did indeed love and need her.

By a stroke of luck, I had brought with me the address of her cousins, recently arrived in Singapore from Amoy. I could go and see them.

Singapore was a huge ragged city, left drab and unpainted after the Japanese occupation, but bustling with life, and not without touches of glamour. I noted with satisfaction that the cinemas were large and smart affairs, prone to giving special midnight matinées. The array of cafés was inexhaustible. From every shop flowed the music of Chinese opera, the outpouring of a sensibility of which I understood little. The whores seemed of an unparalleled elegance. Only on a later visit, after Singapore had set itself up as an independent city state, did I realise how run down the city really was in that immediate post-war period when the Union Jack still flew there; but I was seeing it for the first time with eyes accustomed to almost a year on Sumatra, and its vivacity was astonishing. Later, of course, the skyscrapers went up, and all the music was banished.

The Tans were staying in a green suburb of Singapore, in a fine wooden bungalow which had probably belonged to English traders who — for whatever reason — had not returned after the freeing of the island. Or rather, the Tans had found a home in the garden of this bungalow, for the bungalow was already well-occupied. The Tans, seven of them all told, including a young baby, lived in what had been a summerhouse, against which an impromptu kitchen had been built. They were refugees from the struggle between Chiang Kai-shek's Kuomintang forces and the Communist forces of Mao; in China, the great world struggle was still in process.

Mr Tan Senior spoke some English. Of course he had heard nothing from Medan, but he made promising noises. I left it for a week before returning, by which time the repaired *Van Heutz* was again operating its timetable.

On that second occasion, none of the Tans was about. I returned in the evening. With the resourcefulness of their race, all had got jobs of some kind, leaving the smallest children to be looked after by an old lady in the bungalow. They had an income; they were on their way up again. But they had received no letter from Medan.

Ten days passed. I did not know what to fear or what to hope. I spent some while on guard duties in the abysmal Nee Soon camp, which was either intolerably full, with five thousand men passing through it and all facilities over-strained, or it was almost empty and those unfortunates remaining were tied to duties of various unpleasant kinds.

Meanwhile, 26 Indian Division had been dissolved. Our Indians had all been shipped back to India. There had been no passing-out parade. A post-war lassitude had set in. Over all was that gloomy feeling that the Sumatra operation had been a disaster, reflecting no credit on men or officers, to be forgotten as swiftly as possible.

No posting came through for me, for which I was relieved. There were rumours, those eternal army rumours, that I might be posted to Shanghai — rumours which in ordinary times would have delighted me.

The days went by. Something was wrong; otherwise, why had Mandy not appeared, or at least sent word? The *Van Heutz* laboured into harbour once more after having made her rounds. I was there to meet her, but no familiar figure disembarked. I went back to the Tans' place in the evening.

Of course Mandy had not arrived. But there was a letter for me.

She wrote quite briefly. The ship had been delayed. Then Ginny became more ill and had to go back to hospital. The cancer had spread and she had died there. Ginny sent me God's blessing.

It was impossible for Mandy to leave, at least for a while. She had transferred her booking to the sailing on October 10th. "Then I give myself to you. Please be there for me. Poor Jean weeps."

It was a Tuesday evening when I read this letter. I took it away and wept. On the Thursday morning my posting came up. I was to leave for Hong Kong on the following day, when a lorry would collect me at 0600 hours.

I never saw Mandy again. Circumstances had come between us, and the great grinding machine of the world. I wrote to Mandy from Hong Kong and eventually received a letter back. It was very terse, from grief or because, not understanding the workings of the army, she felt betrayed. She had arrived in Singapore, but there was nothing for her in the city, and she was going to return to Medan. "I did not visit Happy World without you."

Something happened to me. I had kissed the joy as it flies. But whether to be glad or sorry that it had escaped me I knew not, and not knowing was part of the torment I then underwent. After the war, I imagine, many men and women must have suffered a loss of wartime love, the most painful kind of affection, which pits its spark against annihilation's waste.

How my gentle girl fared under the Indonesian Republic without her protective sister, I never discovered.

In Hong Kong, that luxurious commercial capital of the flesh, I fell into a debauched way of life. Every temptation was there, and I applied myself to it. The flesh tried to drown out the soul.

More than once, staggering from one knocking shop or another, in Hong Kong or Macao, the vision of Corporal Jones would rise before me, as he coughed his unused life out in the Medan gutter. At least he had not had to face an existence after the high tide of it had fallen away.

By this time I was an old man of twenty-one. The two campaigns of Burma and Sumatra had been more than enough. After either, I should by rights have been drafted home. But the army in the Far East did not work that way, preferring to drain the young life out of its soldiery. In Hong Kong I fell into the same stained, cynical way of thought that had afflicted the men of 2 Div when I joined them as a pale reinforcement at Milestone 81. Such was the price to pay for being a cog of Empire — an empire which was even then disintegrating, just as I felt myself to be. The sacrifice of years was for little, for nothing. Burma went back to the Burmese. Sumatra went back to the Indonesians. Glory was not to be had. Such disillusion was inevitable in the tide of history, that notorious disrespecter of persons.

IX

Clement shaved in mild good humour. He had no objection to the start of another day. Sheila was still dozing in bed. Peering through the bathroom window at Friday, he saw every sign that sunshine would prevail again. The smell of coffee floated to him from downstairs. He mingled with it the tang of his salvia after-shave lotion.

How blessed, he thought, was domesticity.

Michelin was laying out a few breakfast things when he arrived downstairs. It happened that as he entered the dining room in his slippers, the French woman was reaching across the table, in such a way that he was presented with the long inviting line of her trunk, buttocks, and left leg — all veiled in blouse, skirt, and tights, but pleasing nevertheless. Of course, Michelin was sexless; Clement and Sheila had established that long ago, otherwise there would have been nothing of the stability the three of them enjoyed together.

They had given Michelin a lift while driving about France on holiday in the mid-seventies. She had helped them to find a particularly well-hidden hotel in the Gorges du Tarn, and they had christened her 'Michelin' then, on the flimsy basis that her name was Michelle. Somehow, the joke had stuck. So had Michelin. She was then a delicate little woman in her early thirties, hoping to get to England to teach. The Winters, still suffering from the loss of their child, had virtually adopted her. She came back to England with them, and stayed.

Michelin was now a sturdy woman in her mid-forties, with a regular teaching job at St Emma's just up the road. She acted as a kind of unofficial housekeeper to the Winters in exchange for free board and lodging. She enjoyed a wide circle of acquaintances in Oxford, many of them French.

Within the close confines of Chalfont Road, where the Winters then lived, Clement had entertained luxurious thoughts concerning the young woman they had picked up. On a sunny autumn afternoon when Sheila was away, he had made what for him was a determined attempt to seduce her, after cornering her in the little room he used as a study.

"I like you very well, Clem," Michelin said, pushing him away. He still remembered her words. "But my soul is in China."

He had not understood her meaning. Had she translated an obscure French saying, meaning she was sexless, or a lesbian? He found somewhere that the phrase might imply that she was mad; but Michelin was clearly sane. In any case, the ambiguity served as a barrier between them. With time, Clement and Sheila persuaded themselves that their companion, who never once showed any interest in the opposite sex, was without the normal passions which bedevil humanity.

Clement had several theories as to why Michelin had no sex life, but all had been run through and exhausted long ago. He exchanged a few pleasantries with her and lapsed into his chair with the *Independent*, thinking about adultery and the prestige in which it was still held.

Possibly he had dreamed of Tristan and Isolde. Had he in some way been Tristan, in a gold tunic? After Sheila left for the States and before he followed her there, he had gone with friends to see a performance of Wagner's opera, with its music reinforcing the hopeless passion of the lovers. Although the origins of the legend were obscure, he understood well that it represented the triumph of passionate love over conventional morality. In his student days, he had written a paper on it, *Irresponsibility in the Tristan Legend*.

His brother's love for the Chinese woman, Mandy, had tragic elements. Although neither of them had died on stage, as it were, it was possible that Joseph had sealed Mandy's fate by leaving her in Sumatra. In Wagner's opera, the passion between the couple was represented as a transcendent value, necessitating the deaths of both parties. The passion between Joseph and Mandy had not been strong enough either to overcome all obstacles or to bring about their deaths directly. Life had brought compromises which were not the province of Art. And yet, Clement knew, his brother always considered himself marked by this youthful affair.

Of course life tried to imitate art. What else was there to imitate? Two rival artistic stereotypes held sway over his colleagues and friends, causing much confusion in their lives. On the one hand lay the old Sentimental view of the happy family, with wife and home as the centre of the world; on the other was the Romantic ideal of love — or at least sex — conquering all. Many of Clement's patients subscribed to both as and when it suited them. The torment of these two conflicting theories was reflected in the popular arts.

Even in Sheila's fantasy world of Kerinth, both rival theories flourished, with no attempt made to adjudicate between them. In *The Heart of Kerinth*, the lovely Queen Gyronee had laid down her life for her thankless children, whereas, in *Kerinth Endures*, the noble barbarian Thek died a Tristan-like death for love of the Princess Zimner, who was married to the ruthless Marlat of Cyn, the Dark Planet. He could write a paper on *Confused Moral Attitudes in the Kerinth Novels* for who, except for a few injudicious fans, knew those novels better than he? — apart from the certainty that it would destroy his marriage.

One trouble with Joseph, Clement thought, was that he had been dogged throughout his Sumatra affair by a sense of shame, a false sense inculcated by their parents and the hypocrisies of that generation to which in fact the war would give the kibosh. Had Joseph been able to relish his conquest of the Chinese lady fully and completely, perhaps even to boast of it in the sergeants' mess, instead of keeping it as an uneasy secret, then perhaps he might have been bolder in general and won the lady . . . if, indeed, that was what he really wanted. It seemed to Clement that Joseph fully realised there would have been no place for his and Mandy's union in the forties. By the eighties, such colour prejudice had worn a little thin. Air travel had brought miscegenation into every home.

He could give his brother's story to Sheila, to turn into a suitable Kerinthian fiction. And of course he could use its outline in his thesis on adaptability.

But what to do regarding Sheila's performance as Isolde? That was the question. Clement thought he saw this morning, as he munched a piece of toast, that that Hispanic fellow in Boston had been merely an interlude, a *boffe de politesse* — her coupling with that phantom lover, Fame. Boston, to all intents and purposes, was now as far distant as Joseph's Sumatra. He should be as complacent as Mandy's husband Wang had been. Clement was prepared to forgive the action; it was the words at which he stumbled. *"I'm enjoying it too much to stop. . . ."*

As he was finishing his breakfast, Sheila came down to breakfast in a paisley blouse and a long cream linen skirt. Smiling, she waved the mail which Michelin had left for her on the hall stand.

"Another lovely day," she said, kissing his forehead. "Have you had a swim?" He was momentarily enveloped in her perfume.

"Couldn't be bothered. Got to see the bursar about the heating in my room at ten." He put only a minimal grumpiness into his voice.

She ignored his remark, sat down at her end of the little table, and prepared her bowl of All-Bran and Alpen with milk and sugar, topping it up with a sliced banana and cream. As she ate, she put on her reading glasses and commenced opening her mail.

Opening mail was a serious business for Sheila. Clement immersed himself in the pages of the *Independent*.

Sheila's post contained bills, which she set carefully aside, several periodicals, and a number of notes and letters from her public, her fans, all excited and begging for autographs, photographs, or locks of hair. All the fan letters were full of praise for the Kerinth romances. Sheila made a pile of them, handing them over without comment for her husband to read. This morning, she received as well a letter from her London publishers, Barrage Sims, containing copies of reviews from English newspapers and magazines of her new novel *War Lord of Kerinth*, in its English edition. All the reviews were disappointing, as Clement could judge from Sheila's pained cries as she read: "Oh, no!", "That's wrong, for a start!", and "You bastard!"

The review from the *Guardian* was insulting, brief, and righteous.

"They hate me!" she cried, screwing it up in her fist.

"They don't understand," Clement said.

"They just can't see. . . ."

She sipped at her coffee, freshly made and topped with cream.

Removing her spectacles, she said, without particularly looking anywhere, unless it was at the cornice, "Why do I bother to ensure that my English editions come out first? Why struggle, out of some misguided idea of patriotism? What do the bloody British care? Why do I insist that Barrage send out review copies, simply for these bastards to piss on? I'm just not appreciated in this country. The Germans like me, the Americans love me. In future, I shall sell all rights to Swain, and Barrage can jolly well negotiate English rights from them. To hell with them. Bastards."

Her lips closed in a firm line, revealing the determination that had made Green Mouth the commercial success she was. Clement had put down his newspaper, so that she was able to look him in the eye.

"It's not Barrage Sims's fault," he said. "They've done their best for you. Just the typical English lack of enthusiasm. We still have the genius — as you prove — but the Americans have the enthusiasm."

"It's class, that's what it is. Just because I write genre novels."

In alarm only partly assumed, he said, "You don't want to go and live in the States, do you?"

She laughed. "That depends on the tax situation if they make the movie. New York would be fun."

He did not reply. Leaning back, she took the telephone off the dresser and dialled Barrage Sims, asking to speak to her editor, Maggie Mower. Clement retreated into his paper while Sheila talked. When she put down the receiver, she said, "Whatever the reviews, the sales figures aren't bad. Their first printing was fifty thousand, and eighty per cent are sold already. That's not counting book club sales. So someone loves me."

"According to government claims, the unemployment figures have fallen below the three million mark for the first time in four years."

She looked at Clement with scorn, resenting this irrelevance.

"Yes, well, bugger the government and bugger the unemployed."

He saw that he was dismissed, wiped his mouth on his napkin, and rose. "Me for the Bursar."

"See you," she said, looking up and giving him one of her best smiles.

Fabian Bush, the Bursar of Carisbrooke, was renowned for his economies. In the long-standing grievance of the chilliness of Clement Winter's rooms he had so far managed not to budge an inch, while appearing anxious to please. Clement knew before he embarked on the subject this morning that he was going to get nowhere. Even to him, there was something unreal about discussing the sub-zero temperatures of a room at present immoderately hot and stuffy. They stood in the Bursar's crowded office, pushing back and forth a conversation about the expense of running additional copper piping under twenty feet of parquet flooring, until Clement gave up, knowing full well that if he ventured on the subject during the winter months, when the sub-zero temperatures could actually be sampled, Fabian Bush would claim, with some justice, December to be no time for fetching up floors and draining hot tanks.

Clement worked the rest of the morning and, in his lunch break, phoned his sister Ellen in Salisbury. Perhaps Salisbury had been in her stars at birth. Destiny, Clement felt, had fitted her for the blander parts of fortune. Ellen was now fifty-six, seven years Clement's senior, and still slightly unapproachable. As a child, she had always been closer to Joseph; he remembered numerous occasions on which they had run off together and left him to play forlornly by himself. "Just you behave," as a farewell with a wagged finger, had made the partings hard to bear. Now she was a not unprepossessing, rather sharp-tongued woman in the middle age for which nature had fashioned her, living, as far as Clement and Sheila could tell, alone.

Ellen, somewhat late in her day, had married Alwyn Pickering, a man who had made bank manager before forty. They had immediately had a daughter, Jean, born in 1962, over whom Ellen and Alwyn had made an immense fuss (satirised later in Sheila's *Child of Kerinth*), only to see her — as Ellen had once put it in an extra distraught moment — go to the dogs. Perhaps to pacify her parents, Jean, by no means bereft of a sense of humour, had married the chief dog in 1981. The marriage had come apart three years later, and now she worked in Salisbury, supervising social workers. Her mother's marriage had come apart over the same period. Alwyn had taken to staying away from home for longer and longer periods until finally, Clement had heard, Ellen had requested him not to return. There had been no row, only a financial arrangement to her disadvantage.

"You got the letters safely then," she said, when Clement phoned. "I never know what the post office is up to these days."

"Yes, I like those letters very much. It's really about Joseph's writings I'm phoning."

"I suspected you might be." She added nothing to the brief sentence. He could visualise her standing watchful by her phone in that room with the patio doors overlooking the garden full of crazy paving and the odd concrete statue.

"How are you?"

"Not bad. Just been taking the dog for a walk. Is Sheila with you or in Kerinth?"

"We're both in Rawlinson Road, Ellen. Joseph's letters to you showed the brighter side of his India-Burma experience. I'm sure that was deliberate. You were quite a little girl at the time."

"I was fourteen."

"Yes. Well, I think he naturally wanted to shield you from the harsher experiences. For instance, I know he suffered badly from dysentery, which he doesn't mention. Later, in Burma proper, he hardly mentions the fighting. I wondered if you thought he was always like that, putting the brighter aspect of things forward."

She was silent for a moment, giving the matter consideration. "In the social services they encounter a lot of men who went through the war and survived unscathed. Mostly they're of pensionable age now. Research has shown that many of them found it extremely difficult to adjust to civilian life; some, indeed, claim they never did manage to adjust, becoming alcoholics or chronically unemployable. I would say that some might almost be classified as psychiatric cases — the ones who had a bad war —"

"Ellen, dear, that's my subject," he said patiently.

"War experience certainly caused a great division between generations. Those who returned found that those who had never been away did not understand their problems or want to listen."

"Do you think he tended to whitewash his Burma experience?"

"He never married, though, did he?" Perhaps she had not heard his question. "Joe needed a decent, understanding English girl."

After a pause, Ellen added, "Marriage raises more problems than popularly supposed. Or rather, people know marriage is not the solution to everything, but they still prefer to pretend that it is. Men and women."

Clement laughed rather forcedly. "People don't want things to be as they are. They dream up idealised situations and try to live by them, but sometimes the bottom falls out of the market." He thought of his wife's fantasies, to which he knew Ellen took exception, and tried to steer the conversation into another course. "Do you think there was something of that in Joseph?"

"Poor Joseph's dead, Clem." Again a long silence, as if she mulled over the implications of what she was saying. "Why don't you simply keep all his letters and so on, if you want them, and forget about making them into a book? Let him rest. Live your own life."

"I am trying to live my own life. I feel my brother is part of my life."

"You weren't close. He and I were close. When are you going to sell the Acton flat?"

"A bit more cleaning up to be done first, Ellen."

He exchanged a few more desultory remarks with the distant voice in Salisbury and then hung up.

The baffling quality of his relationship with his sister did not diminish with time or distance. Since they saw so little of each other these days, the matter was no longer of importance: yet it worried him. The will to be friendly, even close, should have had greater effect. He ascribed the problem to the way in which his parents had remained so distant. The failure of their relationship, that abiding mystery, had been central to the emotional development of their three offspring, Joseph, Ellen, and Clement.

Perhaps because of that central loss, Clement felt almost a mystical identification with the institutes round him: his College, the University, Oxford, or more particularly North Oxford — the Puginesque, Betjemanesque half-mile which contained so much diversity and snobbery — and, beyond that ("mistier and mistier") England, the European idea, and the planet Earth itself as a complex ecological unit. He was in some respects a feeble man, yet not an ignorant one, and some of his intuitions, he recognised, had been gained from his wife's half-instinctive, slapdash writings, which he constantly defended, whatever his own private reservations, against the unthinking contempt of the Oxford crowd.

This tendency towards loyalty now attracted him to the preservation of what would otherwise be the forgotten life of his dead brother, and not least to concealed aspects of that life.

Evidence for the concealed aspects of Joseph's life was contained in a binder which the historian had covered with a piece of green wallpaper, possibly to denote a special affection for the book.

It was this book which Clement read through again when he returned to Rawlinson Road at six o'clock in the evening. Sheila and Michelin sat companionably together in the kitchen, drinking white wine with their feet up on the kitchen table. They were watching the news on television.

"How was the Bursar?" Sheila asked.

"Did I tell you he had turned back into a hunchbacked toad?"

He took a glass of wine with him and went up to his study. The book Joseph had labelled LIFE HISTORY was a plastic binder containing badly typed pages of a student's loose-leaf block. Stuck to the inside of the binder was a photograph of the Market Square in Nettlesham, Suffolk.

Joseph's account began abruptly.

This is my life history, which I set down this 8th day of January 1987, being of sound mind more or less. I write it for my own sake, but also in the hopes that perhaps others may gain some advantage from its strange lesson.

It is a history which serves to illustrate two principles: that one may be in grave error for many years without knowing it, and eventually recover; and that, as La Rochefoucauld says, we are none of us as miserable or as happy as we think we are.

Part I really begins before I was born, but we will leave that till later. I first saw light of day, with a thunderous noise, like harsh bells jangled out of tune, in the market town of Nettlesham, in Suffolk. While my arrival was a cause of astonishment to me, I have to report straight away that it was a grave disappointment to my mother, and that from this disappointment much grief sprang.

Part II may serve as a warning to other historians. It tells the story as I fully believed it to be until a short while ago. That story, however, was a curious misreading. I had misunderstood my own life's story. How, in that case, are we to know that we can ever read other people truly?

With such a question mark, I begin.

Nettlesham in the mid-nineteen-twenties, when I was born, was a sleepy little hole. There was not much to distinguish it from a thousand other small English towns, except this: that a minor eighteenth-century poet, William Westlake, famous in his day, came down from London to live with his female cousin in a house on the town square, wrote a few poems sitting at his window, went off his head, and died there. So I claim kinship: I lived there and went off my head.

Not many may boast, as I justifiably can, of having emerged amid the grandiose rattling of galvanised pails at one shilling and one penny ha-penny. It was the first noise to greet my ears on this earth, an unmistakable noise, not harmonious and, as it was to prove, hardly auspicious. As distinguished in its way as the ringing of church bells. And you'd go a long way these days to find as many galvanised pails as we had.

Thus my beginning, and the announcement to Nettlesham, or to anyone who happened to be nearby in the square, that I had butted in on the scene and effected that awful transition out of the nowhere into the everywhere with some success.

> See where these simple country swains appear —
> Well known to Heav'n, tho' little noted here

in the immortal words of William Westlake, in his poem on his mother's portrait. Other remembered gems of his include "The Conversation", "A Summer Stroll Through Parts of Suffolk", the renowned "The Crippled Goat" ("I was a crippled goat that lost its way. . . .") and many other affecting pieces.

Westlake's name was commemorated by the Westlake Memorial Hall and Westlake Street. There was even a *Conversation Arms* in Commercial Street, although its literary associations began and ended with the name. Westlake wasn't a drinking man — no wonder he went mad.

It's clear that Westlake was a polite and conventional chap. My father had the same qualities, clinging to spats and the Sunday sermon with the same fervour that Westlake showed towards the heroic couplet. Also affected by Westlakeitis, he composed a history of World War I — in which he had flown biplanes and ridden mules and various other characteristic vehicles of the time — entirely in verse: it was the last appearance of the alexandrine and the heroic couplet. Unfortunately, this literary relic has not survived. He read parts of it to me when I was young and defenceless. I remember only this couplet:

> "Go forward then," said Kitchener, "ye Grenadiers,"
> And off they marched by way of Armentiers.

I mention Westlake because there was a time when I too longed to be just as dead and as deadly respectable as he. Being spurned by my mother, I had only the death wish to court. The death wish proving as adamant as my mother, I suppose I must own that such writing as I have done probably owes something to the author of "The Crippled Goat". Had it been Constable instead of Westlake who went mad in Nettlesham, I should no doubt be turning out watercolours by now; these childhood influences can be extremely powerful.

But how did I come to misunderstand my own life story? Can there be anything so idiotic? What streak of the perverse entered into me? There must have been some influence more powerful than old Westlake's crippled goat to make me so obdurately lose my way for so long.

There certainly were factors to make even the least shrewd of infants suspect that he was less than popular in the maternal bosom. Take the case when Mater was swelling and I shrinking; she swelling with another infant and I at four years old shrinking under the weight of what was to come. So she wanted a girl with an urgency bordering on the dotty: she did not have to bring me into it. I could have been left in blissful ignorance of the whole reproduction thing, among my farm animals and Bonzo the Dog.

Instead, I was made to get down on my knees with her every evening before beddy-byes (bloody beddy-byes being about six) and pray with her, earnestly and too long, that this time — *this* time, pray God, *nice* God — this time it would be a little girl with a little cunt and cute little skirts and pigtails. Pretty humiliating for a chap, boding no good.

Why didn't God intervene? Lean down and prod her on the shoulder? "Sorry, Mum, but I shouldn't go into all that in his presence or he'll start thinking of himself as a failure. Read Freud if you don't believe Me."

People, and this includes deities, intervene only when they are not wanted. Nature rolled inevitably on, mother found it more and more difficult to sink to her swollen knees. I caught — and how was that for timing? — how, why, did they let it happen? — I caught whooping cough. What's embarrassing is that it sounds such an old-fashioned disease to catch, like curvature of the spine, or ophthalmic spermatorea. Why could I not have caught curvature of the spine? "Oh, the poor little lad has curled into a hoop, let's cancel the pregnancy."

They must have warned me that whooping cough was fatal to babies but, not being up in medical science, I suppose I went right back to studying *Chick's Own* and forgot all about it.

Next thing is, the much-prayed-for infant arrives, proves the existence of God by coming complete with little cunt, little skirts, and pigtails, and I'm flung out of the house. Flung out on the very hour the infant surfaces. Go and live with granny, you little bastard.

On the whole, grannies get a good press, bless them. They're small, they don't eat much, and they view television regularly. In the thirties it was different: they never watched television and they smelt of mothballs. As an additional eccentricity marking her off from the rest of humanity, Granny Scoones wore black: black dress, black stockings, black slippers, black bow in her hair. Black knickers too, for a fiver. Her widow's weeds. Regardless of the fact that the old weed had been dead for about sixty years by then.

Granny lived in a tall house in Lavenham, all of sixty miles away from home and baby. It was called "No. 99", which somehow conferred singular honour upon it. The Late Mr Scoones had gone up in the world; he had been taken away from school at the age of fourteen because his father, a carrier, could not pay a farthing a week for his schooling. "A carrier" — no doubt a euphemism of the time, like those chaps who turn up in criminal court nowadays describing themselves as "a company director". The Late had eventually acquired one or two houses, none quite as grand or quite as semi-detached as No. 99, and become Chairman of the local Budgerigar Breeders and Fanciers Association. He had left behind a great deal of solid furniture, very fashionable with the aspiring classes in the eighteen-nineties, covered all over with carving and scrolling, dotted with tiny shelves, and seeded with mirrors wherever possible. It was all mahogany, of course. The Late Mr Scoones was not the man to venture into oak.

The toilet on the first landing conformed to the same pattern, with a fine high mahogany seat, the moving parts activated by a lever to one side, rather reminiscent of today's ejector seat in fighter planes.

The bathroom, too, had its share of mahogany. The mahogany ran up and around the wash basin, embraced the big misty mirror set too high for me to see into, and completely encircled the enormous bath, as if wood had developed the temperament of bindweed. The bath had a point in its favour. When allowing water to escape, it emitted a disgusting gargling noise which always made me laugh. Since laughing, in chronic whooping cough cases, brings on vomiting, the purpose of the bath was often defeated.

I dwell on these details because I hated everything in the house with — well, not exactly a passionate intensity, but certainly with all the intensity a whelp of that age could bring to the subject. We always remember best what we hate best. Also, in my desperate case, the toilet and bathroom were the rooms to which I was dragged when my illness came on. I had no ordinary whooping cough, like the poor kids down Baxter Row, who always had something so appalling that it's a wonder the working classes of Nettlesham didn't die out in that generation; I had whooping cough with complications. The complications, I realised later, much later, sprang from the bilious attacks which came on whenever something brought to my attention the fact that Mater was so pissed off at having me. A lot of sicking up went on at No. 99, I'm proud to say, and the mahogany took quite a hammering.

In order to cure or at least quieten me, my granny's doctor, a tall sallow man with side whiskers, carrying a bag, and dressed in even blacker black than granny's, and called Dr Humphreys-Menzies — oh, you won't believe it, you'll think I'm getting this out of an old bound volume of *Punch* — Dr Humphreys-Menzies came along and prescribed a medicine of noxious stickiness which was to be taken last thing at night. Probably a mix of laudanum plus cow gum and masses of sugar to taste. I'm certainly right about the sugar, for in no time the mixture had rotted away all my milk teeth. The teeth went brown and green and began to waver in their sockets, like old men trying to keep awake in their pews during the sermon on Sundays. Out they had to come, ha-ha, something else we can do to the little bastard.

I was wheeled down to the dentist in my pyjamas, given chloroform (now reserved for laboratory rats), and twelve of the defective little pegs were whipped out. By the time I came groggily round, the teeth were arranged in a pattern for me to see on a sort of white glass ashtray. Then it was back to No. 99 and bed, and a good bleed over the sheets.

It is not my intention to depict myself as feeble. In fact I was a sturdy kid, give or take a mother or two, well up on the tree-climbing and swift-kick-to-the-bum-of-enemies. It's a tribute to that sturdiness that by four-thirty on the Day of the Great Extraction I was thoroughly awake again, crying aloud for fish warmed in milk, blancmange, and liquorice sticks, and sicking freely over granny's eiderdown.

At last something or other happened. Probably granny refused to keep me any longer, and I was shoved off home. Oh dear, did I weep when I was again in my mother's arms? Oh dear, I did, as far as that was congenial to the little swaddled thing also entangled in the embrace. Siblings? I was well and truly sibbled.

I returned home to my parents on a Wednesday. They couldn't make it on Tuesday, Tuesday being the weekly whist drive over at Mrs Poncer's, as well as (for Pater) the meeting of the Nettlesham Westlake Cultural Society, when no doubt they were giving a public reading of the poems of Baden-Powell.

Anyone well up in amateur psychiatry or do-it-yourself psychoanalysis will recognise that this was danger time for little wowser. Any clued-in

Mater in nineteen-thirty-one would have known that this was crunch time, when little wowser, if he was ever to recover from his psychic shock of displacement, would need special *treatment* (loving being an out-word) for the next week or two; or say even a calendar month. When his poor broken heart might be sutured. What he would not need was an angry shoving aside when two great luxurious tits were brought out for the tiny red-faced one to guzzle at for a half-hour on the trot. That was piling Pelion on the gingerbread, tantamount to inviting him to jump from the frying pan into the Ossa.

If a small child becomes lonely, moody, given to picking his nose, prone to attention-seeking tantrums and periods of withdrawal such as hiding in the wardrobe with Teddy, the signs are there to be read. Mother beware, Father be there. True, in my case, the signs *were* read, and I was given a good clout for seeking attention. Somehow, it had to be made clear to me that it just wasn't my world any longer and I'd be well-advised to get on with my cigarette card collection and not vex Mater. And when I did in fact withdraw into an invisible shell and shuffle and re-shuffle my Fifty Famous Cricketers, then it had to be made clear that I was not to sulk.

It was made sufficiently clear for my behaviour to become more rather than less bizarre. The tree-climbing reached, in every sense, new heights. It was fun to reach a really impossibly high twig and then hang from it, screaming at the top of my voice that I was falling. That did get attention, though it was surely worth a few more laughs than it earned.

So the puzzle was what to do with such a naughty child. And the solution arrived at, after much heart-searching but little consultation with anyone with any fucking sense, was to scare small wowser into submission. Accordingly, at the next lark, wowser was told that Mater would never love him again. Bilious attack followed. No dice. Bed wetting. No dice. Rather the opposite. Minus dice. More threats. If he was going to be naughty, then Mater would run away from him, taking Baby Ellen with her. Oh, no, mummy, please don't leave me! — Ah ha, fatal thing to say, showing what you were really afraid of! Now she had you, vulnerable little rat that you were. . . .

So we come to the central scene of the narrative. The torture scene. It is for this that I sit up late at night, a rug round my legs against the cold, scribbling — just to draw this picture. It happened over half a century ago, yet it remains vivid, vivid as shame, and blood still runs in the gutters.

At that naughty boy's next outburst of misery, Mater was off. She carried out her dreadful threat. Baby Ellie was crammed helpless into her pushchair, wool bonnet was tied under her pink little chops. Arms flying, she was bowled up Ipswich Street, Mater propelling her with maniacal force. I swear that's what she did, doctor. I can prove it. I saw her from our front windows, watched her in despair, my own and only mother, doctor, off almost at a trot in her brown coat, never see her again, never. . . .

Okay, that's it. Lash the strait-jacket back on now. I've told it.

You hear? She actually deserted me. Ran away. She took my little sister — an innocent accomplice — and she ran away from me up Ipswich Street because she hated me so much. What a crime was committed that day!

Okay, it was a bluff. I know it was a bluff. But I'm sure that my learned and aloof brother would tell you that Mater was acting out her secret desires. It was only a bluff, and she sneaked back in again before dark, so that Pater didn't discover what she had done. . . . That makes no difference. A little distinction cuts no ice with a four-year-old. She had bloody left home, carried out her miserable threat to leave me. Come in, Jung, come in, Freud, come in, Dr Spock. You hear what I said? I said my bloody Mater ran away from me, deserted me. I died that day.

They resurrected me next morning. No matter that I had no spirit for anything. The ghastly routines of childhood had to be undergone. There remained the rituals of nutrition, exercise, and neglect. Soon there was infant school. Dead or not, one had to attend. Had to learn to tie bootlaces, had to learn the two-times table, even if to all intents and purposes emotionally extinct.

My fruitless struggles to regain my mother's affections shall not be told, ever. To cut a long throat short, I continued to be nothing but a terrible nuisance to my parents. Since they had no understanding, matters deteriorated. I wouldn't share my toys with Baby, and it was no excuse that Baby, tottering about now like a new-hatched Behemoth, broke them. I was a Bad Boy, and things happen to Bad Boys. Mater again ran away. It was no less impressive than the first time. She did not at all like it when she returned to find urine under the window sill where I had kneeled trembling to watch her go, where I had collapsed when she had disappeared. She must have felt it was an unfair reward for criminal desertion.

So the months rolled by like poison down the sink. Parents came to a decision. He must go away to school. "Right away to school" was the actual phrase. He must go to a place where — this was the next phrase — they would make a little Gentleman out of him. (What ambitions the sellers of buckets harbour in their breasts!) They would make a little Gentleman out of him. Knock the shit out of him, in other words. Not forgetting the piss. And, of course, the sick. And anything else they could find.

Need I say that I was never consulted about this fearful expulsion from the nest, from my first Eden? Even prayer was not used in this instance; no more of the getting down on swollen knees. Keep God out of it. Let the crime be as secret as possible.

Of course Pater knew. He was going to have to pay the bills. But Pater kept aloof, down among his pails and coconut matting, presumably having decided that the intimate dramas of the nest were not to his taste. He distanced himself as far as possible from the squalid bawlings of his son (elder son but, note, not first-born — more of that later), his daughter, and then his second son, as each in turn arrived in this vale of tears. Indeed, throughout the patchy growth of his children, he managed still to stay pained and aloof, relaying such orders as we needed to receive through his wife. She was his mouthpiece. To put it another way, and more effectively, since it mirrors more faithfully the lousy English class system, he was the commanding officer; she was the NCO. Orders were passed down the line to us children, the privates, the conscripts, who were supposed to carry them out without question.

Thus, as we grew, Mater's sentences more and more tended to begin with the words, "Your father says. . . ." They generally spelt doom. The tablets came down from the mountain, wanged with considerable force.

There was some delay in finding an appropriate school for me. None of them was cheap enough. Ironmongers were not made of money. Eventually an establishment was found on a dreary stretch of the Suffolk coast, tucked away from human eyes at the end of a lane in a position forlorn enough to satisfy the most pernickety psychopath.

Father tramped round the premises with the headmaster. This was called "looking the school over". I was dragged behind them, noting the high walls which surrounded the school. To one side was a field where cricket was played. In the stone wall at the rear of the building was a tall wooden gate. The headmaster flung open this gate with a gesture.

"The sea's just there," he said. We could hear the waves scribbling on pebble, not a hundred yards distant.

My father looked down at me. "I hope you teach the boys swimming," he said.

With a kind of cringing geniality to which I would become accustomed over the next few years, the headmaster replied, "At St Paul's, we go in the sea whatever the weather's like. . . ."

The two men eyed each other. They were big men, in sympathy with each other's thought processes.

"Sink or swim, eh?" said my father, and they both laughed.

As well they might. My father had just uttered the school motto.

X

And so I found myself, helpless, with a little kaleidoscope in one pocket, shaking so much that my socks would not stay up over my calves, not weeping even when I kissed little Ellen goodbye, teddy bear suddenly wrenched from my embrace as the car stopped at the gates, a vulnerable seven, installed as one of sixteen young boarders attending Mr Humphrey Fangby's St Paul's Court Preparatory School for Young Gentlemen and Obdurate Little Bastards (Equestrian Lessons Extra).

My parents' farewells still rang lovingly in my ears: "Your father says Work Hard."

My salvation, if it was to be had at all, was to be had at the hands of my companions, the bedraggled fifteen. I cannot say that I came to any harm from them, or they from me, I hope. There was no compassion between us; they were also having a bad time. But a kind of loyalty in adversity did develop between us, and some I grew slowly to love and befriend. Yet even friendship, that most precious quality, was a sickly fruit under the shadow, the ample shadow, of Mr Humphrey Fangby. Let's call the old bastard that.

Fangby was a tall, portly man, imposing if slugs are imposing, with thick wisps of black hair drawn across a dome of bone, a convalescent's fleshy nose ending in a downward sneer, mottled cheeks, and two little eyes like sucked buttons, well suited for detecting lies or happiness in those placed under his care. He wore suits of a ginger bristly material, possibly woven from the pubic hair of Bactrian camels.

Fangby had a Fangby Wife, a pallid little person who occasionally smiled through the dining room hatch at us in a manner indicating that she had been instructed never to say a kindly word to us, on threat of immediate fornication. As to this latter, there had emerged into the world a Fangby Baby. It also never said a kindly word to us. Fangby Baby's only contribution to our welfare at St Paul's was to permit its old huckaback napkins to be used as towels to dry our washing-up. None of our plans to kidnap it came to anything.

Food was of the worst sort. When visitors from abroad complain about the awfulness of English food, the disgusting state of our restaurants, the insolence of our waiters, and the revolting habits of the other (English) diners, I long to take them back in a time machine to St Paul's, to show them where it all began. Our provisions, poor to awful to start with, were cooked by Fangby himself.

Perhaps to persuade himself that he was a good cook, Fangby had imposed a rule upon us: every plateful had to be cleared completely, however long it took. Nothing was to be wasted, not even the most gristly piece of meat. St Paul's fish had gristle too. And the blancmange. Much vomiting went on before we got some especially inedible dish down. Sago would be top of my horror list, perhaps because it reminded one visually of the vomiting that would have to be endured before it all vanished. Fortunately, dining room and lavatory were adjoining. One could be smelt from the other.

Cuisine of course is not the strong point of schools. One goes there to learn, not to eat. Eating is incidental. It is Learning that maketh Gentlemen. Why am I saying this? That's what Fangby taught, so obviously the poison seeped in. Learning doth not make Gentlemen. All it could possibly make at St Paul's, to put things at their unlikely best, was to turn out snotty little trumped-up sons of small tradesmen. Only Gentlemen make Gentlemen. It's a closed shop. You need inherited money, lawns down to lakes, Paters in *Who's Who*, horses in the paddock, friendships with judges, and a fucking blasé accent to be a Gentleman. You also need to steer clear of St Paul's, where a notice in the sports field made it plain that it was a Preparatory School, without clarifying what exactly it might be preparing you for. Not Eton and Harrow, that's for sure.

Nowadays, there are inspectors to see that the Fangbys of this world are denied permission to run schools. Together with Fangby Wives, they run boarding houses and B&Bs instead, from which punters can flee in horror after a one-night stay. No twelve-week terms are imposed.

Of course I'm talking about the mid-thirties, before the war, during the days of the British Empire, when there was a kind of official unspoken consensus that miserable conditions in childhood made the best troops in wartime. It was good thinking on the War Office's part (or whoever it was that planned on such clever lines) — proved to be perfectly correct when the war broke out in 1939. After a dose of Fangby's regime for a few years, it was a positive relief to fling yourself on a German bayonet.

Learning was in the capable if oily hands of whom but Mr Fangby himself. Assisted by two masters, Mr Fletcher and the Rev Winterbottom. Mr Fletcher was the only master to live in. He taught everything and did everything, and all for a pound a week plus lodging, I'm sure. But being an object of pity is not the same as being a pleasant character; and so it was in

Mr Fletcher's case. He took out on the boys all that he hated about Fangby, and was ever ready with a sneer and a crushing witticism. Of the "You didn't stand very near your hairbrush this morning" variety.

The Rev Winterbottom was hardly a teacher at all. He was the local C. of E. minister, as pious as they come, and with a veneer of culture gained, I suppose, from fraternising on a compulsory basis with the local squirearchy. His two boys, Gregory and Hilary Winterbottom, were boarders, and doubtless got in cheap in exchange for Rev Winterbottom's conducting us through the pieties every Saturday morning. He was a conscientious man, and kindly, and we became all too familiar with the buggerings about of the Israelites in the Wilderness. What on earth was it regarding those wandering tribes which made Winterbottom, never mind God, so interested in them in the first place? I soon had their watering places, and the dumps where father was prepared to cut son's throat (I liked that bit) off by heart. I knew everything from Genesis to about Judges. I could tell you who smote whom at Gibeon. Take your average kid of the streets today and ask him before he hits you where a place called Bashan is, or what was built of shittim wood, and he'll look blank. It's the Top Twenty or nothing for him. Not an inkling of old Moab the Tishbite or the Hittites. ("Is that a Group, mate?")

Education has changed.

Any good in that school was brought in by the boys — which tells you how little good there was. Toys were strictly disallowed, on the principle that they provided links with home. I was permitted to have with me my microscope and my telescope, on the grounds that they were something or other that toys were not. Perhaps Fangby thought that Gentlemen used such objects. Be that as it may, I was forever looking up or down brass barrels, and sketching what I saw. What I saw was completely divorced from St Paul's, and therefore welcome and wonderful. My love of science and astronomy dates from that time. Had we been taught science it would have been a different story. But at that date, and previously, only men with left-wing attitudes were attracted to science, so Gentlemen would not touch it.

What Gentlemen learnt were the Classics. Well, Greek was beyond us, but Fangby saw to it that we got a dose of Latin. There in our classroom we sat, learning to conjugate *amo*, learning to decline *mensa*. Thus the first sentence we ever put together in the tongue of those scoundrelly Romans was "I love a table". It was necessary that our sex lives should be warped if we were to go forth and Command, like real Gentlemen.

Fortunately the intended discipline was too insane to be methodically applied. For all his vices, it could be said in Fangby's defence that he was a lazy man. He was given to entering the classroom in the morning with an extra smarmy smile over large areas of his face and saying, "Well, boys, you've been working so well that I am going to give you a day's holiday."

It was forbidden to groan. A holiday meant that we were kicked out of the house into the field until dusk, while Fangby hit the sack, presumably with Fangby Wife — who for that reason probably dreaded holidays as much as we did.

There was nothing to do in the field but sit about and bully each other, or fight off the local boys. The village boys, who knew potential little Gents when they saw them, hated us effortlessly and with true instinct. Since most of them were about fifteen, and hulking with it, and our average age was ten, we were correct to fear them. The first we would know of them was when stones came whizzing through the hawthorn hedge at us — or it would have been the first had they not worn boots shod like horses' hooves and talked in husky whispers audible half a mile off. Many of us had our foreheads cut open by stones ("I must have banged it on the apple tree, Mrs Fangby . . ."). Class warfare begins young.

One other resource was open to us. We were allowed a small strip of field, next to an old hewn-flint wall, to make into gardens. These we worked on quite consistently with the aid of Slaves (boys feeble and consequently gardenless). Fine patches of land they became, every last stone being set carefully aside as ammunition for when the Goths next attacked through the hedge.

Once a week, we were allowed into Miss Araminta's shop, a hundred yards away from the school gates, down the lane. This miserable concession to freedom was always under threat and often withdrawn if a sin was committed (such as dropping a pen in class, which counted about Eight on the local Richter scale). Miss Araminta, oleaginous enough to be indisputably in cahoots with Fangby, sold everything including black knicker elastic at a farthing a yard. To us she sold Carter's Tested Gardens Seeds and penny Milky Way bars, which in those days included Radio Stars (A Set of 25).

We sowed our gardens with seeds bought with our own hard unearned pocket money. If the seeds were sown in the spring term and the plot weeded scrupulously for every last minuscule weed (more work for the Slave) in the last week of term, then when we returned (groan) for our summer incarceration, the carrots, spring onions, lettuce, and radish would be up and doing well.

Our enforced days' holidays were punctuated by either Fangby Wife or Fangby Bootboy coming out with a battered toffee tin full of sandwiches. Lunch. We would fling the gristly old meat over the hedge, lay a young spring onion or a leaf or two of lettuce between the bread, and eat and enjoy. Thus we retained some independence from the Regime.

My feelings for the Earth and the goodness of its fruits, not to mention its vegetables, date from that time. Earth gives you things you can actually eat without being sick. It is a miracle for which we should all be grateful. Pity that no more than sixteen boarders went to St Paul's.

The dreadful years passed. Mr Fletcher was sacked for drunkenness and some wept to see him leave through the school gates. The Rev Winterbottom left us, to be replaced by a Roman Catholic priest with bad breath called Father Chitterling, also well informed on what the Israelites got up to and why. One of our number, a boy we called Old Boghound for reasons long forgotten, came back at the beginning of term with news — rather garbled news — of how children were made and born. His sister had told him. Eggs came into it and it all sounded pretty disgusting. We gave Old Boghound six with his own cricket bat.

Beatings meant little to us, at bottom. Until my last term. One of our number, a large lad called Crouch, who looked like a neatly shaven dromedary, committed an Unforgivable Act. He was immediately expelled. Fangby locked him in a small attic room until his parents could collect him. His clothes were taken away.

We were lectured about this Act, which, we were told, would incur immediate beating and sacking if we perpetrated it. This was alarming and unenlightening, since the Act was never named. It was too terrible to be named. Had Crouch devised for himself the art of masturbation, only to be discovered when at the short sharp stroke stage? Had he been caught puffing at cigarettes? Had he seized on a once-in-a-lifetime chance to rape the Fangby Baby? Had he farted within ear- and nose-shot of Fangby Wife? We were never told, and I still keep hoping to come across old Crouch in some far Salvation Army shelter and get the truth from the horse's mouth. The mystery of his Act increased the atmosphere of terror which prevailed.

Crouch was paraded before us the following day, in pyjamas, accompanied by a very grim and dropsical-looking Fangby holding a cricket stump. The classroom door was locked. Some of our number, sensing blood, asked immediately to Be Excused. Permission was not granted: we were to stay as assembled, to see that justice was done.

Fangby then proceded to give Crouch twelve blows with the cricket stump on his bare bum. Everyone went deathly pale. Each whack brought a fall in the communal blood pressure. Two boys fainted, another we called the Mouse was sick on the floor. It showed there was good in us. Crouch never made a sound, but had to be helped from the room when the beating was over. It was little consolation to think that similar events had taken place in the Navy in Nelson's day. The sinner left St Paul's before sunset, and was presumably doomed from then on. Perhaps he died for England in the war then only three years away.

Whatever Crouch's crime, Fangby's was greater. Strange though it may be to admit such a thing, I had not until the flogging hated Fangby. There was something about his manner, a suspicion of fawning, a hangdog look which came over him, a droop in his shoulders, even a suspicion of apology on occasions when he addressed his little victims, which I found disarming. He was a soft-spoken man. Unlike Mr Fletcher, he did not use the whip of sarcasm on us. Perhaps in some fashion the monster was sorry for the way in which he earned his living. Perhaps — who knows — he too aspired to be a Gentleman.

The brutal flogging elevated him to a different category. He was now the enemy. He had demonstrated how Gentlemen were made — by Fear.

A gulf opened between the teachers and the taught. It was revealed to us as we cowered in our classroom after Crouch had been dragged away that a great division in the world lay between those who had power and those upon whom power was exercised. From now on, and for the rest of our lives, it was to be Us and Them. The Us was rather a solitary role.

The Them were multitudinous.

You may imagine that I was happy to leave St Paul's. You may, but it would not be true. For my parents, ever tender for my welfare, had put my name down for a much larger school, Tremblingham College, which boasted four hundred boys. Since St Paul's never boasted more than twenty, including day kids, the chances of bullying at Tremblingham might be reckoned at twenty times more likely.

I never adjusted to Tremblingham. It proved to be much like a larger scale St Paul's, without the laughs. Perhaps I would have done better if I had not felt I was being sent away as a punishment, as part of what amounted to a continued policy of not loving me. That feeling persisted throughout my school days, being now and then reinforced by one or other incident which showed I was not just imagining things.

While the pitiful round of school term, recovering from the last school term, and preparing oneself psychologically for the next school term, was in full swing, much was going on elsewhere.

The female Winter baby, first seen in these pages red-faced and supping milk, had by now grown up considerably, to the extent of running about and being able to bark like a dog when requested to do so. She had a name: Ellen Mary. She proved to be good value. Whereas I had been reduced to a dreadful lickspittle, hanging around to do anything my parents suggested in order to avoid even more severe punishment (The Hulks? The Inquisition? The Bar?), Ellen, confident of inexhaustible mother's love, was a rebellious little spark, and an increasingly stalwart ally.

The sense of alliance grew when Mater again began to have swollen knees, to wear looser clothes, and to rest even longer in the afternoons. There was an impression that pink bootees were being knitted, new maids engaged, and new cans of powder lined up on the bathroom shelf. I knew these ominous signs of old. Though still blind to the finer points of reproduction, I sensed that another member of the family impended. And the treacherous thought came — it was going to be yet another little girl.

When this suspicion was conveyed to the first little girl, she was furious. Ellie was certainly not having a sister in the house. She'd rather have a big white dog, like Mrs Ravage's. She began to play up in preparation for the event. I was flabbergasted at this show of spirit, which would certainly have involved me in another walk-out up Ipswich Street. Behind my invincible aura of non-confidence, I trembled when the bedclothes were flung on the fire, and when the bottle of Friars Balsam was hurled out of the window, followed defiantly by a new tube of Colgate's Toothpaste. What powers of self-expression this sister had!

Alas, not even a new toothpaste tube can check the onward march of the fallopian tubes. Again the nurse dominated the house, all starched bosom and little pink nose, again the wailings of the newborn and the scent of meconia.

I was transfixed. All the old misery of disgrace went into psychic re-run. Was I again to be whisked off to granny's and lose another twelve teeth? Perhaps it wouldn't be so bad if Ellen were exiled as well. We could have fun in the mahogany-bound bath that made do-dos noises, and Ellen would certainly give granny a run for her money.

A maid brought us the joyous news. It was only a boy. I was saved. Good old God! Well played, Jesus! The parents would not get rid of me for a mere boy. I went back to Tremblingham with a relatively light heart. Ellen was furious, and at first refused to go to school. She had to be bought a little white dog — like Mrs Ravage's but smaller — before she could be induced to venture farther than the front door-step.

This new boy, soon christened Clement, marked a turning point in the relationship between Ellen and me. We now had something we both disliked. It brought us closer together — as close as we could get, considering that I kept having to go to school for two-thirds of the year.

Rebellious boys are popular at school. Quiet boys are unpopular. Quietly rebellious boys are the most unpopular. I could see that once again Tremblingham was up to Fangby's lark of trying to make us into Gentlemen — and with far better chances of success. So everything I did was against the grain, although I could not stop myself learning, since little else offered itself.

War was brewing. Over in Hitler's Germany, the smart money were beginning to pack. Meanwhile, we had our little battles on the home front.

While relations with Mater could not be regarded as more than warm, with an occasional sunny period, father was a figure I admired from afar. He was all I hoped to be, and evidently as he himself hoped, a model son for his father, my authoritarian old grandad.

He had his role in superior Nettlesham society.

Both he and Mater had musical ability. Every Sunday, father played the organ in church. We entered solemnly into God's temple, and nipped solemnly out of the same to the mighty strains he evoked. Evenings, he worked late in our shop, doing the orders. He did not smoke or gamble or drink. I never heard him swear. He was, however, a good man with a gun, won many prizes at shooting, and evidently had God's okay to shoot rabbits and partridges and pheasants whenever they showed their faces in our part of Suffolk.

His brother Hereward was completely different. Hereward cared nothing for church. Every Sunday, Hereward lay in late, recovering from the excesses of the night before. He smoked, drank and gambled. Gambling was a kind of passion with Hereward. He never worked late in the shop, and was over in Newmarket, betting on the gee-gees as often as he could. I often used to think it must be more fun in Uncle Hereward's and Aunt Hermione's house than in ours, had it not been for their three mischievous sons, my cousins, Seneca, Setebos, and Cecil. These large indolent lads were good at football, blowing up frogs with straws, sliding on partly frozen ponds, and other sports for which there was much local competition. They bullied anyone smaller than they (like me) and howled vigorously when beaten. They were all red-faced, with a redness which varied throughout life from acne to high blood pressure. I hated them because they once made another kid and me toss them all off twice in quick succession behind a barn.

Why had my father only one pale son plus little Clement, and Hereward three red-faced ones? It cannot have been just the luck of the draw. God must have had some excuse for making my father so short of male progeny and that progeny so inept at blowing up frogs with straws. The answer seems to be that he and Hereward related to their dread Pater, my grandad, much as Ellen and I did to Mater. Hereward always knew that whatever he did, however awful he and his sons were, he was sure of his Pater's love; and my father, however good he was, however often he abstained from a pint or a drag on a Player's, never could be sure that his Pater loved him.

As I have revealed, my origins were humble. Not that I saw them as humble at the time. Indeed, I thought of them as a cut above most origins, and the family — whatever its other shortcomings — as prosperous.

Grandad Winter's was not any old ironmongery. It stood in the square of Nettlesham right next to the Westlake Memorial Hall. Father said it was the biggest ironmongery business, almost, in the country; which is to say that it may have been the thirty-first biggest. Anyhow, we sold a lot of galvanised pails, I can tell you.

These were the very pails I mentioned as ringing in the new life, my life. Their harmonies, less reckonable than a peal of bells, were awoken by my father's reception of the news of the birth of his first son upstairs. He was at the time adjusting a price ticket saying *Unrepeatable: 1/1½d. each: Bargain*, when the news took him by as much surprise as if he had had no hand — or any other member — in the proceedings which precipitated my birth. He fell off the top of the steps on which he was balancing. Down he went. And with him went a dozen of the one shilling, one penny ha'penny pails, careering over the shop floor in great bucketfuls of sound, some actually rolling cheerfully out into the square. I was, you might say, into ironmongery from the very beginning. Nowadays they use the American term Hardware and done with it.

Grandad ruled over this shop with a rod of wood, which he applied without hesitation to my bare legs if I got in the way of customers.

He spent his days in a small office at the back. Its one window, not much more than a foot square, looked out on the brickwork of the side of the Westlake Memorial Hall. Wedged in with him was our cashier, Doris. In the front of the shop my father and his brother worked. Somehow father always got the dirty jobs and put up shutters, whereas it was Hereward who got to seduce the lovely Doris.

I was not popular in the shop. Things rattled when I went by. Nowhere was safe, nowhere was comfortable. Harsh surfaces threatened. On every side lurked stiff coconut matting, giant scrubbing brushes, blades of saws, bales of barbed wire, down to your humble emery paper. Fortunately, I was welcome in the shop next door, the little milliner's and haberdasher's run by Mrs Tippler and her two daughters, Rosemary and Ruth, among their soft goods.

No harsh surfaces here. Mrs Tippler was delicate and refined; conscious of her unfortunate name, bequeathed by a gent either deceased or permanently living up to his name in the *Conversation Arms*, she never touched a drop. Her two daughters were all peachy surface, pretty and pink and refinedly dressed — and a barrow-load of mischief when Mumsy was not around. I loved Rosemary Tippler. I loved Ruth Tippler. And this was rather odd because when I was twelve Ruth was thirteen and Rosemary was eighteen — at least a generation or two older than I, as it seemed.

But how desirably naughty they were. Since they took an interest in me, I blossomed in their sight. A detestable failing. Ever since, I have blossomed when a pretty woman showed interest in me, and after blossom comes the fruit, which has often been bitter.

When Mrs Tippler worked at her hats in the little room over her shop, or went out to see her ladies (those fortunates who had married Gentlemen), Rosemary and Ruth kept shop. I cannot remember them ever going to school. Perhaps they didn't.

Rosemary loved to tease and kiss me. She had rich brown hair which she, like a smart young thing, had had shingled, whereas her younger sister had a crop of straight dark hair, kept in place by a big blue slide. Rosemary would say silly things to make me laugh and then laugh at me for laughing, and ask me if I was "all there". When she had made me smart enough, she would kiss me. Real kisses. Marvellous kisses, mouth to mouth. Sometimes she would crush me to her tender bosom, when I could sniff how sweet she smelt. She would even permit me, momentarily, to feel her breasts when, excited beyond measure, I put my hand there.

It is really terrible to be twelve years old and not know what it is you wish so frantically to do. Terrible and delectable.

A green curtain was hung to cut off the rear of the shop. We felt ourselves safe behind it. They had few customers, and those often short-sighted.

Rosemary had a way of daring me to do something and being disapproving as I did it, while at the same time seeming to urge me on. Easy enough to say now that she was uncertain of her own sexuality and felt safe only when she could control the situation with a much younger boy. All that's over the young boy's head. He is in love and longing to experiment with all the dangerous forces whirling about him.

She wore a black velour dress on the day I was challenged to undo its little fiddly black buttons if I just dare. Every button undone was an absolute affront, an outrage.

"Do you see this, Ruth? Look just at what he is doing now. Oh, you little devil, there goes another button. I'm going to go right out and tell your mum. What does he hope to find in there, I'd like to know. Eh, Joseph? What do you think is in there?"

It was warm in there. Perhaps from design, she wore no brassiere. Next moment a lovely soft breast was resting in the palm of my triumphant hand. It was a bit like finding an egg when you reach up into a bird's still warm nest in the spring. Almost as exciting.

"There, Ruth, what do you think he's got hold of now? The cheek of it! I bet you didn't expect to find that, did you, sonny? Why, you're looking quite excited, and what exactly do you imagine you're going to do with it now? You mustn't be clumsy with it — it's delicate enough to be set before the king. . . ."

I drew it out into the curtained daylight of their room. Rosemary screamed with affront and caused the breast to pop in again like a startled rabbit. For years after that — all through my adolescence — I had visions of getting that breast out again and kissing it, and much else besides.

Ruth I also loved. Her part in all this sexy teasing was also important. She was the onlooker. She watched, giggled, and commented.

Out at the back of their shop was a small yard, wedged between high walls. It was there she showed herself no mere onlooker.

I had noted how she jumped up and down with excitement when her sister kissed me. Ruth was darker, her lips redder, than her elder sister. And evidently more emotional.

Excited by a tease I had just enjoyed with Rosemary, Ruth and I fell to kissing. Kisses are marvellous when you know of nothing better. Strawberries out of season. Unlike her sister, Ruth was interested in my body. That is how she soon came to be clutching a sausage shape in her hand, and how I came to have my hand in her knickers and to be fingering a little crescent moon of a fishpool, with bewilderment and joy.

Gasping, I let my head roll back — and saw that Rosemary was watching us out of the rear window.

The delight of those two girls, and the harmless play with them, made a return to Tremblingham doubly awful, but warmed many a cold night in my bed when I got there.

I was playing with some friends in Nettlesham Square one day when out came my mother to the edge of the pavement and called me.

"What's wrong?" I asked, fearfully drawing near and feeling guilty as ever.

"Your grandfather's seriously ill, that's what's wrong. I don't think you'd better play out there."

So I didn't, but it served little to improve the old man's health. He was seventy-five and had suffered a stroke just before he left home for work that morning. His sons took him to hospital (in Hereward's car), and father stayed by his bedside overnight. When the old man appeared to be sinking next morning, my father said to him — as mother faithfully reported to us later — "I hope you've divided the business up fairly between Hereward and me in your Will. Otherwise we'll only quarrel over it."

To which grandfather said, or rather husked, these drear words: "You'll have to fight your own battles from now on, Ernest." An hour later, he died, right hand still clutching a book about Scott's Expedition to the South Pole.

After the funeral, attended by all the other acceptable ironmongers for miles around, I returned to Tremblingham. Term was almost over when I received a letter from my mother saying that they were moving to a small house in Lowestoft. Lowestoft was to be home from now on. Hereward and father had quarrelled bitterly and Hereward had bought father out of the business.

Father had fought his own battle. And lost.

It was goodbye to galvanised pails at one shilling and one penny ha'penny, goodbye to red-faced Seneca, Setebos, and Cecil — already away learning to be Gentlemen at a much smarter school than mine — and goodbye, alas, alas, to Rosemary and Ruth, my two loves. Nettlesham was now behind me for ever, and I returned at term end to a saturnine house on three floors, with two small rooms on every floor and a smell of fish emanating from the basement, standing at the fishier end of Lowestoft.

My parents, who so often had no idea, had no idea that I might miss my various friends and enemies in Nettlesham. I was simply left to adjust to the new circumstances on my own. Defeated, I retired to the top floor of the house and played under the sloping roof with my Hornby trains. Ellen by now was old enough to serve as a competent guard or ticket collector. Come summer, we found our way to Oulton Broad, and there we swam together, the best of companions.

That side of life was enjoyable. In the house, gloom reigned. My father felt himself a displaced person. He did not acquire another business for himself, nor would he work for others. Instead, he invested his little nest egg in large decayed houses, in which we would live while he redecorated and repaired them, and strove mightily to get the garden into order again. Then he would sell at a profit, and start the process over again in another old house. So our homes became impermanent.

Father had little to do with us. He became a man of deep silences. We saw him as someone on the top of ladders, painting ceilings, or at the bottom of gardens, laying crazy paving. He was another crippled goat that lost its way.

> These cottagers, in kinship close, yet share
> No words, no joys; before their cheerless grate
> They live apart, though bound by kindred fate.

Father came into his own when buying property. While the owner was extolling the merits of his house, father would stand creaking a board beneath his foot — he unerringly found out creaking boards — and interrupt suddenly, saying, "Is this floor rotten, do you know?" Or he would tap at a wall and ask, wistfully, "Any death watch beetle recently?" His way of looking at guttering or sash windows could reduce a proud owner to silence.

At selling houses, father was equally adroit. He never used an estate agent. So for a while his business flourished. He made money. But the war was approaching fast, and property on the East Coast became very slow. Finally, nothing was selling, and father was left with a monstrous house on his hands. He closed it down in a fit of desperation, and took us off to Cornwall to live — a great swerve in his life, as if to avoid demons. The Lowestoft house was commandeered by the military during the war, and sold off later to the council for a song. It is now demolished. Twenty town houses stand where it once stood.

At this point came a break in the narrative. Using a different pen, Joseph resumed further down the page.

It is impossible to continue as I began. The protective tone of levity has failed, after taking me through the years of early childhood. Long after that, until I was grown up, until after I left the army, I could never communicate to anyone the shame I felt at my mother's desertion of me and my banishment to my grandmother's house in Lavenham.

Much of the pain came from a source quite beyond my control, years before my birth. I have said that I was my parents' elder son but not their first-born. Here's the awful secret. They had another child, born six years before me, which died.

The story of my generation, now getting a little long in the tooth, is set about with war. We were a parenthesis between wars. My parents-to-be, young Ernest Winter and Madge Scoones, met during World War I, when he was on leave and she was acting as temporary nurse in a hospital in London. He was so eager to meet her again after the war that, when the home-coming troopship on which he was sailing was delayed outside Southampton harbour, he dived overboard and swam ashore. This exploit became a family story. It was hard to equate the aloof father I knew with that eager young man.

They were married in Nettlesham, Ernest's home town, in June of 1919, after a brief engagement. In March of 1920, a child was born to them.

How can I best relate this dark story? I never remember a time when my mother was not telling me about that dead child. Father never spoke of it. It was a girl. Mater told me piously, "Your poor little sister is with the angels now."

It happened that an old book I often looked through contained steel engravings of religious subjects. Perhaps it was an illustrated edition of Bunyan's *Pilgrim's Progress* — a book which even as late as my childhood could still be found in every self-respecting religious home. One picture showed a small boy climbing a hill. Over his head — rather uncomfortably close, to my infant mind — floated a small girl angel, with only a shred of cloud to conceal her nudity. This menacing little phenomenon became my dead sister, hanging over me like the Sword of Damocles. The Angel of Damocles.

Nothing I did was ever as good as what my steel-engraving angel would have done. Nor could I in any fashion prove an adequate substitute for her. Mater would in no way allow my coming into the world to appease her grief for the child that had left it. It was her tragedy and she needed to hold it to her.

Her story was that the little creature had lived only six months before fading out. "We just have to believe," she told me, "that she was too good for this world." Six years of mourning had gone by, and then I turned up. She felt herself insulted. "We just have to pray that next time it's a little girl," she told me.

Next time, it was a little girl. It was Ellen. Ellen assuaged Mater's wretchedness as I could never do. Gradually, she became more cheerful, more human, and, by the time World War II broke out, she was able to confront its vicissitudes with amiable courage.

But that wretched little steel-engraving angel took far longer to fade from its position a foot above my head.

My despair at school became worse when father again moved house to buy a small business in Bude, in Cornwall. On that occasion, my parents removed my sister Ellen from her school and took her down with them to a local school. I, however, was left at Tremblingham, despite my pleas to be moved too. Clem was just an infant then.

I took this rejection as a further desertion. Coming at puberty, it went very hard with me, and I suffered a nervous breakdown. The school doctor was a sympathetic man, and sent me nearer home. For some weeks, I was housed in a small private nursing home on the north Cornish coast, and allowed to recover gradually. In the evenings, in a season of calm weather, we were able to watch from the upper windows the first wartime convoys moving out of the Bristol Channel into the Atlantic, the ships outlined against a setting sun.

There I experienced again a recurrent dream which had first come to comfort me at my grandmother's, at the age of five. But my recovery was due as much as anything to a woman called Irene Rosenfeld, who lived only a few minutes away from the nursing home.

Irene was in her mid-twenties. Of course I thought of her as much older than I. In the October of 1941, when we set eyes on each other, I was fifteen, and in many respects still a hag-ridden little boy. We met on my daily walks along the cliffs and at first we only talked together. Then Irene invited me to her house for tea.

She was completely alone. She had a big complicated family, but they lived elsewhere. She was married to a man now serving in the Air Force, who came home on leave only occasionally. She was lonely but did not actually want the burden of a love affair. I was her substitute — her victim, I suppose, in some ways. So I can see the situation, years later. At the time, however, I fell into her embrace and her tuition with gratitude.

> They best can learn, who court the Muse
> When learning doth with gentle joy infuse

as old Westlake remarked of more academic matters.

The days at the nursing home became transformed. I lived in a golden daze, to think that I would be with her all afternoon and evening, that we would be naked to each other and in bed together. I could not believe my luck. Here was someone who really did love me, and showed it abundantly. Later, it became possible for me to see that, in her kind way, Irene was merely enjoying sex with me, and passing empty hours in a manner she thought safest; but for me it was a full-blown love affair, tinged with some pathos to think that my poor darling was so old.

The threatened return of Irene's husband on leave happened to coincide with the nursing home's declared intention of returning me to school. I bought her flowers, I made her speeches, I felt my heart breaking, I suppose I was as absurd as a fifteen-year-old can be. Irene took it all seriously and sweetly, and kissed me over and over, even weeping prettily as we finally parted.

Somehow, the remaining school years passed. In fact, I was happy at school for the first time. I had something positive to set against all the previous negativity. I talked smut like the rest of the boys — but that pure affair (as I regarded it) with Irene remained my precious secret, to be shared with no one.

In the autumn of 1943, I was conscripted into the army, and went straight from school into a barracks at Prestatyn. The days of my childhood were finished. Within a year, I found myself in Burma.

Joseph's "Life History" ended there. Part II, mentioned in the opening paragraphs, was missing. There, Joseph had promised to show how he had misunderstood his own story.

The meaning of that curious remark as yet remained obscure to Clement.

Book Two

ANIMA

XI

"You have been a bit absent-minded since we got home, darling," said Sheila, with a calculated amount of indulgence in her voice.

Clement was on his hands and knees, picking up the pieces of a cup and saucer he had knocked on to the kitchen floor.

"It's partly because I've so much to cope with at present," said Clement, realising how sorry for himself he sounded. He kneeled up and looked at his wife over the top of the table. "Joseph."

It was a code name.

Sheila settled herself comfortably beside Michelin and continued to arrange flowers in a glass vase. "But you weren't all that close, were you? He was too much your senior. The war came between your childhoods."

"Still there was a brotherhood," said Michelin. "Sorrow has to come out."

"Mourning is often a matter of guilt as well as sorrow," said Sheila, in one of her writer's intonations. "He probably feels guilty because he was not as close to Joseph as his sister was."

Clement did not relish hearing himself explained. "I've no reason to feel guilt," he said. He put a hand to his left knee to help him rise, clutching the shards of cup and saucer in his other hand.

"It's essential to be practical after a funeral," said Michelin, addressing him rather than Sheila, as if now taking his side. "One has to do something after a funeral." She was drinking a spritzer, as was her evening habit. The kitchen television set was tuned to Channel Four. A domestic drama was on. They had taken up an incident in the play for discussion and, as so often, sharing little of the public humility before the medium, they found their own opinions more interesting than Channel Four's offering.

"I am doing something," Clement said. "And more than just breaking tea cups. I'm always doing things. The puzzle is the small effect they seem to have." He piled the broken pieces of china, with their crisp edges and interesting shapes, on the draining board.

"After a funeral," Michelin continued, "one holds a memorial service — at least we do in France. Or orders a stone angel, or polishes up the photo frames. And of course goes round talking endlessly regarding the dead —

163

favourably at first and then, as the flowers on the grave wither, more freely and scandalously. . . ."

"I did think of a memorial service," said Clement, "but I couldn't be quite sure who would come. Do you think that universities in Singapore, Medan and Bangkok would have sent representatives, because I don't."

"You're fortunate, Clem. You have plenty to do. You don't have to polish up photo frames," said Sheila. "You have all Joseph's junk to look into, all his secrets to nose out. You can find out if you will all his scandalous relationships with women. That Lucy Traill woman, for instance. It's of moment to you if no one else. As you say, people in Singapore are hardly interested, but now that your brother is dead, you can turn his life into your hobby."

"You're being unpleasant."

"No, it's a perfectly legitimate hobby. Why don't you go over to that flat of his in Acton again and sort out the rest of his things? The sooner you sell that place, the better, after all. Just don't be made miserable. Why should his death upset you? You saw little enough of each other. You disliked his political views."

"No, I didn't, I admired many of them, though I felt he held some of them for the wrong reasons. If you'd been nicer to him, he would have come over to see us more often."

"I was nice to him, most of the time. He was jolly, but whenever he came over for the weekend, he used to booze and get argumentative. At your mother's funeral in Nettlesham — well, you both went out and got thoroughly plastered, didn't you? Like a couple of overgrown boys."

He remembered the occasion, and frowned. "I certainly don't forget how you attacked Joe that evening. I'm amazed you choose to mention it. No wonder we didn't see much of him after that."

Sheila remained unperturbed, smiling conspiratorially at Michelin. "It's true I told him a few home truths that evening. Also, I didn't care much for some of the women he brought over here. You remember that Filipino girl — Carmilla, was it? I swear she stole that pair of gold earrings off my dressing-table." She laughed at the memory.

Clement laughed. "And she was sick in the lavatory. Carmilla was a disaster, admittedly." He helped himself to more white wine.

"Then there was that physiotherapist of his. You remember her, Michelin? Lucy Traill. The unmarried mother, right?"

As it happened, Clement had taken a fancy to Lucy Traill, liking her spirit. He knew, too, that she had a more permanent place in Joseph's later years than any other woman. So he said, "Not an unmarried mother, Sheila, please. Lucy was a one-parent family. Keep your terms up to date."

Ignoring this, Sheila continued, "Joseph brought her over a couple of times, the first time with that awful child of hers. The second time, she'd only been in the house for half-an-hour when she started manipulating my shoulders! It was like being seized by a mad wrestler."

They all laughed. Clement said, "You thought she had gay aspirations towards you."

"She said I was suffering from something or other and needed Alexander technique. I thought it was something to do with sex."

Amid laughter, Clement said, "She was quite sexy. She used the word 'posture' rather adroitly, I recall."

"Oh, and we heard them arguing in the bedroom at night. That was because Lucy wanted to go off on some CND march, wasn't it?"

"She tried to speak to me in French, and wasn't at all good at it," Michelin said. "After family deaths in Languedoc, there often follows increased drinking and risks of suicide. It is related to a tendency to stay indoors more, so as not to meet other people who will fail to comprehend your grief. Then the lack of blue sky overhead tends to promote mental illness, and pretty soon the house of grief is again a house of illness. What's the word? Terminal illness."

"In England, too, one marriage partner tends to follow the other to an early grave," Sheila said. "The bereaved often suffers a heart attack. It must be the same in France, and elsewhere."

"There's more drinking in France than here." Thus reminding herself, Michelin gave them all a refill of wine.

"Those drinking statistics are highly suspect. I've always thought so. French drinking is mainly wine and aperitifs. Over here the stuff is harder. The further north you go, the more fiery the liquors consumed."

"I'm not exactly suffering from grief," said Clement, "and can manage without fiery liquor, thanks. I would just like to be able to put my brother's life in order, that's all."

"You mean put his papers in order, Clem. Putting your brother's life in order is a big commitment."

Clement nodded at Michelin to show that she had made her point, and said to Sheila, "I think I will take your suggestion and drive up to Acton to the flat. Will you come too?"

She spread her hands. "Oh, I have so much to catch up with here. No, no, I'm just so busy. I'd only be in your way. Acton depresses me. There are so many letters to answer and I'm still feeling the effects of jet-lag. Besides, you like to be there alone — you can be as melancholy as you wish. One thing I have against Joseph was his attitude towards his parents. I suppose you might say I am no judge because my childhood was so idyllic. But he was very vengeful towards them, blaming them for all sorts of things that were his own fault. That's a token of weakness of character. From what I saw of your parents, they were perfectly nice ordinary people. You thought so, Clem, you know you did."

"We may have been brothers but we were born in rather different circumstances. In this notebook" — he indicated the green-covered book — "Joseph makes the case against our parents very clearly. I consider he was treated with monstrous insensitivity as a child. When I came along, family circumstances were different, and they behaved rather better towards me."

"I can believe that," agreed Michelin. "Very often in a family there is one child on whom all the family anger is visited. It may be a boy or a girl. The other children are treated kindly, even spoilt, yet the one unfortunate child is given a very bad time, is not loved, is starved, or whatever the special beastliness of the house may be. We have a lot of that in France, too. Nothing seems to explain why one particular child should be treated so."

"My brother has an explanation," said Clement.

"You admire him, don't you?"

"I admire him because, despite the way he was treated, he never exhibited the slightest jealousy towards Ellen or me. She and I failed to realise how he suffered, how desperate he was, but he never showed us other than his gentlest side."

"He probably thought it was his destiny to suffer," said Sheila.

"Destiny is rather an old-fashioned word these days. We talk about genetic inheritance instead."

The heatwave persisted over the south of England. After only a week of dry weather, there were already warnings of drought and water shortage. Householders were urged not to use their hoses. Standpipes were installed in the West Country. There was a plague of ladybirds in Kent. Inspired by the heat, British holiday-makers went abroad in their thousands, in quest of even higher temperatures. A bomb exploded in a tourist hotel in Tunisia, injuring ten British tourists.

Acton looked cheerful in the sunshine. When Clement Winter arrived towards noon the next day, men and women were already standing on the pavement outside pubs, drinking and taking in the sun, enjoying the start of the weekend. He parked the Mercedes in Chesterfield Street. His dead brother's flat occupied the upper floor of No. 22, a house which had been built in some indeterminate period either before or after the first World

War, when people had said that house-building had reached its nadir, simply because they had not the gift to see into the future. The street had been designed to provide cheap housing for an upwardly mobile lower middle class. Although the houses almost touched each other, they were detached within the strict meaning of the term. They had bay windows and a small porch with a half-hearted Gothic decoration. The front door of No. 22 contained stained glass offering a vague memory of some mullioned pile from which it was remotely descended. The front garden, although no larger than a senior executive's desk, boasted a holly tree.

The ingenuity of the builder had been taxed when it came to the matter of class distinction. Yet, even with the limited space at his command, he had solved it, as far as anyone could tell, to the satisfaction of many generations of denizens of Chesterfield Street. The narrow brick facade of each house was crammed with a porch and front door, a bay window, and a second door, designed solely for the use of tradesmen, maids, bootboys, or similar inferior species. There being no access to the rear of the house, the builder had inserted the back door at the front, making it lower than the front door, to which one step led up, by three steps which led down, thus plainly denoting its reduced status.

This inferior door still bore on it a legend saying TRADESMEN ONLY, despite the fact that many of the houses in Chesterfield Street were now occupied by the tradesmen themselves. Beside the legend on the inferior door of No. 22 was a note on card in waterproof ink, but smudged nevertheless, saying J. WINTER. Clement had no doubt that Joseph had enjoyed this wry joke.

He went to unlock the door but found it ajar. Proceeding inside cautiously, he ascended the narrowest of stairways, carpeted with worn staircarpet, and became conscious of the smell of the place. It comprised a mixture of dirt, nutmeg, and imprisoned heat. It halted him for a moment on the stair, as if he were trying to remember something. Then he heard a noise above, and went slowly forward.

He reached a narrow upper hall from which four doors led. One door was open. A burly man poked his head out and asked of Clement in a suspicious voice, "Who may you be when you're at home?"

"I should be asking you that. And how did you get in?"

For answer, the burly man fished in his pocket and triumphantly produced a key, which he held upwards, rather as if it had been a small sword.

"You'll be the posh brother from Oxford," he said. "Cheers."

"I'll have that key, thanks, and I'd still like to know who you are."

The burly man came out on the landing. He wore trainers, jeans, and a blue shirt open almost to his navel. There was a casual, open-air look to him. He bore a tattoo and a gilt bracelet on his left arm. He held out the key to Clement, grinning as he did so.

"Possession being nine points of the law and the law being nine points about possession," he said. "I'm Ron Mallock, good friend of your late brother's, known him many years."

"You weren't at the funeral."

"I'm an atheist, same as what Joe was. He'd have laughed if he saw you giving him a Christian burial. I come here to pick up some disarmament pamphlets I should have got hold of before."

He retreated into the rear room. Clement followed, feeling slightly at a loss, still conscious of the heat and scent of the flat.

"None of this stuff is your property, you know," he ventured.

Ron Mallock flashed a smile. "Funerals, property. . . . What next? I'm not trying to rob you, chum, I'm just looking for a few pamphlets. I don't imagine you're a member of CND, are you? — so I can't think it would hurt you if I collected them. Your brother and I ran the local branch, you know."

"We're still waiting for probate," Clement said, becoming conscious at once of the inadequacy of his reply.

Ron Mallock gave a half-grin but made no answer. Instead, he got on his knees and crawled under the gateleg table which occupied the centre of the room, where stacks of *Marxism Today* and other periodicals had found a resting place.

There was little furniture in the room. In one corner lay a pile of grey blankets. Papers were everywhere. Conspicuous among the books were many volumes of B. Traven who, Clement knew, was a favourite of Joseph's. Where not occupied by bookshelves, the walls were covered with threatening-looking posters in various languages; the Polish Solidarity sign was among them. In contrast was a delicate Korean Buddha, standing on a window sill. A desk by the window and a side table were covered with more pamphlets and papers, some in Eastern alphabets. Half-empty bottles of wine and stronger liquor stood on the mantelpiece, together with a mug lacking a handle.

Everything was as Clement had last seen it. It was a comfortably squalid room. He had visited many like it in Oxford, rotting here and there in old mansions which had once been family houses. It was a place where book-work was done. Its stuffy yet curiously inviting smell made Clement think of drugs. As if to emphasise the heat, flies buzzed about the room or darted their little dynamic bodies against the windows.

Seeing Ron Mallock sink back on his heels and begin to read through a book on the Vietnam War, Clement made impatient noises.

"Sorry, don't mind me. I'm having the day off. I'll be sad when this lot goes. This place has been a home-from-home for me. I've got a place over in Brentford. You don't mind me being here?"

"Well, not a lot, I suppose," said Clement, seating himself in an old wicker chair with rather more force than necessary.

"Here's the morning paper." Ron took a folded copy of the *Daily Mirror* out of his rear pocket and threw it across to Clement. "You might like a read. Take it easy — you look pale."

Clement accepted the newspaper rather shame-facedly, thinking that after all this man had probably been a better friend to Joseph than he had.

The front page of the paper carried a huge headline, TUNIS TRAGEDY. and an account in various weights of type of how bombs had exploded in four luxury hotels in Monastir, on the Tunisian coast. Six English people, all women and children, had been injured. Despite reassurances from the Tunisian government, British tourists were now flocking home by the hundred, cutting short their holidays and heading for safety.

"Terrible, i'n't it?" said Ron, catching Clement's eye.

"Yes, it is. Innocent holiday-makers."

"Terrible the way they panic and all start rushing home at one little spot of bother."

"The Arab world is rather in ferment at present. What reassurances can a government possibly give that more bombs won't be planted? Agreed, Tunis is pretty peaceful, but you can't take chances. If I were there with my family, I'd bring them back home pretty promptly. It would not be a case of panic, rather of simple caution, surely."

"These people don't know anything. Rich tourists. They're selfish." Ron spoke as if he had not heard Clement's reply. "They just panic and rush home with never a thought that they might be ruining the tourist trade on which the Tunisians depend. So the Third World gets poorer and poorer and suffers a further decline. More victimisation by the Developed Countries."

"If I were in one of those hotels, I would think of my family before the local tourist trade, wouldn't you?"

"There you go, the extortion of the Third World. This will scare off the American tourists, you'll see, and they will all stay at home. It's the Americans' fault in the first place, all this."

"How do you make that out?"

"Obvious, isn't it? Start a lot of oppression, gang up with Israel, this is what you get."

"I feel I mustn't take up any more of your time. If you can find those pamphlets, well and good. I must have the flat to myself, since I hope to tidy everything up. Besides, I'm hoping to write a book on my brother. . . ."

Ron stood up. "And what sort of a book will it be, may I ask?"

"That's what I haven't quite decided. I'm keeping an open mind until all the evidence is in."

"An open mind, eh?" Ron appeared to think about it. "Yet I gather from what you say that you're a Tory?"

"As a matter of fact, no, I'm not. I'm a socialist — a socialist with rather a small 's' these days, I'm afraid, but still a socialist."

Ron laughed, showing a lot of white teeth and looking amazingly well. "You're kidding. Listen, Mr Winter, your brother was a really good man. There was a side to him you maybe never saw. He worried greatly about the rotten social system in this country, and all the misery it brings. And he cared about the Third World — especially the nations of South East Asia, which he often visited. Such as Kampuchea, ruined by American Imperialism. You'd better put all that in your book."

"I intend to."

"And put in that he was a sensitive man who cared for the spiritual side of life. Not a man of action, you wouldn't say, more your dreamer, but none the worse for that. A scholar and a gentleman."

"I thought he didn't have much time for gentlemen."

"It's just a saying, isn't it? He had revelations, your brother. Which is more than what I have. Or you, I daresay."

Feeling his temper rise, Clement said nothing.

Ron hefted the volume he had been looking at. "I'd better be off if my presence offends you. Let's have my paper. I don't see the CND pamphlets anywhere, but I'll just borrow this book, if you've no objections."

Clement made a gesture and opened his mouth to speak.

Ron said quickly, "Oh, I know, don't tell me. Probate. Keep the book, and good luck to you. I'm not a thief, you know."

As he left the room, Clement shouted, "Take the bloody book if you want it." He felt rather feverish.

Clumping down the stairs, Ron Mallock shouted a response which Clement did not hear. As he left by the tradesman's entrance, he slammed the door shut behind him.

Clement wandered round the room, vaguely vexed. He opened a window where a fly buzzed and stared out over the unappetising prospect of back yards and broken roofs. He could hear his heart beating and wondered why he was so upset.

Perhaps he was not the sort of man to write his brother's biography.

It was true he did not have revelations. Life had to be lived on a low plane, without sudden glimpses of the numinous. The survivors of the war, chief witnesses in his work on adaptability, testified to finding God in merciful escapes from death among ruins. There had been no similar challenges for Clement, barely seven when the war ended; he remembered nothing of it, only the return of bananas when it was all over. His was a peaceful peacetime existence, without especial exhilarations.

Of course there was Sheila, the great consolation. Her pleasantness, day by day and year by year, was a form of revelation for which he was grateful.

At last he turned away from the window, conscious of the stuffy silence of the flat surrounding him. Death — the ultimate in probate — had immobilised it. He walked uncertainly through the other rooms, the poky bathroom/toilet, the kitchen/diner where Joseph's body had been found, the bedroom with its unmade bed. Each room had an individual silence and individual smell.

On a shelf in the bedroom stood a large framed photograph of Lucy Traill, Joseph's last girlfriend, standing her ground while a small child tried to wrench her arm off. Tucked into the frame of this photograph was an old snapshot — rather surprisingly — of Ernest Winter, Joseph and Clement's father. In his early fifties, he was standing by a privet hedge, holding a large pair of shears and smiling uncertainly into the camera. His appeared an intelligent face, although Clement never ceased to be astonished at how little of their owners' faces gave away. Even hands were more revealing.

Ernest Winter had died at the age of seventy-one, when Clement was thirty-one. Clement tucked the snap back where he had found it.

Going down to the car with some boxes, he came up again carrying two empty suitcases, into which he started to pile his brother's clothes. There was nothing he wanted himself. It was cheap stuff, well worn. Michelin could take it to Oxfam. He hesitated once, when he came on Joseph's bush hat, moth-eaten souvenir of his years in Burma, the Fourteenth Army flash still sewn on its brim. Joseph would like him to keep that.

The journeys up and down stairs made him feel weak. A certain delicacy prevented him from stretching out on the bed. He sat in the cramped living room, with its curious drugged scent.

In the ancient, battered roll-top desk, bought doubtless from a local junk dealer, he found various CND leaflets, probably the ones Ron Mallock had been seeking. With them was a bundle of letters, secured by a rubber band. Clement bent over to lift them out into the light. Again that smell came to him, strong as a herb. He found himself incapable of moving from the stooped position. Time passed in dull, thick pulses.

He saw that it was in fact a long way across the room, a distance hardly to be measured, which wound its way through barricades of books. They were depicted in a vivid purple light which he felt did not deceive him for a minute. Through the open door lay another extravagant vista, seen as if through a weight of water, attended by bar-like wooden banisters and a shabby rug which lay in wait for an unwary footfall. It took time as much as anything to observe these things. At the far end of this distressing view was a strip of wall and another open door, painted dull brown. Through the dull door, a fragment of the kitchen could be seen, and there a man was standing at the sink, washing his hands with slow and portentous industry.

It was crucial that this man should not turn round and see Clement, who had become small as well as immobile. The likelihood was that the man would turn round, since the fatal scent in the air, which found its way to Clement, emanated from this figure.

Somehow, Clement found himself able to see the porcelain sink, and the stream of water falling, falling from a thin tap down on a pair of veined white hands, and a bar of soap revolving slowly over and over in the grasp of the hands, foaming terribly as it went, as if it bled. This he was forced to watch, all the while fearing that the man would turn round — he would be bound to turn round slowly, but turn round he would — and look at him. That was to be avoided at all cost. The flies in the room were making a terrible noise.

The bar of soap went on foaming and revolving, in some way independent of anything else that was happening, for the man was now drying his hands on a towel, his veined white hands now repeating their previous movements under the tap into the folds of towelling. And he was turning round.

Clement thought that it was time he took another breath, an action that proved laboriously difficult to carry out, stooped as he was. He caught the sounds of his own lungs and imagined them down below somewhere, sponge-like and flapping in a strong wind.

His brother had now turned completely round. He still held the towel. Now he was advancing on Clement. Considering how far there was to come, he advanced with terrifying rapidity. The towel trailed behind him, leading all the way back into the kitchen.

He entered the living room. Clement remained bent over the open desk.

Although his brother's face was pallid, it bore a smile. He was near now. He stood over Clement. With a great effort, Clement rose to his feet and confronted Joseph.

Joseph said, "Everything worked out all right."

Then he was gone.

For a long while, Clement stood where he was, listening to the flies buzzing against the window pane. The strange scent had disappeared. With automatic movements, he went over to close the window he had opened.

Still clutching the bundle of letters, he moved down the stairs, down the steps covered with their old brown carpeting. Outside, the street looked unnaturally bright, the Mercedes against the curb unnaturally large. Somehow, he locked the tradesman's entrance of the flat behind him and crossed the pavement to his car.

He sat there for several minutes, breathing slowly, before driving away.

XII

Sheila was sympathetic.

"You poor darling, it's not like you to see things."

"There Joseph stood, as close as you are to me. He said 'Everything worked out all right' — almost like a voice from the grave. I couldn't have seen him more clearly. He had been washing his hands."

"You poor darling," she said again. "It's the heat. Temperatures were over ninety in Somerville when they took the noon reading. Why don't you go up and get into bed and I'll have Michelin bring you up a nice light supper.

"Perhaps I'll do that," Clement said. "It sounds a bit feeble."

"You're allowed to be feeble once in a while."

"'Everything worked out all right. . . .' I can still hear his voice. It was amazing."

"Would you like me to get Dr Lloyd?"

"No, I'll go and have a bath as you suggest."

"Have a nice cool bath. Not too cool. Perhaps I'll take your temperature."

When he lowered his flabby bulk into the bath, Clement lay there half-submerged. He was unable to wash himself. Staring at the tablet of bath soap, his mind returned to that other bar of soap in Chesterfield Street, slowly revolving, foaming its substance away in Joseph's hands. What had it signified? He tried to answer the question clinically, imagining it posed by Mrs Emerova. Answer would not come: only the vision of the soap rotating, its colour now forgotten, and the minute linked bubbles of foam falling away from it, regularly.

After the bath, he slid into bed between the sheets, to find himself shivering. He could not get to grips with himself or with his recent experience. The functioning of his brain seemed oddly affected, although he could not explain how. Nor was it possible for him to decide whether he had actually received a visitation from his brother, or whether he had had some sort of illness, say a minor stroke, which had caused a vivid hallucination. The latter possibility left him unmoved; strokes were part of the rational world. Far more alarming was the prospect that his brother might actually have come back from the dead to speak to him; the rational world had no place for such events.

Suppose, against all belief, Joseph had returned. The meaning of "Everything worked out all right" was still obscure. Probably Joseph was referring to his own life. Or was he referring to Clement's problem with the book, or with Sheila? Perhaps he meant that the whole confused world worked out all right, on evidence from some superior time-annihilating position of vantage granted those who had died. . . .

It was more comfortable to suppose that the whole episode had been a delusion. Heat may have played a part. Clement remembered the smell of the flat; it might also have had a disturbing effect on the mind.

He dozed lightly, hearing traffic go by in Rawlinson Road. When he roused, his head felt better and he noted that he was less uneasy, at least until the thought of Mrs Emerova came into his mind. It would be difficult communicating this new episode in his life to her.

"It was a vision of some kind. One hates using the word because of its Biblical connotations, but a vision is what it was: something between reality and unreality."

"Do you mean between objective and subjective? Is there such a state?"

"Why do you look at me like that? I suppose you think the whole thing was just an outcrop of disturbed sexuality?"

"Is that what you feel it was?"

"It was just a joke. Maybe I was just having a kind of brain storm. I was rather upset by the friend of Joseph's I met there, Ron Mallock."

"Why did he upset you?"

"Oh, he was just talking about the Campaign for Nuclear Disarmament. . . ."

Suddenly, Clement remembered that a psychotherapist of his acquaintance at Carisbrooke had told him over drinks that two of his patients were high-ranking members of the CND who had come for treatment, in conditions of utmost confidentiality, because they found that competing with their wish to ban the bomb was a strong desire to see it dropped. Wish and fear were close neighbours; opposites attracted.

In a similar way, his vision in the Acton flat seemed to incorporate opposites, fear and reassurance, or his love of his brother and his hatred of him. Joseph had excluded him from his life.

Feeling slightly perked up, Clement sat up in bed and adjusted his pillows. The untidy bundle of letters he had brought from Acton lay on his bedside table. Taking them up rather feebly, Clement began to shuffle through them.

With one exception, the letters were from Lucy Traill, the last of

Joseph's long succession of girl-friends. He knew Lucy was a physiotherapist, from the disastrous occasion when she had tried to practise her art on Sheila. He also remembered, as soon as he started to read the letters, that she was an ardent supporter of CND, and that Joseph had met her on some demonstration or march. She worked in a hospital in Richmond, and lived with Joseph only at weekends, which explained both the letters and their highly-charged sexual content.

Lucy was good at describing in detail what she and Joseph had done the previous weekend, and what she wanted them to do when next they met. The uninhibited nature of the correspondence caused Clement to stir uneasily in the bed.

He and Sheila rarely talked much about sex. Nor was there much in the way of description of sexual activity in Sheila's Kerinth novels. Yet vivid and happy memories came back to him of their early years of marriage, when they had both discovered in themselves a desire for sexual intercourse out of doors. They had done it wherever and whenever they could, sometimes tumbling out of cars to perform in a lane or a field, quickly before anyone saw them—Sheila had always been fast off the button. They had done it in parks, in woods, by roaring motorways, on beaches. They had done it lying down, or had enjoyed knee-tremblers against trees in the rain.

Thought of those happy years brought a gush of pleasure to him. How close they had been! — And still were, perhaps because of that carefree, randy time. It had ceased with the birth of their daughter, Juliet, in 1970.

He sighed, still not willing to think of Juliet, and opened another of Lucy's letters.

After a long description of their next encounter in bed, she wrote, "But all these joys may never be. You have been increasingly strange lately, not even coming on the last demonstration. We put on a great show outside the base at Lakenheath, yet you weren't there. And that remark of yours about the Pershings — that they weren't pointing at us. Okay, I know you were drunk. It was in *The Queen's Arms*, remember. There was a sudden hush. Everyone suddenly shut up and stared at you. I felt such a fool. We have to be united, firm in our beliefs. Every missile in the world points at us. If you're going to give up now, just when we seem to be succeeding, don't count on me to be around."

Her next letter showed that Joseph had given a reply she found unsatisfactory. Her tone was abusive.

Joseph had made a pained and elaborate response. That it had been important to him was indicated by the fact that he had typed it out on an old manual typewriter and kept a carbon copy. It was dated January 1987.

My darling Lucy,

We've always been honest with each other. I know the taste of your mind as well as I do the taste of your fanny. You're a zealot — as I am, but it appears our zealotry sometimes goes in different directions. I just hope we don't. I love you madly and would even overcome my rooted objection to marriage if it suited you, and adopt your kid, I suppose.

I'm older than you by quite a bit. You're a child of the Cold War, born early fifties, whereas I did such growing up as I was ever going to manage in the World War. So I'm going to bore and irritate you (in a good cause) with MY story of the BOMB. I want to try and set it all down. You clearly confuse sex and CND, like many of our comrades. I confuse the Bomb and Life. Like this. Darling, I dig your deepest depths, please read this. Don't be impatient. Assume a Zen posture.

You know Japan only as a distant country which showers down upon us all the electronic gadgets we now take for granted. You can't imagine what a different face Japan showed to those who fell within her power. I fought against them in Burma, when our commander-in-chief referred to the Japs as "fighting insects". They were rightly feared as pitiless — to themselves and others. They struck the first blow. They were an enemy who had to be fought and conquered.

After the Burma campaign, while the war was still on, my division, part of the Forgotten Army, was sent back to India and there disbanded. I was posted to a camp near Bangalore, and from there to Madras where, in hot and primitive conditions, we were set to practising amphibious landings.

We used landing craft which had been returned from operations in the Middle East. Old boats, good enough for South East Asia Command. These were the craft we were to employ in an assault on the Japanese armies ensconced in Singapore and Malaya.

This assault had a code name. Operation Zipper. The rumour was that we were to attack Singapore from the sea — this vauntedly impregnable fortress — and to invade the complex western coast of Malaya. Much later, it was discovered that some of the designated beaches in the Port Swettenham area were impossible places in which to land, with dangerous currents sweeping the beaches and mangrove swamps behind the beaches. Training for Zipper caused severe low morale, particularly for those of us who had served in Burma.

I tell you this for background to what follows.

Some luck came my way. I was unexpectedly posted from Madras to Bombay, to act as Out Clerk in a signals office there.

For the first time, I had some idea of what it would be like to be detached from the army, which by this time I hated. Instead of sleeping in a mildewed Great War tent on a strip of Madrassi desert, I found myself in a private house standing in a private road near Breach Candy, the luxurious bathing pool by the sea. I enjoyed that blessed luxury, a room to myself, and a bearer to look after me. I also enjoyed an unconsummated love affair — you don't even know what the words mean, but life was different then — with a WAC(I) called Mary. The initials stand for Women's Auxiliary Corps (India). I can't tell you the racist and sexist insults poor Mary put up with in our signal office, where I was her defender, and fought a dispatch rider who insulted her vilely. This little affair went some way to satisfying the hungers of the soul. Oh, the hungers of my bloody soul. But on, on to the Bomb. . . .

Despite all my manoeuvres, I found it impossible to anchor myself to Bombay. After a month, I came under orders to return to Madras, as if the dread Operation Zipper couldn't start without me. I went back to my division (now the 26th Indian Div.). It was early August, 1945.

We woke one morning to find that the atom bomb had been dropped on Hiroshima.

Ever since then — since that merciful time when Operation Zipper was cancelled — I have been a student of what manoeuvres went on on the international scene. It was a crucial period in the history of the war.

So much savagery was unleashed on the world. That savagery is always there, in war or peace — something has to contain it. All we know to contain it so far is the threat of retribution. The way Mater contained me.

Japan in 1945 was a country slowly succumbing to starvation. American B-29 fire raids on Tokyo were killing 80,000 civilians and injuring over half that number in one night. Yet there were high officers in the Japanese military who believed that the war must continue at all costs, for honour's sake, if necessary to the last man, woman, and child. They thought like that.

However, Japan's foreign minister, Togo, was suing for peace. He sued in the wrong place. He directed his efforts at Moscow, capital of what he took to be a neutral country as far as Japan was concerned. But devious plans were in the making. Stalin was secretly preparing to attack the Japanese in Manchuria and then to press on to the home islands. He wanted a presence in Tokyo itself. So his foreign minister, Molotov, found it convenient not to see Togo's ambassador.

On the 2nd August, Togo cabled that ambassador, ordering him to speak to Molotov. A note of desperation breaks through the stiff diplomatic politeness. Togo said, "Since the loss of one day relative to this present matter may result in a thousand years of regret, it is requested that you immediately have a talk with Molotov."

It was not to be. The nearer the weir, the faster the water. The slow and secret preparations to manufacture an atomic bomb — the Manhattan Project — to be dropped on Germany were complete. The bomb was ready, but Nazi Germany was already out of the war.

You're supposed to know all this, but you refuse to bloody think about the past.

On the 5th August, the crew of a B–29 christened the *Enola Gay* ate a midnight breakfast of eggs, sausage, toast and coffee, and then attended a church service. In the early hours of the 6th August, the *Enola Gay* took off. This was from a small airstrip on Tinian, an island near Guam. They had the bomb aboard, and were accompanied by a weather plane.

Their target was Hiroshima, an army centre and military supply port. The flight was without event. The bomb was dropped from an altitude of 31,600 feet on a city just going about its morning business. A peaceful city, an enemy city. 71,379 people were killed or just went missing, 68,023 were injured.

The world changed, Lucy. Never has there been such a clear-cut division between one age and the next as that marked by the mushroom cloud boiling up over Hiroshima. All that savagery and hate had found technological embodiment.

This first bomb, code name Little Boy, was a uranium bomb. On the 9th of August, a plutonium bomb was dropped on the seaport of Nagasaki. In the time between these two bombs, on the 8th of August, the Soviet Union declared war on Japan. (Did you know that? What an hour to strike!) Japan surrendered unconditionally on the 14th of August.

It's a bit of a platitude now, but you see that the last military act of World War II was also the first political act of the peace that followed — or rather of that uncertain state between peace and war we call the Cold War. The Russians could go no farther, and Tokyo did not become the Berlin of the Far East, quarrelled over by the major powers.

At the time of the armistice, a Japanese report stated simply, "The whole city of Hiroshima was destroyed instantly by a single bomb."

Is that what we've had to face ever since, or the savagery and hate which conjured up the bomb in the first place?

Do you know what we did when we heard the news from Hiroshima? "Fucking great!" we said. We rejoiced. They had it coming to them. That's what we thought.

A third bomb would have been ready from 15th August onwards. Even on the 13th August, the day before the Japanese surrender, the war was still very much in progress. The Soviets were advancing across Manchuria, American naval and air attacks were carried out against Tokyo and Kyushu, and I was jumping from a boat into four feet of water with a 22-set on my back. A Japanese war party was opposing their government's attempts to terminate the struggle. In the Japanese cabinet itself, fierce dissension raged; only the concession by the Allies that the Emperor Hirohito could retain the throne decided the Japanese to sue for peace, and not to fight on despite the bombs.

Hirohito himself said, "I cannot endure the thought of letting my people suffer any longer. A continuation of the war will bring death to tens, perhaps even hundreds, of thousands of persons."

So it was all over, and we were supposed to become ordinary people again.

Forty years on, and consciences are still troubled about this dramatic conclusion to the biggest show of the century. They are mainly post-bellum consciences. At the time, peace at any price was the cry. Britain had been at war for six years.

You may think this is special pleading, but, if the war had continued in the East, it would have entailed many more fire-bombings of Japanese cities and most probably an invasion by sea of the Japanese mainland. Losses on both sides would have been formidably high.

Earl Mountbatten and Commander Slim, on the British side, inherited large parts of what had been the "Greater East Asia Co-prosperity Sphere", where 128 million people awaited rehabilitation after the War's end. Among them, spread over a wide area, 750,000 Japanese were still at large, often prepared to fight on till death (some who never heard the news of the surrender were still on standby twenty years later.) Some 125,000 Allied prisoners-of-war were also awaiting rescue from death by starvation or torture.

As for the Americans, whom all good followers of CND are supposed to mistrust, it was different in 1945. Grave responsibilities faced them. There were already signs that the Soviet Union would turn at any moment from untrustworthy ally into enemy, and might be disposed to sweep westwards through an incapacitated Europe when it was denied Japan. It was foreseen that, in the coming winter of 1945–46, millions of Europeans would die of starvation if America did not promptly shoulder the responsibility for feeding them — a responsibility it would hardly have been possible to undertake if the war in the East were still raging.

On every count, the sudden armistice procured by the two A-bombs was a life-saver all round the globe. Not least to those of us on Operation Zipper. To this day, I believe that most of our lives were saved by Little Boy and its sinister companion. Many men who survived the War in the East will carry that same belief with them to the grave.

After the Japanese surrender came the immense task of putting things back in the boxes where they belonged. 26 Indian Div was part of that mopping up operation. We put to sea from Madras and, on the 4th of October 1945, islands loomed out of the fog before us. We had crossed the line. Ahead of us lay Sumatra, and a peace that was not peace.

Perhaps there's no such thing as peace. There's too much hate and savagery. You know how much of those emotions we meet with in the ranks. Don't we generate hate to keep our morale up?

All this explains why I had to have a very deep change of heart before I went on my first Ban the Bomb march to Aldermaston. I had to suppress my emotional response to the bomb and allow my intellect to win. My intellect told me that it was insane to drop nuclear bombs on anyone. Even the Russians. (Sorry!)

But you see really my stand regarding the bomb was about something else, deep down in that part of us which construes its own version of reality. The hatred of authority came into it. Ever since my schooldays, I have hated authority. They rule by force, whether with canes or nuclear arms. It's an Us or Them situation. I'm always the underdog. As the Far East experience wore off, I began more and more to interpret the country's nuclear policy as an excuse for authoritarianism. Something against which to revolt.

And another persuader. I had a grudge against England. It let me down. I fought for this fucking country and it paid me off in pennies. I came back here from the East pretty well destitute, and have had to fend for myself as an underdog ever since. Let's face it, all this history over which I sweat, year in, year out, brings no reward, in terms of money or respect. It didn't even bring me you — you came to me through CND, where many of those with some grudge or other against their country find refuge. Some of them long to see the bomb dropped on Mrs Thatcher.

Hatred of authority, grudge against England. Emotive reasons for screaming Ban the Bomb and singing We Shall Overcome. How wonderful to have the pigs grab you up by your duffel coat and dump you in their van. Through the veins goes pure cleansing hatred. Very cathartic.

So I was as keen a marcher as anyone. It made me feel good. And I pulled women. I'm funny, I know. Can't resist a female body, can't establish a lasting relationship. Some fundamental mistrust driving me. . . .

Shit. Anyhow, I also made pals like Ron Mallock. A good drinking friend. And met you.

When you took me to Greenham Common to see the women living rough and laying siege to the base, I became even more emotionally devoted to the cause. That was just before Christmas 1983. The women sang that carol — "Peace on Earth and Mercy mild" — as they rattled the wire. They wore their kind of informal uniform, wrapped up against the cold in woollen hats, bright scarves, heavy coats, striped leg-warmers, and boots. They didn't use make-up. They had something going between them: they were a tribe. They lived in those tattered improvised tents among the trees and bracken, some with kids. Camp fires smouldered among the leafless trees, the smoke filtering up towards a clouded sky. We saw one woman pull up her clothes and shit among the ferns, careless of who might be looking. They were a tribe. I understood; it was their Burma.

And they were laying siege to an RAF camp. The RAF! In my schooldays, the heroes of the Battle of Britain, the country's saviours. . . . All that forgotten by a new generation. What a reversal. This is that fatal phenomenon at the heart of the sodding world, enantiodromia, the incessant and inevitable turning of all things into their opposites.

The women didn't want me around the Common. They only tolerated me because they knew you and respected you. You'd been with them. You were one of them.

They had a cause. And to prove it helicopters roared overhead, photographing them, and police guarded the perimeter, and troops waited inside the perimeter. And we stumbled across a posse of mounted police, sitting silent on their horses in a straggling copse of silver birch, awaiting word over their intercoms to charge.

I felt in my bones the women were right. That whatever the pros and cons of the international situation, nuclear weapons were too obscene ever to be used. Someone had to speak up against them — and of course it would have to be the underdogs, who would die in their hundreds of thousands if the weapons were unleashed.

How those women moved me! That day I was whole-hearted. Remember how we clutched each other. Here at last was a spirit that would vanquish war. All your feminism made sense then. Laughing, I quoted to you the old poet of my youth, William Westlake:

> Those men forget who pray for arms to cease
> War but enacts the mischief sown in Peace.

It seemed then, in that encampment already half at war, that Westlake was talking through his hat.

That day I was whole-hearted. Just to be whole-hearted filled me with energy. Perhaps you remember how we screwed in the back of my van, clothes and boots still on. God, I enjoyed that. Somehow love and revenge were all mixed up in my fucking head.

We've had such good times. Don't leave me now. Please. I need you. Forget ideology, remember me.

. . . It's four in the sodding morning. Another glass of whisky and perhaps I'll finish this — whatever it is. I know nothing about life, nothing. I'm as ignorant as the day I was born.

Lucy. I no longer feel as I did that day at Greenham Common. Useless to camouflage the fact. You know I had that amazing revelation on the night of the full moon, November last year in Dorset. In a few short weeks, it has changed my life. I told you about it, or tried to.

I saw then that all my years I had somehow been mistaken. I'm too tired to go into it, and in any case why should it matter to you? It concerns only me, my little dot of consciousness which, I'm well aware, is of such small consequence to anyone but its possessor.

But the result was — still is, the process still goes on — a complete revision of everything I have lived. Christ, that's about sixty years of life and still I'm not tired of pursuing some phantom of perfection, of trying to make myself . . . complete, perfect? . . . No, make myself into something I can't clearly see until I get there. But a person who lives and breathes truth. . . . (Don't laugh.)

For all its miseries, I have lived life so passionately. You've felt it, or you'd not have cared, for you too have passion — and not just sexual passion. Your job is the manipulation of human bodies, trying to make them better.

I've been like that, but all the time I have operated under a bad misconstruction. A self-inflicted misconstruction, set up in self-defence by the unhappy child I once was.

It has warped my emotional life. I am now rethinking the habits of a lifetime. That includes my attitude to England and authority. I never wanted authority. So why should I hate those who want and get it? They are in a different category from me, just as bank clerks are. Let them get on with it; why waste my time in hatred?

England, too. It's as neutral as the jungles I fought in. It's an abstraction, largely, apart from the physical land area. To hate it is to admit to a hatred of one's parents — and that was at the bottom of all my problems.

The Bomb was my parent. It once gave me life. It was my father. Some such distortion had taken place in my psyche.

And for the first time I have been seeing that the idea of unilateral disarmament is an emotional phantasy. Any country that disarms itself voluntarily — as Czechoslovakia was persuaded to do by Britain and France in 1938 — writes itself out of history. It is overcome, because it has given up its will to live. There's a Darwinian logic which operates. We cannot give up our arms. We must negotiate the arms away from a position of strength. (God, but you'll laugh at that.) The disarmament negotiations now in progress, hellish though they may be, have a grasp on reality that unilateralism doesn't. It is realistic to haggle and argue and threaten and orate; that keeps the hate and savagery within barriers. Dropping your trousers to the enemy doesn't.

I'll put it simply in other terms. All my life I have had to fight for my inner identity and existence; unilateralism is not part of my make-up. I'm an old soldier. I actually would rather die than give in.

And I'd rather face the truth about myself, however shabby it may seem to others, than deceive you. I want you. I will still come to meetings with you and Ron, because I consider that the pressure CND exerts on governments to get on with negotiations is valuable (as long as it never gains its true objective!); but you will know now that it is just intellect moving me, and not emotionalism any more.

Here's where I'd better stop. If you don't show up next Saturday, I'll understand.

Your storm-tossed
Joseph

Clement dropped the letter on the blanket and began to weep. Again Joseph was saying that he had misunderstood and misconstructed his own story. What exactly he meant by that, Clement could not yet comprehend. Some of his tears were for his own lack of comprehension.

XIII

When Clement awoke next morning, Sheila had already left the bedroom. He could see that the sun beyond the curtains had resumed its unexpected reign over Rawlinson Road. Making a mental check of his anatomy, he discovered that he was in moderate good health; the pain in his left leg and the slight tremor in his right forearm were distractions of long standing, and not to be considered.

It was Sunday — a week since they left the madhouse in Boston.

He dressed and came downstairs slowly, seeming to float in the dimness, for Sheila had drawn the curtains over the long window on the landing in order to keep out the heat, creating unfocused semi-shadows on the striped wallpaper. From Sheila's room came the steady click of her word-processor: Kerinth was being reborn and he did not disturb her. His mind was still full of yesterday's worrying experience.

As he was about to descend to the hall, a sound at the front door attracted his attention. Accelerating his step, he was in time to see a glint of daylight and fingers at the letterbox, as a piece of paper was pushed through. The paper dropped to the doormat. Even as he hastened forward to pick it up, Clement recognised it as a copy of the vindictive review of *War Lord of Kerinth*, cut from the *Guardian*, which had greeted them on their return from Boston.

At once, Clement unlocked the front door and flung it open. He ran down the steps and the path to the street. He could see the traffic trundling by on the Banbury Road. On Rawlinson Road, no one was in sight. He went out on the pavement and stared this way and that, clutching the review. He looked into next door, beyond Mrs Farrer's pseudo-acacia. Had someone just disappeared down the sideway? He was convinced that the horrible John Farrer had struck again. Why wasn't the little bugger in church, praying forgiveness for his sins?

His savage glare at the Farrer roses failed to wither them. Retreating to his own territory, he went slowly inside, shaking with anger, and closed the door behind him.

There were voices in the kitchen. Two of Michelin's friends had come round to take coffee and Maison Blanc cakes with her. They greeted Clement politely when he entered the room.

Michelin was wearing lipstick for once. This was a detail Clement only later realised he had observed.

He helped himself to a bowl of mixed Shreddies and All Bran and took it out to eat at the garden table, away from the chatter of the ladies. After a little while, Michelin came out with a cup of coffee for him. He smiled at her and then made himself read the adverse review.

". . . What is disturbing about such fantasies is that they present arrant impossibilities as if they were fact, thus stepping up the power of the drug. In the silly world of Kerinth, a dead race comes back from a million years ago and interferes with present-day activities whenever the plot demands it.

"None of the characters is surprised at this remarkable phenomenon, because the effect the author is aiming at is sedation rather than enquiry."

This extract contained several mistakes. Its general air of condescension was also a mistake, in Clement's eyes. He screwed the scrap of paper up and heeled it into a flower bed, so that Sheila would not see and be disturbed by it again. The sheer malice prompting someone to push this idle squib through the door nearly made him sick.

He imagined doing many violent things to Farrer until the savagery of his thoughts frightened him, and he resorted mentally to Mrs Emerova.

"If it was that little bugger next door, what does he know about it? He's no literary critic. Who's he to agree or disagree with the prick in the *Guardian*, whoever he is?"

"How do you know it is the person next door? Why so close?"

"What's that to do with it? He'd destroy my wife's work if he possibly could. I know her books have no stylistic excellence. She's no Nabokov and doesn't pretend to be, but they bring her peace of mind and happiness, and delight others, and here's this little bit of dirt. . . ."

"Does all this hostility mask your own dislike of Sheila's books?"

"Really, you say the silliest things. I'm happy if Sheila's happy. This little cretin next door can have no real valid opinion of his own. Who's he to judge what the Kerinth novels are worth? He's only a sodding little insurance agent. Don't you agree that this was a low and vindictive thing to do?"

"Mightn't there be another way of looking at it? A friend meaning well? After all, the review goes on to say that Green Mouth is mistress of her craft, so it is possible, isn't it, that someone else might carelessly think of it as rather a favourable review?"

"Look, he hates the novels simply because they are written in the house next door. He hates them because sometimes Sheila types on a manual in her bikini by the swimming pool, and he can see her at it if he stands on a chair in their spare room and cranes his head out of the window. He hates them because there aren't any insurance agents on Kerinth. He just hates the thought of creative activity. He even came round once to complain that the sound of the word-processor kept him awake at night. He hates them because they've got wrap-around picture jackets with bronzed people on not at all resembling his own little contorted frame.

"He hates the novels because they are extremely successful. He hates them because you can buy them in airports all over the world, and in Papua New Guinea. Not for any literary reasons. He knows bugger all about literature. He can't tell the difference between Tolstoi and Trotsky. He probably thinks Gorky is a Park. Who's he, after all, to defend literary standards? All right, he's seen Frank Delaney and Melvyn Bragg on television, but that's as far as it goes. He takes the *Reader's Digest*. Do we comment on his fancy insurance policies? Who's he to comment on Sheila's prose? Besides, I always check her grammar for her.

"He hates Sheila and me simply because we are happier than he is, and much richer. He hates us because we've got a villa outside Marbella. He hates us because we have the house repainted every four years. He hates us because we've installed Victorian fireplaces. He hates us because we have parties. What if a guest once slung a bottle over the wall and smashed one of his cloches? Didn't we go round next day with a bottle of wine to apologise? When's he ever come round here with anything? He hates Sheila because she's bigger than his little mouse of a wife and wears fashionable clothes. He hates her because she gets her photo in Blackwell's shop window. He hates her no doubt because he secretly desires her. Some hope!

"He hates other people's success. He hates me. I don't have a thing against him. He's just a little shit who ought to be squashed."

"And do you see yourself doing that?"

"Often."

The interior dialogue went some way towards cooling Clement's temper. Draining his coffee, he looked at his watch. He might as well go along to his room in college and work on *Adaptability*; he liked the silences Sunday brought, with Arthur presumably off taking his nubile little wife out in their Zastava Caribbean to have lunch in Burford or Henley. He felt perfectly well this morning, although the traumatic visitation from his brother remained vivid in his mind. The bar of soap still revolved. He made a resolve not to go over to Acton alone next time.

Before leaving the house, he went upstairs to say hello to Sheila.

Sheila, in her role as Green Mouth, had taken over all the first floor of the house. Of the two front rooms, bedrooms under a previous ownership, one served as a sort of library-lounge-art gallery, while the other was her study — her Room, more simply. It was the powerhouse of Kerinth.

A secretary, who had a small room of her own at the rear of the house, also worked in Sheila's study. The study was dressed in cream. Being in it was rather like being in a huge meringue. The walls were cream, the long heavy curtains were cream. Even the Chinese carpet on the floor was cream, with brilliant green edges. Her desk was also cream. The chairs in the room were upholstered in cream, as was the large Victorian sofa, on which green cushions were piled.

The secretary, Mrs Florence Flowerbury, also sat at a cream desk, half-concealed behind a four-panel cream screen.

Seeing Clement enter, Mrs Flowerbury half-rose and gave him a gracious smile. "Here we are, you see, Dr Winter. How are you?"

It was her little joke that she stuck to Sheila — in a phrase she had once used — "through thick and thin", though very little thin had affected the Green Mouth career.

"I didn't expect to see you here on a Sunday, Mrs Flowerbury."

"A lot of work to catch up with, Dr Winter. I wouldn't do it for everyone" — said with a sweet smile towards Sheila.

The general effect of being in a clotted cream factory was mitigated by a brilliantly painted panel on the rear wall of the room, executed somewhat in the manner of Douanier Rousseau. Amid riotous foliage, lifesize *mazooms* and *crichts*, the owl-like inhabitants of Vinto, Kerinth's moon, gazed down with huge cat eyes on their creator.

Their creator, evidently not yet entirely back to Earth after the adulation heaped on her in Boston, wore one of her striking green embroidered robes. She was working at her word-processor. On a corner of the sofa lay Green Mouth, the lizard-like doll and companion of Sheila's childhood, much worn by years of infantile caresses, from which Sheila had taken her trade name. The doll was her secret talisman, without which she could not write. It was clear she meant business now. Her somewhat heavy face was set in lines of concentration as she sat, elbow on desk, considerable cheek resting on fist, peering into the screen of her purring word-processor for inspiration.

"I must get out into the garden," she said, absent-mindedly.

On her desk she had gathered, conventionally enough, a series of objects of problematic relationship. They lay strewn beside a photograph, framed in silver, of the Winters' dead child, who, staring as if deep in thought at a toy ambulance from which protruded the legs and feet of a doll, formed a striking little figure in a short-skirted dress and picture hat. The surrounding objects included a small bell from a Mexican church; a matchbox advertising a restaurant in Bath; a postcard view of the Potala Palace in Lhasa; a block of Duplo Lego; an Italian miniature scent bottle without stopper; a netsuke of a man and woman copulating, gift of an admirer in New York; and a smooth stone, streaked with wafer-thin evidence of bygone geological events, which had been picked up on a distant seashore. It might have appeared — say to an interviewer who came to talk to Sheila Winter in her home — that these items presented some kind of methodical reminder to the author of the so-called real world, necessary while she ventured into the realms of her imagination; but from their casual disposition, and the way in which most of them were half-buried in paper or scribbled notes, or other vital adjuncts of her profession, it seemed they had accumulated merely through an idle acquisitive instinct. Sheila was a conventional woman.

As her husband came closer, she glanced up and smiled.

"How are you feeling, darling? I was up early this morning. I had an idea."

"You must have thought me out of my mind yesterday. It's ridiculous to say that Joseph's flat is haunted, but there he was." He went to her side, and she took hold of his hand. "There he was. It was a real shock. He was washing his hands in the kitchen. I can't tell you the effect of it all. The hand-washing seemed to be going on for ever. . . . You aren't about to tell me I imagined it all, are you?"

Sheila half-smiled. She stood up and held his face between her hands. "You old silly! 'There's nothing but thinking makes it so.' Isn't that what you've often told me? It's real to you, so it's real to me."

"Well, it was most extraordinary. Joseph definitely spoke to me. 'Everything worked out all right.' It's a genuine message from the Beyond, isn't it? How are you feeling? Are you entirely over your jet-lag yet?"

Even as he asked the question, he wondered if Joseph's supposed appearance had not been a product of his own jet-lag.

"That reminds me. Mrs Flowerbury, we must ring the Boston committee and thank them for their hospitality." She seated herself again on her cream chair, her mind slipping back to her work. "I suddenly had a marvellous idea as I was in the shower. An image. It must have been something to do with the milkman. He was delivering yesterday with a new van. When I was a child in the country, the milkman used to go on his rounds with a horse and cart."

"Good, yes, well, I'm just off. I didn't mean to disturb you. Don't forget it's drinks with the Fender-Lieversohns this evening."

"Good. I had the image of three hooded men galloping at full stretch along a shore. The tide had retreated, leaving miles of sodden sand reflecting the blue sky. Some way out to sea was a small island, volcanic, with smoke rising in a plume from it. A wonderful opening. A wonderful cover. I felt I had to write it down. We'll see where it takes me. Keep your fingers crossed."

"That's fine. Remember, you don't need to work on a Sunday, nor do I. I must get the booze for the party from Bottoms Up tomorrow. Well, they'll deliver as usual, of course."

"Don't forget to order plenty of glasses. I thought this time I'd make more of the *Rajjimi*, give them a bigger role in events."

"I like your *Rajjimi*. Don't overwork."

"I'm supposed to be Sunday-lunching with Maureen. I might just put her off. She'll understand."

He kissed her and they stroked each other's faces.

He did like the *Rajjimi*, he reflected as he went downstairs past Sheila's pictures, among the soothing shadows, hearing the keyboard of the word-processor already beginning to click. The Golden Age of Kerinth lay far behind it. The planet had once been ruled by a noble and powerful race, the *Rajjimi*. It had disappeared. A quarter of a million years (and not a million years, as the man had said in his *Guardian* review) of barbarism had elapsed before Kerinth became — at least in part — civilised again. The ruling *Rajjimi* materialised to the new rulers of the planet, appearing like apparitions from the dead, to advise, to counsel, to warn. Some of the new rulers heeded them, others deliberately flouted the ghostly advice.

At first, the *Rajjimi* made few appearances but, when their popularity was certain, Sheila began writing them into every book.

Well, it was not such a preposterous idea, Clement thought. Just a post-Freudian idea. . . . We were all ruled by the dead whispering to us. The *Rajjimi* functioned rather like archetypes.

Juliet's death came back to him. He closed the front door carefully on the house and its contents.

The car crash had happened in the summer of 1974, thirteen years ago. Juliet would have been sixteen by now, in the fifth at Oxford High School. Instead, she remained forever in his mind — and Sheila's — at the age of three and a half, delicate, dependent, dear. He had been driving. That was what made it so awful. And the country had been so green and heavy with leaf. The details had always been vague, except that he did not see the other car as it pulled out of a side lane in front of them.

Then he had found himself being carried, and had no idea where he was. He shouted for Sheila. Shouted in a whisper. Things faded. He was in a moving vehicle, prostrate, and Sheila's face was near his, deathly white. His thought was, "I've killed her." That terrible moment still resurfaced at intervals in his mind. He had not immediately thought of Juliet then. At the Radcliffe Infirmary he had learned that both Sheila and he were relatively whole, but their child was dying. She had been sitting on Sheila's knee, and had gone through the windscreen during the collision.

They had been sedated and patched up before they returned to the house. They lived in Chalfont Road, then, in a roomy upstairs flat. They had avoided friends for a long while. How many times had he poured out his guilt to Sheila. How many times had she forgiven. How many times had they both wept. That beastly summer, full of irremediable pain.

Ice cream. That was all they seemed to want to eat. Endless maple and walnut ice cream from the new delicatessen in Summertown. And both being all in all to each other. They had endured each other's silences, each other's fits of wailing. Somehow they had clung to the idea that they still loved each other, despite a tendency to fly apart, to flee to the other ends of the world to escape from the one person who most reminded them of the dead.

They sated themselves with music as if it were a kind of drug, in particular playing records of Bach chorales over and over. Clement never heard "Ich ruf zu dir, Herr Jesu Christ", in the sombre key of F minor, without recalling that desolate time. Slowly the mania left them, along with the need for ice cream, as the winter's rains came down.

Then one day she had started typing on the manual Hermes they shared. "I'm going to write a fantasy novel," she said.

There had been no dead child in that first Kerinth novel. All had been excitement and sunlight and it had ended happily. But the mysterious *Rajjimi* had made their first appearance, coming back from death, trailing clouds of a vanished glory. "Arrant impossibilities" indeed. . . .

Clement tried to dismiss the past as he came to the Banbury Road and the challenge of its traffic, dense even today. In a city of obfuscations, the Banbury Road was one of Oxford's more definite statements, blunt rather than equivocal. For most of its length, say from St Giles to Summertown, it had been built before the age of the motor car, or at least during the mere dawn of that terrifying age. The great houses which flanked it, angular mansions of brick, had been designed for ample families; provision had been made in basement and attic for plural servants. Carriages had conveyed the families into town, to shop at Elliston & Cavell's emporium. Young rustic men in waistcoats served as gardeners, in response to the Edwardian penchant for *rus in urbe*.

But the Kaiser had proved too much for stability. Young England had gone first to the war and then to the dogs. Now these Oxford gardens were under-tended and overgrown; models of Darwinism, they had become places where only the fittest plants survived. The houses themselves had been given over to trumpery schools of English or divided into flats where untenanted milk bottles congregated on crumbling doorsteps. The carriages had gone, swept aside by automobiles. Arthur Stranks lived in one of the little flats into which No. 82 Banbury Road had been sliced, and would drive his Zastava Caribbean regularly into the streams of traffic which ran north and south through all daylight hours and long after. This was where Clement and Sheila had once walked in agony, mutely clutching each other's hands, as far up as Squitchey Lane, after their Juliet was killed. The great houses, behind their great trees, lay back from the thronging cars, blind, wounded, extinct — yet living on, their carcasses turned over to contemporary fashion and lusting estate agents.

Catching a period without traffic, Clement hastened across the road and soon took a side street to college, but his trail of memory persisted.

How vulnerably young they had been then!

It remained a source of pride to him that he and Sheila had seen each other through that period of mourning, although at times her grief had been nearly impossible to bear. The very smell of her had changed for a while. Had anyone ever done a medical paper on that? *Changes in Olfactory Signals During Periods of Grief.* He had made love several times to her friend Maureen Bowler — looking back, he appreciated Maureen's immense understanding: she had agreed, he could perceive, not for his sake but for her friend's. This was in Maureen's pre-feminist days. The affair, lasting hardly a month, had put him back on the road in running order. He had been more able to look after Sheila. Ever since, they had remained close, devoted, although Sheila would never start another child. They had been examples of the adaptability round which Clement was compiling his record.

Kerinth was Sheila's child. She had her escape routes. No one could bear too much reality. Even at this moment, she was writing about three hooded men galloping along a deserted seashore on an imaginary planet. He smiled to himself. Good for her.

By an inevitable and painful association, Clement's thoughts ran to another dead child, his mother's first-born, born long before he himself saw the light of day. That ill-fated little creature, that "steel-engraving angel", had had a malign effect on Joseph's childhood, haunting his early years. He recalled Joseph's strenuous attempts to lay that ghost on the occasion of their mother's funeral in Nettlesham, three years previously.

It was a suitably bleak occasion. Madge Constance Winter, widow of Ernest Winter, had died one cold April day in 1984. She left behind a wish to be buried beside her husband in the town cemetery of Nettlesham, Suffolk. Her two sons carried out her wishes.

Nettlesham lay in the midst of flat uninteresting country, a market town which had lost touch with its countryside. It stood cold and grey within a ring of treeless new estates. An east wind moved through its streets. Clement, accustomed to the legend of Nettlesham as the old family home, took a dislike to it all over again. Although he and Sheila arrived at lunchtime, the town gave an appearance of obstinate stagnation, like something washed up on an elderly beach. On the outskirts, they had driven through some light industry, kitchen designers, agricultural machinery hirers, bamboo furniture importers, and such. The centre, despite the injection of a hideous shopping centre, had fossilised in a dull bygone time, cramped and crotchety. Young people with red hands ate their lunches from paper bags in the street.

Nettlesham's one claim to fame remained the poet William Westlake, the minor eighteenth-century figure who had gone mad and died there. In the market place was a Westlake Tea Rooms, which sold postcards and scarves, as well as dusty buns.

Sheila and Clement drove up from Oxford in the Mercedes. Ellen drove up in her Mini with her daughter Jean, even then undergoing a divorce. Joseph drove up in his van. Sheila and Clement had booked to stay overnight at the *Gryphon*, the only hotel for miles recommended in the *Good Hotel Guide*, thinking to have a look at the coast the next morning. The others planned to drive home that evening.

Despite the solemnity of the occasion, Sheila and Clement arrived in Nettlesham in good humour, amused at the prospect of seeing some of the family again. Clement had driven; Sheila did not drive. He sometimes wondered about that. She had refused to learn. In many things, she had come to be the dominant partner in their marriage. Above all, fame and the earning-capacity had become hers. Most of the time, he was content enough that this should be so; it was a state of affairs compatible with the times, when women played an increasingly confident role in life. But in the car and in bed with Clement she was content to play a passive role.

They all met by arrangement in the *King's Arms*, near where the old Winter ironmongery shop had once stood — new developments had swept the shop away with a lot of the other junk of the past. It now had a fragile existence only in the memory of Joseph Winter and possibly one or two others.

Joining the two brothers later would be Ellen and Jean, and Madge Winter's two younger sisters, Mary and Doris, together with their husbands and assorted offspring. They had all agreed to meet in the bar for a drink before visiting the dining room for a meal.

Directly Clement and Sheila entered the bar, all yellow pine and plastic avocado upholstery, they saw his elder brother there alone, drinking. Joseph sat hunched on a swivel stool, elbow on bar and glass of beer in his hand. He was neatly dressed in a dark grey jacket and black trousers. As Clement advanced, he saw that Joseph's tie was slightly awry and the top button of his shirt undone. He wore a CND badge in his lapel. Clement smiled and extended his hand.

"How are you, Joseph?"

Joseph climbed down carefully from his stool. His untidy hair was greyer than when they had last met, and his face more lined. He grinned.

"Right as a cricket, and no regrets at the prospect of seeing the old girl shovelled under. You're looking as neat and upright as ever."

He turned to Sheila and kissed her cheek, standing back to survey her dark dress.

"Plenty of embonpoint, Sheila, dearest."

"I know your preference is for less of that."

Joseph laughed. "Touché. Puissant as always, and selling even better than before, no doubt."

Clement smiled rather hard at his wife to encourage her to accept this greeting, but she merely said, with a fugitive gleam, "I saw a book of yours announced last week in a bookseller's catalogue."

"Oh, that! Let's have a drink. Same old stuff that no one wants to buy — King Sidabutar of Sumatra, very obscure. Isn't it amazing that I still keep going over the same old ground? You'd think I'd be discouraged by now, but not a bit of it." He laughed heartily, and then changed tack, clutching Clement's arm in mock earnestness. "Well, young 'un, what do you think to this ancient town in which I was born and bred?"

"Not much. It looks as if it has been ruined since the war."

"No, not at all. Improved if anything. When I was a lad, everyone used to go about in creaky boots, with straw in their hair."

"I'd grow straws in my hair if I lived here for long."

"Where's Ellen, may I ask? She can't have thought better of it, can she?"

"Perhaps she's staying at home to look after the dog."

"She'd better be here, and that pretty daughter with her. Ellie was always mother's little pet. Can't plant the old lady without Ellie here to wave her goodbye."

He's now fifty-seven, Clement thought, surveying his brother with lively interest. Quite a raffish old man. His skin is rather blotchy, his hair needs a trim and a wash. But cheerful, or at least in his usual sort of bantering, self-deprecating humour. "How long have you been here?"

"Propping up this bar? Not long. I drove over early. Decided to seize on the chance of looking round my birthplace. Don't ask me why. I don't suffer from nostalgia. I suppose you take no interest in William Westlake, Clem, renowned author of 'The Crippled Goat'? Well, William's my literary mentor. I had my first orgasm only a semen's throw from where the old boy lived. He knew the folly of birthplaces.

'. . . Pride is in all, e'en in our Birth.
How much we count it where and when on Earth
We happened — though all came by merest Chance. . . .'"

He laughed. "There was a lot of sense in the eighteenth century, not to mention sententiousness. Yes, I've had a prowl around. Went to the cemetery. Revisited some old haunts. Even sought a girl I used to know. Well, two girls, in fact. Rosemary and Ruth Tippler. My first loves — or second, or third. . . . They lived over their shop next to our shop. I was twelve when I fell in love with them both. Ever since then, to enjoy two sisters at the same time has been my ideal, but I've never come across a pair as lovely as Ruth and Rosemary. 'Course, they've been married for years — left bloody Nettlesham, if they had any sense. All very carnal, Sheila, but of course I don't shock you."

"Keep trying," she said, and smiled.

"Worse things happen in Corinth, I bet — or whatever your pet planet is called."

"Much worse." She was not going to allow Joseph to win a tease. "Where's this drink?"

After a while, Ellen arrived with Jean. Jean was now twenty-two, a pretty girl with dark curly hair and something of the Winter features. Joseph got off his stool, and began to make up to his niece. Clement, while talking to Ellen, observed how much Jean resembled Joseph as he had been when younger, and wondered whether, in her unfortunate love life, she did not also resemble him.

At fifty-three, Ellen looked spry enough in her dark two-piece suit. She dyed her hair. She cradled her handbag in the crook of her left arm and put her right hand daintily on Clement's shoulder as she kissed his cheek. For Joseph she had a kiss on the lips and a swift hug.

"Drinking again," she said to him. "Still, you don't look in bad shape. You're a bit thin."

"I ran out of money and had to walk all the way back from Bangkok. Those CND marches proved useful at last."

"And you're wearing a suit — almost a suit!"

"A last-minute bid for respectability. I should always go about togged up like this. Your daughter gets prettier all the time. How are you?"

While they were uttering phatic expressions of pleasure, in came the rest of the party, a man in front, a man bringing up the rear, with Madge Winter's two younger sisters, Mary and Doris, and their grown-up offspring, in between.

"This way. Here we are," old Claude Vernon was saying, unnecessarily, proclaiming himself leader of the pack, as they entered.

"What a tragic occasion, dear," said his wife, Doris, opening her arms wide before flinging them round Ellen. Doris Vernon's past history had given her a taste for the dramatic and a tendency to slope to the right which the years had not quenched.

Mary Overton, her sister, managed to look mournful at the best of times. Ellen's arms being occupied, she took second choice and headed for Joseph. Evading his aunt adroitly, he left her with no option but to collapse into Sheila's arms, where she managed a creditable spasm of sobbing.

The younger Overtons and Vernons milled about among themselves. Those with initiative rapidly ordered themselves drinks. Last came heavy-bodied Hugh Overton, Mary's husband, struggling to escape from the clutches of a heavy overcoat. Clement helped him. "Always beastly cold in East Anglia," he grumbled to the company in general.

"How's the shrink trade going?" he asked Clement. "Still sooth-saying to the sexually repressed?" In his youth, Hugh had gained a small reputation as a wag.

After a reasonable amount of milling about, and resumés of the journey they had just undergone, they all moved together in a crowd up two steps and into the *King's Arms* dining room. As they passed through the glazed double doors, Joseph grabbed Clement by the elbow.

"I know I'm the senior and all that, but I'm not able to go treat, I'm afraid. I can pay my whack and that's about all."

"Don't worry, Joseph. This meal was Sheila's and my idea, so we'll pay for it."

"If father hadn't been so spineless, we might have owned this town by now. Isn't life a bummer? Full of 'might have beens', along with all the other nasties."

"You'll probably have the lunch to complain about too. I don't suppose it's anything special."

"Pity we couldn't have had a curry."

"I don't eat curry, remember?"

This was said as Clement surveyed the dining room. It was an old room. One might have suspected that, the arts of hospitality having been practised on this site for three or four centuries, tippling, gluttony, gossiping, and other gregarious human failings having filled its spaces to the rafters since the times of Good Queen Bess, something bonhomous might have remained in its atmosphere. But it had been redecorated in the nineteen sixties, and now was merely an old room.

"I say, our niece Jean looks good, doesn't she?" said Joseph. "Divorced so young. . . . Pity she drove her husband away — nice chap, I thought."

The guests came to the table in clusters, with feigned or real reluctance, and Clement directed where they should sit, making sure that his brother sat next to Jean.

"I'm glad you're in command, Clem," said Ellen, waspishly.

He grouped the younger people of the Overton and Vernon clans at one end of the table, so that they could make cryptic remarks among themselves. The older members sat at the other end, assembling themselves rather moodily in their unfamiliar clothes as Sheila said, "We can be happy together, although it is a sad occasion. Madge wouldn't want to see us looking miserable."

No one answered her, although Joseph glanced across and gave her a nod of approval before plunging back into conversation with Jean.

They kept their voices low. The chilly atmosphere of the dining room got to them. The table had been laid with a white cloth. Withered white carnations drooped in two silver-plated vases. There were white bone china side plates and paper napkins, and white china salt and pepper-pots in the shape of imitation igloos. The impression was of a table set more for an ice age than a meal.

Sheila began talking calmly and remorselessly to Doris Vernon and her husband sitting next to her. Launching out on the price of vodka in various Oxford shops as compared with the Duty Free shop in Heathrow, and taking relative proofs into consideration, she moved easily into the psychology of flying long distances, pointing out that motivation as well as the basic technology was needed. With this example to encourage the party, a thin trickle of talk emerged from them; good humour developed as a thin waiter poured a thin red wine.

April rain came scudding down outside, an element twinned with the clear soup served inside. Jean laughed at Joseph's jokes. Someone in the kitchen was having a violent fit of coughing.

Both Mary Overton and Doris Vernon resembled their dead sister. They had been tall, although now they were beginning to crumble, gazing out on what was left of their world through thick spectacles. In repose, Mary's face had a mournful expression of surprise, as if she was saying, inwardly, "Oh dear, that's what's happened, is it?" The younger of the two, Doris, looked rather more formidable, although still mournful when not imbibing the soup; her expression inclined more towards, "Well, don't let this happen again."

These two slightly differing expressions, etched on their respective faces with increasing emphasis over the years, owed much to the influence of their spouses. Hugh Overton, Mary's husband, was known as a moody man who had long outgrown any notoriety as a card; with the years, his jests had turned to jibes and his jibes had turned against his wife, perhaps because she excelled him in an area where he had expected little competition, intelligence. He had conducted a furniture business in North London; now, in the years of his retirement, he haunted secondhand shops and auctions, making occasional purchases which Mary neglected to polish.

Doris's fate had been more dramatic than her sister's. Her husband, Claude Vernon, had been a young lawyer in Bury St Edmunds. After she had borne him three children, he had run off with one of his clients, a South American lady called Dolores Beltrao do Soares. They had fled to a small island in the English Channel, Elbit, the property of Dolores's uncle, to escape the lady's husband. There it had been love among the sheep, until the husband arrived by motor launch with a rifle, in a well-sustained jealous rage.

The intruder had threatened to shoot both his wife and Claude, but they had somehow fallen to talking, possibly about sheep-breeding, with such intensity that Dolores, whose interest in sheep was at a low ebb, had snatched the rifle and shot her husband. He had been taken to a hospital in Weymouth, where he died; Dolores was arrested for murder. The trial, with its romantic ingredients — lust, weaponry, small island, adultery, and sheep — had received wide and sensational coverage. Claude Vernon had been expelled from the Bar. Dolores got a two-year sentence for manslaughter.

Claude went back to Doris and the three children. Far from being apologetic, his attitude was that of a man who had instigated high and desperate adventure. He persuaded Doris, at least temporarily, to take the same point of view. She accepted him back into the family home.

But the high and desperate adventure, coupled with difficulty in finding a suitable job, had unsettled Claude's disposition. Doris's mood of acceptance slowly changed to one of resentment, coupled with some envy. She gradually withdrew herself from her husband and children; rheumatism had taken her like a rusted weathervane and frozen her in that attitude. She walked and now sat at the table with a perceptible tilt to starboard, leaning away from what she loved and hated.

Although this adventure had taken place in the late thirties, when such affrays were as common as record-breaking flights across the Atlantic, and when Doris and Claude were in their early thirties, the mark of it was still on them, half a century later — and upon the relationship between the sisters; for Mary's life, despite the jibes and the furniture, had been very dull. She still showed some envy of her sister, whose photograph had appeared in the *Daily Graphic* and other newspapers, as if Doris had been the one run away with rather than from. Doris, too, was able to luxuriate in her brief fame, when not punishing her husband for it; so that the pleasant sibling friendship they had enjoyed as children had long drained away. In Mary's presence, Doris came more than usually to resemble the celebrated Tower of Pisa.

Stepping up the "Well, don't let this happen again" expression, Doris now addressed the company in general, saying, as pallid translucent strips of fish were brought in on cold plates, "Madge's was a long widowhood. She was a gentle creature who deserved better of life, in my opinion."

"I wonder what God's opinion was," said Jean, and then looked horrified at what she had said. "I mean, Granny wasn't at all what you would call religious. She never went to church."

"She went to church a lot when she was young," replied Doris.

"We all had to go to church then, Doris," said her sister, speaking in a reproving tone as if for the entire C. of E. "If you can remember those days."

"And she went to church a lot after she married Ernest," said Doris, in a conclusive way, ignoring Mary's remark.

"That would be when her first child died, wouldn't it?" asked Joseph. "I mean, that poor little thing, which would have been my elder sister. . . ." He looked poker-faced at Jean as he spoke. "Mater remained heart-broken about that until Ellie was born. The Almighty is a bad listener and made the mistake of sending her a boy — me — as replacement first time round."

"That's no way to speak, Joe, really," said Doris. "Madge cried her eyes out for that poor little darling."

"Prayer should be an end in itself," said Joseph. "It's an end, not a means. The Buddha knew that. If you get an answer, it comes from yourself, and it's a miracle."

"Well, it would be a miracle if you got an answer from yourself, wouldn't it?" said Hugh Overton, with a laugh. He was not attending much. Senility was setting in and he was assisting it with an overdose of the thin wine. Clement summoned the waiter for another bottle.

"We haven't any more," said the waiter.

"What do you mean, you haven't any more?"

"What I say. That was our last bottle." The waiter spoke as from a deep sense of injury, and sucked his mouth in, as though he would say much more, were he so minded, and were it not so chilly.

"Bring us something like it, then."

"Well done, Clem, but don't over-tax the local resources," Joseph said, nodding across the table. "Remember, this country lapsed into barbarism when the Romans left and has yet to recover."

"Of course, you're a socialist, aren't you?" said Claude, scowling. A cheer came from someone at the other end of the table.

Silence descended. In due course, the beef was got through, and they were served something called "gateau". This was the first time they had warm plates. The gateau was white in some parts and brownish in others, rather like decomposing flesh, with a grey imitation marble topping which broke into gravestone-shaped segments when tackled, thus preparing the diners for the ceremony which was to follow after the meal.

"Nice wine," said Hugh. "Some brandy would help fend off the cold."

"Brandy at the bar," said the waiter, over the guests' heads, rattling the dirty plates as he started to clear away.

The Nettlesham cemetery, like the *King's Arms* dining room, held little comfort for the living. Nor did it reflect much credit on the dead, who might be reckoned indifferent to ecological niceties. Unlike the great mortuary enclosures of France and Italy, little grandeur flourished here, and no sense of occasion. The monuments raised were mainly skimpy and conventional, pocket having triumphed over piety in the minds of the recently bereaved. Neither flowers nor stones were deployed with imagination. Instead, the defunct had been interred within little oblong prisons like disused men's toilets, outlined by kerbs the colour of frozen pig's liver. The memorial stones carried only names and dates — rather less information than an identity card. It was hard, looking about Nettlesham's windy cemetery, to imagine that anyone buried there had been much loved, or that anyone attending their burial had been much moved. The more recent the stone, the more this seemed to be the case.

Madge Winter's coffin went down into the gravelly ground close to where her husband lay. Clement stood clutching Sheila's hand. She gave a great sob.

He also felt close to tears which the bitter Nettlesham wind encouraged. His parents' history was now closed. His father had decided to stay in Cornwall when war broke out, for safety's sake, fearing that in Suffolk they would all be bombed. Such property as he held in Lowestoft had to be sold for a song. Such money as he had had been invested in a small newsagent's and tobacconist's business in Bude. The family lived in cramped conditions over the shop, putting up the blackouts every night.

Ernest Winter worked and scrimped throughout the war, growing more taciturn as time went by. The lady now being lowered into the gravel, however, had flourished. In the shop she was always able to find someone to talk to. She began to organise things about the town. She became, in a small, parsimonious way suited to the times, a social success. Clement remembered her from that period, when he was still in short trousers, as delightful company, full of jokes and stories. His mother had also been a good cook. The war served as a challenge to her culinary expertise. By using the barter power of the shop's stock, some of which was on ration, she could procure for her family prime hams, salmon, turkey at Christmas, and a regular stream of eggs. Barter was a joke to her. Everything that happened in Bude could be turned into a joke in Madge Winter's reckoning. This was her manic phase. After the war, she ran out of steam.

The shop flourished in a meagre way throughout most of the fifties. Ernest Winter bought a small bungalow nearby, in which the family could live more comfortably. Anchored in the thirties as it was, the shop and its trade did not survive the sixties. Ernest sold up and retired. His wife, missing the company, got a job in the large newsagent's shop, one of the chain which had put them out of business. Ernest was furious. The couple lived for some years on bad terms. By that time, Clement was doing psychiatric work in London, and rarely made the journey down to Cornwall to see his parents. His father died in 1969 — "in a bit of a huff", Joseph had said. His widow again managed a new lease of life, and went to live in a flat near her sisters, where she took harmlessly to drink. Latterly she had shown little interest in her sons, though her old affectionate link with Ellen was maintained.

The sisters, Mary and Doris, wept in chorus as the coffin went into the hole, perhaps foreseeing that their turn was next. Ellen also cried for her mother — the person in the world who had doted on her most — but in silence, as Jean held her hand.

The parson went through the traditional service, a cleverly compiled series of condolences and veiled threats. Afterwards, Hugh Overton took a photograph of them all, just before they began to straggle towards the distant yews and lych-gate which marked the cemetery entrance.

Joseph caught up with Clement and Sheila, thrusting his hands deep in his pockets for warmth.

"Well, that's seen both of them buried," he said. "Whatever the rights or the wrongs of the case, they're gone, and now it's our generation in the firing line."

"Go easy on the relish," said Clement, grumpily. "Let's at least get out of the cemetery before you start sneering."

"Don't go pious on me, please." After a moment, Joseph said, "You notice anyone missing in the roster of the dead, Clem? Perhaps you have no cause to recollect, as I certainly have, that our dear deceased parents spawned four children, not three. There was also the little steel-engraving angel, their first child, who died after six months, remember? Aren't you a mite astonished to find no stone raised to her, considering the misery her death caused mother at the time?"

Clement looked curiously at his brother, whose tone contained both jocularity and bitterness. The chilly breeze had blown Joseph's hair across his eyes, giving him a desperate look.

"I never thought about it." Not for the first time, his brother's intensity made him uneasy.

"Grandfather and grandmother are buried here. Mother and father are buried here. This is some far corner of a foreign Nettlesham that is forever Winter. Where, then, is the little steel-engraving angel buried?"

"Why do you call her that?" Sheila asked.

"Old associations. She's the prime cause of this pilgrim's regress. And because as far as I know the little paragon never had a name. Or mother kept it secret."

They dawdled while this conversation was taking place, so that Ellen, dry-eyed now, and Jean, could catch up with them.

"There's a bird singing," Jean said. "Isn't that in rather bad taste?"

Joseph turned and took Ellen's arm.

"That little dead sister which had such an effect on our lives when we arrived reluctantly on the scene — what was her name?"

Ellen looked puzzled. "Oh, I don't know, Joe. Does it matter after all this time? I know you've always had this kind of grudge against Mum and Dad, but they did the best for us they could, by and large. It's an awful subject. I think so. Always blame the mothers. . . . Mothers are only human like the rest. I keep telling Jean. Mothers have their troubles too. You ask too much. We all meet with disappointments. Here we stand. . . . If Mother's poor dead baby had a name, she never spoke it to us. Perhaps she never spoke it to Dad, either. Perhaps if she spoke it at all she'd have burst into tears."

She clutched her coat to her thin frame and looked reprovingly at Joseph.

"Oh, Christ," Jean said, and sighed.

Joseph brushed his hair back from his eyes and looked at the distant memorial church.

"You've given in, Ellie. I haven't. I have a surprise for you. In fact, I know the answer to the questions I've just been asking. I've almost laid the ghost of that little steel-engraving fiend. Just this morning I did it, before lunch. . . ." He struck his chest with an open hand. "'Art thou weary, Art thou languid, Art thou sore oppressed? Come to Me, said One, and, coming, be at rest. . . .' That doesn't mean what you may think," he said, with a sly look at Jean, standing next to him. "I've been busy laying demons to rest which have been torturing me for half a century and more. I'll tell you all about it if we can go round to your hotel, Clem and Sheila, and get a civilised drink. Failing that, we could have an uncivilised one at my van, where I have a bottle of whisky stashed. How about it?"

They stood in a rather English way, indecisively on the gravel, discussing what the chances were that the *Gryphon* would provide drink at three in the afternoon. They said goodbye to Mary Overton and Doris and Claude Vernon and their relations in a way indicating warmth of heart without enthusiastic liking.

"We want to get away from Nettlesham just as soon as we can," said Doris, as if condemning those who stood chatting at the entrances of graveyards. "This is a chilly part of the world." She gave them a farewell wave. Hugh straggled after her, still trying to deal with his ill-fitting coat.

"See you next funeral," he said, as he passed Clement.

"Well, what are we going to do?" asked Jean, with a touch of impatience. "I support Uncle Joseph. I vote we go to the *Gryphon* and see how we get on. The least they can do is give us a cup of tea."

Agreeing that funerals made them thirsty, they moved on, and drove in their three vehicles to the hotel.

There, because the manager was agreeable and Sheila was carrying the *Good Hotel Guide*, they were served a round of drinks in a snug back parlour, the manager himself presiding.

He was a small rotund man, built round a tomato nose cleverly underlined by an upwardly mobile moustache. His blue eyes, also round, peered out on his little world with nervous intensity. He had evidently decided that, despite his build, he was the stuff the military are made of, since he sported commando-style boots, cavalry twill trousers, and a club tie on a white shirt under what appeared to be an old deflated life-jacket. He spoke a strangulated English pepped up with the odd French word, to indicate the tone of his establishment.

"I'm without auxiliary assistance this p.m., *malheureusement*, life being what it is. But don't let the thought decommode you. Think of me as entirely *à votre service*, *n'est ce pas*? Enjoy yourselves, drink away." Snatching a covert glance at Sheila's *Good Hotel Guide*, he addressed her more particularly. "Your wish is my command. Give me a bell and I shall appear *toute suite* from the nether regions."

He disappeared. They heard him scuffling behind a curtain. Next moment, muzak filled the room.

They looked at each other round the table, said "Cheers", and drank.

"I didn't think Claude looked at all well," said Ellen, stealing a glance at her watch. "We mustn't be long before we start back, Jean. I'm worried about the dog. He hardly said a word over dinner."

"Is it true he once ran off with an Argentinian woman?" Jean asked. The company understood that Claude Vernon was under discussion, rather than Ellen's dog.

"Brazilian, and only as far as the Channel Islands," Sheila said, and all but Ellen laughed.

"Well, Joe, are you going to tell us about this ghost you've laid?" Sheila enquired, putting her head on one side and managing to frown and smile at him at the same time. "I'd like to hear a good story."

"Yes, what's the mystery, uncle?" asked Jean. "What have you been up to?"

Joseph hung over his drink. He shook his head slowly. "This won't mean as much to Clem and Sheila, or you, Jean, my girl, as it will to Ellie and me. Every family has layers of history — little dark corners where others can't penetrate. I've had to hug some bits of my early life to me in secret for years, and I'm glad enough to get rid of them. You might think they'd be buried, but no, they go on and on. Every so often, one surfaces, as today."

He looked rather challengingly at them. The only one to speak was Jean, who showed lively interest.

"I'm longing to hear what you're going to tell us. Surely it's true that every time someone dies some awful secrets spring out? I'd hate to think I died with a totally unblemished record, as if I'd been a nun. Wasn't Granny married, or something dramatic like that?"

Joseph turned smiling to her. "Madge got married right enough, and to Ernest, your grandfather. They were spliced, as the expression used to have it, just after the end of World War One. Nine months later, they had a baby — a girl.

"It still pains me to talk about that child. It received the affection I never got, like a sponge that sucked up all the nourishment available before I appeared on the scene."

Ellen said, "Joe, I wish you wouldn't talk in this way." She tapped the table, as if in a feeble attempt to bring her brother to order. "I know you suffered a hurt, but — well, it doesn't do any good to go on like this."

"Oh yes, it does. It's a relief just to talk about it. For too many years I kept silent. I never said anything to you when we were kids, close though we were. I was too ashamed. Why did I suffer guilt for their negligence?"

As he was taking a drink, Jean patted his hand.

"What about this child, then?"

Joseph turned back to his sister. "You remember how that child was held up to us as a paragon, one that could never be excelled? How good it was, how it never cried? Remember all that crap?"

"No, I can't say I do exactly."

"I had four years more of it than you did. . . . Anyhow, Ellie, you surely remember that we lived with the legend of the good darling daughter who died tragically at the age of six months?"

"Oh, I remember that. Of course mother was sad about it."

"Six months, right? *How* the creature died we were never told — how she went to join the angels, in mother's immortal phrase. Somehow, I used to imagine her carried off by autumn winds, turning blue and blowing away. . . ."

Sheila said, as Joseph paused, "What year did this unhappy child die? You have no need to grieve about it any longer, surely, Joseph? Can't you put it behind you?"

"I hate the child, Sheila. I always did. It stole my happiness. My parents didn't want *me*, because they yearned for *it*." He covered his face briefly, and then said with forced cheer, "Can't we get *monsieur* to drag up some more drink? A bottle. *Une bouteille, nicht var?* You see — I don't know how I can explain this. Well, old Westlake, that great neglected bard of Nettlesham, had the right idea. *His* mother died young — i.e., she forsook him, just as mine did. William went mad in the end, but not before knocking out the immortal couplet

> Grief unlike Joy ignores the tick of clock
> 'Til later generations feel its shock.

"If this cherished little wretch lived for six months, then it must have been christened and given a burial in Nettlesham churchyard. Presumably a stone was raised to it by its inconsolable parents. When I turned up here early this morning, I had a snoop round the churchyard. What we military types term a recce. . . . No sign of any stone. Not a marble angel in sight. Ah, *monsieur*, another round, and turn off the muzak, if you please."

The manager of the *Gryphon* did a slow scuttle to the table and bobbed his head. "*Enchanté*, of course. Just as you wish. And may I say that cakes and tea will be available from my good wife within the next few minutes, for those desirous. . . ."

"That is odd," agreed Clement, diving back into the conversation as soon as the manager had rolled away. "The child must have had a stone. Would it — she — have been buried anywhere else?"

"Where else?" asked Joseph.

"Oh, she would have been buried here," Ellen said. "Where our parents worshipped. They were devout churchgoers at the time, as most of the middle classes were until the war."

They looked at Joseph.

"Yes, I solved the mystery," he said. He lit a cigarette and sat back, tilting his chair back with him. "Since I drew blank at the churchyard, I went to the Town Hall and asked to check in the parish records. I enlisted the aid of a helpful lady clerk who dusted off the register of burials for the year 1920. We know our little angel was born in March of that year, so it should have died six months later, in September. But no entry in the records. Not a sausage. I began to wonder if the little horror had existed at all, if she wasn't just some ghastly hoax that the parents had decided to play on me, to rob me of the dubious honour of being their first-born.

"The clerk lady was resourceful. She thought to look in an old ledger they had preserved in which were logged payments to gravediggers. The Burial Fees book. This will all sound like Victorian England to you, Jean. To be honest, it does to me too. The book was quite a Victorian relic. Entries in ink, in copperplate. . . . Well, it was sixty-seven years ago. Another age." He sighed, then turned the sigh into a laugh.

"So what did it say in the book?" Jean asked.

"I found it: 'Stillborn female child of Mrs Madge Winter, 6 The Square, Nettlesham. Entry No. 5115. Fees taken: Board Fee, 1 shilling, Grave Digger, 1 shilling.'"

For a moment they were silent, and then all started talking at once. "Stillborn!" exclaimed Ellen. At which point, the manager rolled back with the tray of drinks and an enquiry as to whether they required *la musique* to be switched on again.

"Stillborn," repeated Joseph, when he had left them. "And the date of the entry — 20th March 1920. And attached to the entry was a certificate signed by a doctor to show that the delivery of the child had taken place on 18th March, 1920, at 6 The Square. . . ."

"So it didn't live six months," Sheila said.

"Mother always claimed it lived for six months," said Ellen. "I remember she had preserved a little pink nightdress it was supposed to have worn. You're sure you've got this right, Joseph?"

"At that time, it appears that stillborn infants were buried without a funeral. Because they had not been christened. Great, eh? They could be buried in the cemetery, but only in unconsecrated ground." He shook his head in disbelief at some profound wickedness. "Do you wonder she haunts me? Unconsecrated ground! And the graves were unmarked. I suppose they just shovelled the little corpse in under the chestnut trees. . . . In a box, I suppose. . . ."

"Oh, uncle, I'm so sorry. . . ."

"No, Jean, I feel all the better for knowing. To know is like laying a ghost."

Ellen said, "So they lied to us about the child. . . ."

"They? Father never lied. Father never said anything at all about the child. It didn't exist as far as he was concerned. It was mother who kept on about her."

"But why *lie*?"

"It doesn't require much psychological penetration to see why she lied. What do you think, Clement? You were too young. By the time you were born, long after Ellie had come along to console everyone, that storm was all over."

"I wouldn't call it a lie," Clement said thoughtfully, looking at Sheila. "I'd say it was a fantasy. A protective fantasy. Mother was editing her past in order to make it bearable."

He caught something in Sheila's expression, and stopped speaking. They looked into each other's eyes. Sheila said, "Yes. Not a lie. A kindness. Her child was born dead, but in retrospect she could give it six months of life and a Christian burial. That would mean that at least she had held it alive and kicking in her arms, and sucking milk. . . ."

Joseph rose from the table. He went to the window and stood with his back to it, drawing on his cigarette. "Sorry, I realise this is a tender subject for you, Sheila. I'd forgotten for a moment how you lost Juliet. But I'd say you've hit the nail on the head. That six months we always heard about, in which little Blank was such a paragon, was an invention, a protective device. Pathetic, really, wouldn't you say?" He looked round challengingly.

"Touching would be my word," Sheila said. "Tragic."

"Oh, well, you're a popular novelist. So that was my discovery today. I discovered that my little steel-engraving angel was truly dead and gone. The knowledge slightly abates some of the torture they put me through. . . ."

"Joe, you are a bit unfair to them," Ellen said. "They weren't that bad, were they, Clem?"

"Oh, to you they were great," Joseph said. "You were the little spoilt apple of mother's eye. Couldn't do a thing wrong, got everything you wanted —"

"You're jealous! You're still jealous!"

"Not a bit. Ellie, honestly, I pity you. It's almost worse to be spoilt than neglected. Look how you grew up. Nothing ever satisfied you. Then you married Alwyn, who treated you as if you were his baby rather than his wife. And poor Jean here — haven't you spoilt her rotten, so that her marriage collapsed after a couple of years? Jean, that bloke of yours was okay. You ought to go back to him and leave your mother to sort out her own problems."

"You bastard!" Jean exclaimed. "It's none of your bloody business why I ditched Bob. He was no good, wasn't he?"

"I daresay if you told him he was no good often enough, he came to believe it."

Ellen stood up, steadying herself with one hand on the table. "If that's really the time, then Jean and I must be on our way. Joe, I'm sorry you see fit to spoil a pleasant occasion. . . ."

He laughed. "Mother's funeral — a pleasant occasion! You said it, I didn't. Sorry, Ellie, you know me, can't keep my mouth shut."

"You should learn to. Silence is golden, especially in families. How else can they stick together? I've certainly had my troubles and I've learned not to complain."

"You sound like the Mater," he said coldly.

Ellen and Jean went round the table, kissing Clement and Sheila. She then turned towards Joseph, hesitated, and held out her hand. "I don't want to quarrel, Joe. It's been a trying day for all of us."

He took her hand. "I'll give you a ring some time. You know you were always the favourite of my two sisters. . . ."

"Come on, mum," Jean said, and led the way past the manager, who bobbed out with a quick *au revoir*, into the street.

Clement and Sheila sat where they were, clutching their glasses and looking downcast.

"That's what happens when you seek wisdom and completeness," Joseph said, sighing heavily.

He went and sat down next to his brother, putting a hand on Clement's shoulder. "Shall we get this joker to bring us another round?"

XIV

Sheila, her husband, and his brother dined together in the *Gryphon*. The meal was good, and served by a young waitress, while the manager presided over his bar, *bon soir*ing all and sundry. The food, wine, and service all had a benevolent effect; the trio was cheerful, and avoided the painful topics of the past.

After dinner, Joseph indicated that it was time he started to drive back to Acton. Clement and Sheila moved towards the hall with him, when he grasped his brother's arm.

"Here we are in my home town — not yours, I know, but it's where our little clan originated, in a way. When are we likely to be here again? God knows, I don't love the place, but there's not another Nettlesham. Let's have a quick canter round the back streets. Sheila won't mind, will you, Sheila?"

"Well . . . I take it from the locution that you'd rather be on your own with Clem. Do go, and don't get lost."

Nettlesham was rather dark and rather cold. Nettlesham was the eggshell left over when the chick had hatched, lying abandoned. It had known prosperity of a sort in the days, long past, when wool was important. Bygone people in Nettlesham had found wool interesting. Things had changed in the world; Nettlesham had remained. It wasn't even on the road to anywhere. People came to Nettlesham to retire.

The brothers walked down a street of meagre houses interspersed with shops. "There used to be an advert featuring a Red Indian on that gable end," Joseph said. "It frightened me. I was easily frightened."

He strolled along with his hands in his pockets. He had no coat. Clement was wrapped in a black overcoat. They walked in step.

They passed a modest Chinese take-away. A Chinese woman stood awaiting custom behind a wooden counter on which a small TV glittered. The woman stared blankly past it into the street.

Joseph gestured dismissively. "When I first got back to this country from Sumatra, Chinese and Indians were very scarce in England. If I saw one, particularly a Chinese, particularly a Chinese woman, I would follow her, just to get a look at those extraordinary planes of the face.

Well, shit, that's also all dead and buried. I hate talking about the past."

"People do it all the time as they get older. There should be another name for it." Clement laughed. "Something of the order of 'The Present', or 'The Environment'. I've ceased to be amazed at how people love talking to me about the war. It often seems to be the most vivid part of their lives."

"It's the jungle through which we move. I think about Burma as it was every week of my life, curse it." He pointed ahead down the street, to where a line of decorative red and blue lights burned. "Hey, Clem. The corner of Commercial Road. I'd forgotten. The *Conversation Arms*. It used to be pretty rough, or so father said. Not that he ever went in to drown his sorrows. Let's pop in and have a pint."

"It's getting late. You've got to get back to Acton."

"It's the *Conversation Arms*, Clem, named after old Westlake's poem. His most famous poem, or one of them. Come on, just a pint."

The *Conversation Arms* presented a square, shiny exterior to the world. Up to the level of the first floor, it was clad in brown tiling broken here and there by bands of cream tiling. It looked like an ill-designed fancy cake. Its windows, small, frosted and barred, might have served on a prison were it not for the encouraging legend "Ales & Spirits" engraved on them. The upper storey, in yellowing stucco, bore the words "Bullard's Ales" painted out, and an inn sign framed in wrought iron which showed two gentlemen with red noses *tête-à-tête*. They wore periwigs and tricorn hats.

The pub was already well occupied when the brothers entered. In the small room inside the door a group of youths of both sexes were standing shouting amiably at each other while drinking lager and smoking. Beyond — the pub was narrow but deep — was another room with a more extensive bar, where a number of men, mainly middle-aged, were talking more quietly over their drinks. Two women sat together on a bench, not speaking, surveying the scene with a docile air. Joseph bought two pints of bitter here and pushed into a third and rear room, where round tables and chairs were provided. A group of red-faced men were laughing heartily over a joke while asking each other if they "had heard that". The brothers took a seat beside an empty fireplace in which stood a large jar bearing the words "Grimsby's Foundry, 1903".

Beside the fireplace hung a printed paper, framed in a walnut frame.

"Look at that!" exclaimed Joseph. "Literature — you see, Clem. Nettlesham remembers its most famous son. I like that. A touch of piety in this godless town."

"A copy of 'The Conversation', is it?"

They went over to look at the pamphlet. On close inspection, it proved to be merely a photocopy of the original poem, published in 1781.

"Well, that's typical. Everything's a fake nowadays. I suppose they flogged the original and thought a copy was the same thing. Another symptom of tranny-culture. At least they still remember a good native poet. That's something."

"He was a pretty awful poet, wasn't he?"

Joseph eyed his brother suspiciously, before going to sit down, offended, by his glass.

"Who are you to judge? Are you an expert on poetry, Clem? Why do you find him *pretty awful*? Did you ever read him? Doesn't he rhyme? Doesn't he scan? What's your objection?"

"Oh . . . he's a bit sententious, isn't he?"

"Did you ever read him? No. Yet you judge. I happen to like Westlake. At least, that is the position I took up many years ago, and it's too late to change now. It's true he thought peasants led a happy life, but that was a common eighteenth-century illusion. I happen to have a tolerance of sententiousness, and all the poor sod's other imputed faults."

"I don't read much poetry."

"You ought to try Westlake's 'A Summer Stroll Through Parts of Suffolk'. Really. He sets sail from the old iambic pentameter, defies Alexander Pope, and even looks forward to poets like Hardy."

When Clement made no response, Joseph shrugged his shoulders and laughed.

"He was a poet and he went mad in Nettlesham, and that's good enough for me. I drink to William Westlake."

They drank in silence, elbows on table. The silence extended itself uncomfortably until suddenly Joseph plunged into talk.

"I suppose you'll mourn mother. I shall, despite all I may say. Bravado speaking. I'll miss her. This whole pathetic business about the dead child — 'stillborn'. . . . Funny to discover that little bit of truth on the very day we bury her, funny the way these secrets leak out. I'll be very happy to work all that business out of my system.

"Twelve years difference between us — we've never been very close. You don't think much of me, do you?"

"That's not so, though it's true we've not been close. I suppose you don't think a great deal of me."

"Oh, you're so cautious, Clem. There's one thing for which I admire you very very greatly, if you want to know." Joseph leaned forward and tapped the table with a finger for emphasis. "I admire you for the way you stuck by Sheila when your daughter died in that car crash. I admire the way you comforted each other. That sort of thing goes beyond marriage. People are almost incapable of fucking comforting each other. I speak as one uncomforted. You two comforted each other. There was no blame about who was driving when it happened — or not as far as I know. You simply comforted each other, and so you got over it, and so you have achieved — I say this seriously and not without envy — a good marriage."

He drained his glass and, as he rose, said, "Now we'll talk about father, but first we'll fortify ourselves with another pint of the same. At least the *Conversation Arms* has Adnam's Ale. . . ."

Clement sat rather helplessly where he was until his brother came back. As he set his beer down neatly on the wet ring left by the previous pint, he blurted out, "Before you say anything, I was very fond of father. Of course I remember him only in Bude, when he was getting on in years. There was no doubt that losing his share of the business here to Uncle Hereward told against him. He lived for the shop."

"I've always thought there was more to that than met the eye. Father was swindled in some way — that's what I think." Joseph laughed. "When I was in Burma, father wrote to me precisely once. To tell me how Uncle Hereward and Aunt Hermione had been up in London with their three sons, at a Noel Coward play, when a bomb fell on the theatre and killed them all outright. Father made no comment beyond relaying the bare facts, but I could tell he thought justice had been done."

"It does seem to say something for the war."

"And for Noel Coward." They laughed.

"That probably wouldn't stop him feeling that he had let grandad down. Grandad being a self-made man and all that. I say 'probably' because he never talked about it. I respected him —"

"There you have the whole key to father's character. He never talked about anything. As an analyst, you must have your opinions on that. Don't you remember how, even in your time, all his remarks came to us through mother? He was the officer, she was the NCO. We were the bloody privates. Why he was so silent, we'll never know, I suppose. But that seems to have been his character. Very withdrawn. Maybe it was his experiences during the first war.

"Immediately after the war, marriage. Then that bloody stillborn kid. God, the mess that accident made of our lives. How all my days have been tarnished — never mind, you've heard that tune before. The fact that sticks out a mile is that mother had to make up a fantasy that the kid lived for six months. She had to console herself. Why? Because father didn't console her. He couldn't bring himself to do as you did when you lost a child. You have to forget yourself a bit and *give* in such circumstances. He

213

couldn't give. I can just imagine it and I swear that's what happened, that he simply went back to the shop and got on with work. Never said a word about the matter again. Not a word. They probably didn't even screw each other for years after the death."

As Joseph paused to drink, Clement said, "This is all your imagination. Of course he'd have tried to comfort her. They were only just married, they'd have been in love. You don't know —"

"You think it's mother I hate, for all she did to me. It's not. It's father, for all he didn't do.

"I worshipped him, modelled myself on him. I wanted to be his little slave. My ambition was to be just like him, take the dog for walks, go shooting rabbits, church on Sundays, smoke a pipe with a jaunty air. Even sell buckets. Everything he did, I wanted to do. I craved to learn. I craved to be in his company. He had no patience. He didn't want me there. To him I was a perfect nonentity, a blank. He took me into an outfitter's once, to buy me a shirt — I can't remember why, because mother used to do that sort of thing. I tried on one of the shirts — I suppose I was about eight years old — and for some reason didn't like it. I said, 'It doesn't suit me, daddy.' He put his finger between my neck and the collar and gave it a sort of impatient wrench, saying, 'Of course it suits you if I say so.'

"You see, he had no concept of *me* at all. It never occurred to him that I might possibly have an individual life."

Clement listened as his brother went on in the same vein, often laughing as he spoke. Outside the window near which they were sitting was a wooden post, standing at an angle and illuminated by the light from the pub; for the rest, the darkness allowed only a vague impression of the walls of a back yard. The two women on the bench came within the line of his observation; they were talking confidingly together over their gins, the slightly older woman, wearing a pink coat, dominating the conversation, while the younger one, who wore trousers and a sweater with the word "Oklahoma" across her breasts, confined her contribution to a series of nods and exclamations of disgust. It occurred to Clement that the younger one was quite pretty, despite fashionably straggly hair. The red-faced men drinking at the round table nearby kept casting glances at her, glances of which the Oklahoma lady seemed totally unaware.

"Do you want a whisky?" Joseph asked, interrupting himself. "The cup that cheers and inebriates?"

"No, I don't want to get drunk, Joe. You've got to drive back to Acton, haven't you?"

"Christ, I must have a smoke. Where's their bloody cigarette machine?" As he asked the question, Joseph rose and plunged towards the far end of the pub, where the youths were still in voluble conversation. At almost the same moment, the Oklahoma lady said something to her companion and rose; she too headed towards the door. Clement, draining off his pint, watched as his brother and the woman met at the cigarette machine. Joseph immediately began talking to her. Somehow, they became entangled with the youths. One of the bigger lads exchanged words with Joseph, who gave, even at a distance, a convincing imitation of a very angry man. The lad backed off and returned to the chatter with his mates.

Joseph and the woman, who was possibly in her late thirties, stood talking by the machine, and moved together towards their seats, joking amiably and smiling as they lit their cigarettes. The *Conversation Arms* was now filling up. Joseph took the woman's arm and guided her back to her bench, sitting down beside her, smiling, as Oklahoma introduced him to the older woman, who did not look particularly pleased at the intervention, to judge by the way she wrapped her pink coat more tightly round her middle.

Finding himself abandoned, Clement was so annoyed that he went up to the bar and ordered himself a whisky-and-soda, by no means his usual tipple, standing there to drink it with his back to the room.

He had almost finished the whisky when Joseph nudged him on one arm, saying cheerfully, "Sorry about that. What are you drinking?"

His manner had changed. He puffed away on a cigarette in obvious good humour. His jacket was unbuttoned, his tie slightly awry, his hair slightly ruffled. He ordered himself a whisky on the rocks, saying almost at the same time, by way of an aside to his brother, "Come on over and meet a couple of nice women. Iris and — Christ, what was the other one's name? Susan, I think she said. Sarah. No, maybe Sophie. Josie? Anyhow, Iris is mine."

"Come on, Joe, you must be pissed. You nearly got into a fight then, didn't you? Bit old for that sort of thing, aren't you?"

Joseph laughed. "If you've got grey hair or you're wearing a tie, they think they can take advantage of you. Iris is the one with Oklahoma written across her tits." He sang a line of song and laughed, "'You're doing fine, Oklahoma. . . .'"

"Let's get out of here. You are pissed. Picking up women at your age. It's ridiculous!"

"I'm not picking them up. I simply got talking to them. That's what pubs are for. I liked the look of her. She's a nice girl. It's always been easy for me to get friendly with women. Women are very approachable. They don't have the hang-ups — I mean, you should hear women talk about how difficult it is to get friendly with men. Men have all the hang-ups. Women see the world in a completely different light. I admit it's true of me, too. I'm as bad as the rest. I find it easy to get friendly with women. I love women. My trouble is, that I'm terrified of them leaving me. So I always concoct some difficulty, some quarrel or other, so that we break up. I can't tell you. . . .

"Well, yes, I can fucking tell you. That's really why I admire you, Clem. You and Sheila have stuck together, despite everything. Do you reckon she's easier to live with because she's got writing as a hobby? Well, hardly a hobby. . . . Now, me, I suppose you think I'm a terrible womaniser, nearly sixty, ought to settle down. It's not so at all. Sex soon palls, don't you think. Perhaps you don't think so? It's better in anticipation, like most things." He looked glancingly into Clem's face as he said this, with a smile. Clement felt himself charmed; even behind his brother's most cynical remarks lay a kind of spirit resembling light-heartedness.

"It's just my terrible insecurity forces me to chuck them out just when everything seems rosy. I suppose it's because — this only recently dawned on me — this is juvenile experience fucking me up all over again. I'm always secretly afraid they'll desert me, just as mother did. Until recently, I didn't even realise I had that fear. That's progress, at least, identifying the thing. No doubt it helps a bit. If only I could get over it. Don't think I wouldn't have been married long ago." He paused and drank.

"I don't know what to say."

"You mean you don't know what attitude to take to me," said Joseph, with a sudden flare of anger, bowing his head to light a cigarette. "You never did. You're buggered up, not me. Your profession has buggered you up. We'll never agree, I'm Dionysiac, you're Apollonian. I don't want pity. I'm proud of it. Well, not proud. But you have to fill a lifetime with something, don't you?"

Blowing out smoke, he remembered the women. "I'm supposed to be buying them gins. Come on over and meet them. Iris and Sophie. I think it's Sophie."

It was Josie. Clement sat with Josie on his right and Iris on his left. Joseph was on Iris's left.

"I'm Apollonian," Clement told Josie with dignity.

Josie had her problems. Her husband was working for the Saudi-Arabians, while she was left in Nettlesham with two young teenage children to look after. She lived in a semi-detached, and the people in the other half of the semi, the Dowkers, were making her life a misery. Mr Dowker had three strong teenage lads, about whom Josie had been to the police several times. She had proof they had killed her cat and hung it from her clothes line. They drilled holes through the bedroom wall in order to spy on her daughter.

Joe had his arm round Iris and was telling her of ways to be happy. "I don't want to be *happy*," she said, protestingly. "Don't get me wrong. I just want to enjoy life. I'm still young, but this bloke Eddie won't let me alone. He keeps popping up. I told him, I said, I am not interested any longer, and I hate the smell of kebabs, but he said to me, Where I come from it's never a case of not being interested, you can't be not interested once you've started. So I told him, I said, Well, this is England, and in England it's quite usual for people not to be interested any old day of the week they please, but then you see he says —"

"Why don't you look at it this way, Iris? I've had a lucky life, really, done a lot of the things I wanted to do, though sometimes I think it has been a pretty miserable one, until I see how other people are getting on. And I believe that you have to fill your life with something. The truth is that in evolutionary terms, the human race was not properly created. We're neither animal nor angel, and we just don't know what to do with our lives. I'll get you another gin in a minute.

"Your generation wasn't brought up on the Bible, but I was, and I think that human life's like the Third Day. You know God is supposed to have created the world in seven days. On the Third Day, he created the sea in one place and the dry land in another, and he caused grass to grow everywhere. It was a terribly boring dump, and evidently the Almighty had to have a bloody good think before he decided what to do next. The human mind's like that. Just grass and dry land and the odd patch of ocean to begin with. We each of us have to think what else should go there. And we actually have the option. We stock it with obsessions, assumptions. I won't go into mine, but basically I was rejected at birth and from that rejection I've managed to fill my mind. The point I'm trying to make is that we're actually in charge from the Third Day on — we can choose what to put in all that space. We have to choose unless we're to become basket cases. We have to choose whether to be educated, to accept education, we have to choose whether to be good or bad, we have to choose whether to be happy or miserable. As a French philospher once said, we are neither as happy nor as miserable as we think. We really do make choices in all the vital areas DNA doesn't predetermine. The difficulty is, that the choices we make are based emotionally on all the chance things that happened to us on Day One and Day Two, which we don't remember because we were too young and unformed. Do you see what I'm getting at?"

"Sort of. You mean the Bible's true, after all?"

"No, I bloody don't. Look, I'll explain. You're so involved with this Eddie because whether you realise it or not you need to be. Something in his foreignness attracts you, but you could chuck it all if you really wanted. Throw it off like a coat. Be someone different tomorrow. Character isn't permanent, choice is. I nearly married a Chinese girl once, just because she was so unlike my mother I thought she wouldn't skip out and leave me." He roared with laughter.

"What do you do?" Iris asked. "What's your job?"

"I'm a historian of the Far East."

"I think maybe Josie and me had better be going. It's getting late."

When the pub closed, and Clement and Joseph were ushered out into the cold, they proceeded up the dark street arm in arm, Joseph at least in the best of spirits.

"I don't know what Sheila will say," Clement remarked.

"She was nice, wasn't she? Iris. Sweet little person, easy-going at heart, I'd say, but pretty stupid."

"What on earth were you telling her?"

"What she needs is a good man. No, maybe not — who knows what people need? She wouldn't come with me. What *was* I saying? Just trying to cheer her up. She's got problems."

"You should hear Josie's problems. One feels so compassionate. You were giving Iris some nonsense about choosing the way you live. It was nonsense, utter nonsense — well, I thought it was nonsense, although I didn't catch exactly what you were saying. Anyhow, you were very optimistic."

"I'm always optimistic. This parental stuff — it isn't going to bite so hard from now on. I'm determined."

"Why don't you go and see someone?"

Joseph did not answer. He gave his brother's shoulders an affectionate squeeze. They turned a corner and the *Gryphon* lay ahead.

"Glad I left this fucking town." He sketched with a free hand what passed in the gloom for an airy eighteenth-century gesture. "Remember Westlake — 'I was a crippled goat that lost its way. But took delight in being all astray'."

Sheila was sitting in the cosy bar of the *Gryphon*, saying farewells to a young couple who were about to leave. Joseph went up to her and became heavily gallant in a drunken way, clutching her about the waist, while Clement looked on, laughing.

"Get off me, Joe! You'd better not drive back to Acton in that state."

He persisted. "We've just been celebrating the great event, Sheila, dear Sheila — burying the old girl, you know. She'll be with the angels this evening!" He put his hands together in mock-piety and rolled his eyes upwards, allowing Sheila to stand back and confront him. Something changed in the generous planes of her face. Suddenly, she was Green Mouth, standing no nonsense from anyone.

"Joe, I'll tell you something. You are just a baby, and a rather noxious one at that. Why can't you show some love, or at least respect, for your mother? Have you ever had a moment's pity for her, poor woman? You're a self-dramatising bastard, entirely self-centred —"

"I know all this," he broke in. "Known it ages. . . . Not again, old girl. Virtue makes me want to throw up."

She pushed Clement away as he moved to her side.

"Throw up if you like, but first listen to me. The way you go on and on about that dead sister of yours! The first Clem ever told me about you was that you had this hang-up. It's become your signature tune, your cue for sympathy, your cue to grab centre stage. Can't you think of something better? Do you like going about acting the cripple? Do you do it so that women can mother you? God, you must be a real mess in bed! You never spare one single thought for how your mother might have felt when her first little baby died, do you? Do you know that the death of a baby is about the worst thing a mother can ever suffer, worse than losing a partner, worse even than rape? Feelings of guilt, inadequacy, failure, utter loneliness —"

"Sheila!" Clement took her arm. He could see that she also had been drinking. A tear rolled down her cheek, and she was winding herself up to say more. The young couple stood by the door, ready to leave but longing to hear.

"Keep out of this, Clem. You only encourage Joe. He has never made any attempt to understand how callously his mother might have been treated by everyone, back whenever it was. It was regarded as a disgrace to give birth to a dead baby. A disgrace. Ernest's attitude was all important, and he may have blamed her, who knows? Instead of consoling her. The doctor certainly didn't even let her see or hold the little baby — it would be taken away and shovelled under, and she'd be left to grieve with no memory of it. And then the agony for her, a religious woman, of having the burial in unconsecrated ground. . . ." She turned on Joseph. "When I saw you, when I watched you today, telling your pathetic tale with such relish, such venom — oh, such delicious excitement, I realised your true character —"

"Stow it, you pompous, preaching woman," said Joseph, clenching his fists. "You love a scene, don't you? You're jealous because I took your precious husband off for a couple of hours. Get back to your best-sellers and leave the legions of the lost to look after themselves."

Making a disgusted face at Clement, he turned, barged past him, and staggered out into the darkness of the Nettlesham night.

XV

An old moon was waning above the roof-tops of North Oxford. The sky over Linton Road was of a purplish blue special to the hour between summer day and night. Even the noise of Sunday traffic on the main road seemed to attune itself to the sensuous pleasure of the moment, as the Winters came away from Carisbrooke. A thorny hedgehog could be heard snuffling in the gutter, hoping for grubs and starlight. The gardens of houses on either side of the street, masked by dusk, so that their general air of neglect did not show, were voluptuously clad in green. Nature was not incompatible with old brick. This suburb had been established long enough for saplings, staked out by Victorian hands, to have developed hearty trunks, and branches which looked in at upper casement windows. They had been generous, those early botanisers, planting out not merely flimsy trees and ornamental cherries but what were now, in effect, grand forest giants, their roots, burrowing through clay under old walls, eventually defining metaphorical ways across ceilings in the form of hairline cracks seeking exploratory courses over coving and plaster. At this silvery hour, appearances suggested that North Oxford had been built in a wood. Oberon and Titania might have emerged from the leafy grounds of Carisbrooke, clad in their academic gowns, without untoward effect.

Clement walked back from college with Sheila beside him. He found that the pain in his left leg was eased if he progressed more slowly than usual. Perhaps in sympathy, she clung to his arm. He was glad of the solid feel of her against him and, enjoying her companionship and the warmth of the evening, felt disinclined to talk. Sheila was conversational; parties always energised her.

"Nansey Fender-Lieversohn has had such an interesting life," Sheila said, and proceeded to regale Clement with some of the details. He half-listened, observing the dying light in the trees while trying to gauge how much pleasure he derived from it. He thought he remembered a performance of *Tristan und Isolde* in Salzburg, some years ago, where the advent of evening in Act II had been achieved more poignantly. With the recollection came the distant sound of hunting horns.

He and Sheila were returning home from a small party given by Aaron Fender-Lieversohn and his wife Nansey in Fender-Lieversohn's rooms, before his return to Israel. Fender-Lieversohn had spent a year at Carisbrooke, working on a study of Husserl and phenomenology. Over the year, he and Clement had enjoyed several pleasant conversations. Fender-Lieversohn was a frail man in his late seventies; Clement wondered if they would ever see each other again, and if Fender-Lieversohn would finish his work on Husserl — or even if he wished to finish, while continuance implied creativity, that hallmark of life.

Whilst trapped *tête-à-tête* with one of the Fender-Lieversohns' more tedious guests, Clement had been able to overhear part of a nearby conversation between Sheila and Nansey Fender-Lieversohn. Nansey was some years younger than her husband. He already knew — as did most of Carisbrooke — of her involvement with Jean-Paul Sartre, when Aaron's interests had taken him to Paris, and of how the bright-painted creature had been kidnapped by Sicilian gangsters, had corresponded with Chou En-lai, and enjoyed other enlarging episodes. Her adventures had, in fact, become a topic to be avoided around the college. Her sensationally awful girlhood in Poland was also common knowledge. An anti-reminiscence mafia had sprung up to evade her anecdotes. In Sheila, Nansey had found a new listener, and out came the terrors once again, delivered with glittering eye, while Sheila responded with chirpy cries of, "Oh, and to think how happy my childhood was!" As she retold Nansey's tales, Clement listened with patience, checking on how accurate Sheila's short term memory was. It seemed in good fettle this evening, despite a considerable amount of the Fender-Lieversohns' white wine.

Once they were home, Clement and Sheila went through into the kitchen to make themselves cups of tea. Michelin appeared to be out, which was nothing surprising. They refrained from switching lights on, preferring to be together in the half-dark, enjoying the voluptuousness of dusk, the softening into ambiguity of day's outlines.

"You all right? You were walking a bit slowly. Still worrying about what happened to you yesterday in your brother's flat?"

"I certainly wonder how exactly to categorise that experience, yes."

"Does that affect your leg?"

"Old Aaron's interested in phenomenology and how Husserl's trail led to existentialism, but he doesn't seem to have investigated the psychology of perception very thoroughly."

"Nansey hinted that she had once been the mistress of Martin Heidegger. Was he a phenomenologist?"

"I don't think she could have been. She likes to embroider her tales, you know."

"You didn't tell Aaron about your experience yesterday, did you? Wouldn't that come under the heading of phenomenology?"

"That's private. Don't go spreading it around, will you, or people will think I'm cracking at last. I could have touched Joseph. He was so real."

"But you didn't touch him. So he remains an unclassified phenomenon. Sit down and rest. I'm a bit worried about you, seeing ghosts."

The kettle was coming to the boil and making a song and dance of it. He sat down, surreptitiously rubbing his calf. He said rather loudly, "Significance doesn't lie in the object itself, but in the object as perceived, however erroneously or distortedly. Husserl appreciated that. And that seems to be as true in science as in analysis."

"And that applies to Nansey's early life?"

"To everything. To a cup of tea. We regard tea as benevolent. The tannin is actually a deadly drug."

Sheila laughed, pouring boiling water on to two tea bags, watching the clear water colour as steam rose to her eyes. She said, not looking at him, "You don't really believe that. You're just saying it for effect. Why do you always try to impress me?"

Despite the wine he had drunk, he was taken aback by the unexpected challenge.

"That's the Oxford manner. Everything's effect, effect is everything. I'm surprised you haven't contracted it yourself, living in this house in your fantasy world, immune from outside influence. Even at the party, you weren't talking to any of my colleagues, only to outsiders like Nansey Fender-Lieversohn, who will be leaving Oxford in a week or two anyway. I've had to adjust to the environment. Even if it's only protective camouflage, some of it gets through. Doesn't matter how foolishly you behave, as long as what you say is either frivolously intellectual or intellectually frivolous."

She stood immobile in the middle of the kitchen, milk jug in hand, half-raised in the air, as if about to pour a libation.

"Your colleagues don't like me. Timid rats! That's why I talk to outsiders. They're all male chauvinists and they absolutely hate what I write. Even Maureen criticises my novels, and says they are not politically aware enough, although my central characters are women. As if Queen Gyronee wasn't a real independent —"

"You pay too much attention to Maureen. Ever since she's made feminism pay."

"Oh, shut up. Don't think I don't know what people say about my . . ."

Feeling slightly dizzy, Clement rose from the chair and said, "I have to live with these people. If I may quote, we all have our crosses to bear. We all have our John Farrers living next to us. It's a conformist place, the University, by its nature. No wonder there's so much mental illness."

"Even in Carisbrooke, they only read spy stories. And you love it, Clem, don't deny it. Oxford was made for you and you for it."

He fell silent, not happy with the tone in which Sheila delivered this remark. So preoccupied were they with each other that in the dusk they missed the letter awaiting them on top of the refrigerator.

Carrying their cups of tea, they made their way slowly upstairs to bed. The street light outside meant that the front of the house was never dark at night. An antiseptic imitation of moonlight seeped round the curtains on to the landing, throwing shadows of pictures and their frames slantwise over the walls.

They sat down on the side of the double bed in near-dark, not bothering to draw the curtains.

"Did you have lunch with Maureen, or did you work as planned?"

"Inspiration ran out early. We went to the *Perch* for lunch. It was crowded."

"So you've been boozing all day. What a good preparation for Nansey Fender-Lieversohn. And how's feminism these days?"

He could see in the dimness that she lowered her eyes, looking away from him as if moved by instinct to protect her thoughts.

"Oh, we had a long talk." Said with studied carelessness.

"Oh? What about? Love? Fecundation?"

"Maureen was in fine form. Lots of ghoulish sexual anthropology stories as usual. She has nearly finished her latest book on women." Sheila folded her hands and looked across them sideways at her husband. "It's to be called *People with Breasts*."

"*People with Breasts*. . . ." A sudden gust of laughter took him. Sheila joined in. He sank back on the bed, laughing and protesting that he was sloshed. She lay back with him, giggling and cuddling him.

It was while he was brewing himself a cup of coffee on the following morning that Clement observed the white envelope on the top of the refrigerator. As he took it up, he saw that it bore his name, written in Michelin's neat handwriting. At once a premonition of dread filled his mind. He tore the envelope open.

The message inside was brief.

Dear Clement,

This is to tell you I shall leave now. I have enough of acting as your housekeeper. You have taken me for granted too much. It is final.

Not all of my things are with me. One will come later to take away more of my possessions. Good-bye to you both.

Michelle

P.S. You can see I sign with my proper name.

Clement brought a carton of single cream from the refrigerator and poured some into his coffee. He sat down with the note by his cup. He tried as calmly as possible to put aside guilt feelings, which he perceived to be contradictory: on the one hand, self-reproach because he had once tried to seduce Michelin; on the other, self-reproach because he had not tried often enough. He told himself that in some way he had let her down, searching for a sexual reason for this abrupt departure, since sexual motives lay behind most human activity.

When he had finished his coffee, he went slowly upstairs, taking the note with him. Sheila was just emerging from the shower, stepping naked and powdered into the bedroom. When Clement entered, she hurriedly covered her nudity with a bath towel — an unexpected gesture which registered on him only later.

"A bit of a shock, love," he said, holding out the piece of paper. "I'm afraid our Michelin's left us."

"Don't be silly," she said, glancing sharply at him as she snatched the letter. "That can't be."

She read it hurriedly, in a flurry of perfume.

"I don't believe it. How can she leave like this?" Dropping the note on the floor, she tucked the towel more firmly round herself and went to look out of the window, as if hoping to see Michelin there. "The woman doesn't even mention my name. It's an insult. I've always been so careful of her feelings."

"She was one of the family." He wanted to go on to say, "She was like a daughter to us," but checked himself, not wishing to cause Sheila unnecessary pain. Like a daughter, he thought, she suddenly decided to up and leave. We mustn't think of this as final. She may come back. Poor Michelin, something's troubling her. But what a damned nuisance.

"Fuck her," Sheila said. She flung her blue towelling robe over her bare shoulders and rushed from the room. He stood where he was, listening as she ran upstairs and banged open the door of Michelin's room. After a while, she came downstairs again, frowning, biting a finger.

"Well, this is just too much. She's done a bunk. What does she mean, 'acting as our housekeeper'? She lived here free, didn't she? We looked after her when she was ill. Bloody bitch. Oh, if she's pinched something. . . !"

"I don't suppose she's pinched anything."

She rounded on him angrily. "You're defending her? What's the meaning of such a stupid letter, after twelve years? Twelve years! We've arranged our lives round her. She's stayed on in the villa in Marbella — had free holidays at our expense, met our friends. . . . This is a fucking insult. Why didn't she mention me?"

"We don't know what's behind it."

"Oh, god, you're always so calm, Clem! How are we to manage now? Have you thought about that? Am I supposed to do the housework, like an ordinary housewife? Is that what you expect, because I'm not!"

He said helplessly, "We'll just have to get someone else. Probably Arthur will know of someone."

"Arthur?" She stared at him blankly, frowning.

"Arthur, yes. Arthur Stranks, or his wife. I think they have someone. . . ."

She walked about the room, saying to herself, "Well, this really mucks things up. How thoughtless can you get? What got into the woman? What's this grumble about her proper name? I suppose she was jealous of me in some way." She sighed deeply, "We'll have the police round here next. They'll have fished her body out of the Isis."

"Yes, I'm also slightly concerned for her safety. . . ."

Again she turned on him with a look of contempt. "Are you trying to be funny at my expense? God, you're irritating. Trust you to be 'slightly concerned'! I don't care what's happened to her, not after she treats us like this. What kind of creature have we been clutching to our bosoms all these years?"

"You're being melodramatic. We must look for some explanation. There may be a man involved."

"What man? You know she isn't interested in men. Never has been. You found that out for yourself, didn't you?"

"Well, there must be some explanation. I must get to work. I'll ring St Emma's and see if they know anything about it."

She looked almost pityingly. "Life has to go on as usual, eh?"

It was Clement's turn to sigh. "I fear it always does, Sheila."

"Oh, no, it doesn't," she said.

"Gordon Bennett, that's awful," said Arthur Stranks, briskly. "I know how upset Cheri will be when I tell her. Er — she knows how much you and Sheila depended on Michelin."

"Well, we gave each other mutual support," said Clement. On arrival at Carisbrooke, he had not been able to keep the impact of Michelin's dismal note to himself and, rather to his surprise, had told everything to his research assistant.

Arthur now stood in the bay window, scratching the Scrubbing Brush Cut and trying to look for all the world as if something awful had happened to him.

"You hadn't had any kind of row?"

"Certainly not. We never had rows."

"Let me drive you round to St Emma's. I've got the car. We can find out straight away what they know about her. I'll just ring Cheri and let her know what's happened."

"Oh, no, Arthur, really, that isn't necessary, is it?" He was disturbed by the way his assistant seemed to be taking over Michelin's disappearance, and waved his hands to reinforce the seriousness of his protest.

"Perhaps there's something Cheri could do to help. She could go round and see Sheila, perhaps. She's free this morning because, as I think I mentioned, the library's putting her on part-time. They're having to make some cuts."

"Another of the government's blows against culture?"

Even that remark failed to stop Arthur. Bouncing in his trainers, he led the way across the quad to the car park, where his new blue Zastava Caribbean waited. Clement found himself cramped into the front passenger seat, remembering his last lift, when Arthur and Cheri had taken him to see Tina Turner, in the days of the Mini with the printed jokes in the rear window.

"She wasn't — well, funny, or anything? Michelin?"

"She told me once that her soul was in China."

"Soul in China? What does that mean?"

"Arthur, sometimes I wish I had taken up a different career and was even now digging up dinosaur bones in Wyoming. I'm no good at dealing with people."

"That's cool, coming from you!" As he spoke, Arthur shot a quick smiling glance at Clement. To Clement, it came as a shock. Good God, he thought, he actually admires me. Or makes a good pretence of it.

They negotiated the Banbury Road traffic to the sound of Radio One.

The single window in St Emma's secretary's office looked out through leaded windows to an enclosed stretch of lawn, where a bust of someone once illustrious took shelter under a laburnum tree. The diamond pane motif was carried over in the embroidery on the secretary's cotton shirt, while the glazing was continued by the spectacles she wore on a gold chain about her neck. Two small breasts lay concealed beneath the shirt. She was a birdlike creature of no particular age, with quick movements, glimpses of spiky teeth, and bony little hands which seemed poised as if about to attack an invisible piano. They ceased their foray on a typewriter as she darted a look at the two men. The spiky teeth were revealed in a momentary smile as she said, unhelpfully, "Yes?"

Arthur stated their business in an efficient way.

The secretary sat down on her hands, as a preliminary to not being helpful, and shook her head, as if she had practised these difficult movements many times. Forestalling her, Arthur, who had Clement firmly in tow, introduced him with full titles.

"Oh, sorry, Dr Winterman, yes, I'm afraid to say that Michelle Bouyat has left St Emma's," the secretary said, retrieving her hands from her sparrowy buttocks.

"When did she leave?"

Feeling called upon to answer this question standing up, the secretary rose to her sandalled feet, saying, "It wasn't very convenient for us, really, her leaving before the end of term. So inconsiderate. She went last Friday. Would you like to see the Warden? I think she's available."

"Three days ago. . . ." While Clement and Arthur exchanged thoughtful glances at this evidence of iniquity, the secretary resumed her chair, perhaps as an indication that her duty was done. "Just tell me, miss, have you a forwarding address?"

She rifled through an antiquated card filing system. Arthur, computer born and bred, rolled up his eyes in horror. Peering short-sightedly at a large pink card, the secretary said, "We've got an address in a place called Saint Enemy."

"*Sainte Enémie*," Clement corrected her, without thinking. "That's on the Tarn. It's an old address — her aunt's, I believe. Did she tell you why she was leaving?"

"Oh, yes. She was going to get married."

"*Married?* To whom?"

"She didn't say." The hands were firm about that, and alighted on the typewriter.

"Someone must have asked her that all-too-obvious question. When a lady in her mid-forties gets married, it's quite an event. Who would know?"

But the secretary could help them no further. Her manner indicated that she was offended by the assumption that there was something going on to which others were privy and she not. Further questions were met with helpless shrugs and one further glimpse of the front teeth. In the end, Clement and Arthur left, and walked back to the Zastava.

"I'll ring the Warden later," Clement said. "I have some slight acquaintance with her. We've met once or twice at dinner."

When they got back to the College, he phoned Sheila, but their number was engaged. Sighing, he turned to work, and was soon engrossed in the early weeks of 1940.

Arthur presented him with three new letters, one from a correspondent in New Zealand who had been a child in Coventry when that city was bombed by the Luftwaffe and remembered the cathedral burning. The other two were from correspondents who had written before, answering Clement's forms, and had essentially nothing fresh to add. They wrote for the pleasure of talking about what one correspondent referred to, without apparent cynicism, as "the good old days". It was a matter of conjecture as to how much these correspondents could be said to have adapted, not to the war and its upheavals, but to the peace which followed.

On his way home that evening, he visited the post office in North Parade to buy Sheila a box of her favourite Belgian chocolates. Directly he let himself in the front door, the emptiness of the house struck him. Closing the front door softly, he stood for a full minute in the hall, listening to the silent signals emanating from various rooms.

He directed his gaze up the stairs. Here were ranged some of the Victorian and Edwardian oils which Sheila collected: a Leighton, a Peacock, and a Stone, leading towards her two favourite John Collier puzzle paintings which hung in her sitting-room upstairs. At the top of the flight of stairs, he could just see from where he stood an etching of Poynter's sinister "Faithful Unto Death". He looked, however, not at the framed pictures but at the shadowy vacancy before them — expecting, for a superstitious moment, that his brother might appear again.

Clement felt tired and dispirited, and went through to the drinks fridge in the kitchen to pour himself a Cinzano on the rocks laced with vodka. He observed that the bottle of Smirnoff he and Sheila had brought Michelin from New York had gone. Walking into the conservatory, he dropped the chocolates in a wicker armchair. He picked up the *Independent*, but dropped that too after a minute's desultory scanning of the headlines.

Gyronee, Queen of Kerinth, was still staring into the future from her alcove. The doglike thing by her feet appeared to be looking direct at Clement. He had never trusted it.

If only Juliet had lived, she might have been here to greet me.

Making an effort, he forced himself to go and inspect Michelin's room. She had folded her duvet neatly and piled her used towels, also folded, on top. A calendar of France for 1987 hung open at June on one wall. All her personal effects had been removed, except for two large suitcases standing by the door. A faint scent of perfume was traceable in the air. He reflected on the nature of the person who had shared his and Sheila's lives for so long. She had entered their existence casually, one day on a mountain road, and had as casually left it. Was she happy about the prospect of marriage, or did the abruptness of her farewell note indicate otherwise?

Not to have her help during the party on Thursday was going to be difficult. Perhaps they should cancel the party. No, that would be to give away their precious privacy, to start rumours. Perhaps Cheri Stranks would come and assist.

He thought of Sheila. "I'm enjoying it too much to stop. . . ." Well, she had stopped, and no doubt Arthur Hernandez was as absent from her mind as he was from Clement's. The upset of Michelin's disappearance would drive him even further. Right now, she was most likely at a SOW meeting. SOW was the Society of Oxford Writers she had helped found. Even distinguished writers like A. N. Wilson had joined, to her delight. They would simply have to grow accustomed to Michelin's absence.

In his study, he rifled through Joseph's papers rather aimlessly, then lay on his couch and dozed for ten minutes, the Cinzano beside him.

In contrast with his wife's Colliers, all that Clement's study had to offer in the way of the pictorial was a severe 1927 Kandinsky, which Sheila had bought him at a New York auction.

The silence of the house weighed on him. Joseph seemed to be in a dream he had, but when he woke the contents of the dream eluded him — as perhaps after death, he thought, the contents of life might elude one.

He went over to the boxes containing Joseph's literary remains, conscious of a slight resentment of his brother. Michelin's unexplained disappearance gave him a feeling of being incapable of managing his life; the present had to be negotiated, without these encumbrances from the past.

He sat down on the edge of his couch with a hardbound notebook labelled "Book of Dreams", to which Joseph had stuck a Chinese gift tag. The tag showed an undulant Chinese lady carrying a fan and trailing long flimsy silk scarves from her wrists. She appeared to be beckoning.

His intention was to study again one of Joseph's dreams to which the latter had attached special significance. But, flipping through the unlined pages, he discovered writing at the back of the book. Turning it upside down, he began to read. Here were more of Joseph's eastern jottings. He opened with fragmentary accounts of what he called Three Great Disasters, the killing of perhaps ten million Chinese by Soekarno's and Suharto's governments in Indonesia, the Rape of Cambodia, and the Chinese Catastrophe under Mao Tse-Tung. These appeared to be preliminary notes for a longer treatment, which Clement had in his possession.

The notes ended. Next, the pages were filled with a small script where Joseph had written accounts of his visits to brothels and his affairs with women. Each entry was dated. The years covered were the early seventies, when Joseph had been abroad preparing contributions to a guide to the East. Some entries were several pages long. Joseph had noted down things of interest the women said, together with details of their anatomies and descriptions of their breasts and sexual organs.

The entries were interspersed with aphoristic cries like, "Predatory man always turns victim", "In every love affair there is one who pursues and one who falls flat on his face: both are I", and, in imitation of de la Rochefoucauld, "We are neither as whored nor as abhored as we think."

Although he had settled himself to read, Clement soon grew impatient. Box File No. 3 on his window sill contained similar accounts of sexual adventure in a variety of cities, from Rangoon, Saigon, Penang, and Phnom Penh to Palembang, Djakarta, Hanoi, and Hong Kong. Box File No. 3 also revealed that Joseph had put some of his reminiscences together and sold them to the Luxury Life Limited Edition Club of Elizabethtown, New Jersey, under the pen name of Michael Meatyard, Duke of Suffolk, England. The resultant book bore the title, *Eastern Arousals: Memoirs of a Dissolute Duke.*

Joseph had travelled farther than his brother from the stifled respectabilities of Nettlesham and Bude. While Joseph, unlike some Casanovas, appeared genuinely to like women and enjoy their personalities, it was open to doubt whether he knew any of them as intimately as Clement thought he knew Sheila. Pondering this contrast, his thoughts went to his old father, forever at work in his shop and rising at five each morning to collect the day's newspapers from Bude railway station. What would Ernest Winter have made of the careers of his two sons, had he known of them? What would he have made of Kandinsky, come to that? Both he and Joseph had escaped from their father's narrow way of life.

And yet, Ernest Winter had had little to say in those long years of his working life. He had never complained. He had spoken of nothing that Clement could remember beyond the immediate affairs of the newsagent's shop. As far as his family could tell, he had no imaginative life. He had remained closed. The rest of the family had pursued their own emotional concerns, virtually ignoring Ernest. He had died of lung cancer in the end: or rather, Clement thought, cancer, work, disillusion. Joseph had hated his father. Yet Clement had found something to admire in that long-sustained silence; and something in it he had unwittingly imitated and incorporated into his own character.

He turned to the series of dreams in Joseph's book, leafing to the final entry. This he now re-read, concentrating with effort and having occasional recourse to his Cinzano.

There is a flaw in the universe (Joseph had written in his neat longhand). The Greek dramatists knew it. The good and the innocent suffer along with the rest. I have suffered so much that I am now neither good nor innocent. But being moderns mean this: we understand that the flaw in the universe is inside us. What Aeschylus could have done, had someone explained to him about genetic inheritance and the eternal artistries of the DNA spiral!

Yet a flaw is not a fatal wound. However much I have suffered, I have not been utterly destitute of hope. I am visited by a cheering recurrent dream. This I set down now in some doubt, fearing that to drag that precious dream into the open may drive it away for good.

There's one curious feature about the dream, apart from its persistence over nearly half a century (how's that for permanent transience?) — the way in which I have never woken immediately afterwards saying, "There was that dream again". One or two days have always had to pass before I could say "I dreamed it again". In other words, the dream came, in some way I do not understand, slowly through consciousness, instead of direct from the sub-conscious, like an ordinary dream.

It first appeared to me, so I believe, when I was enjoying the enforced stay with my grandmother in Lavenham, as a vulnerable child of four. It has returned ever since, at intervals — perhaps once every five years — developing as I have developed. On paper, there is little startling about it; yet it has always given me comfort and hope. I told Lucy about it when we were quarrelling, and the quarrel ceased.

In essence, all the dream contains is a garden and a gateway. I am wandering in a vast, disconsolate garden. I am small, perhaps still in short trousers. I do not know where to go. There is a threat in the garden which I cannot understand. Looking about, I see no one.

After a while, I come to some steps. The steps are wide and paved, with ornate balustrades. The balustrades are all of a certain number, I know not what. I ascend the steps. The flights are punctuated by terraces, with nine steps between terraces (yes, that number I do remember, I believe, even from the earliest dream). I feel safer.

At the top of the steps stands a perfect wall. In the wall is a perfectly circular hole or entrance, its diameter taking up nearly the whole height of the wall, its circumference ornamented with stonework. A yard behind this entrance is another wall, a screen blocking the view beyond.

Perhaps someone speaks to me at this point. In any case, I am delighted and full of expectation as I approach the gateway.

There the dream ends.

I am sure of the details of this first dream, as far as they go, because I was so taken with it that I got out my water colours, with which I used to play, and painted the scene. My grandmother declared that the result was a masterpiece.

Aren't dreams amazing? I was a kid, an infant. I knew nothing about anything. Yet this archetypal dream came to me and prepared me for much of my life, all the emotional part of my life.

About this time I was learning to read swiftly and easily. That was how I filled the time spent by myself. Newspapers in those days — the early nineteen-thirties — devoted a lot of space to children. There I read a long tale about a little boy who lost his shadow. He made a walking pattern with his shadow on a sunny wall, and the shadow simply ran away from him and was lost. The boy was inconsolable, and sought it high and low. He travelled to the far ends of the earth after it, and eventually found it, I forget how, in China, in a palace.

Although I was already familiar with Grimms' fairy stories, this was the first story I ever read that seemed to say to me direct, pointing a finger, "This is about you — the real you — the secret you!"

Perhaps the story influenced the dream. Where else did I get it from? All its furnishings were Chinese. When first I saw one of those circular Chinese entrances, in Medan, I was overwhelmed by a sense of recognition.

As I grew older, the dream altered according to circumstance. On one occasion, for instance, the steps had flattened into a paved path. The path led through a dreary pine wood. On another occasion, I was in danger from floods. But always at the end of the track stood this confining wall, with the circular entrance and, beyond the entrance, a white screen.

I interpreted the entrance as symbolising the female sexual organ.

Sometimes I met someone along the way. In my adolescence, the dream once took on the aspect of nightmare, for a maiden met me near the wall, a slender maiden, pale as paper. I drew near her and looked into her eyes. She was death. Shortly after that, I went into the army. More often, when the female appeared, she was a tutelary spirit, guiding me to safety.

The richness of that dream can't be conveyed, any more than words can convey the richness of life. The dream enriched my life. Gradually I came to understand how Chinese the dream was. Desultory reading revealed to me that the multiples of nine, into which the dream steps were divided, represented the celestial number which divides the Chinese heaven. The square wall, the circular entranceway, conform to the ancient belief that Earth is square and the heavens round. I understood that the entrance was the entrance to heaven, or at least to happiness.

Also, the entrance, with the white blocking screen behind it, was built according to the Chinese belief that devils and evil spirits were notoriously unable to turn corners, and so would crash into the screen and be unable to enter beyond it.

Sometimes, it appeared that I was dressed in ceremonial vestments when I approached the entrance. Sometimes I was merely a lonely wanderer, my one ambition to get into whatever lay beyond the entrance. I had the impression that the hour was always the same, possibly at the first glimmer of dawn.

I cannot say how much this dream interested me, and how I longed for each successive visitation. It was as if I in some way partook of an ancient ritual, in which the ceremony was invariable. There was a negative aspect to the dream, in that if I could never get through the round entrance, then I must myself be an evil spirit, but this interpretation felt weak and did not appal me, as perhaps it should have done. For the dream came from my very being, that healthful biological centre within even the most desperate of us — the psyche, as the Greeks used that word, to mean the consciousness of all living things, and not only of human beings. This primitive, faraway aspect of the dream was not its least attractive feature.

The last time I dreamed that dream, it remained in its essentials the same, although I approached the wall across a desert, riding on horseback. I think it was a horse. I could see that beyond the wall lay a great complex of buildings and trees. Before the gate stood two tutelary spirits, as I have called them, both beautiful pale women, who came towards me with graceful gestures. They were the most lovely women I had ever seen, waking or sleeping. They spoke sweetly to me, beckoning me to enter the gate. I awoke, trying desperately to recapture what they had said, but without success.

This dream prepared me for a wandering life. Indeed, it may have set the pattern for a wandering life. It also prepared me to love a Chinese woman.

*

Clement grunted as he put the book aside. His brother was not so different from him as he sometimes imagined; both of them, having discarded their father's religion, had become preoccupied with the inner life, bestowing on it a kind of sanctity. The times were uncertain; who could say if the sanctity was justified? Like God, the mind was easy enough to make use of, but almost impossible to understand.

Clement regretted the gulf that lay between him and his poor wandering brother, a gulf which had widened after their mother's funeral in Nettlesham, when Sheila, normally so placid, had berated Joseph for his self-indulgence. They had not seen him for some while after that — not until they were next in Marbella, spending the Christmas holiday in Sheila's villa. Michelin accompanied them. And Michelin it was who had announced Joseph's unexpected arrival, after lunch on Boxing Day.

"No room at the inn, Sheila dear," Joseph had said. "Have you a place to lay my head? A stable would be ideal."

He looked at his worst. His clothes were filthy and worn. A small pack was slung over one shoulder. He had a long, incoherent tale to tell them of his wanderings. As they might have expected, a girl had been involved. He had been returning home from the East. The girl had stolen his wallet in Cairo. Joseph had managed to get a ship to Gibraltar, working as crew, and had hitched by road from Gibraltar to Marbella, hoping to find his brother at the villa. They had a spare room for him, but that night Joseph had been at his worst, getting hopelessly drunk "for Christmas", as he put it, and cursing them all three for bloated capitalists.

"Why don't you throw me out, Clem?" he asked next morning, when he finally made an appearance, his face pallid, his hair still lank from the shower. "I'm useless. I should've finished myself off long ago. Not that I haven't tried. If I ever get in *Who's Who*, like your lovely Sheila, I shall list 'failing suicide' as my hobby. I just haven't enough courage. Or else I can't believe that the world wouldn't wink out if I ceased to exist. There's egotism. . . ."

"Your trouble's not egotism, Joe," Clement said. "It's a certain lack of self-esteem — something with which women can't supply you, apparently."

Joseph gave him a dark look. "Typical clever shrink-talk. Stealing my wallet was a symbolic castration, was it? But you're right. Clever boy! I'm easy to see through. I certainly lack self-esteem. Those bastards of parents, they robbed me of that one natural biological quality which even a tadpole enjoys — self-esteem. But I mustn't start on that tack or Sheila will be at my throat again. Lend me some money and I'll be off — I can get to Madrid, and there's a friend there who will look after me."

Clement had given his brother a wad of pesatas and Joseph had disappeared, as so often he had done before.

He tried to recall more of what had happened on that occasion. Memory was, as usual, selective. He could not remember what Sheila had said. He could not remember how Joseph had intended to get to Madrid. He could remember a cat that Michelin had befriended. And he could remember his selfish relief when Joseph left.

"I shouldn't have let him go," Clement said now, savouring the taste of fruitless regret. "He was my brother and I wasn't even his friend.

"The time will come when I shall be Joe's age when he died. One advantage of growing older is that one gets to appreciate more the living minute. Small pains creep up on one, pains in the joints and so on, but it is amazing how little they detract from happiness. Happiness can be such a good solid quality, although it wasn't for Joseph, with his indwelling insecurity. He acted like a fool, yet at heart he was wise. Perhaps it's the reverse with me; I did tell Sheila that it did not matter how stupidly you behaved as long as you said sensible things. I was a bit tiddly; nevertheless, I may have meant it, and it may have been the truth. . . . Memory is so uncertain: not at all the mind's equivalent of a filing cabinet, more like a compost heap from which unexpected plants grow. Take this old photo of the Winters, snapped by mother in the very hour war broke out. Even that is not reliable. It has usurped real memory and become memory. It has stopped past time. Because of photography, we have made our memories come to resemble family snapshots, static and posed. Yet the unique ingredient of the living moment is its malleable, transient quality, the fish swimming downstream, a glint of sunlight on its twisting body. No one has ever caught that evanescent moment, that dear thing, that solemnity in sunsets. All the world's diarists are hotfoot in quest of it, yet it remains its own tricksy self, there and gone. Gone. Gone, only to be immediately replaced by another tricksy moment. I wish Sheila would come back. I love having her near. Why, I can't even recall to the inner ear the timbre of her voice. Yet how often have I recorded it in mind — often listened to its music rather than to what it was trying to tell me. She's so ordinary, my dear Sheila, so extraordinary. Perhaps I missed something in life by being so unadventurous, yet I found her. That was a bit of luck. She doesn't seem to fret about the passing moment as women are supposed to — and perhaps it's worse for them. How many images of her could I honestly conjure up from all the years we have been together? Out of the millions, precious few.

"These minutes that go by now, where do they vanish to? It's somehow against nature to think they're lost forever. Yet they've gone beyond recall and I'll never remember them from this moment on. What was my train of thought just a moment ago? I suppose Joe wished he could forget his early years. For some people it is an absolute curse how those memories linger. Perhaps memory is the seat of all psychological disease. But that's a thought I've had before. No thought is entirely new. That one's staler than most — except for the one that wonders how Joe's state of mind was when he knew he was dying. He surely didn't really want to die. . . . Perhaps the hour will dawn when I shall wish I could forget Joe. But that's a base thing to say."

He was sitting idly, spinning out his drink, with Joseph's dream book by his elbow, when he heard a car draw up outside and Sheila's key in the door below. He went downstairs.

She appeared flustered. He had the impression that she was trying to avoid looking directly at him.

"Are you all right?"

"I'm fine, absolutely fine."

"It's quite late. Did someone drive you home?"

"Maureen drove me back. I went round to see her."

"It was only yesterday you had lunch with her."

"I'm sorry, Clem, she's a friend of mine, as you know. I really don't want to talk. I'm tired, I have a headache, and I want to go to bed."

She stood impatiently before him, formidable, and yet as if in some way awaiting a signal from him. Clement was the first to change stance.

"Well, let me get you something. Have you had supper?"

"Oh, don't fuss. Please leave me alone. I'm fine, absolutely fine."

She looked angrily at him. "Please, Clem, I just want to be quiet. What is all this, anyway? What have you been up to?"

"Nothing. I've been up in the study. Something's wrong, isn't it?"

She brushed past him and rushed to the rear of the hall, fair hair aflutter, crying that she couldn't stand any more interrogation.

Clement did not follow. As he stood at the foot of the stairs, he found himself listening to an unusual noise outside, like a long-protracted sigh, gentle, yet regretful. Oxford was being visited by a shower of rain.

On Tuesday, the weather was considerably cooler. The sky was cloudy but the threat of rain seemed to have passed. Clement decided to walk into town to his clinic. He wore a light suit and carried a raincoat over one arm. He adopted a slow pace, conscious of the pain in his left leg which he was unable to diagnose, although a list of more or less unpleasant possibilities ran through his head.

His walk took him down the Banbury Road, past the old cumbersome

Victorian houses still disregarding the traffic as if their lives depended on it, through St Giles on the St John's side, and along Cornmarket, making his way with difficulty among the crowds of people there. The people all seemed to him young, and dressed in tawdry fashion, although he realised that this was a subjective view which owed much to his age. If he stopped to think, he could remember how dingily and with what lack of variety his generation dressed in the early sixties, before Style had visited the multitude, and how they had probably smelt badly in the days before roll-on deodorant. By this intellectual effort, he could think well of those about him. But he could not like their habit of pushing by on their own rude course, without regard for others; he had been brought up to step aside for his elders, and such old training did not easily die — rather, became stronger with the years, like bands of ivy round a decaying tree. He found himself breathing heavily. Couldn't these young barbarians see he was almost fifty, and slightly distinguished? What were they doing? The answer seemed to be, Nothing. Cornmarket had become a precinct of loafers.

One token of the loafing was the rubbish and filth which lay on the pavements. Young girls were smoking and eating in the open air, throwing down their litter, using the world as their ashtray. He sighed at his own disapproval. Of course, even the fourteen-year-olds would be having sexual intercourse every day. He overheard their use of swear words — forbidden when he was a boy — as he went by. Once he had hoped such freedoms would come about. They had arrived, and they did not please him.

Sheila was never far from his thoughts. She had made every effort to appear as normal at breakfast, so that he had not dared to bring up the incident of the evening before. So rare was it for them to have a difference, that he was disturbed by it; but he would not permit himself idle speculation on a subject he could not resolve. The cause of her unhappiness would no doubt emerge in time. Meanwhile, he turned his contemplation to the sessions which lay ahead of him, as far as that was possible among the jostling crowd.

It was hard to understand the state of Britain, he thought. Either it prospered or it was going downhill. But nobody could look on the Cornmarket with much favour, certainly not Britain's European part-ners, the Germans, the Dutch, the French, whose own city centres were clean and decorous.

Turning into Boots, a garish shop containing all perquisites for brothel life, he purchased a packet of his favourite blackcurrant throat pastilles and proceeded down The High, congested with groups of tourists all looking for somewhere to sit and rest, or for even older colleges than those already visited. From The High, after lingering for a moment before the windows of the Oxford University Press, he turned right into King Edward Street. This grandly named street, which in Clement's early days in Oxford had appeared friendly, containing lodgings and old professors versed in the Napoleonic Wars, was now coldly schizophrenic, with health shops on one side and on the other, the east side, grim offices of lawyers, solicitors and accountants, thus catering, in Clement's eyes at least, to some of the less appealing features of the English character, crankiness and litigiousness.

On the east side of the street, however, Clement had his room, which he shared with two other analysts. Tuesday was his day of occupancy. This room, situated on the first floor, and overlooking from its windows the health shop opposite, had, by a legal trick, been saved from the encroaching lawyers; it catered to the minds and souls, rather than the pockets, of the locals. On every side, one had only to drill through a wall to overhear discussions of tax matters, dividends, and disputed wills: but in this room, dreams, fantasies, and selected snatches of the past were allowed.

Despite his worry regarding Sheila, he looked about the neutral room with some satisfaction. He might have been dominated by his brother, but here at least he was in control and could help people. The light in the room pleased him; the cloud having dispersed, sunlight slanted in with a rather artificial aspect, reflected from the windows on the opposite side of the street. With its hint of warmth, it recalled to his mind a hired room in which Sheila and he had once stayed, in a town in France, on their way to the Mediterranean. He remembered that they had been in high good humour, having just eaten a meal that began with a plate of delicious *haricots verts*. The old bed had creaked when they made love.

Punctually at ten o'clock, only shortly after Clement had arrived, his bell buzzed, and he admitted his first client into the tiny waiting room. Clement crossed to the inner door and ushered into his sanctum a plump cheerful man in his early eighties, who entered the room clutching a stick in one hand and a string shopping bag in the other, his head held high in order to see through thick glasses.

"How are you, Clement?" the newcomer said. He stomped here and there about the room, laid down his stick and shopping bag on the couch, peered out of the window, commented on this and that, admired Clement's gloomy Piranesi print as he had often done before, finally coming to rest in the armchair by the electric fire and saying, with his habitual optimistic air, "Things much as ever?"

Captain Charles Parr was the oldest and most faithful of all Clement's clients, a record tacitly acknowledged between them by the captain's familiar use of Clement's Christian name. He had been consulting Clement since the mid-seventies, with intermissions only for Clement's or his own excursions abroad.

"Much as ever," Clement now replied. "And with you? When did you get back from India?"

"Just yesterday. Terribly sorry to be back here. Bombay was as pleasant as always." He launched into an enthusiastic account of his trip, to which Clement listened without giving it his complete attention. Captain Parr's history was no stranger than that of many others; yet it was of interest. His endorsement of Bombay, a city from which other Western visitors often recoiled in horror, was of a piece with his boyish outlook on life, which had survived eighty years of stress.

One of Captain Parr's most admirable traits was his openness to experience. He had begun life humbly, one of a large family brought up in the slums of Pimlico. Getting work in the offices of a minor shipping line, he had spent his pre-war years of adolescence holidaying in Belgium and Holland. The shipping line had allowed him discount fares over to Zeebrugge, and there he had cycled about the Lowlands, picking up fluent Flemish. One day, on the ferry returning to Harwich, he had encountered an Indian lady in some trouble, and, with his knowledge of the intricacies of immigration regulations, had been able to help her and her father. They had invited him to visit them, an invitation the youthful Parr had accepted, but the war came along and put a stop to the friendship.

The war was the making of Charles Parr. The number of Englishmen who could speak Flemish was small. He volunteered for service and, after the Nazis invaded the Netherlands and Belgium, was made an officer in the SOE. From London, he helped conduct the operation which air-dropped secret agents into Holland. He also went twice to wartime Holland himself, on one occasion getting captured, escaping only by shooting two of the enemy and returning to England in a stolen fishing boat.

Clement had never discovered when, if ever, Captain Parr had left the secret service. After the war, however, he had become a travel writer and journalist, ostensibly to see more of the world, possibly as a cover. Shortly after India gained its independence, he was in the Indian Embassy to make some travel arrangements, where he met Sushila, the Indian lady he had helped some years earlier. They fell in love and married within a few weeks.

The newly married Parrs settled in Lathbury Road in North Oxford, and there raised two sons and a daughter. Captain Parr, however was often away on his mysterious trips, which took him to the Far East, the Antarctic, and elsewhere. On his return to Oxford, he was always united with his family and with Clement Winter's armchair. He had discovered, however, that Sushila's relations in Bombay were as prosperous as they were amiable, and often appeared to spend more of the year with them than with his wife in North Oxford.

Sushila left him abruptly in the early eighties, when the three children were adult, to go and live with a fox-hunting stockbroker in Gloucestershire. But Charles Parr, who quarrelled with no one, took his wife's dereliction in good part, remained friendly with her, became chummy with the fox-hunting stockbroker, and returned regularly to Clement's chair, sometimes bringing with him the present of a Gloucestershire pheasant. He had also become friendly with Sheila and Joseph.

And why did he return regularly to Clement's chair? It was a question Clement often asked himself about his oldest client. Of course, old habits were hard to break. Captain Parr had nothing particular on his mind; he perhaps enjoyed the chance to talk, being somewhat lonelier than he would ever care to admit.

"How's your book getting on?" the captain asked now, companionably. Clement replied with a few generalities, reflecting that there was, after all, something on the other's mind, the subject which had first drawn him into Clement's orbit. His wartime operations were known as Operation North Pole; the Germans having acquired knowledge of the British codes, every agent Captain Parr's organisation parachuted into Holland had been captured and often shot by the Wehrmacht on landing. It was this — rather than the two soldiers he had had to kill in the line of duty — which occasionally preyed on the captain's mind, and drove him into reminiscence.

The prescribed hour was drawing to a close when the captain said, "Look, Clement, I know I owe you for a few sessions. I'm afraid I can't pay up until I get a couple of articles published in the States."

"Don't leave it hanging about too long."

Captain Parr heaved himself out of the armchair and collected up his belongings in a brisk way. "I'm sorry about your brother's death, by the way, Clement. He was a bit of a blighter, your brother, but we got on well. He presented me with a copy of his dirty book, *Eastern Erections*, or whatever it was called. He was another Far East buff, although he didn't exactly share my passion for India. It was funny how he completely changed during the last few months of his life, wasn't it?"

Not wishing to admit that this remark took him unawares, Clement turned towards his desk and murmured, "In what way do you think he changed?"

"I'm sure you as an analyst noticed the difference. He became much more contented. There was a whole lot of Jungian stuff he spouted to me, the last evening we spent together. Joe set more store by that sort of thing than I do."

Clement said nothing, and the captain rattled on in his cheerful way, "I rather liked his girl friend, too, didn't you? What was her name?"

"Lucy."

"That's it, Lucy. Very attractive girl, very vital. She knew a lot about the thing Joe went through — revelation, he called it. I got the impression they had plenty of sex. Joe was a bit of a randy bastard, wasn't he? What's happened to Lucy now? I'd quite like to see her again. She must miss Joe a lot. It was rather sudden, wasn't it? His death, I mean. Well, mustn't keep you, Clement, old boy. See you next week."

He waved his stick in an authoritative way, his gesture of goodbye, only to pause in the doorway. Diving one hand into his string bag, he came up with a little bundle, wrapped in greaseproof paper, which he pressed into Clement's hand.

"I brought you a present from Bombay, old boy."

Clement saw him out, smiling, and clutching a dozen spiced papadoms.

He went back into the inner room to phone Lucy Traill.

XVI

Clement entered the hallway of his house to find a suitcase standing there.

The time was just after five, and, as it was raining, he had taken a taxi home from King Edward Street. The rain, slight at first, no more than a whisper round the city, had persisted, gradually raising its voice, as roofs of colleges, pavements, and multitudinous gutters added their liquid commentary, until water everywhere was pouring into the many throats of the Isis and Cherwell in a continuous shout. Clement didn't like noise or wet; he phoned Luxicars to drive him home.

His mind was so taken up with thoughts of a college meeting he had to attend that evening that he allowed the suitcase little attention. At first assuming without great surprise that Michelin had returned, he was almost past it when he realised it belonged to Sheila, although it was not one of her special green Green Mouth cases.

"Sheila!" he called.

She came immediately out of the living room as if she had been waiting for him. She was dressed in what he thought of as her London clothes, a rather pretentious new costume consisting of a deep blue wool wrap top over a blouse and emphatic gabardine trousers, with a mock tortoiseshell necklace wrapped twice about her neck. Her face was strained and anxious.

"Clem, I don't want you to say anything. I'm going. I'm leaving. Please don't say anything. I can't explain. I don't want to hurt you, but this has to be."

"It's raining."

"That's got nothing to do with it. Please don't try to stop me. I don't like doing this."

They stared at each other.

"Do you mean — you're leaving me for another man?"

"Don't ask me questions. It's all over, Clem. I can't help it."

"Is it that fellow Arthur Hernandez?"

She hesitated, as if contemplating a lie, and then said, "He gets into Heathrow early tomorrow morning. I'm going to meet him."

He felt himself to be quite calm, chiefly because he could not believe what he heard. Pushing past her, he walked into their living room and set down on the table the little greasy package Captain Parr had given him. Then he turned to her again — she had followed him in.

"You're trying to tell me you're leaving me for that little wretch you met in Boston?"

"I've known him for some time. We're terribly compatible. I don't have to explain anything to you."

"Has this got to do with Michelin?"

"Of course not. I loved her and I'm sorry she has cleared off. You'll have to look after yourself. A car's coming for me."

"Now you're clearing off." He found he had difficulty swallowing. "This is a delusion. It's part of your fantasy life, Sheila. You want to be Green Mouth all the time, and it can't be done."

"I thought you'd say something like that." She sounded miserable. "You were bound to say something like that, weren't you? That's why I will not discuss the matter with you. There's plenty of money in the bank; you won't go short."

With trembling hands, Clement unwrapped the papadoms and held the package out to his wife.

"Would you like one?"

As she shook her head, he said, looking down, "Please don't leave me. You're so dear to me. You always have been, ever since we met. Who'll find you as dear as I do? There's so much stored between us, stored up against winter and bad weather. . . . Our relationship has been so intense — well, I thought so — to break it now would injure you as well as me."

He bit one of the papadoms and tried to chew it.

"Don't be a fool, Clement, those things aren't cooked. I have to do this. I'm not your little lost girl any more. I'm independent. I want to live, be free — I'm just sick of our relationship. I want to see something of the world, travel, meet new people. Put those disgusting things down."

"You know I don't like Indian food." He put the bitten papadom down and removed the piece he had chewed into his handkerchief. She looked on, unmoving, in contempt. "Sheila, we know what happiness is — let's not lose it." He spat into the handkerchief.

"I'm trapped. I feel trapped. I want to get away and meet new people."

"Perhaps it would be useless to tell you that you really don't." He looked at her searchingly. "You're happier in your fantasy world. You just have to decide where its boundaries lie. I know I have many deficiencies, Sheila; I'm all too aware of them, but by now you are used to them — hardened to them — and against them you must set the fact that I love you as much as ever I did — no, that really we love each other as much as ever. It's a miracle, and it is real. Ours is the most enormous luck. You're my life. Shall I tell you how eagerly I open my eyes in the morning to see your face again, how I miss you if —"

"No, you shan't tell me. You're always telling me things. I knew it would be like this. I should have left before you returned, but I wanted to do the decent thing. I couldn't just leave a note like that bitch Michelin." She glared at him from her position of immobility as he paced about the room. "To hell with it, to hell with you, you and your claims on me. I want to be free, to be my own self for once —"

"You mean you want to go off with that seedy little Spaniard!"

"All right, call him names. Art's American, anyway, not Spanish. Art has capabilities you've never dreamed of. Look at you — you're more interested in your dead brother than you are in me. That's what you like, you feel safe dealing with the dead. Your whole life you've kept people at arm's length. You've kept me at arm's length —"

"Sheila, careful, some words can destroy a marriage."

"So can some silences. Now I'm speaking out. This is my turn, at last. Art is a wonderful talker, just as he's a wonderful lover. Yes, I am going to go off with him, to be an equal partner. He's flying over to get me. I'm going to escape at last from under your wing, if you want to know — rejoice in being a free woman."

He sank down on the arm of the chair during this speech but, in his pain, immediately stood up again.

"Oh, it's being a free woman, is it? You've been talking to Maureen too much. This is her idea. She dominates you far more than I do. Your problem's not me or this Spaniard, it's feminism. Can't you see that we've got a good equal partnership here? Don't let all the Maureens in the world persuade you otherwise."

Her face was dark. "You keep bringing Maureen into the conversation. Don't think I don't know you had an affair with her, just when I was at my most wretched. What right have you got to criticise me?"

"That was ages ago, best forgotten." Hostility was naked between them now. The swords were out. They were on the battlefield.

"Well, I haven't forgotten it. You do what you like now — and I'm going to do what I like."

"If you leave here now, you never come back! I warn you."

"I don't want to come back. I'm sick of the damned place, sick of Oxford, sick of you!"

"And I'm glad you're going!"

The front doorbell rang, signalling from another world.

"Don't answer it," Clement said. "Bugger them."

"Shut up," Sheila said. She went through to the front door, and in a moment Cheri Stranks was in the living room with them, smiling and silently confused, pretty as a peacemaker and scenting blood in the air.

"I'm sorry, do tell me if it isn't convenient. I didn't mean to interrupt anything. Are you going away?"

"Just for the weekend," Clement said, shooting a glance at Sheila. "Come in, come in. How are you keeping, Cheri? No signs of the baby yet."

"We're going to London," Sheila said, with a ferocious look at her husband, as if adding under her breath, "and you're going to hell."

"Oh, I expect you're going to the opera," Cheri said. "I thought I'd just drop in and see you." She gestured to the road, where the blue Zastava Caribbean stood out in the rain. "Sorry to butt in. I wondered if I could help in any way, really in any way at all. Arthur told me you'd lost your housekeeper. Can I give a hand? I was passing this way."

"Thanks very much, but —" Clement began, when Sheila cut him off, moving forcibly in front of him and saying, as she took Cheri's arm, "That's very kind. Very kind. We are in a bit of a pickle, as it happens. The surface of the pool hasn't been skimmed today — that was always Michelin's morning job. And I'm afraid there's a stack of washing-up. If you could help. . . ."

She manoeuvred the younger woman out to the back, shut the door on her, and returned, picking up a brown wool coat from an armchair, throwing it across her arm in a business-like way.

"There you are. There's someone else to see to all your needs. You always land on your feet, don't you, Clem? Now I'm off. A car will be round at any moment. I think I hear it now."

He caught her arm. "I love you, Sheila, please don't go. He's not worth it."

"He is worth it to me, and that's all that matters."

"But you don't know," he said desperately.

"I'm going to find out," she said, with a kind of grim gaiety, but he plunged on. "Listen, you are always pretending to everyone that you had a happy childhood. I never contradict you, do I? I know how you live in this fantasy world. Well, you'll smash it all up if you aren't careful, and then you may not like reality when it hits you."

"I'm not on your couch any more, and I can look after myself. I'm not one of your fucking sick, though you may like to think it."

There was a car at the door, and the rain was stopping.

"I didn't mean that, Sheila. Please don't go, please don't leave me!"

She had opened the front door. A uniformed chauffeur was approaching up the path. She snatched up her suitcase, but he smiled professionally and took it from her. She walked down the path behind him, not looking back. The rain petered out. Eaves were dripping. Alice Farrer appeared in her front garden and pretended to prune something. The suitcase was stowed in the boot of the car, the door was opened for her. She got in. The chauffeur got in. The car moved forward down Rawlinson Road. He stood there in the doorway, staring, hoping she would wave. She did not wave.

He was lying flat on the couch in his study, thinking of the years that had gone by, so many, so soon, when there was a cautious knock on the door and Cheri Stranks entered.

"Are you all right, Clement? I wondered if there was something wrong?"

Faintness had overcome him. He smiled, a mockery of a smile, and sat up, planting his feet carefully on the floor.

"Aren't you well? You do look a bit sick. Can I get you a gin or something?" She looked alarmed. She was a well built girl, today allowing the world a glimpse of her good legs, her jeans having been discarded for once in favour of a tight black skirt. The best feature of her face, a certain pleasing sharpness, was more observable in profile than from the front. Her eyelashes, thick and artificially darkened, framed two lively brown eyes. Her hair was brown and floated freely about her face; there was nothing of the Scrubbing Brush mode which afflicted her husband.

"Sheila's left me," he said, adding, so that there should be no mistake, "for good."

She came closer. As yet the pregnancy did not show.

"I can't credit it. Left you — at her age!" Immediately realising her error, she went on, "I don't mean she's old at all, it's just that. . . ." But the damage was done, and in a moment she stopped speaking. "It's a real bummer, and I'm sorry. Arthur and I have always admired you as the sort of couple. . . ."

Again she stopped. Clement saw how ancient he was in her eyes, and that she had come round, perhaps with some urging from Arthur, to see if there was anything to be done for this poor old couple. He stood up and tried to show a little vitality, but reaction to the scene with Sheila had set in, making him tremble and look older than ever.

He cleared his throat. "It is a bummer, you're right. Whatever a bummer is, it's this. Oh, I'm sure she'll come back."

"But your wife's so famous. Everyone's read her books. Has she — I mean, did she say why. . . ."

"She's leaving me for another man, Cheri. He's younger. He's flying over from the States to meet her. He's got the same name as your husband, Arthur. He edits books in New York. Well, he's Sheila's editor, as a matter of fact. He stands about five feet nothing. And that's all I know." He laughed feebly, holding his forehead.

"Perhaps you'd rather I went."

"I expect you'd rather go." He held out a hand to her. "It was sweet of you to come round, Cheri."

She took his hand and almost immediately let it go in embarrassment.

"I couldn't have come round at a worse time, could I?"

Recovering from her startlement, she was now beginning to enjoy the situation, as he could see.

"I'm glad you're here. Come down and have a drink with me."

She looked sceptical, but accompanied him as he made a rather shaky way downstairs. They sat in the kitchen; she drank a white wine and Perrier while he sipped a deep brandy. She sat with her legs crossed. She wore patterned net stockings.

"I suppose in your profession — well, such things are pretty common," she said, breaking a silence. "Marriage bust-ups and so on."

"I had an elder brother. He died earlier this year. He had a fear of desertion. Perhaps that was the biggest fear of his life. His mother — our mother, I should say — deserted him when he was a small child. She came back, but she always held the threat of desertion over him. It is a terrifying thing to do to a sensitive child. By the time I came on the scene I got better treatment; my mother's neurosis was in remission. But somehow that fear of desertion by the one one most loves has rubbed off on me. . . . I wasn't at all prepared. Well, one never is. . . ."

"My parents never got on too well. Always rowing. There were five of us kids." They talked for a little while, but, despite her evident intelligence, it was an unequal conversation.

"I'll have to get back to Arthur. He needs the car this evening. He's got to go over to Abingdon, to a meeting. Why don't you come back and have supper with us?"

"You're enormously kind, Cheri." And more than kind, he thought, but of course not always kind. She would have her moods too, docile as she might seem now. She had rested her soft right hand on the table, and he saw there were gilt rings on each of its fingers. It was a beautiful hand, the nails of which were enamelled shell pink. At present that hand slept as far as he was concerned, after its little exercise in being held out to him.

And it was accustomed to beckoning husband Arthur towards her. But the day might come — who could tell? — when the hand would be raised with all the force of a policeman's to halt Arthur's approach, or to catch another passing man. And then the dainty nails would appear more like claws, and no doubt heart's blood would flow. But there was no denying it, at this moment she was enormously kind, though the hand could never reach out and touch him with the warmth of Sheila's.

"We've always admired you, Clement, ever since you came with us to the Tina Turner concert and enjoyed it so much. Generally speaking, your age group doesn't go a bomb on rock'n'roll. Don't say no, have supper with us. It's macaroni cheese."

"No, I'll stay here, thanks. I'd rather. Another time."

She looked hard at him, then offered a smile. "You'll be okay?"

He laughed. "I won't do anything desperate. Promise."

When she had gone, he walked about the house, brandy glass in hand. He picked the packet of papadoms off the living room table and threw it in the waste bin.

A plan formed in his mind. He could phone Swain Books in New York and get the number of Arthur Hernandez's flight. He could check with Heathrow and find what time it landed the next morning. Then he could drive up to Heathrow and shoot both him and her as they came out of Terminal Three.

However, he did nothing. He sat in Sheila's favourite chair, as unmoving as she generally was, going over the dreadful scene in his mind, trying to analyse it. In retrospect, he was able to appreciate the tension and apprehension in her.

It was his own fault. It was his own fault that Sheila's hand, the hand that typed all the stories about the fantasy world of Kerinth, had been raised against him. He had never expressed his love enough; oh, he had done all that a husband should or could and possibly more; but Sheila lived by words as well as deeds; her real world, like her fantasy one, must be largely built of words and the need of them. It was a human need. He had never said to her — for instance — for instance, for he was putting himself to an inquisition — he had not talked enough about her novels. He had defended them and her against the prejudiced, had at times been fierce as a tiger. But he had failed to like them, or perhaps just failed to take them seriously enough for her taste. Arthur Hernandez, now — there was a man who took the damned books seriously, who could be said, in his position, to be almost dependent upon them. Creature of Kerinth. The title rose spontaneously to mind. He had emerged, her Latin hero, sparkling from the sugary foam of her fantasy. And there was nothing Clement could do about that.

"I must not fall into the trap of blaming myself," he said aloud. He stood up and sat down again. She was so dependent on her audience. He had seen that in Boston, without realising all its implications. The novels, which had begun as a substitute for the dead daughter, for little Juliet, had become a substitute for other relationships. She loved Clement, but even more she needed her audience, those warm hearts who found no fault with the Kerinth fantasies and who sent her presents and cards and love. Arturo Hernandez was merely an embodiment of that audience. Rises and falls in sales were received by her as the ardour or coolness of a lover. And here — winging across the Atlantic even now — was the man who had his finger on those sales, the maestro of salesmanship, the astute commercial little man of Swain who had not one word of adverse criticism to offer as long as the product was right.

"I could have warned her."

But of course that was impossible. People were not to be warned. He had encouraged her by keeping quiet. He had profited by the enormous worldwide sales. After the poverty of his childhood, had they not been ever welcome?

Besides, keeping his trap shut was a habit. Analysis had not changed that. It had appeared that his habit of holding back had been agreeable to her, one of the reasons they had been happy together. Instead of holding back, he should have held her when she tried to go, have been more physical, as Joseph would have been.

And why had Clement held back? What had kept him from ever saying enough to her? Of course it went back to childhood, as everything did eventually. His thoughts returned to that old dull time, as an escaped prisoner's thoughts must return to his cell. His older brother and sister not wanting him about; then their sudden absence as they got sucked into the global war. His parents, committed to tedious work, rendered more tedious by their religion. Brought up strictly, with everything in short supply. Not like now. The endless preaching that people were wicked and sinful, that happiness was reserved for some vague after-life, and then only for a few, a minority to which he could never persuade himself that he might belong. The conviction that the world was a vale of tears and God had it in for him. The sense that his parents saw it God's way.

Why had he gone in for analysis, if not to banish that diseased vision of life? How delighted he had been when, in his teens, he had come on one of Freud's works dismissing religion as neurosis. It had led him on like a torch to new thoughts, new ways of life, better ways.

But, despite his analysis in Berlin, despite the easy adult life he had lived, so full of surface pleasure, that infernal picture set up in childhood had evidently persisted. He had known secretly that life was grim, and had its revenge on those who smiled and drank wine and made love, and that one day . . . one day, unsuspecting, a man would discover that the whole easy fabric would be torn from the place where he lived, to reveal the bare stones of misery. And those who had lived the easy bourgeois life would feel it worst, and be flung down hardest.

What was he going to do now? What was left for him? His father would have said, glowing with *schadenfreude*, as his way was, "That's what you get. . . ."

That's what you get. . . . As if the phrase contained a profound truth, beyond which nothing could fruitfully be said.

He wished he had told all that to pretty Cheri, a little earlier, to warn her. There must be some way of warning people what to expect.

That's what you get. . . . He found he was standing looking at his widespread hands, as if to convince himself that what he got was nothing. He ran upstairs, ignoring the pain in his leg, and stared into Sheila's study, assuring himself she was not there. Everything in the clotted cream factory was as usual, except that the room did not live without Sheila's presence. It had become a photograph of itself. On the rear wall, the large painted *mazooms* and *crichts*, inhabitants of Kerinth's moon, stared at Clement with their large cat eyes. That's what you get, they said.

He went listlessly downstairs again, wandering about, wondering what could possibly be done. It came to his memory that he had arranged a party for Thursday evening. Friends would be arriving at six o'clock to celebrate Sheila's return from the States and to drink to her new novel. He dismissed the thought irritably. He would worry about that in the morning. There were more important issues to worry about. Of course he would be disgraced; he took that for granted. Going to the patio windows in the rear of the house, he looked at the dull evening trapped between the walls of the garden. The sun, striking through a band of cloud over Walton Street, lit the maple in the Phillips' garden nearby so that all its wet leaves gleamed. Its shadow fell on the Winters' garden. The swimming pool lay motionless, its surface blank as a sleeping face.

He felt a sudden unity with Joseph, who had been pursued by a fear of desertion for ever after his mother's betrayal, and had fought the fear, leading as vivid an existence as possible — preferably in the Far East, as distant from the scene of the crime as could be.

He saw more clearly than ever that it was not only the desertion and that expulsion from the family home on the day — the very hour — of Ellen's birth which had so scarred Joseph, but the way in which those heedless acts had come as confirmation of a whole prior history of maternal deprivation, dating from his birth, that birth over which the steel-engraving angel had presided so decisively.

The dreadful thoughts would not allow him peace. He could no longer bear to stay in the house alone. Bursting through the silent rooms as if pursued, he ran out of the front door, slamming it behind him — to the evident satisfaction of both Farrers, alert in their front garden — and walked with uncharacteristic rapidity in the direction of the Woodstock Road and Wolvercote, as if all the steel-engraving angels in the world were pursuing him.

XVII

Clement's night was a restless one. Often he imagined Sheila, lying somewhere in a hotel bed in London, must also be restless. He slept in fits and starts, waking late after a vivid dream.

After showering, he dressed and went down to eat a piece of toast in the kitchen. Memory of the dream returned. He had been in Australia, an hour before dawn, waiting for the sun to rise. Already it was hot. Other people jostled by him. He could not see their faces. In the tall, dead, brittle, elephant grass, a creature like a dog roamed. He had looked towards the west, where a great black rock loomed between him and the sky. The dawn, because this was Australia, was postponed several times, but he knew it would come, and this knowledge filled him with happiness.

The question he asked himself was, why did this fragment make him happy, and how did he connect it with Sheila?

He set the question aside for a time, while he sorted out the mail. Most of it was for Sheila, as usual, many letters in familiar American air mail envelopes. There was a bill for him and a letter addressed in writing he recognised as Michelin's. He slit it open with a buttery knife.

Dear Clement and Sheila,

It is necessary that you think badly of me to leave in my hurry without informing you both. I deeply beg forgiveness. But I cannot bear your questions.

You know my age. Time goes by. I have fallen in love with a man of a year less than me. He is rich, in fact a lawyer, and from my region of France. We know each other only since a week, but it is the REAL THING! This I need so desperately. But I could not stand your eyes upon me when I tell these things.

We will fly to Nice in only a few hours. Then I will write to you again. Now, my thoughts are in a tempest!

Sincerely,

Michelin

"Poor dear Michelin!" he said aloud. "There seems to have been an outbreak of love here. Perhaps I should have the house fumigated before I catch it. . . ."

He stood there, thinking, absently making himself a cup of coffee as he worried about this uncharacteristic impulse of Michelin's. If only she had confided in Sheila earlier in the week, perhaps after comparing notes neither of them would have left, and he would not now be alone. . . .

The doorbell rang. As he went to answer it, he thought, "She's back." But on the doorstep stood Mrs Flowerbury, neat, ample, smiling her rather fixed smile and clutching the handbag she always carried.

"You look startled, Dr Winter. It's Wednesday and it's ten o'clock, or am I a bit early?" She smiled with her head on one side, as if this was her patent way of smiling, to which she stuck through thick and thin.

"Oh, Mrs Flowerbury, I'm afraid Sheila isn't here this morning. She has had to go up to London."

"It would be about the film business, I expect. Never mind, I can get on with my work." She made to enter.

"Well, I'd rather you didn't, Mrs Flowerbury. I'm going to have her study cleaned professionally while she's away. See you next week."

"Oooh, everything will be turned upside-down." She backed away, as though an offer had been made to clean her professionally, and turn her upside-down into the bargain. She retained enough self-possession to wave to Clement as he shut the door.

"Of course," he thought. "Sheila is also down-under slang for 'woman'. That's why the dream was set in Australia. It was all about her, and she is the sun about to return to my life."

Perhaps the doglike thing in the dry undergrowth had been a vague memory of the pet Sheila had owned in Berlin. He went back to his coffee, thinking of an occasion when they had encountered each other in a park in West Berlin. It was spring. Sheila wore a neat fawn coat and a hat. She was slender in those days, even thin. She had been walking her little dog on a lead.

She was reserved; he was shy. But he had induced her to sit on a bench with him. She had nursed the dog while they talked, running her long fingers through his fur, and once or twice kissing him on the head, with a gesture of unconscious coquetry.

The doorbell rang. He thought, "She's back" but, when he opened the door, Arthur and Cheri Stranks stood there, Arthur looking business-like and standing on his toes, Cheri back in her stone-washed jeans and clutching her husband's arm proprietorially, as if to demonstrate who had brought whom. Behind them in the road the Zastava Caribbean was parked.

"Er — I just had to come round and say how sorry I am," Arthur said, stealing a march on his wife — stealing such a march that he had moved forward and was entering the house before either Cheri or Clement could forestall him. "Cheri and I have been talking about it all night. If there's anything we can do — for instance, if you want to go somewhere and don't want to drive yourself. . . ."

He was inside now, adjusting his spectacles and nodding, with Cheri following nimbly behind.

"Please don't mind us intruding," Cheri said, "but we had the notion that we might just nip in and be of use. That's what friends are for. You have only to say the word."

"Creative people are known to be sensitive," Arthur said, looking as if impressed by his own insight. "Er — creative people in particular. They're more dependent on the old bio-clock. More dependent than is comfortable, sometimes. It would be a hell of a world if men menstruated as well, wouldn't it? No, no, it's easy to quarrel at such times."

"We didn't quarrel."

"Oh, er, I don't imagine you did. Cheri and I think of you as far too gentle — well, too wise, really — too mature — for that. Still, the male psyche's under threat these days, isn't it? When the social order is disrupted and the NHS is having to cope with AIDS victims and is breaking down under so many people demanding heart operations."

"He's maddening," said Cheri, placidly, interrupting her husband's demonstration of understanding. "He never went on like this till I got pregnant. What about the vulnerability of the modern woman, under threat from all sides, her role questioned? Listen to Arthur or read the papers and you would think the modern woman was off her rocker. There's passion, you know, and that's what decides what happens, not just feminism."

"You may be right there," Clement agreed.

"It's generous of you to say so," Arthur said, "but to my mind, er, financial independence comes into it. That's what's caused the breakdown of family life. Women out to jobs, women earning more money than men. . . ." He paused dramatically, to let the relevance of this remark sink in.

"Arthur talks like something out of the Old Testament sometimes," Cheri said, excusing him. "Don't listen to him, Clem."

Thinking this was excellent advice, Clement said hastily, "There is one thing you might do for me, Arthur. Sheila and I were going to have a party here tomorrow evening. I've got a list of the people invited in my study. If you could phone them and say the party is off, owing to unforeseen circumstances, I'd be grateful. Don't say more than that. Say I'm not too well, or something, if you must."

"I'll do the washing up," Cheri said. "There's a liberated woman for you." She struck out in the direction of the kitchen as Clement proceeded upstairs with Arthur.

"It's funny how women behave," Arthur said, in a low voice, inviting man-to-man confidences.

"Men have been known to run off from their wives."

"Yes, but — er —" Perhaps Arthur sensed he was treading on delicate ground. "You and Sheila seemed so stable. Cheri and I admired you for that."

"I'm sorry to let you down."

"But what do you make of it?"

"I don't make anything of it, Arthur. I simply hope that she will come back."

Arthur halted in the doorway of Clement's study, his solid form blocking the entrance. He turned back, the expression on his face obscured by the dimness on the landing. "Er — but I mean, you being an analyst, doesn't this rather upset your ideas, if you didn't see it coming?" A hesitation in the way he phrased the question removed some of the impertinence from it.

Clement saw the force of it. If an analyst, whose business it was to understand others, got into such messes, what hope was there for research assistants?

"I didn't see it coming."

"Does that make you question — well, I'm no judge, but Jung's ideas always struck me as rather airy-fairy. . . . I thought you perhaps. . . . No, I shouldn't be saying this. But what price the archetypes now?"

"Arthur, I don't really think you want a lecture, but archetypes aren't just airy-fairy ideas. They're modes of functioning. The chick pecking its way out of the egg obeys an archetype. A woman loving her newborn child is probably obeying an archetype. Ethology shows us how every species has a whole range of suitable behaviours. Archetypes have evolved through natural selection and are no more airy-fairy than biological entities. Sheila at the moment is trying to escape a wrong archetype, an archetype of dominance, embodied for her in the figure of a threatening stepfather. I'm convinced this is more a question of dominance-avoidance than of Eros. If so, she may come to that realisation soon, and return. If I'm wrong, I may not see her again."

"Gordon Bennett," Arthur said. "What a mind you have, Clem." And he gripped the older man's arm in a spasm of admiration.

Clement managed to settle Arthur in front of the phone with the invitation list for the party. He went slowly from his study into the bedroom, where he sat on the bed, head bent, reflecting.

It was lax of him to have mentioned Sheila's overbearing stepfather to Arthur. He had an unspoken agreement with Sheila, which had grown up over the years, to edit that man from her life. When talking to others — even when talking to him on occasions — Sheila pretended that she had enjoyed a happy childhood. He always listened with sympathy; the pretence might be regarded as her protective entitlement. He knew all too well the terrors of her early adolescence, and feared only that she might come to take the lie for the truth, unpalatable as the truth might be.

She had slowly reconstructed her own biography to suit her needs as a successful writer of romances. He had seen it in print, in articles about her: "Green Mouth enjoyed a radiantly happy childhood in Somerset, on her father's estates."

Sheila's father had been killed in the Ardennes, in the closing stages of the war. Her mother had married again, after the war, to one William Harstow, a friend of her late husband's and a regular soldier. When he was posted to West Berlin, Harstow's new wife and her daughter went with him. It was an ill-advised match. Harstow was a rigid disciplinarian, and ruled over their uncomfortable home with a heavy military hand. He frequently beat Sheila and her mother, starved them, and humiliated them in front of others. On occasions, when drunk, he sexually assaulted his ten-year-old step-daughter.

One dark night, Harstow came to the bad end his army friends had long been predicting. He was set upon in a dark Berlin alley and battered to death. The incident reached the papers. Had some German vented his anti-British feelings? The matter was never cleared up. No one was charged with the murder. Sheila and her mother returned to England under a mystery, a cloud, and some debts.

But Harstow left behind a sister, Sheila's adopted Aunt Anna. Anna Harstow had also gone out to Germany, and secured a job in army welfare, which she left after a while in order to work for a German civilian firm. Anna was a different kind from her brother, as gentle as he was rough. Moreover, she took a liking to Sheila, and visited her whenever she was in England.

It was Aunt Anna who brought Sheila to Clement Winter, at the clinic in Berlin where he had just started out as an analytical psychologist, under the aegis of T. F. Schulz.

That was in the autumn of 1969. Sheila was twenty-nine. She was fair and slender, with blonde hair hanging straight to her shoulders. The style of her clothes was dated, but she had an innate elegance. Her manner was polite and reserved. There was little animation about her, a trait that was to persist, as though she had been born to an indoor, sedentary life.

She fixed the impressionable young analyst with a radiant smile, showing irregular teeth — which would be properly fixed in the Kerinth days which lay ahead. The smile was maintained even when the aunt handed her over to Clement's care and retired to a waiting room — although he observed her increased rigidity and the tighter grip she took of her handbag.

Yes, she told Clement, smiling apologetically, there had been some trouble with her step-father, but the poor man was dead, so it was all over. She had a flat of her own in England. Well, a room, really. She was on fairly good terms with her mother. Well, better terms. And she loved staying with Aunt Anna in West Berlin.

But Clement had been slow to perceive how much the girl suffered. This pretty young woman, with her sweet expression and gentle air, concealed her sorrow well. While she admitted that she had mentioned suicide to her aunt, that of course was all past. Last year, when she was ill. A misunderstanding when she happened to be feeling lonely.

It was the aunt, Anna Harstow, who had understood that her niece's loneliness went deep, and still continued, to the point of anomia. In some ways, the caring Anna saw Sheila more clearly even than Clement did — for he had fallen in love with her. It took him many months, and another of her suicide attempts, to see how obsessively Sheila tried to conceal the depth of anguish she was experiencing. He had not encountered a smiling depressive type before.

Years later, in the early eighties — he and Sheila had been married for over ten years by then — when he saw photographs of Chinese smiling blankly into the cameras of foreign journalists, shortly after the death of Chairman Mao, he could comprehend something of the tragedy which had overwhelmed China and its population.

The Berlin analysis had proved seminal for Clement as well as Sheila. Week by week, sometimes day by day, he had been in his room with her, gaining her confidence. Once she had begun to talk, it was easier.

At last she had been able to speak of the times when, as a child, alone and frightened in the dark, she had heard her step-father stagger home, the quarrels, the cries of her mother, sometimes the sound of china being broken. She lay upstairs in her bed, ten years old, clutching the friendly little felt lizard her real father had given her before he went off to the war, the lizard she called Green Mouth. Sometimes her step-father would come to her bed. And in her fear, all she could do was to lie there and let him behave as he wished.

Gradually, she talked the terror and shame away. Life again became possible for her.

After she ceased to attend the clinic, Clement sought her out and proposed to her. And was accepted.

He felt, he hoped, that Sheila and he had forged such a bond between them that they could not be happy with other partners. But of course financial independence had come her way. She might want to exercise it. She had exercised it.

Feeling a headache coming on, he took an aspirin. He was going slowly downstairs when the front door bell rang.

"She's back," he thought, and a shaft of daylight seemed to play through his being.

Outside, however, stood three figures, none of them remotely resembling his wife. All belonged to the armies of the jean-clad. A heavily built man with a shirt open to his navel and his sleeves rolled up to reveal tattoos on his arms was trying to anchor a struggling child whom he held by one hand. Smiling at Clement, he gave a mock salute with his free hand. The child, running fast backwards without moving, trying to drag its anchor, was red in the face and resembled a small version of the man as to rig-out, except for the tattoos. In front of these heroic figures was a woman of decided features, sharp looks, and blue eyes. Her hair was in interesting disarray, while something in her alert stance suggested that she was equally prepared for flight or attack, as the occasion might require.

"Here I am, bang on time. You'll have to excuse me bringing along Ron and the bairn, but we fancied a look round the colleges while we were this way, didn't we, Ron? Okay if we come in? Stop that, Pat."

A few seconds late, Clement recognised Lucy Traill. It had been some while since he last saw her when, as far as he could recollect, she had been wearing the same clothes as now, and sporting the same CND badge on her faded jacket.

"Come in, all of you," he said. He could not for a moment think of anything else to say. He had phoned Lucy only yesterday, before Sheila had taken it into her head to disappear, since when the appointment had gone completely out of his mind. "Sheila's not here at present," he added.

He thought that Lucy gave a slight sniff. She and Sheila had not become friends.

The man addressed as Ron made a great show of dragging the child into the hall, while the child made a great show of going insane as it entered. Getting a closer look at the creature as it swung in an orbit about Ron's body, Clement saw that it was female, though its hair was cut as short as a boy's. It was protesting its lot in a high, unmusical monotone.

Apparently unaware that his arm was being torn off, Ron said, grinning, "You sorted your brother's gear out yet?"

"Not quite." Belatedly, Clement realised that this was the man claiming to be Joseph's friend, whom he had found inside the Acton flat, on his visit at the weekend. Ron Mallock.

"I expect you'd like some coffee."

"Yes, coffee'd be okay, great, cheers," Ron said. "Give over, Pat, will you, for crying out loud?"

"I don't want to be here I told you I keep telling you I'm not meant to be here why did you drag me here why did you make me come why can't you let me go why can't you lay off I'm not meant to be here I'm meant to be somewhere else I don't want to be here I'm going to spew up if you don't look out I'm supposed to play with Daphne why don't you leave me alone why did you make me come," said the child, in a kind of unpunctuated shriek, evidently feeling that at least she could kill off grammar while biding her time on Ron.

"She wanted to stay home," Lucy said, by way of elucidation. She was not tall, and stood looking up into Clement's face as if watching for his next move.

He was in the presence of the woman who had found Joseph dead. The vitality in her, in the way of walking and in her stance, seemed to negate death. The movement of her clearly defined lips and the positioning of her head when she spoke, as if a question lurked behind her every statement, was immediately familiar to him, as if it had not been a couple of years since they had last met — apart from Joe's cremation, when she had come and gone without speaking to anyone, standing alone at the rear of the crematorium, wrapped in a black plastic raincoat.

Sheila and Clement had just returned from a dinner in Thame when the phone had rung. Lucy was on the line. He knew immediately that something was wrong.

"I'm ringing from a call box," Lucy said. "It's going to be rotten news. Are you ready? Joe's dead. I've just found him up in his kitchen. I mean, he's still up there, just lying by the sink. I can't go back, sorry. I blame myself not being with him. I can't say how long he's been there. He's quite cold."

He interrupted her flow. "Stay there. I'll be right over."

"The point is — well, I've got to get back to my kid. You know how it is. It's a bit of a journey by tube. . . . Should I ring for a doctor?"

"Leave it to me. How did you get in the flat?"

"Oh, Joe often didn't lock the door. If only someone had been with him, someone to comfort him. Me."

"Don't fret. It's a shock, of course. Go home, have a drink of tea — maybe something stronger. I'll take care of everything. Thanks — thanks for phoning."

"I didn't realise he was that bad. He was okay last week when I was with him. . . . Poor Joe." And then she had allowed herself a few sobs.

Now she looked fine. He took it she had been sunbathing, making the best of the good weather. He did not believe that weeping formed part of her ordinary repertoire. Although the child was still howling, Lucy appeared calm and alert, her clear gaze fixed on Clement as if she was coming to some decision about him, a decision which might or might not be favourable. The thought made him nervous.

He led the way through the rear hall into the kitchen. Although the child fought Ron every inch of the way, he still found the chance to observe his surroundings, saying, in the genial voice which seemed to be habitual to him, "You done better in life than your brother, by the looks of things."

Such remarks embarrassed Clement but, before he could express that embarrassment, the child began to kick Ron and anything else within reach, including the table.

"You'll break a leg, Pat," Lucy said, without making it clear whose leg she was referring to. At which point, Cheri emerged from the walk-in larder and was introduced in a sort of way, the proceedings drowned out by the child's rapid stream of protests.

"Do you think Pat would like a swim?" Cheri asked Clement. This was such a sensible suggestion that even the child could not resist it, and took up a great cry of, "Wannerswim wannerswim."

"It's in the back garden. Cheri will show you," Clement said curtly, dividing the remark equally between Lucy and Ron, since he was not yet certain to whom the child belonged. "There are towels in the changing hut."

"I'll take care of her," Ron said, with a nod at Lucy. The child was now dragging him after Cheri, who smiled and made playful scurries at her, perhaps getting into practice for when her own child was born. "I'll have that coffee in a bit, cheers."

As he switched the kettle on, Clement asked Lucy, "Is Pat your child? I mean, not Ron's?"

"Yes. I'm living with Ron now, since your brother died."

He recalled that a silent and sulky Pat had been with Lucy on her first visit to the house with Joseph. It was difficult to concentrate on anything but Sheila's absence.

He was silent. Perhaps sensing unspoken criticism, she said, "Ron's a caring guy." After another silence, she added, "He's good with Patricia. She's been quite upset since her dad left us. She didn't get on with Joe."

Clement did not intend to show approval or disapproval of this revelation. Instead, he passed her over a mug of instant coffee. He pushed the demerara sugar towards her but she shook her head. He put more coffee and boiling water in the mug he had used earlier and sipped at it appreciatively.

"I thought a lot of your brother," Lucy said. "But Ron's been good to me, there's no denying. Things aren't easy for those who don't fit in with Mrs T's notions of progress."

He construed these remarks as mainly defensive, and grunted sympathetically. He assumed she was still doing physiotherapy, but did not enquire.

"Anyhow, it was good of you to come over."

"I told you on the phone I would. I've brought along the notebook you might like to see. You've been talking to that Captain Parr." Lucy perched close to him on the edge of the kitchen table.

"Yes."

"He's a bit of a lad. How ever old is he?" She laughed with amused pleasure, and for a moment he saw something open and delightful in her rather anxious face.

"Lucy, Captain Parr was telling me that Joseph had a revelation of some sort. A spiritual revelation. I'm afraid I saw very little of Joseph after our mother died, which I regret. I've been trying to finish a book, and goodness knows why we should set books above people —"

"Sometimes books are more accessible to us," she said.

He was surprised by the remark. "That's so. Can you tell me what exactly Joe's revelation was? Parr said that it changed his life. Is that so?"

Since she took some while to respond to this direct question, he had time to study her face and lips. He remembered his wife, angry when Lucy, uninvited, had laid hands on her, had described Lucy as "thin-lipped". He saw that those narrow lips were perfectly shaped and turned very prettily at the corners, and were of an attractive light pink, without make-up.

"I had a couple of holidays on the Costa Brava, before Pat arrived. I didn't like it much. It was too full of English nutcases. Once I went to Paris with my sister. That was all right. But I'm not a great one for going abroad. One thing I liked about Joe was that he knew abroad so well. Really foreign places, I mean, not like the Costa Brava. He could tell you about China and make it really interesting. I hope to go there one day, if I can ever get the cash together. But I'd have loved to have gone with him."

She was silent again. Clement sipped his coffee and waited.

"Tell you another thing I liked. It was part of his love of foreign things. I liked all his awful family history. He used to laugh about it. I mean, that school he went to by the seaside. Did you get sent there too?"

"No."

"You were lucky, I should think. But Joe could be so funny about it. He'd so developed his personal history — all the hardships and everything, the way no one at home loved him, the way his whole life was blighted by a dead baby sister — it had become a sort of mythology, you know, which he let me share. It was really like a wonderful story, and his triumph over misery. I liked that."

He reached out and touched her hand.

"People feel guilt about such early miseries. Joseph did. He was able to share it with you because you were sympathetic."

"It's true he didn't open up much when we first knew each other. We got to trust each other, although we often had rows — over political issues and that. Anyhow, I suppose you know he found out that this little dead sister had been buried in an unconsecrated grave?"

"In Nettlesham cemetery, yes. He found out on the day of mother's funeral."

She nodded. "Yes, I remember. He said it was more than a coincidence. Your mum had been able to keep her secret until her funeral but no longer. Not a day longer. That discovery, the discovery that the baby had been buried and finished with, I mean, set him to examining his early life all over again. He took to studying up psychological literature and so on — I don't know what. I had no patience with those tomes."

"He should have come to me."

She looked him in the eye, and the shapely lips curled into what was not quite a smile. "Ah, but there was that long-standing difference between you. Besides, brothers aren't like sisters, are they?"

"Not quite." He laughed.

"Sometimes he was very down, reading the books. Other times, he'd be happy, and lark about, and say he was beginning to understand."

"Understand what exactly? Can you say?"

"He used to have a recurrent dream." As she spoke, screams broke out from the direction of the garden. Clement jumped up and ran to the kitchen window.

Outside, in the sunless garden, a small naked girl had just plunged into the swimming pool. A lumbering hairy man stood naked on its edge. As Clement reached the window, he jumped. A great splash. More screams.

"They're enjoying themselves," he said.

Lucy gave no sign of having heard. She looked down at the gingham tablecloth and traced one of the lines with a nail, as if finding a path through life for some absent person.

"This recurrent dream of his. It was about walking through a wilderness towards a circular gate. It doesn't sound much but it used to give Joe encouragement in bad times."

"Yes, I know the details. It was a Chinese dream. Joe wrote an account of it."

"He wrote accounts of everything," she said with slight sarcasm. "He was always writing, rather than watch the television."

Screams and shouts came from the direction of the pool. The Farrers would not like that if they were at home. Lucy took no notice. Cheri came into the kitchen with a look of surprise on her face, hand over mouth, possibly because she had been confronted by Ron Mallock in the nude. Tactfully, she did no more than nod to Clement and pass through into the front of the house. Lucy continued her account uninterruptedly.

"The dream was all part of Joe's mythology. I can't help thinking of him — even now he's dead — as a kind of mythological character, though you'd probably know a better word. The prodigal son who refused to go home. It was November of last year that he got a cheque from some learned society or other and decided we should go off to the south coast for a break. I parked Pat on Ron and Ron's mum — her and my mum used to be neighbours a long time back. We ended up in Dorset and put up at a little pub smack on the coast. It was cold but we went for walks on the cliffs. I love Dorset.

"It was there Joe suddenly hit on a new interpretation of his old dream. You know the circular gate with the white screen behind it? At the top of the steps?" She spoke as if she and Clement had personally visited the site. "He suddenly thought that he had got the idea the wrong way round, and that it wasn't a circle or white screen. It was the moon. The gate led direct to the moon. The circle of perfection, he called it. The dream had always made him happy because it represented an escape to another world, to a higher sphere. That was what he said."

"The moon can also represent a great many other things. As you know, in classical mythology —"

"Yes, Joe knew all that stuff. He used to quote 'Diana, huntress, chased and fair. . . .' However it went. Joe was fond of poetry. But what he said was that the moon represented his anima. I still don't quite grasp what an anima is, but it's the female component of a man's mind, is that it?"

"In the female mind it's the animus. Animus and anima are contrasexual archetypes. When a man falls passionately in love, it is because the woman embodies the qualities of his anima, or appears to do so..The anima acts as mediator between conscious and unconscious, which was also the function of Joe's recurrent dream. Go on."

Lucy said, folding her arms, "These things frighten me. I can't see how such ideas got into our heads in the first place. . . . Anyhow, Joe interpreted his dream as meaning he had to make an approach to his anima. The message, he said, had finally got through to him. Throughout all the years previously, he said, he had been mad."

" 'His soul had been in China. . . .' Sorry, that's another quotation. Go on, Lucy, I'm extremely interested."

"Well, that's what he said. He'd gone — I forget what word he used — bonkers — the day his mother ran off and left him. Yet always at the back of his mind had been this dream, a communication from the anima, the sane bit of his brain, trying to get through to him. Is that possible?"

"Yes, though the words may not be exactly right; he suffered from an anxiety state rather than insanity."

Lucy hardly seemed to be listening as she concentrated on the next stage of her story.

"That night, it happened there was a full moon. Joe said it was no coincidence, but that was the way he thought. Crazy in a way, but it related to his view of the natural world, and if it got somewhere it couldn't be crazy. . . . So he was all kind of elevated. Our little pub was on the coast road, and our bedroom looked out over the cliffs to sea. We knocked back a drink or two after supper but then he was eager to get to bed. He didn't want sex that night.

"When we put the light out, there was the full moon, shining over the water. Really beautiful. He made me keep quiet. What he did was quite sort of daft, or so I thought at the time. He got down on his knees and prostrated himself — like a Muslim or something, and asked his anima to visit him." She laughed at the memory of it, a short laugh, rather rueful, without looking directly at Clement.

"I couldn't sleep that night. The bed was lumpy. Joe slept like the dead. He never moved. When he woke up in the morning, his face was youthful and full of — I don't know, joy, certainly, and he said, 'Luce, the anima visited me. Jesus, I never expected her to, but she really and truly visited me.'

"He wouldn't or couldn't say anything else then. He was like a man stunned. I didn't press him. I was — oh, it sounds corny now, but I was sort of excited and frightened, all at once. There was a feeling, you know, that something really strange had taken place. Certainly there was a difference in him. Only when we got outside after breakfast and were up on the cliffs — no, we climbed down to the beach that morning — did he say to me — I warn you, you may not think this sounds like much. He told me at the time it wouldn't sound like much."

"Go ahead, Lucy. What did Joe say?"

She took a sip of her coffee. "He explained that he had seen nothing in his dream, so it hadn't been a dream. Or if it was, it was strictly non-visual. But he had heard the anima's voice as clear as he heard mine, and what she said was simple and unmistakable. His anima said to him, 'Your mother did love you'. That was what the anima said. 'Your mother did love you.'"

She looked challengingly at Clement.

Arthur entered the kitchen, with Cheri close behind him. He adjusted his glasses as he spoke.

"Most of your guests are not at home and haven't got answer-phones. Er, I'll come round this evening and have another go. I take it you won't be at college today? You don't want me to phone the police?"

"Certainly not."

"We'll see you later, then," Cheri called. "Come on, Arthur! I've got to go round to the clinic."

Clement saw them out to their waiting vehicle. Then he and Lucy were alone in the house.

XVIII

Inset in the front door of the house in Rawlinson Road was a stained glass panel. In the middle of an abstract lozenge arrangement was a circular design consisting of three elements: a small boat with a white sail skimming over a blue sea towards an imagined haven ensconced between two thickly wooded green hills. Clement had called the picture "The Soul Returning to its Home"; Sheila had a more boisterous title for it.

The sun, shining through thinning cloud, cast the white, the blue, the green, on to Lucy's face and shoulders as she and Clement stood looking at each other in the hall. He recalled the sunny sexuality of her letters to Joseph.

"There's been nothing but interruptions this morning," he said. "Let's go up to my study."

She gave him a sly glance. "Do I get to lie on your couch?"

"That depends on how you behave."

He perceived that she was the sort who could not resist flirting with men.

"I can see how good you are at handling people, Clem. I'm good at handling their bodies, and that's all. If you knew the mess. . . ."

Since she left the sentence trailing, as part of the hesitancy that was ingrained in her manner, he said, taking her hand, "Let's get some more coffee and go up. Ron and Pat will be quite happy in the pool for a while."

The hand was small and its skin tough. He felt a quickening of his pulse. "Everything worked out all right. . . ." Perhaps it would do.

In the kitchen, she picked up the woven bag with which she had come and slung it over her shoulder. They refilled their mugs. Politely indicating that she should go ahead, he followed her up the stairs, conscious of the movement of her thighs and buttocks encased in her old patched jeans. She stopped several times on the way to look at Sheila's pictures, with a particularly long pause before "Faithful Unto Death", though she made no comment.

In Clement's study, she would not settle at first, but prowled about, looking at this and that, regarding the Kandinsky, fingering the spines of some of his textbooks, as if identifying their titles by touch, poking at

Joseph's papers on the window sill. Then she sighed deeply and sat down, folding her legs, on the seat Clement had indicated.

"You live a learned sort of life."

He smiled. "I was never much good at games."

"My life's such a mess."

"Most people feel the same way, Lucy."

As if with a sudden intuition, Lucy asked, "Where's your wife gone?"

"She's in London."

"I see. . . . Just as well, perhaps. She didn't like me. She's a famous writer, right?"

"Yes."

She fumbled in her bag, looking down into it. "You're so different from your brother. Joe was very emotional. Sometimes he'd fly into rages, you know."

"That was fortunate for him, if not perhaps for you. He must have induced himself to fly into rages; expression of anger is important — women in particular, I find, tend to repress anger, and there are clear indications in his writings that there was a time when Joseph could not release his anger, or could release it only masked as humour. Anyhow, I want to hear more about Joseph's visitation by his anima. It said, 'Your mother loved you.' Is that correct?"

"'Your mother did love you.' He told me about it down on the beach and he suddenly roared with laughter. Oh, he ran about like a child, and he caught me up and kissed me. He was so funny. I said to him, 'You're like a great dog.' Then he was very serious and said, 'It means I have got to rethink my whole life. I shall begin today.'"

Lucy pulled from her bag an A4 notebook bound in a William Morris floral pattern cloth. She held it out to Clement.

"You'd better read what he says about the whole business. Joe was great at telling these things. It's my recipe book, which he lifted. Trust him!"

He looked at her, then accepted the book. It opened to a series of recipes, some hand-written, others cut from columns of newspapers and magazines. True to form, Joseph had turned the volume over and started to write from the other end.

His account took the form of a letter — presumably a draft for a letter never sent — to Ellen, and began in characteristic style.

My dearest Ellie,

There you sit, or maybe stand, down in Salisbury, with that faithful

268

hound of yours by your side. Here stand I, or maybe sit, with a far rarer animal in my grasp. A visionary animal, a metaphorical hound which, by my following, will lead. . . . God knows where.

We've suffered hard knocks in our time, Ellie, as have most people, but now a bit of luck has come my way, and I must tell you about it. I must tell you about it in a way that will not too far strain your credulity. You try so hard to live on the textbook level, but that's never been my way. And you go to church services — and are a Friend of the Cathedral, aren't you? — just as our dear parents brought you up to do. You know I'm the rebel, the defaulter, and you forgive me, don't you? Because I once used to love and cuddle you when you were a tiny person in soggy nappies. In my heart I love and cuddle you still, so you will have to accept that I have had what in Christian terms would be a miracle. I've had a Visitation. St Paul on his way to Damascus couldn't have been more knocked out than I've been.

This was last November, and I am still trying to reorient myself.

Oh, Ellie dear, life's so strange. . . . Why don't people just throw up their hands and admit it?

That day, I had to go and see a solicitor. He's a rogue who knows how to deal with rogues. I'm trying to sue a publisher, to get a miserable sum of money he owes me. My solicitor has moved from Harrow to Oxford. I was in Oxford and I did not go to see Clem and Sheila. Would Clem forgive me if he knew? He's such a dry old stick — my guess is that the voluptuous Sheila does his living for him. But I don't know what goes on in any marriage, do I? Having had that one failed marriage under my nose all my childhood — and it's still a mystery to me — I'm not likely to set another up for myself.

Anyhow, Oxford. Home of the young. I like it. It's like the East in that respect — everyone is young and hopeful. Tranny-culture, maybe, but the new generation has style: they swear and screw without being self-conscious about it. Frankly, I envy them. I sat in a coffee shop and watched them, setting up their plans and pretences so whole-heartedly. Girls very pretty, swearing like chaps.

Then I took refuge in one of the college chapels. It was more my age. Clem took me there once. New College — built in Plantagenet times, I believe. The carved misericords under the seats are my delight: little bursts of brutal peasant life as counterpoints to all that solemn upraising of eyes to God and the roof beams. Acrobats, people dancing, men gambling, a chap fucking a sow. That brute life of the centuries, not much tainted by mind; and allowed there in the church. That's where I belong, in the gutter life, being sat on. But I too have had a vision of lovelier things, and not in a church either.

There must have been a time — perhaps in Plantagenet centuries, who knows? — when gutter and heaven were close. Our old Nettlesham poet Westlake, in "The Conversation", has something of the same thought (you see I still read him):

> However dark the gulfs that ope, the days
> That 'whelm me, still I feel the Maker's gaze.

From chapel to solicitor. He seemed to think we might extract some money from my back-street publisher. You see, back-street authors have back-street publishers. The thought of solvency went to my head. I buzzed straight back to Acton, collected Lucy from her hospital, and drove off to the south coast.

We found a little place in Dorset, near Lulworth Cove. It's years since I was at the English seaside. I like palm trees and mangusteens and warm water. But the Dorset coast looked superb, like a film set; November had washed it clean of tourists, and the great chalk cliffs stood out into the waves as if creation had made chalk, rather than Homo sapiens, the highest form of intelligent life. The air turned me very spiritual. We got a neat little room under the eaves of a quiet pub, with a sea view out of the foot-square window. We took a long walk, arm-in-arm, along the cliff paths.

Everything there was simple — none of your middle-class-isation in that pub — to match the great gentle forms of the cliffs. Lucy and I felt so good, and were in harmony (English for not rowing for once). The meal that evening was okay and, after a drink and a chat with the landlord, we went out to look at the night before going to bed. The moon was up, sailing in a clear sky like a sparrow's egg in a fit of hubris. Another simple form in the immense beauty of the universe.

On the beach were pebbles as smooth as the far-shining moon. As I chucked one of them into the foam dashing up to meet our feet, as I had the feel of it between my fingers, it occurred to me naturally that a recurring dream I had was about the moon, and that the moon was a female entity with which I was in communication. About the night was a unity that made this leap of thought entirely natural, as if something from a much more primitive way of life, long forgotten, had slipped through a panel in the universe and presented me with its visiting card.

This thought — it was something much more basic than thought — this illumination filled my mind like sunshine (it's generally very dark in the brain, you know). We shook the sand from our shoes and went inside, up the wooden stairs to bed.

That nut Jung said that the crux of today's spiritual problems lay in the fascination which psychic life holds for modern man. Or, alternatively, he might have said does not hold for modern man. . . . But suddenly I was filled with a radiant psychic hope — I can't tell you — quite unlike me. You're religious and you'll interpret it your way, but I felt it as a great pagan force, almost *geometrically* plain and pure, like cliffs, sea, moon, beyond our window sill.

Lucy was marvellous. She must have thought I was mad. We sleep naked. There she was in the nude, in the dim white light of the room, before creeping into bed. I didn't touch her. She was a catalyst that night, a numinosity rather than the flesh. I was in a trance. There has never been a night like it in my life.

I recalled Muslims in Sumatra, prostrating themselves during Ramadan. The urge came on me to do the same. I flung myself to the floor. The light of the moon poured in on me like a white syrup. Without words, I addressed the anima, my female tutelary spirit — wayward priestess — beseeching her to speak to me, to emerge from behind the veil. I was complete, on the spiral, beyond myself, a creature, a flung pebble.

How I slept. Like a dropped pebble. Ellie, something wonderful happened to me. My anima did indeed visit me. Perhaps her face had always been turned elsewhere. Okay, it wasn't like that, but it felt like that. I tell you some inarguable persona of female gender came unto me during that night while I slept and said —

Can you think of the most momentous thing she might have said? The most unlikely, the most tiny, the most illogical, the most inescapable? You can? Okay, well that's what she said. I awoke with these words in my head: "Your mother did love you."

You see, she was putting me right, putting everything right.

Your mother did love you. So I was worth something, after all.

It's possible to be full of faith and joy and yet almost fainting. I told Lucy about it when she woke. And again she was great. She seemed extremely moved. At least, she didn't laugh, and was strong enough to stand back and give me air. Somehow I managed to eat an enormous breakfast downstairs in a little back parlour, and then we went out into the morning air. There I tried to explain everything.

She listened and kissed me and did not run from me screaming.

Ever since that clear November day, I have been trying to rearrange my life according to the truth as delivered by that wondrous voice. Well — rebuilding rather than rearranging. It's like arriving from Mars to try and live on Earth. Long, long ago, before geology happened, while you were still running about with a rusk in your mouth barking like a little dog, I came to the conclusion that the parents, sweet folk that they were, did not love their only little son. I had to come to that conclusion. It protected me from the uncertainty that was destroying me.

You won't remember how you were kidnapped into persuading me how hateful I was. But mother grabbed you and strapped you into your pushchair and rammed on your bonnet and rammed on her bonnet and rushed off in the direction of eternity up Ipswich Street — simply in order to persuade me that I was such a little shit she had run away from me for good. Maybe that was the actual moment you got religion. You know — Teach Love Through Fear and all that. It was the moment when I got mad. I could not bear the nervous strain and found it as a matter of survival necessary to remain forever sullen, unmoved by kisses or threats, sheltered behind the doleful fortification of her assumed unlovingness. I mean, part of me knew even then that she did in a way love me, but was too much up the pole to admit it.

And ever since I have had to live my life behind that barricade. It has twisted everything out of true. All those whores in the east, all my attempts to cut my life short, all those fears of the permanent bond of marriage, all those delusions, all those broken hopes . . . all have sprung from that fragile defence erected at the age of four or five. Of course she was off her rocker, and she threw me off mine. I think she buggered up your life just as much, but I know you won't have that.

Anyhow, somehow, I have survived sixty years of torture to be — it's your word — Redeemed. I am a different chap. Lucy sees it. She knows there's a touch of magic about me. Understanding follows forgiveness, blossoms follow drought.

As to what it has cost. The universe itself

There the letter broke off.

Clement closed the recipe book and laid it down on the desk, scarcely able to look at Lucy, who had sat by on the sofa, covertly studying his face as he read and crossing and re-crossing her jean-clad legs.

To break a silence that threatened to extend itself, she said, "Joe had some funny ideas — comparing the moon with a sparrow's egg. He read too much poetry, Joe did."

"Did this letter get written out?"

She shrugged. "Are you annoyed? I know he's not very complimentary about you. . . . I think he wrote it only a week or so before he died."

"I'll have it copied out and sent to Ellen, since it was intended for her. If you don't mind."

"Why should I mind?" she said, in a tone of voice that implied she was never going to fathom the Winter family.

He said, speaking to himself, "Perhaps he felt in the end that everything did work out all right."

Another long pause came, in which both of them sighed heavily.

As if putting many complex thoughts behind him, Clement brushed his hollow temples and looked directly at her with an intense gaze, smiling. "I'm so glad that you were with him, Lucy, at such a taxing time."

"Ever since I first knew Joe, times were taxing for him. But that bit about living on Mars is just an exaggeration. Being with Joe helped me quite a lot. He sort of gave utterance for both of us, really. . . ." She paused, but Clement's grave yet friendly glance encouraged her to go on. "I felt a bit out of my depth — this talk of the anima and everything. But he relied on me. I quite liked that. He said that I would have to help him, but I didn't see how I could, except by being with him. . . ."

Clement nodded. "What more could anyone hope for? Why didn't he come to me?"

Lucy said, without intending cruelty, "You asked me that before. You would have been the last person Joe turned to."

Clement propped his elbow on his desk and covered his eyes, recognising the truth of what she said. Always there had been a barrier between him and Joseph, a barrier not of their own making, compounded of the age difference and the effect of the "steel-engraving angel" and the secretiveness of their parents. But his attempts to demolish the barrier had been singularly ineffective. It occurred to him now, as he shaded out the room with his hand, that an early awareness of and sensitivity to that barrier, to his brother's predicament, had influenced him to follow his career in analytical psychology. All that he was was owed mainly to Joe's suffering.

The chief witness to his brother's latter days had moved round the desk and stood beside him. She put a hand on his shoulder and said, "I didn't mean to upset you."

Touched by this unexpected display of affection, he put an arm round her lower waist, causing her to move closer against him. Feeling her warmth, he rose and put both arms about her. For a moment, he set his lips against her shapely mouth, and then withdrew.

"You're not entirely unemotional, then," she said, looking up at him.

"Lucy — I'm being silly. You're very kind. Let's sit on the sofa together. I don't know why I put the desk between us — force of habit, maybe."

Without moving, she said, "You reckon I'm an easy lay, I suppose?"

"I thought nothing of the sort."

"All right. No funny business." She sat down as he had indicated, contemplating him, not without a certain look of amusement in her eyes. "Perhaps the desk was between us for safety's sake. . . ."

"My safety, then, not yours." They smiled at each other, as if something had been agreed with a delicacy beyond words.

"Look at me, I'm carrying on with you," she said, with a mischievous smile. "The truth is, I'm glad to talk to you like this. How can I put it? I'm always snarled up in the minute — in everyday things. I've always got to be at the hospital or looking after Pat, or arranging for someone else to look after her, or shopping. . . . Well, a thousand and one little things. Most people I know are like that. It's a rubbish life. A cop-out, isn't it? Sometimes it all seems unreal, as if my real life was going to waste. Does that make sense to you at all?"

"Oh, it's 'everydayness' — that's what H. G. Wells called it. We're all victims of everydayness. Routine. It's easier than thinking."

She pulled a face in her endeavour to get an idea across to Clement. "That's one thing I liked about Joe. He didn't suffer from that sort of thing. He may have been a slave to his miseries, but he was free otherwise from — well, what you said, I guess, 'everydayness'. I never met anyone else like that. But perhaps you're like it too. Your parents can't have been all that bad. . . ." She laughed.

"We're all given the means of refuge. Through dreams, for instance, which link us with our world of inner feelings, at least some of the time. Joe paid attention to his dreams, and they directed him to stability." He felt he was beginning to lecture, and added, more conversationally, "We're so proud, as a species, of our big brains, yet they aren't really all that good for thinking with, at least to judge by global results. What they really are good at is fantasising. Most people do large amounts of fantasising every day — by watching TV or videos if nothing else."

"Joe wouldn't watch TV. He said he preferred the Far East."

They both laughed. "Not everyone is as individual as Joe. Now, after this seminal dream, he set about rethinking his life, yes?"

She took a sip of her coffee and pulled a face. "I feel a bit guilty about this. You see, I did stay with him for a bit, then I didn't. You're used to all this mental stuff, and so was he. I wasn't. I'm a physiotherapist, I'm physical. It's everydayness, I suppose. Anything else I find — well, a bit freaky, to be honest."

"People do. That's why analysts are treated as a joke."

"Also, I had my own troubles. Joe and Pat didn't get on. He always said he couldn't work with her around. He hated kids. He just wanted me. I couldn't have that. I mean, she's my child. He said to me once, 'Shove her

274

in an orphanage.' Fancy! 'Shove her in an orphanage. . . .' After all he'd suffered in that respect. He could be very hurtful. It wasn't just me. . . .

"Also we had quarrels over CND. Oh, trivial things, really. So they seem now, now he's dead. I got a room nearer my job, but Pat didn't exactly take to the day centre. Cash was tight. Then I moved in with Ron, over in Brentford. Ron's very easy-going."

"What does Ron do?"

"He's a sort of builder. I did go over to Joe at Christmas time, just for a couple of days. We were supposed to go on a march, but he wouldn't come. Like a fool, I cleared off again. I know it was bad for him. It was bad for both of us. He wrote me a long letter in the New Year, and that persuaded me I loved him and should stay with him for good."

"I think I have a copy of the very letter."

"All the political stuff about what the Americans had done didn't cut much ice with me, but I liked the trouble he'd taken. He was really quite a lot different when I moved back in — gentler with me and more patient with Pat. A sunny, gentler side was coming out. He allowed himself to be less guarded. You see, he meant what he said. He'd started to rethink his whole life. What a task — at sixty! There was nothing for it but to believe the message from his anima — the visitation had been too serious to ignore. He felt compelled to act on it. After all, the anima wasn't the moon — wasn't outside him. It came from within him, from something he had previously suppressed. You see what I mean?

"He'd lived by the assumption that your mother did not love him. She'd wanted a girl to make up for the dead one and had only been happy when Ellen came along. Hence her treatment of him — all those threats that she didn't love him, and her running away from him. Did you know she even threatened that she was going to die at any day? She was a right one, your mother! How come she didn't behave like that to you?"

Despite his training, it was a question still capable of inducing guilt feelings. Clement clasped his hands together as he replied.

"Joe bore the brunt of her mental disturbance. Illness, if you like. I came along twelve years after him, don't forget, when mother had largely recovered. She'd had Ellen to console her, and so on."

"Mental disturbance. I should think it was. I see red when I think of a mother behaving in that way. To be honest, I don't think she did love Joe, or she wouldn't have done what she did. What do you say? I mean you're the expert."

Clement stared at the ceiling. "She had a neurosis. She was primarily preoccupied with her own life, rather than with anyone else's. A diagnostic label isn't very useful. She was unable to establish emotional boundaries, and was sexually unsettled; hence, in part, her rejection of Joe and over-possessiveness towards Ellen."

"But did she love Joe?"

"Of course. If he said so."

Lucy regarded him searchingly, as if she felt he had raised a barrier to further questions. Then she glanced at her watch and spoke in a deliberately casual tone.

"Well, love is a whole bundle of things. . . . Anyhow, after last November, Joe began to count up all the signs of love and affection she had shown him, totting up the positive side of the bill, as against the negative. How she had written to him twice a week when he was at that barbarous little school — St Paul's. Even how she wept for joy — Joe said it was either joy or remorse — when he returned from that fatal stay with his gran at Lavenham. Lots of plus items like that.

"But even the minus things. You see, what this rethinking process came down to was this — I guess it was the crucial bit — that he had to forgive. Forgive his mother and his father. Then he could forgive himself. He laughed and said he was getting as bad as Christ."

"I can imagine him saying it. The question of forgiveness would have been a crucial element, as you say."

"He was reluctant to do it. He fought himself. He had a fit of smoking and drinking hard, although he had been off the booze. I suppose you'd say he was mad?"

Clement shook his head. He saw that she wanted approval of Joe for reasons of her own, and spoke firmly. "Joe was never mad, Lucy. Far from it. Those infantile traumatic experiences, which destroyed the security he should have enjoyed, compelled him to recognise the insecurity of the human condition. So he grew up wise and unhappy, but not ill. Wartime suited him, for instance, because everyone shared the sense of insecurity which had become his lot. But, no, Joe was one of the sane."

She smiled. "I think often it's hard to tell. Often I wonder about myself. Thanks. What a good father you'd make, Clem. Anyhow, it was hard for Joe to accept that his mother had loved him after all the terrors she'd put him through, but he trusted in the communication of his anima, and pushed on. I could see the strain. . . . Oh, I left him again, sod me. Just for a month. I couldn't really grasp. . . . It was wrong of me — I knew it at the time. Yet there I was, doing what his mother had done, deserting him. But I realised that if he couldn't rely on me there was no one else. . . . So I went back. . . ."

"Good for you. And for him. How did he receive you?"

She shook the curls at the memory. "He cried. He was very sweet. But next day he was angry and said he couldn't stand me coming and going like that — he'd really rather I stayed away for good. Then — well, it was as if he stood back from what he was saying. He started to laugh, and said that that was simply an old pattern. Now discarded. He kept saying it. 'That was the old pattern.'"

"Meaning?"

She sighed and put a hand on Clement's knee. "He'd worked through the crisis on his own, while I was gone. He understood that the infant Joe had been unable to tolerate all the terrifying uncertainties of life with his mother. Did she love him? Didn't she? He had to decide that she didn't, and leave it at that. That was the old pattern. Signs of love, indications of love, had become unbearable — they just stepped up his anxiety. So much so that when she threatened to run away, he began to wish she really would. And me ditto."

Clement nodded. "And when she said she would die, he wished she really would. All guilt-inducing."

"So by the age of six, he'd decided that neither of his parents loved him. A terrible thing for a kid. It also meant that he was unlovable. I know he was under terrible pressure, but I can't see how he could have been so wrong — about such an important thing, I mean."

Clement was silent, wondering how best to explain a case he had yet to understand fully himself. The question of phenomenology came into it. This attractive woman and the room they sat in undoubtedly had objective existence; yet his cognisance of her and the room was a subjective one, contained within his head. It was our perceptions, rather than reality, which determined what we perceived. The perceptions of the infant Joseph had been directed towards all that was threatening in the behaviour of his dominating parent. But there was also a transcendental reality, and towards that Joseph had been able, finally, to fight his way. His escapes from England were unconscious elements in that fight.

"He had to choose between conflicting signals of love and neglect. When his mother did actually desert him — though only for a short while — Joe not unreasonably assumed that she did not love him, and decided in self-defence to cling to that decision. He kept his sanity at the expense of developing a depressive psychopathology."

"I don't know about that. I wish I had read more. . . . I read a bit of Dickens, following Joe's example, because he was interested in Dickens's orphans, feeling himself an orphan of sorts — but Dickens isn't intellectual, is he? Anyway, he said he was stuck in a kind of limbo, a paralysis, from the time they sent him off to his granny until he met a girl older than him, someone called Irene, during the war, when he was still at school."

"Yes, Irene Rosenfeld."

"She gave him love, poor kid, love and a little confidence. Then there was his time in the Far East — his initiation rite, he called it. I hate the mere idea of war. The thought of the bomb petrifies me. That's why I joined CND — women have to do something if men won't. But Joe seemed to have enjoyed his war, as you said. . . ." She looked questioningly at Clement.

"There's a mythological component to the mind. Being involved in the heroic campaigns in Burma restored Joe to a sense of his own significance he had lost as a child. Being involved in great events is perhaps necessary for psychic health. My wife's novels sell well because they deal with great, if highly fictitious, events. It may have been good for you to be involved in the great event of Joe's personality adventure."

"I don't know about that." She laughed uncertainly. "Then after Irene there was Mandy, the Chinese woman, and his passionate affair with her. That set him on the road to emotional recovery, didn't it? Was that mythological, too?"

"In both cases, the woman was older and more experienced, and Joe's role, at least initially, appears to have been rather passive — a token of his depression."

"He certainly wasn't passive by the time I met him, on CND marches, let me tell you. . . . So that was where this recurrent dream eventually led him. It was very dramatic. He saw that he had entirely misinterpreted his life — had been forced into a false position by his early bad treatment. And he came to realise that his mother was to be pitied, that in fact she was in the grip of some awful misery that could not find expression except when acted out on him."

She turned her head to look out of the window, so that Clement was able to study her wild hair, short and curled at its tips.

"He had to keep on telling me the tale over and over again. When Pat was asleep we used to go down the road to an Indian restaurant to eat. There he'd go over the whole thing in great detail. I think the waiters wondered what on earth we were talking about."

Clement laughed. "You must have been bored. You didn't go away again?"

"Joe took me seriously. So I listened. I knew I was being useful."

"To listen is sometimes the best thing anyone can do. He would have needed your attention. You have no cause to blame yourself. Joe should have made a new will and left you something."

Lucy made a gesture and laughed in a displeased manner. "Wills? No, we weren't careful in that way. He'd found new life in himself. He didn't think of dying. He was full of a kind of glow. . . . I can't convey it. He said that the whole — the whole emotional coloration of his life was altered, as a result of his forgiveness. . . . Oh, I'm no good at explaining this, Clem — you'll have to study what Joe set down. You and he have learning. My education was rubbish."

"You had the great thing, though, a sympathetic understanding of his troubles."

"I don't know about that." She lay back against the arm of the sofa, and stared up at the ceiling. "Joe became very calm and relaxed, as if a great prison door had been flung open. We had a lovely New Year — he was sure it would be good."

"And four months later — the heart attack."

At that, Lucy got up and walked about, looking at Clement sideways to say, "I'm sure all his emotional struggles wore him out. Of course, he smoked too much. You know, he wasn't resentful or anything about what had happened. Just grateful to be free of it at last. And of course proud of having solved the problem. I don't know if he was what you'd call *happy*. Not many people are. I remember he told me that some foreigner — perhaps a Frenchman he'd met — said to him that we are not as happy as we think we are, or as miserable either."

When Clement said nothing to that, she asked rather timidly, standing before him, "You don't think Joe was mad, do you, I mean, in any way? Even to the last?"

"I admire Joe. He learnt to cope admirably with a difficult psychopathology."

"I don't see exactly what that means. He did really have the vision, didn't he? If so, there's hope for all of us!" She gave a brief laugh.

"Oh, he lived by what he perceived — often a very healthy sign."

Dissatisfied with this response, she folded her arms, and then settled again on the sofa, saying, "Pity the two of you weren't closer. I wish I'd had a brother."

"Joe had almost nothing to do with me when I was a child, and I'm afraid it stayed that way."

She appeared restless now that she had told the story. As she set her coffee mug down on the desk, she bit her lip — displeased, Clement thought, with the turn the conversation had taken.

"Well, he's dead now," she said.

Boisterous cries of "Luce!" came from downstairs.

"That's Ron," she said, getting to her feet again. "Listen, Clem, I'm having problems with little Pat, always have done. Can I come and see you some time — about Pat, I mean? Would you charge me the earth?"

He got up. "Come to my consulting room in the centre of Oxford. I'll give you my card. I'll fit you in and I won't charge you."

"Oh, bless you for that." They moved together and kissed each other, touching only for a moment, as shrill cries from below redoubled.

"I'm grateful to you for coming over, Lucy."

"It was my day off. I couldn't have poured it all out over the phone, could I? I miss Joe so much."

"So do I, believe it or not."

They went downstairs together. Ron Mallock and Pat stood together in the hall, hair spiky from the water. He was not holding the child, who swung energetically from his tattooed arm.

"We had a lovely swim, mum," Pat said. "Next time, you've got to come in with us."

"There may not be a next time, love," Lucy said, taking hold of her daughter's hand.

It was almost twelve noon when the trio left Rawlinson Road. Clement Winter went indoors, locked the front door, and returned to his study. His coffee mug and Lucy's stood together on his desk. Her presence seemed to hover in the air.

She had engaged his sympathies. Sheila's and his earlier perceptions of her had been mistaken, he considered; her clumsy attempt to knead Sheila's shoulders had been compounded of social awkwardness and a genuine desire to help. She was a woman, no longer young, struggling to survive in a harsh society, a one-parent family. She needed help and advice. Her attitude to Ron Mallock suggested that she regarded him as only a temporary prop in her life. . . . He reined his thoughts abruptly. He was also sexually attracted to her. In their farewell kiss, she had darted a thin tongue into his mouth.

He relished the memory of it. Yet their meeting had not ended in too satisfactory a way. He had withheld something, in characteristic fashion. What she had wanted, perhaps the covert reason for her visit, was to hear praise for her unusual lover. A requiem of sorts. She had needed that beacon in her difficult life, and he, the weak brother being weak again, had not provided. Her magical tale — important to her — had not been adequately rewarded.

Clement walked about unhappily. Holding people at arm's length presented a difficulty; the length of arms required varied. He could still make amends by writing his brother's biography. And Lucy would have to be a star witness. Sheila, if she came back, would have to put up with that arrangement.

In any case, he would see Lucy again. For the moment, staring out of the window at the horse chestnut, he allowed his fantasies free play. There were other things he had inherited from his brother — why not his bedmate? The incestuous nature of the idea was not unpleasant, spice to the dish. *It would be a way of getting his own back on Joseph.*

"Oh, God!" He held the heels of both hands to his head. So that was the reason for all the indecisiveness. . . .

He saw again the bar of soap turning, endlessly turning, the suds dripping like saliva into the basin. Had he all along wanted to wash his hands of Joseph, and of everything that was Joseph? What mysteries we were — especially to ourselves.

This was something to discuss with Mrs Emerova on his next visit. Not that answers could be expected, but new, interesting questions would be raised.

Poor homeless Lucy. Perhaps he should sell her the Acton flat cheaply — even give it to her? That would make her grateful. His reveries flowed, thick and rich, into the new channel. If Sheila had left him for good, then he was free to do as he pleased.

He hummed a tune to himself and recognised it as a snatch from Humperdinck's opera *Hansel and Gretel*. The two children had been left to perish in the forest; a Hansel without any Gretel, Joseph had been left in the same way. The problem of parental cruelty was one which, for Clement, far outweighed in importance any political questions. The matter of the oppression of the powerless by the powerful in fact had strong bearing on world politics.

Impatience seized him. How typical of him it was to be pondering a general question, when he was a man newly deserted by his wife. Here he remained in the house alone, while she had gone off to play the *femme fatale* with a New York publisher. Bloody Sheila! Money and success had gone to her head. But if that was all there was to it, then why hadn't she run off with someone glamorous, someone powerful? Not with little Hernandez, a jumped-up copy-editor. . . . Green Mouth should have had more ambition. Her fans would be disappointed.

He began pacing about the study, going over the long history of his marriage. Of course he'd taken Sheila for granted. After seventeen happy years, that was part of the deal.

But it wasn't. Not these days. Marriages were breaking down everywhere. There were more homosexuals, more lesbians, more confused, more homeless, more suicides. The nuclear family — which he and Sheila had failed to establish — was breaking up. Society was in trouble. He was victim of a trend, and rebelled against the role; it was an indignity as well as a misery.

Bloody Sheila! Why am I so slow to find my proper anger against her?

By this time, she would have met her lover off the plane. They would have had time to get from Heathrow to central London. They could have checked into a hotel by now. She liked to stay at Brown's: perhaps they were in Brown's. In bed. Little Hernandez would probably be underneath, as in Boston. . . . "I'm enjoying it too much to stop. . . ."

Well, never mind Joseph and his forgiveness. He was not going to forgive Sheila. She had thrown too much away, had thrown real things away for a dream, a fantasy. The nature of the real world was such that it required forgiveness; but the hard fact, against which so many of his clients wrecked themselves, was that imaginary worlds were so much more delusory, ultimately so much nastier.

He would ask Lucy back. He could find plenty of pretexts. They would have an affair. She seemed willing enough, and he could help her. Her and that slender little tongue. . . .

He went slowly downstairs. The ache in his left leg was back. He had resented the invasion by the Strankses; now he missed them. The house was eerily silent. Still, he would not let Sheila in when she came back. If she came back. Even Mrs Flowerbury did not have a key to the door; only Sheila and he had keys. He would get on to those people in Walton Street and have the lock changed.

Thought of action cheered him. He went outside, locking the door behind him, and got the car out. Happily, he saw no sign of Alice Farrer next door. Making a conscious effort to drive slowly, he took the Mercedes down Walton Street and arranged for a locksmith to come in the morning and change the front door lock.

And if she never returned. . . .

In his estimation, the chances were that she would return. She was basically a sensible woman, who would soon realise that she had fallen victim to her own fantasies. Facing reality would be painful, but she could do it — as she had in Berlin, long ago.

He could not bear to go home. He was too sick at heart to feel hungry. Driving up the Woodstock Road, he took the ring road round Oxford and headed for Swindon. In a short while, he turned off the main road and drove up the winding way on to the White Horse Hills.

Only a half dozen cars stood in the car park. Nobody was about: an ancient pre-English silence brooded over the scene. Clement went to look at the view towards Swindon. It was unexpectedly hazy, and little could be seen. He was isolated on a bleak grassy island. He walked about, but the chill wind usually haunting this part of the world chased him back into the car. He sat there, drumming with his fingers on the steering wheel, staring out at the immense supine mound before him. The thought occurred to him that he might drive over a steep edge with some convenience to himself and everyone else involved, but he found he was not desperate enough to do it.

Blank misery settled over him like the haze in the valley. He thought of everything and of nothing. Nothing coherent came through. He wanted to leave this isolated place but could not find the motivation. His misery drove him from the car again, and he trudged up to the site of the old Roman fortress, over the close-cropped grass. A man and a boy, well wrapped up, were flying a two-string kite. When they called to him, Clement did not answer. He came back down to the Mercedes, chilled to the bone.

Goaded by cold, he drove down the hill, past sheep nibbling in the hedgerows. The time was gone four-thirty. He drank a cup of tea at a thatched tea place in Uffington. Then he walked, wandering along the network of small roads lying at the foot of the downs.

When he returned to his car, it was almost nine in the evening, and the light was going. He had no idea, no memory, of where he had been; all he knew was that he was tired and sick at heart.

"Sheila," he said brokenly, but could formulate no sentence to go with her name.

By the time he tucked the car into the garage in Rawlinson Road, it was all but dark. He entered the silence of the house and locked himself in.

In the kitchen, he poured himself a glass of Mouton Cadet, more from force of habit than from desire. He found he had no taste for it. Out in the garden, two sopping brown towels lay by the side of the pool. He kicked them into the water, where they floated like drowned bodies.

Taking a book, he settled with it in a chair, only to throw it down after a few minutes, unaware of a word he had read. There seemed nothing for it but to get to bed and take a sleeping pill.

As he was approaching the stairs, he heard Sheila's key in the front door.

The wind tugged at his locks. A lone
Rose tore from off the tower wall.
    He saw that in *FORGIVENESS* all
Redemption lay. His Parents' stone
    Their carved Names bore where ivy gnawed.
Then cried he, "Just to be forgiven
    Or to forgive: both are to *HEAVEN*
The Key. I do forgive them, *LORD*" —
    His words shook like the riven tree —
"Who never have forgiven me."

"The Storm" from
A Summer Stroll Through Parts of Suffolk
William Westlake, 1801